Esther's
Violin

Ellen Hansa

Publisher: Ellen Hansa
website: transfiguration942.blog

First published in Australia 2019
This edition published 2019
Copyright © Ellen Hansa 2019

Cover design, typesetting: WorkingType (www.workingtype.com.au)

Hansa, Ellen
Esther's Violin
ISBN- 978-0-646-80486-6

pp504

The story is set in a small European town on a river.
The town is fictional, as too are all the characters.

A dream is unrehearsed.
Yehudi Menuhin

BOOK ONE

ONE

Holding on to his precious coins, 9-year-old Tom Dolmer entered the Saturday market. His step was light and rhythmic. He had a tune in his head. He did like it. It did not want to go. While his mother looked for the weekly groceries Tom slowly and systematically scanned the book stalls. Did he have enough money? Whistling quietly, he contemplated if and how he should spend those coins.

There was a short, sharp pull on his shirt.

"Whistling in public is rude!"

Tom's mother had caught up with him.

"What do you want another book for? I can hardly get in your room now!"

Margret Dolmer had put her basket of vegetables next to Tom.

"Look after that, will you?"

Tom watched his mother, tall and straight, walk away to continue her shopping. Her walk was soldier-like, stiff but purposeful. As she disappeared behind one of the stalls, he laboured to pick up the full, heavy basket with both hands, then kept on walking along the bookstall, now with the music back in his head. Having arrived at the end of the stall, still contemplating if he should buy another book, he could hear music.

The tune was very familiar. He knew that music from the radio. Partially dragging, partially carrying the heavy basket he moved down the row of stalls, looking for where it came from.

In front of one stall, decorated to resemble an old caravan and displaying all sorts of small antique items, stood an old lady playing the violin. She seemed totally immersed in the music, swaying to the slow rhythm, bending her knees for the lower notes and standing tall, almost on her toes, when playing the higher ones.

Tom knew this music and he started singing. First quietly, but soon enthusiastically, louder, mimicking the movement of the musician. Soon he found himself holding a pretend violin. The old lady smiled, watching him closely, but continuing to play. He came to the end of his knowledge of the music and stopped singing, but he kept on following the old lady's movements. He was in a different world. With a flourish, as if ending an intricate minuet, he gestured with his imaginative bow, finishing almost at the same time as the elderly violinist.

She took the instrument off her chin and held it at the end of the fingerboard on the beautifully crafted scroll between the fingers of her left hand. With utter concentration Tom copied every move she made.

She took hold of his hand and bent down to his level. He noticed her soft white hair, held together on the back of her head with an over-large comb. Some of the hair had escaped. It framed her wrinkled face. She was surrounded by the most bewitching smell. It made Tom slightly giddy.

"You have a lovely voice," she said, looking at Tom with her pale-blue, sharp eyes. "And you sing in perfect pitch!"

Immediately he fell in love with her.

Her watching husband smiled. A crowd had gathered.

"My name is Esther," she said. "What is yours, my little virtuoso? Do you play?"

"No, I am sorry to disturb you. I just love this music. I have heard it on the radio. I want to play like you," he said, "I want to play the violin!"

"Good for you!" she kissed him on both cheeks. "And I am absolutely sure you will."

Over the clapping of the small audience one could hear an announcement from the loudspeaker: "We are looking for Tom Dolmer. His mother is waiting at the market-office."

"That's me! I must go. My mother will be furious."

Esther stood up. She whispered, "We will be here again next week, then we can continue our music making."

Getting help with the heavy shopping baskets from a young woman, Tom hastily made his way to the office and his angry mother. The beautiful music of the violin was still rolling about in his head and the thought of being able to see Esther again made the little smack his mother gave him feel less intimidating.

TWO

Margret Dolmer slid into her heavy overcoat, pulled her sensible, cold-weather hat on her frizzy hair and looked at herself in the hallway mirror.

There was the reflection of Tom in the long mirror, dressed in readiness to face the cold. She rearranged her hat and sighed.

"Yes, that will do."

Turning around she noticed her son.

"You are keen."

"I thought I could come and help you carry."

"My goodness, you do look determined! There will be no books at the market today. It is just too wet and cold. Well, let's get a move on then. I haven't got all day."

She opened the heavy door to their flat and they started to descend the staircase of the old house. In the narrow street the icy wind almost blew Tom off his feet. Even though he was almost ten years old he decided to hold on to his mother's thick coat. The tall houses of the old town created a wind tunnel and the badly maintained footpath made it hard for him to keep up with his tall mother. She had no time to lose and did not slow down.

They had to wait at the tram stop. Tom's mind wandered as he sat on the cold, hard seat of the little shelter. He thought of a story he'd read about a hare and a tortoise. How they both somehow got to the goal at the same time. One running, resting often from exhaustion, the other just slowly trotting along. He thought of his dad, who was never in a hurry but still seemed to get all of his work done. Then of his mother in constant motion: always moving, always running.

"Hello, Tom! Daydreaming again? The tram is here."

There was no music at the market and no bookstalls. Tom followed his mother, watching how she argued with the stallholders about almost everything. He did not dare think of music. He might have whistled and made her angry. There was not even any music in his head, no matter how much he looked for it. Her aggression towards everything had killed the music inside him. Walking all over the market looking for bargains and good quality she filled one bag after another, passing them on to Tom who felt like an overladen donkey. He'd seen a picture in one of his books. All one could see were four spindly legs and the two rather large ears. Yes, he felt like an overladen donkey carrying mother's shopping and filled with the sadness of not seeing Esther and her beautiful violin. He wanted so badly to smell her wonderful scent again.

On the tram he tried to forget his unhappy state by making up a tune in his head to the rhythm of its rattling ride.

"Tam, tam, taa, tam, tam, tatam…"

"Did you say something?" his mother barked at him.

He stared at his hands then gazed at the passing townscape through the tram window. He looked but did not see. His mind was with the thoughts of Esther's broken promise. He could still hear her violin and now the music had filled his whole being. Sadness filled his eyes with tears. The streetscape started to swim and went out of focus.

At home, Tom scrolled the radio dial up and down. His father sat by the fire watching him.

"There," Tom said, "listen to that music! If I could only make music like that."

"But son, you have a beautiful voice. Your voice is an instrument. It can make all sorts of music. And you can whistle. Not everyone can whistle. I can't!"

Tom moved to sit with his father in one of the large armchairs.

"I met this lady, her name is Esther, at the market. I think she was very old, almost like gran. She played the violin, oh so beautifully, it was almost singing. She said she would be back at the market today. But no matter how hard I looked and listened, I could not find her. She promised to be there, and she was not. Why do grownups do that sort of thing, not keeping a promise?"

His mother came into the room with a tray, interrupting the boy and his father. With an aggressive movement she turned off the radio.

"Do we only have one armchair? Look, Theo, the boy is almost ten years old! Can he not sit in his own chair?"

Margret put the tray on the table.

"I made some afternoon tea. There were some nice little cakes at the market. Some hot chocolate for Tom. He needs warming up."

She poured a little milk into the cups and topped them up with tea, then vigorously stirred some sugar in, making the delicate cups clink and jump. After that the only sound was a little slurping from Tom, trying to cope with the hot chocolate.

"Cake?"

Margret put the small cakes on little plates and handed them first to her husband, then to her son.

"Well, Tom was a real little helper today at the market," she said with a smile.

"Mum, why do grown-ups not stick to their promises?" he asked her over the rim of his cup.

"Circumstances. Circumstances can change situations, can change your life!"

Her reply was cold and sharp.

She looked at her husband and then at the boy. She felt the love between them, the closeness, the father-son relationship. Margret Dolmer's soul was empty of love. She was as cold and rigid inside as she looked on the outside.

There had been love once and laughter, then the boy was born. It seemed as if he took it all away. There was a time of great happiness. That was when she met Theo. He took her away from a life Margret had decided to forget, to rub out.

After her mother's death, Margret was adopted by her childless aunt. She was only four years old and her aunt became the mother she remembered. But the novelty of having a little girl wore off and Margret was sent to boarding school, where everything inside her was slowly destroyed. Her laughter, her love of singing, all slowly erased.

At the end of her education she went back to her father's sister, a dark and unhappy household. Now and then her father would visit and take her out to a small café where he would get her an enormous ice-cream in a glass, topped with lashings of cream. He tried to make Margret happy, to find the joyous little girl he left with his sister all those years ago. When she was sixteen, he stopped coming. During one of the visits to the cafe, she met Theo and his parents. She became friends with the Dolmer family.

Margret fell in love with Theo, with his warm, caring, steadfast character. When she visited his home, she was welcomed with warmth and kindness.

Theo worked in his father's small engineering factory. Soon his father offered Margret a job in the office. On her eighteenth birthday she and Theo got married. She never went back to her foster mother. Margret pushed away all her memories from that part of her life. A new life began. A life of happiness and laughter. They danced every Saturday. Oh, how he made her dress fly!

Until ten years later when the boy came.

Margret felt the love between the boy and his father grow, and Theo's love for her diminish.

"Circumstances," she repeated, looking at her husband.

Tom got up and fetched the dictionary. It took him quite a while to find the word. The boy's whole being was full of wanting to know.

Circumstances, Tom read, *An event or fact that causes or helps to cause something to happen.* He looked at his mother, then at his father.

"So, something important could have happened to Esther and her husband. That's why they did not come to the market. Maybe she was called away to the big concert hall in the city to play? The Golden Concert Hall maybe! Maybe she had to fly overseas? Oh yes, there must have been something important!"

"Maybe the weather?" his father replied. "Don't be too disappointed, son."

"Yes, it was rather cold." Tom continued drinking his chocolate. "What does disappointment mean?"

Again, he picked up the dictionary.

Failure to fulfil the hopes of expectations.

He thought of the words he had just learned.

"Yes, it was far too cold. Circumstances created my disappointment."

The rhythm of the two words put a tune into his head and he started singing.

"Do you have to?"

Margret picked up the tray. The room went cold. Tom tried to disappear into the big armchair.

Theo looked at his wife. What had made her so bitter, so hard, so unloving? Did they not have everything a family could wish for? Yes well, he thought, circumstances. His mother's illness was a blow to them. But then Margret offered to look after her. She did say that she was the mother she never had. Mother could have gone into a home, she could have had the best. But no, Margret left her job to take care of her.

Theo looked over to his treasure in life, his boy. Why did she not love him? What's wrong with a bit of whistling or singing? The boy had a beautiful voice. And did she not once love to sing herself?

Again, he looked at Margret. With a big sigh, he picked up the newspaper and started reading.

Tom went to his sanctuary, his room. For a long time he sat on his bed with his knees pulled up tight to his chest. It seemed that he sat like that forever, feeling lonely. In front of him was the big, exciting book of the world. His favourite: The Atlas. By looking at the different maps of foreign countries, he could dream of distant places, of their stories, their music. He suddenly spread out his arms as if he were hugging, encircling, taking in the whole world. Then folding them tight around his drawn-up knees he hid his head, and started dreaming, accompanied by music. He felt the sound of a violin encircling him.

THREE

The room had not changed much; on the wall a large map, looking old and well-used. Pinned in the middle a long strip of paper with large, childlike writing: CIRCUMSTANCES — DISAPPOINTMENT = PAIN.

Sitting on the bed Tom, now a young man of twenty-four, had his knees drawn up. In front of him, an array of books. On top of the books, sheet music. Tom had his head resting on his knees. He was humming a tune that had entered his head from nowhere. With the music always came the feeling of a presence, a shadow of someone he might have known. It made him always feel good and safe.

"Dinner is on the table!" the persistent voice of his mother called down the corridor.

The kitchen table was laid for two. Tom's father had died after a long illness. Now the dining room was seldom used. Margret felt it was easier eating in the kitchen.

"How are your studies going? Haven't you got an exam soon?"

Tom nodded. He had his mouth full. His mother despised people talking with a full mouth. Margret had become thinner, brittle. Her thick mop of unruly, curly, charcoal-grey hair looked unkempt. Her back not as straight, her walk not as brisk. She poked her food and slowly started eating. The only noise came from the road. From cars and laughing people. She closed the window.

"Too much noise," she said, picking up her half-empty plate to put it on the sink.

Margret Dolmer looked at her son. He was so much like her

Theo when they were young; when life was easy and full of fun and love.

She stretched out her hand across the table towards her son. "Some more?"

"No, thank you, Mother."

Tom got up. He had grown tall, like his mother when she was young. His father's face topped off by blond curls on broad shoulders. He slowly walked into the living room and sat down in one of the armchairs. He lit a cigarette, took a deep drag, put his head back and slowly pushed the smoke straight up in the air.

"Must you?"

Margret had entered the semi-dark room and turned the standard lamp on.

"Yes," was the answer, "I enjoy it." With that, he took another deep drag and blew rings playfully towards his mother.

Margret moved away, got out some mending, and said nothing.

The evening was spent in total silence. Margret nervously mending, Tom relaxing, smoking. He had slid into his father's old armchair, his long gangly legs stretched out in front of him. His head was resting on the back of the chair, his eyes closed.

It was only six months since Tom's father had passed away. Tom was sad to have not known his father better. To not see him through the eyes of a man. To not communicate with him as a man. Tom pressed his head into the back of his father's chair. He could feel the gentleness, the encouragement, the enfoldment of his father's love.

And then suddenly there was this melody, soft, oh so soft. With it the feeling of someone near him.

"Who are you?" he softly asked.

"Sorry?" his mother barked. "Did you say something? You know I don't hear too well anymore."

"Nothing, nothing. I'd better get on with my studies. Do you need any help?"

With that, he left his mother, her mending, the room full of his father's memories; and the silence, the eternal silence.

In his room the radio quietly played. On his desk the books for university, the books he should study. On the bed, books on travel and sheets of music, his silent dream for his future.

Tom sat by his desk looking at the textbooks. Suddenly there was the music again, the same tune: soft, oh so soft. He closed his eyes. A smell drifted in. It was enchanting, it created a longing he did not understand. Putting his elbow on the desk he upset one of his books and it fell to the floor. The noise brought him back to his studies. Back to the promise he gave his father; the promise of looking after his mother. The promise to get good marks at the university.

Tom got up and opened his door to let the noise of the flat come in. The clanking of dishes being washed floated down the corridor and into his room. With it, the tender, unsure voice of his mother. She was singing. It was a tune from the time when she was young and dancing, whirling in her wide dress round and around. Holding Theo's hands. It was a beautiful song. Margret had a bewitchingly sweet voice. She sang to the rhythm of the swishing dish-wash brush. Or was she washing the dishes to the rhythm of the song? Tom listened very hard, but he only could hear her sigh, "Yes. Yes."

Then the sound of rubber gloves being taken off. With a clank she put the kettle on to make their evening drink. He returned to the numbers and graphs in his textbook, straight and sharp.

Tom knew that he had to finish his engineering degree and he did like working with numbers and graphs. He was to take over the family's small, but quite successful, engineering firm. It was what kept him and his mother financially comfortable.

"No more music. No more interruptions. Until I have finished the exams. Please!"

With that he sorted out his papers. Two more years, he thought. Yes, two more years and I will have to take over the firm: relieve

Douglas Henshall, his manager and mentor, become the boss of Dolmer's Engineering! Tom felt a slight dread thinking about it.

He hadn't noticed his mother sneak into the room and place a cup of cocoa on his desk.

FOUR

Two more years had passed. Tom sat at the desk in his room. On the bed lay a violin and some sheet music. He could hear his mother slowly shuffling down the corridor towards the kitchen. She had collected the mail from their little mailbox attached to the front door. Automatically he covered the violin.

It was his big secret. He had bought the violin with funds from the firm. She must not know that he was about to fulfil his big passion in life. All he wanted to do was to make music. To make the violin sing, just like Esther did on that beautiful day at the market.

He heard his mother call,

"Aren't you going to open the mail?"

Then the phone rang. It was Jason, the music shop owner.

Picking up the mail he told his mother that he was needed at the office.

"You better change then. You cannot go to the office in those clothes!"

His mother never went into his room. He had to get his suit from his mother's sewing and ironing room. She would ask for his office clothes and get them ready for him, as she had done for her husband. Everything was neat, clean and ironed, from his underwear and socks to his white shirt. The jacket and trousers brushed, the trousers with a sharp crease. He smiled, feeling a great affection toward her.

"Let me look at you."

Margret Dolmer had to stretch to reach his collar, which needed straightening.

"You'll do. Give my regards to Mr Henshall."

Tom rushed down the stone staircase of the old house and out into the narrow street. Looking up he could see the blue of the sky between the tall houses. He felt good. He felt as if something special was awaiting him. Whistling, he started walking down the familiar uneven footpath towards the tram stop. Coming to the main street he suddenly stopped.

No, he thought, I am not going to the office. I am going to the music shop. With this thought he took off his suit jacket, slung it over his shoulder, loosened his tie, turned around and started to walk towards the music shop.

On the corner, where the small street met the next main road, was the music shop's door. As he opened it a lever hit a bell hanging from the door jamb.

With a loud "ding" his arrival was announced.

"Good morning, Jason, you have something for me?"

They shook hands, smiling.

"Good morning, Tom. I'd like you to meet Mr Goldmark; your music teacher."

An old, short man, sporting a carefully trimmed white beard, stood up from a chair and walked briskly towards Tom — who seemed to tower over his teacher-to-be. The old man wore an antiquated black suit. The silver-white hair needed a cut and a comb.

"Rubin," he said and held out his hand, "Just call me Rubin. Being called Mister makes me feel terribly old! Show me your hands. They seem to be strong and, yes, long fingers. Well, I might just make some sort of a violinist out of you. Have you played at all? Ever held a violin? Have you got a violin? Can you read music?"

"Yes, yes, and yes. But I have never played. My mother hates every kind of noise, especially music. I cannot practise at home. Is that a problem?"

Ignoring the question, Rubin rummaged about in his coat pocket and found a tuning fork. He hit it on the side of the counter and held the end against the belly of a guitar, which amplified the sound.

"Can you sing this note for me, please?"

Tom precisely repeated the sound.

"Spot on. What a beautiful voice you have. Why don't you take singing lessons? Not as hard as playing the violin."

Tom told Rubin why. He did touch on his experience at the market as a little boy, where he met an old lady making her violin sing. He had fallen in love with the beautiful sound and all he ever wanted was to do the same.

Rubin seemed to ignore Tom's tale and carried on with his questioning.

"How old are you now, son?"

"Twenty-six."

"A bit old starting to learn the violin, I think."

Worried, Tom looked at his friend, Jason.

"Don't listen to him," Jason said, "He's only testing you."

Turning towards Rubin he continued,

"Tom is absolutely keen. He spends every spare minute here in my shop!"

"And how much is that? I need to know what I take on. I don't just take anybody!"

For a long time, Rubin looked at Tom.

"You seem to be honestly keen. I'll give you a try. Jason will tell you where I live. Maybe today after lunch?"

The tram took Tom into the centre of town. He thought of the day he went with his mother to the market. The new trams did not make the rhythmic *tam-ta-tam* noise anymore. They just soundless travelled down the road towards the centre of the town, past the large park with its colourful flowerbeds and roses. Tom decided to get off and walk through the park. He had plenty of time. Spring was in the air. His heart was full, almost bursting. Everything seemed to be exaggerated. The sky bluer, the smell of the roses sweeter and melodic bird-songs brilliantly loud.

He sat on one of the park benches. Looking at the violin case he whispered, "We are going to make Esther proud of us. We will work hard. We will sing together."

The thought of Esther always made him feel confident in his musical journey.

He found the very narrow little side street and the century-old house of his teacher. Well-worn stone stairs took him up to the top floor. He could hear someone playing behind the door. He knocked. No one answered. There was no doorbell.

He sat down on the top step. With his knees touching his chin he waited, his mind wandering. He could just look out through a little window towards the house next door. It was overgrown with ivy, a little bird busily flying in and out with some nest-building material.

The music stopped and the small door opened. Tom jumped up, almost hitting his head on the ceiling.

A young woman stood in the doorway.

"Tom, meet Clara. She is an excellent student."

The girl bent down and gave Rubin a kiss on the cheek. Still bent she manoeuvred herself out the low door, trying to make room for Tom. She straightened up and offered him her hand in greeting. She was tall and slim. Her hair was held together with a large comb in an untidy knot on the back of her head. Tom looked at her, feeling a tingle going through his body.

"Ok, ok. Greetings finished. Let's start your first lesson, Tom."

With that, Rubin disappeared into the darkness of the little flat. Tom took one last look at Clara's head and that untidy knot of hair as she descended the stairs. She glanced up at him and smiled.

Rubin took Tom's violin. Putting the case over the arms of a wooden chair, he opened it, removed the silk scarf covering it and took the instrument out. Slowly he ran his finger over the strings. A terrible sound escaped.

"G, D, A, E," he murmured as he dug in his coat pocket in

search of the tuning fork. His hand reappeared with a number of them. Looking over his glasses he found the right one, tapped it on the chair and held it onto the body of the violin.

"E. That's your high string."

With that Rubin started plucking the top string and turning one of the pegs. Higher and higher the note went. Tom was waiting for the string to break.

While Rubin tuned, Tom looked around the semi-dark room. His eyes had adjusted to the dim light. There was a window, but neat stacks of papers blocked most of the light. Markers at different intervals were protruding from the piles.

"Sheet music, write-ups, revues and other papers I find important and interesting, all sorted and marked. Well, your violin is in tune. I'll just compare it with the piano over there."

Rubin turned on a light. It shone on a baby grand.

"I only like to illuminate the subjects I am working with. That way I cannot be distracted. I have a bit of trouble with attentiveness."

With the piano lit up the room suddenly showed its entire size. Tom was amazed how big it was and by its odd shape. There were two windows and two doors. One open, showing the black tunnel-like entrance hall.

Rubin had put the violin back in its case. He had totally forgotten about checking the tuning with the piano, or did he know it was not really necessary?

"Strange shape this room," he said as he turned around. "It is very old and there is talk about completely renovating the interior by gutting the building. But as long as I live here, the authorities cannot do anything. You see, I own this old flat. They'll have to carry me out. I am the only one living here. It's absolutely wonderful! I can make as much noise as I like. I have no idea what this building was used for. Easily found out by going to the council. But I don't want to fill my head with such things."

Rubin ruffled his silvery hair and made a stubborn face.

Tom had noticed some paintings on the walls. All of them, except one, were covered with black paper. He pointed at them.

"Why?"

"Oh, less diversion that way. I only shine a light on items I am involved with in the now. When I am tired of this painting or change my mood, I will cover it and uncover another."

'I do like that', Tom thought. 'But I don't think mother would agree'.

The old man looked approvingly around his living space. Turning toward Tom he pointed at the floor.

"Would you like a coffee? There's a great café on the ground floor. Mr Hawelka knows how to make a good coffee. His wife makes lovely little cakes."

Tom wanted to know when the lesson would start.

Rubin did not answer. He had disappeared into the blackness of the hall.

The front door opened, and a strip of light ran over the floor.

Tom was amazed how agile the old man was, managing the decaying stone steps. Rubin stopped at one of the windows and pointed at the building next door.

"Look! Those little birds come every year and make a nest in the ivy. Spring must be here."

The birds disappeared into the vine and Rubin continued down the steep steps.

He seemed to have forgotten that Tom had come to have his first violin lesson.

There was no one in the café. They chose a table by one of the windows and ordered their drinks and some small cakes. The coffee arrived on individual little trays accompanied by a glass of water.

"I believe that is how they do it in Vienna. Mr Hawelka does not talk about his time in Vienna. Who wants to live in the past when there is so much future to fill? I have been to Vienna, a beautiful city. You know they don't dance the waltz in the streets. Do you dance?"

"No," was Tom's despondent answer. "What is the building overgrown by ivy? It looks very grand in a sombre sort of way."

He was trying to change the subject.

"Oh, that's the synagogue. We are in the Jewish district of this town."

They both fell into silence, nursing their own private thoughts whilst drinking their coffee.

Abruptly Rubin got up, stretched his hand towards Tom and bid him goodbye.

"Come tomorrow morning and we will continue our lesson. Please leave your violin with me. I need to play it. I will take good care, trust me. Please excuse my sudden departure. I have to meet someone. What I need is a secretary or an appointment book. I think I'll settle for the latter. Less troublesome."

Rubin smiled at Tom who was getting his wallet out.

"No, no, I don't want any money, but you can pay for the coffee. See you tomorrow."

With that he was off out the door and across the road.

'What a strange little man', Tom thought.

The next day was as beautiful as the one before. Far too early Tom left the flat, his mother wondering where he was going in his everyday clothes, leaving his tie behind. He was out the door before she could ask.

He thought he might have a coffee and maybe something to eat at the café Rubin had introduced him to before going to his second lesson. Would there be a second lesson? Tom wondered if he could work with a man whose mind never seemed to be focused. Tom thought of Rubin's method of avoiding being distracted by covering items of no importance. And yet his thoughts seemed to be all over the place. Thinking of his teacher-to-be, he slowly strolled through the park, with his hands in his pockets, whistling, trying to be calm. But he was not. His legs were tense, his chest wanted to explode.

Rubin was sitting in Hawelka's café having breakfast, a big

mug of coffee in front of him. Wiping a few crumbs from his carefully trimmed grey beard, he waved at Tom and invited him to his table.

"Mrs Hawelka makes a great breakfast. Would you like some?"

Without waiting for an answer Rubin called and ordered.

They ate in silence. Rubin had picked up his large cup of coffee. Looking over the rim he slowly asked Tom how he knew Esther.

Tom had not mentioned Esther to anyone. She was his secret!

"How, how do you know her?" Tom half-shouted at Rubin. "How?"

Rubin put his cup down. He made himself comfortable in his seat. His pretentious behaviour disappeared.

"When you mentioned an old lady bewitching you with her music, I knew that this could only be Esther. It felt so like her. Playing at a market? Well, that was news to me. I know everyone in this town who plays the violin. There is only one person I know who can wrap you up in her music. Wrap you up tight with her sweet musical ribbon."

Rubin made fists as if he were tightening up this imaginative ribbon.

"Did you say, tall and slender, her hair tied into an untidy bun on the back of her head? Held together with a large comb? Did you say that some of the hair was hanging down, framing her face? Did you not say she was kind and beautiful? Did she not bewitch you with her playing? Did the sound of her instrument not make you fall in love with the violin? Is that not the reason why we are now sitting here together?"

His eyes looked out into nowhere. Was he visiting the past? Something he always considered to be a waste of time.

"She bewitched me. That was a long time ago when we were both very young. Oh, did we make music together! Music with our instruments. Music with our bodies."

His expression changed.

"Tom, do not allow her to bewitch you with her music. You

21

cannot follow her. None of us could. She will make your life a misery. Like the Pied Piper she will lure you!"

Rubin started moving his cup about on the table. Slowly, as if he was trying to remove a memory, he pushed it towards the edge.

"No one could follow her. No one could keep her. She would sweeten your life with her beauty and suddenly leave. One day she was gone. I never found her. In the end I stopped looking."

Blackness filled Tom's heart. Esther was his deep secret. How did Rubin know? How could he know who he was talking about? The blackness turned into a deep jealousy. The jealousy into anger. Trying to stay calm he found himself saying,

"What happened to her?"

"No one knows. She just left, taking her bewitching music, her beautiful self, away from us all who loved her deeply. Oh, so deeply. Oh, how I loved her. Oh, how I hate her!"

Tom felt the rage fill his chest. There was no way he could speak. He thought of her broken promise, his deep disappointment. He thought how she surrounded him with music. Turned his life into confusion. Lured him to stay with his violin.

Esther and her music are mine. She is mine! How dare Rubin stake a prior claim to her! Rage welled up in him.

Tom stood up and hit the table with his fist, using all his strength, making the breakfast dishes jump. He thought he heard himself screaming, but there was no sound. He just kept on hitting the table.

"I love Esther so much! She poured water on a little seed in me and made it grow. She introduced me to my first love, music, the violin. She was my first disappointment, my first big hurt."

Coming up behind him Mrs Hawelka put her hand on Tom's shoulder, "We all loved her. She was a beautiful woman inside and out."

Tom shouted, "You all knew her? How? When?"

For the first time in his life, he felt what it was like to be deeply jealous. He thought she was his, only his. With rage in his eyes, and confusion in his soul, he looked at them and left the café.

Rubin wanted to follow Tom.

"Let him be." Mrs Hawelka held Rubin back. "Let him be."

On this beautiful spring day, surrounded by his own thundercloud, Tom walked and walked through the city, through the park and onwards. Suddenly he found himself in front of a familiar building, a familiar sign: *Dolmer's Engineering.*

He walked through the front door of the two-storied office building and up the stairs to his office.

"Good morning, Tom. We did not expect you today. Is everything OK?" His secretary greeted him, cheerful as ever."I'll tell Mr Henshall that you are here."

"Thank you, Joyce."

He walked into his office and sat down behind his desk: his father's desk. Didn't his dad have a good life? A wife, a son, a flat, food. 'Should I not concentrate on what I have? I am good at my job. So why, oh why do I hanker after the impossible? Dream myself into a different life.'

The door opened. Douglas Henshall, the manager, came into the room, behind him was Joyce.

"Are you OK. Tom? Is something wrong with your mother?"

Douglas had known Tom since his birth. He knew him as well as his own children. Never had he seen Tom in such a state.

"There is nothing wrong with my mother! I am fine, thank you."

He looked at his concerned manager, friend and, at times, father-figure.

"Yes, well, I have just managed to upset some people I know. I was jealous that I would never know her the way they did. I lost my temper. And now I have lost them!"

Douglas had brought a chair to the desk and sat opposite Tom.

"Look, Tom. If they are true friends, they will understand. And I am sure you will over time learn more about the person you're talking about. If I were you, I'd go back, buy them all a drink and apologise for your behaviour. Why don't you do that?"

Rubin Goldmark was still sitting at the same table. He was looking out the window, down the narrow street, as if he was waiting for someone. Then he saw him. The sun was behind Tom. It lit up his curly, blond hair. Rubin could not read any expression in the shaded face.

Tom stood in the doorway pretending to look calm and self-confident.

"Well?" Rubin examined the young man. "Sit down. We need to talk."

Like a statue, Tom stood looking at his teacher. Over and over he had practised what he was going to say. Now it had all gone! His tongue and legs did not want to work.

"Please, Tom, come and sit down."

Rubin patted the chair next to him. On the table was a glass of white wine. He pointed at the glass.

"Would you like one?"

Tom shook his head.

"My dear boy, this incredible, angry outburst of yours has made me very happy. Let me explain."

Rubin had a sip of wine, then stroked his beard. Looking hard at Tom he continued.

"Every artistic person carries anger inside of them. Anger and quite a bit of madness. Without that, one cannot step outside the square of the ordinary life. You looked to me like a man in a square. A man who makes lists and follows them. A man with an appointment book. You are probably too young to have a secretary."

He lifted his glass towards Tom.

"My dear boy, today you have shown me that you possess anger! Also, we have a common love. We will never talk about her again."

He put a little book on the table.

"Appointment book! So, let's make a day for our next lesson. I am looking forward to teaching you what I can, but you will have to do as I say!"

Tom suggested Monday afternoon.

"Excellent! Come at about three. No, come at three! By then young Clara will have finished her lesson."

Rubin noted the time in his empty little book.

FIVE

"Tom, do you have to sit like that? Please take your feet off the chair. It was after all your father's and he would not approve. No, he would not!"

Margret Dolmer looked sternly at her son, then carried on mending.

With his feet on the chair, clutching his knees, Tom felt safe. He always sat like that when life put problems in front of him. Until a few days ago everything was so easy. Now it was total confusion. A few days ago, he lived with a dream. Now his dream was turning into reality. Tom was scared. This crazy little old man who was going to be his teacher, what did he know about him? How did he meet Esther? He made him so angry. Tom had not been that angry since he was a little boy.

And Rubin thought it good to be angry.

Tom held his legs, clutching his knees tight to his chest, trying to make himself small.

"Douglas rang. He was worried about you. Are you OK, son? You went to the office on your day off."

Margret looked over her work at Tom. She was concerned.

"Douglas said you had been quarrelling with a friend. Which friend was that? He said it was over a young woman. I have never met any of your friends."

She took up the mending and quietly continued,

"Have you got a girlfriend? You have been going out a lot lately."

Tom let go his knees and stretched out his long legs. Looking at his mother he lit a cigarette.

"No, I do not have a girlfriend."

How could he tell his mother that he was in love with a violin? Could he tell her about his dream? Could he tell her how frightened he was to stand in front of that open door leading him towards his lifelong ambition?

Is the doing going to be as wondrous as the dream? Would she understand? Could she help?

The light shone on her mending. He could not make out her face, her thoughts. She somehow felt sad and lonely. Here they were living together, not knowing each other's thoughts. Not knowing each other. Never really talking.

"I promise I will let you know when I have a girlfriend and make sure you meet her. The people I had a quarrel with, well, you will meet them too, if they turn out to be friends. That's a promise."

She looked up. The light shone on her face and showed him a pair of slightly wet eyes. Putting her mending back in her basket, she asked Tom if he would like a drink before he went to bed.

They both sat with their hot drink in the semi-dark living room, not talking, but both of them could feel that there was a bridge being built. A bridge that one day might bring them together.

Ding! The little bell over the door of the music shop announced Tom's arrival. As his eyes adjusted to the dim light, he noticed Jason talking to a young woman.

"Hi Tom! Meet Claire."

The young woman glared at Jason.

"Sorry, meet Clara. She hates being called Claire. Sounds too girlish, she says!"

Clara looked at Jason and stuck her tongue out. Jason did the same. Then they laughed. Tom did not know what to do. He felt deeply embarrassed.

"Yes, I met Clara at Mr Goldmark's."

"Isn't Rubin a darling?"

Clara's blue eyes scanned Tom. Her tall slender body was

dressed in tight trousers and a sloppy oversized jumper, her hair was very long and completely unruly. She kept on hooking the long strands behind her ears, but they always seem to escape. Tom took her hand in greeting and bowed. Clara laughed and gave him a hug and a little peck on his cheek.

"Hey, Tom, she likes you!" Jason laughed.

Tom blushed.

"Did I say I like him?" she said teasingly. "We are going to be fellow students. We need to like each other. Or at least like each other's music making."

Clara went behind the counter and got her little rucksack.

"I have a class. Yes, some of us have to go and get an education! See you around."

With that and the 'ding' of the door, Clara was gone, her hair flying.

Tom stood mesmerised. He was totally bewildered. He wanted to be in the safety of his room, alone with his violin and his dream.

"Hey Tom, isn't she gorgeous? Quite a bit egocentric. But she can play the fiddle! Rubin seems to be very pleased. He says her technical skills are excellent, though sometimes a bit of emotion would improve her playing. I suppose she uses all her emotions in her daily life. By the way, you could do with a bit of emotion. Be a bit less stiff. Put on a large sloppy jumper and see how you feel!"

Tom looked at his pressed trousers and hand-knitted jumper.

"Well, Tom, what can I do for you? Where is your fiddle? You never go anywhere without the Steiner."

"Mr Goldmark, I mean Rubin has my violin. I feel quite lonely without it. I've forgotten why I came to see you. All this greeting with Clara and hugging made me forget."

"Tom, you must loosen up a bit. You know, sort of relax, get rid of all those inhibitions you carry around with you."

Backing towards the door he just said a quick, "Maybe", and before he knew Tom found himself standing on the footpath outside the music shop, totally confused and not quite knowing what to do. Not remembering why he came. Meeting Clara had unsettled him. She felt so familiar. Had he met her before?

He turned around and walked back to his apartment.

"Home already?" his mother asked.

"Would you like to go out for coffee?" he called down the corridor.

"What, like to a café?"

"Yes, come on, let's go for a coffee and cake."

Margret Dolmer was still a handsome woman. She had put on a little make-up, pulled a comb through her frizzy hair and put on shoes with little heels, which made her just tall enough to be able to hook her arm through her son's. She tried to put a spring in her steps, but her sore hips prevented it. They walked slowly towards the café, where they sat outside in the garden. The old chestnut trees were starting to set flowers. Just like little candles standing up straight. It was a glorious spring day.

Tom scooped the cream off his coffee, putting big dollops into his mouth.

"You are supposed to mix the cream into your coffee!"

"I know, but I like cream and I like my coffee black and strong. And dear mother, I am 26. At my age, I am allowed to take my coffee the way I like!"

He looked at his mother, laughed and took her hand.

"Mother stop treating me like a little boy!"

She was stirring and stirring her coffee. It took far longer than necessary.

"It is not easy," she whispered.

She did not look up. What did he know? How did he know what it was like? She had never understood his silence, his quiet inner world. He never opened a door to let her in. She knew he had a big secret. A secret that occupied his whole being. A secret not to be shared with her. Was it her fault that he had closed up? Had she been too strict with him when he was a little boy? Oh, how she wished she was not so alone, so lonely. How she wished Theo had not left her. He was so good with the boy.

Margret did not realise that she had slowly demolished her cake into small pieces. It looked like crumbs surrounded by cream.

"Mother, what are you doing with your cake? That's not the way to enjoy a good cake!"

They looked at each other for what seemed ages. Then they both started laughing.

"Oh, son!"

Rummaging about in her handbag she found a handkerchief.

"Oh, my dear boy!"

Tom was not sure if the tears were happy or unhappy ones.

"If you stop treating me like a child, I will tell you my secret."

Not being in the flat, full of past memories but in the café garden surrounded by trees and with the feeling of spring in the air, made Tom feel relaxed and free. He would have never let his private thoughts escape his room to fill the rest of the flat. But here? In the garden, amongst the old trees, he felt he could talk about them.

Her big fear was that Tom might go and start his own life, maybe with his love, his girlfriend. This had always been her biggest dread.

"Are you in love? But will she look after you? Cook, clean, knit you jumpers, iron your clothes?"

He smiled at her.

"Yes, I am in love. I have been in love with her since I was nine years old. But not with a person; or with a spirit or something weird like that. I am in love with music. I am in love with the violin.

For years I have been looking at instruments through the window of the music shop down the street. I used to make a detour from the railway station to be able to pass the music shop. Then one day, Jason, the man who runs the store, called me in and we started talking music. We started listening to records. This amazing instrument mesmerised me! I became infatuated by it. So, after I finished my degree and started working, I bought a second-hand violin.

I was terrified that you would find out. You did not like me making a lot of noise and you always stopped me from singing and whistling. You always turned off the radio in the living room. You obviously did not like music!

Never have I played. I dream that one day I will play as well as.....”

He stopped talking, not being able to say Esther's name. ”I just want to make the instrument sing. One day I will.”

Please don't misunderstand my love for the violin, my love for music. It is not like being in love with a person. You probably remember the girl I was going out with during my university years. This is a different kind of love. You know what I mean. You were in love with dad.”

Tom blushed.

His mother had completely demolished her cake, the plate was full of crumbs. She stared at him. How could she not have felt her own child's yearnings? How could she have rejected his love for music? How, how? Was she so occupied with her own misery? Before she could carry on tormenting herself with her thoughts, Tom continued,

“As a boy I dreamt of two things. Music and travel. Dad had given me an atlas and a number of maps for Christmas. Do you remember?”

She looked at the young man opposite her, the boy, the baby she carried for nine months.

Theo had called him, the miracle. She had called him inconvenient, disruptive. Over ten years they'd been married. Then their circumstances changed. The motorbike was sold. A car was bought. Going dancing on Saturdays stopped. Oh, how she loved dancing with Theo. But now she stayed at home with

31

the baby. Theo went to the office. She started to despise life and people and music and laughter.

"No, I do not remember your father giving you an atlas."

She pushed the plate of scrambled-up cake away. The short magic between them was broken.

The evening was slowly creeping in. The outside lights had been turned on.

Tom looked pleadingly at her. He could feel the bridge between him and his mother crumble. Could he save the moment? Or was it lost.

"Let's have a glass of wine, mother."

"No, I do not want a drink!"

"A cup of coffee? Tea? It is so lovely to sit here with you. At home we never talk!" Tom took his mother's hand. "Please?"

"I must get home and cook dinner. We do have to eat! I have things organised. Everything is ready..."

"I don't need any dinner. I need you to stay here with me. It is such a lovely evening."

With that, Tom called the waiter and ordered two glasses of wine.

Margret Dolmer pulled her hand away from Tom's and stood up.

"Please!" he whispered.

She turned towards the door and walked out.

The waiter arrived with the two glasses

"Looks like I will have to drink them both. May I smoke?"

He lit a cigarette and drank the wine. Slowly Tom's anger and disappointment faded away. He had managed to catch her and hold her for a moment. Surely, he would be able to do that again. Tickle her, like a trout. Hold her for a short time only to have her slip through his fingers, back into the dark depths of her pond, her life.

SIX

Outside the large ornate iron gates was a small stand with cut flowers in tins. The old man greeted them. Margret chose a short-stemmed bunch of mixed flowers. She said nothing, nor did she acknowledge the old man. Tom smiled, nodded and paid for the flowers.

It was a small, intimate graveyard with its graves meandering up a gentle slope, so that the gravestones overlooked the town. They walked to the gravesite. It was situated almost on top of the little rise. Margret, kneeling on a small mat, made herself busy, straightening up her husband's grave. Tom picked up the tin vase and walked to the tap. On his return Margret put the vase back on the now tidy grave and arranged the flowers. Not a word was spoken. They never did speak by the grave.

Tom put up the small folding chair for his mother. He decided to sit down on the verge of the grave. It was on this day two years ago his father was buried.

Margret had put her face into her hands. She let go a little sigh. Her thoughts flew to her husband.

"Oh Theo, oh Theo. What to do! What to do! I just do not know how to communicate with my own son. Yesterday, well you probably know about the situation at the café. I really want to get close to him. He is a good boy. He is no trouble. I do love him! You were so good with him. You had such an easy relationship. I will lose him and then I will be all alone. Yes, I know, treat him like a man. Learn to communicate with him. Meet his friends. Try to fit in. Oh, Theo."

She felt a slight touch on her shoulder and then a little kiss on the back of her head. It was Tom. He thought she was crying.

"I miss him too, Mum. We just have to do the best, you and me."

Tom walked away. Under a group of trees were some benches. He wore his good trousers. As if his dad minded what he wore, but his mother insisted on getting dressed up. Tom brushed away the spent flowers which had fallen from the tree onto the bench and sat down.

"Oh Dad! It is so very comforting talking to you. Life has confronted me with a long corridor; at the end a door slightly ajar. A strip of light is escaping from within. A streak of new life! So many years have I dreamt and schemed and planned for my wish to come true. Music. Oh Dad, music. It fills my body, my soul, everything. I am frightened, Dad. Is the reality as the dream? I am frightened I might wake up! I am frightened of losing this feeling inside. I am frightened of losing Esther's music. Oh Dad, I wish you could talk to me. You were so good and patient in answering all my questions. Do you remember when I asked you why the sky was blue? You told me that it was blue, because that is the name people gave it. I often think about the names we give to things around us. You laughed and gave me a big hug. Then you told me why the sky is blue. Oh Dad, I wish I could talk to mum, I wish I had someone I could talk to about this."

Tom pulled his long legs up against his chest, clutching them tightly, his head resting on his knees.

Margret slowly walked up to him. With a stiff, tentative motion she put her hand on his shoulder.

"Let's go home and have a cup of tea."

"No thank you, I'd like to stay on a bit longer," he said.

He listened to her slow steps on the gravel. Suddenly the crunching noise ceased. His mother had stopped. She called to him.

"What about a cup of coffee? There is a nice little place just down from here?"

As they walked out from the cemetery through the iron gates, Margret nodded and smiled at the old man. She bought another small bunch of flowers.

"For home," she said as she paid.

The old man looked at her with astonishment. In all these years she had not spoken a word to him, never given him a smile.

Margret hooked her arm into Tom's and, in step, they walked down the path towards the town. Next to them a little brook confined in concrete walls chatted and gurgled. As soon as they came to the main street the little waterway was covered over, never to be seen again, to merge with the sewage, with the waste water of the town.

Tom stopped and looked at the water being swallowed up under the road. Margret did not notice. She pointed at a building on the other side of the street.

"Look, Tom, there is the café."

As they were waiting for their coffee Margret suddenly said:

"Will you take me to meet your violin teacher? I would like to meet your friends."

SEVEN

They got off the tram one stop early and walked towards the large iron gates that led to the narrow streets of the old part of the town.

As they passed through the big gates they walked into a different century. There were no cars, no public transport in this part of town. Margret had not been here since her schooldays. She slowed down and smiled.

"See this strange round building. That used to be a tower of the old wall encircling the town. There were four. Only two remain. I do remember a bit of my history lessons. History was my favourite subject."

"My teacher, Mr Goldmark, lives in the other one," Tom replied "Close to the Jewish part of town. We'll have to go to the other end. And we're a bit late!"

With that Margret hooked her arm through Tom's and they strode through the old streets, Margret pointing at buildings, giving Tom a history lesson.

Rubin was sitting at his café table by the window, facing the street so that he could see Tom and his mother arrive. Tom's violin-case was on the table next to his. He was correcting something, stabbing the paper with a pencil.

"Ta ta ta tam ta…..Oh, my dear God, this is terrible! Oh why, oh why do I, Rubin Goldmark, have to be punished by correcting exam papers?"

Tom held the door open for Margret. Rubin looked up.

"Mrs Dolmer, I presume. Oh, thank you for saving me from suicide! I was just about to stab myself with this pencil!"

He jumped up and walked briskly to Margret, who was just about to turn around and leave. Tom gently pushed his totally bewildered mother through the door into the café.

Rubin took Margret's limp hand and gave it a good shake.

"Rubin Goldmark. I am, I will be, Tom's teacher. Please have a seat."

He made a little bow and pulled the chair out for her.

"Mr Havelka. Service, please!"

They sat around the little table. Coffees and a plate of small cakes arrived. The whole scenario felt rehearsed. Margret sat straight and stiff on the edge of her chair.

"Did we disturb you? Are we stopping you from important work?"

She was ready to spring up and leave.

"No, no. Please relax. I was just correcting some so-called compositions from so-called music students. They get a test to write a duet. There is not a hint of harmony. Well, I suppose they would call it modern. We are after all in the second half of the 20th century. This so-called music is tickling my ears the wrong way. Terrible, terrible!"

Rubin kept on talking about his involvement in music. He used big words, musical terms, and talked a lot about composers like Wagner, dissecting the compositions, singing parts of them.

Margret could not contribute to the conversation. She felt left out and closed up completely. She would have rather strolled about the old city, remembering her schooldays, feeling young amongst the old buildings. She wondered what her school friends were doing. Looking at the synagogue across the road she suddenly said,

"But that building was destroyed?"

The conversation was broken. They both looked at her.

"Was it not?"

Mr Hawelka stepped to the table, filled her cup and told her that she was quite right. The synagogue was rebuilt with the material of the old one.

"Did you know the old one? It was a beautiful building. This one looks like a fortress, very foreboding."

Margret quietly told them about her school days and history lessons.

"I did like history," she said.

Rubin looked at her.

"History? Did you? What about the future?"

Tom was worried that Rubin would voice his theory and his feeling towards the past. He did not want his mother hurt, not now when she was trying to talk.

"Did you like music?" Rubin looked sharply at Margret.

"I did once, but that was a long time ago."

Turning towards Tom she said,

"I would like to go home now."

Rubin gestured at Tom's violin case.

"It is a very fine instrument, your Jacob Steiner. Of course, it is a copy, a good one though. It is in tune, and it holds its tune very well. Practise long strokes and see if you can get some good sounds instead of horrid scratchings. Keep your bow light and soft. *Loooong* strokes, light and soft."

Rubin was standing, pretending to hold a violin. His whole body-language changed as he played the phantom violin. Suddenly stopping, he said to Tom,

"I see you in a week. I am busy marking these horrid exam papers. I will get some music for you. Just practise, long strokes, light and soft and make that lovely instrument sing for you."

He looked at Margret. In a slightly sarcastic tone he said,

"Tom put the mute on. It will soften the sound."

Then he took her hand, made a little bow, and sat down at the table with the students' sheet music, carrying on stabbing the paper and asking God why he, Mr Rubin Goldmark had to be punished by correcting something that offended his ears.

The walk back to the tram was silent. Margret walked stooped, as if she was fighting against a strong wind. Tom, clutching his beloved violin under his arm, trailed behind, whistling.

Suddenly she turned into a narrow side street. With long strides, Tom soon caught up with her.

"The tram stop is down that road!"

Tom stood in front of his mother looking puzzled.

"I would like to go back to the park, where it is green and quiet."

They walked through the large iron gates into the green oasis. Margret found a bench and sat down. She was hot and out of breath.

Close to them was a large round fishpond and fountain. In the middle a figure shiny from the cascading water. She noticed some ducks paddling about. The fountain created a roundabout for the paths coming from all directions. There was no one walking. It was just after lunch and the park was almost empty. The sun was high; it was warming up.

When she had regained her breath, she angrily snapped at Tom:

"That little, old, arrogant man. That teacher of yours. My God, what a self-centred little man he is. Who does he think he is? First, he is all over me, full of charm and then I was just treated like a bit of nothing to be totally ignored. Then sprouting about all those musical terms, trying to show my ignorance. Then bringing up Wagner. Really! Oh, Tom, must you get involved with people like that? They are not our kind of people."

She slid into the back of the curved bench and looked at Tom standing in front of her. He did not know what to say. The memories of his childhood came back. The way she barked at him when he sang or whistled. How he always was terrified of disappointing his parents. How he put his love for music aside to pass university.

He started walking up and down in front of his mother.

"I made a mistake, I should have never told you about my love of music. I should have never introduced you to Rubin. I will not give up my music. I can move out if noise and music revolts you so much. I have arranged with Jason from the music shop to practise in his shop after closing...Oh, Mum!"

Long did mother and son look at each other. Then, with difficulty, Margret stood up and limped towards the tram stop.

EIGHT

"Where are you going?" Margret was sitting in the kitchen. "The office. We are having a meeting, I need to be there. After that, I am going to Jason's music shop. I will not be home for lunch. Not too sure about dinner."

Before she could answer, the front door slammed, and Tom was running down the steps, his violin case under his arm, his briefcase in his hand.

He dropped the violin off at Jason and hailed a taxi. Quickly he skimmed over the meeting's agenda. Tom had slid into the skin of his other life.

He walked into the boardroom and sat down in his father's chair at the end of the table. Douglas Henshall, his manager, to his left. Gary, the foreman, came into the room, embarrassed to be in his work clothes. Tom pointed at the seat next to him, to his right. That's how it was in his father's days.

He remembered those days well. The many times Tom, as a little boy, had to sit quietly on a chair in the corner waiting for his mother to get some time off from the office.

Continuing the tradition of his father and grandfather gave Tom a feeling of security. This was his first client meeting since taking over the company. Even knowing that his staff was very supportive he was extremely nervous. He desperately wanted a cigarette, but smoking was not permitted in the boardroom.

He took off his jacket and hung it on the back of his chair. Stretching out his long legs he leant back and relaxed. Slowly he pulled his fingers through his curly, blond hair. Douglas smiled.

41

'Just like his father,' he thought. 'But so young and with such big responsibilities.' He gently touched Tom's arm. 'You will be fine, lad,' the touch seemed to say.

The door opened and Joyce ushered their prospective new client into the room.

After the meeting he asked Joyce how she thought it had gone.

"Very well," she said. "He was clearly impressed by the company and particularly by its young Managing Director and his grasp of the business."

Tom blushed and looked down.

"Are you going home?" she asked him.

"No Joyce, just order a taxi, thank you."

He asked the driver to take him to the old city, close to the tower facing the river. The briefcase was on his lap. He gave it a little tap, which started a slow drumming rhythm. The drumming became louder and Tom started whistling.

"You got a good whistle there, sir. Musician? Well, here we are."

Tom pushed the door to Hawela's café open. He took a seat at Rubin's table and sat with his back to the window, reading the paper, sipping his coffee, smoking. The briefcase lay on the table. It had belonged to his father. The shiny dark-brown leather showed off a little brass plaque with the initials TAD.

Rubin walked in and sat down at another table. He was annoyed that some stranger, some businessman, was occupying his regular space.

Tom looked up and Rubin stared in astonishment.

"It's you! What happened to you? Are you going to a job interview?"

"No, I have just come from work."

Rubin picked up his cup and sat down with Tom.

"Work. You have a job?"

"Yes, but I am not here to talk about that. I am here to talk about your attitude towards my mother. She was deeply hurt."

"Did I have an attitude?"

42

Tom ran his long fingers through his blond curls. Rubin stroked his finely trimmed beard. He was clearly amazed by the accusation.

"Me? What did I do?" He stared at Tom. "Me?"

Looking at his teacher Tom felt intimidation creep into him. This was different to his other life, his work and the boardroom. He had rehearsed a speech. He was going to tell Rubin off. It was easy to reprimand one of his apprentices, but his teacher? The words did not want to come out.

Rubin pointed at the briefcase.

"What does the TAD stand for?"

"Theodore Andreas Dolmer and Tom Alexander Dolmer; my dad and me. "

"And pray, tell me, Mr Dolmer, what do you do?"

"I am the Director of Dolmer's Engineering."

"Oh my, a numbers man!"

"Yes, a numbers man."

Rubin was mocking him. Tom felt anger creep in. But he did not want to make a scene. After finishing his coffee, he asked Mr Hawelka to call for a taxi.

Turning to Rubin he smiled while inside he was boiling with rage.

"I'll see you next Monday. I will practise, soft and slow. See you then."

After Tom left the house that morning Margret put on her hat and a smart jacket. She looked up music shops in the telephone book and found the one Tom frequently visited. Jason had answered the phone. She remembered his name.

Bling! said the little bell on the door as she entered. It took her a while to adjust to the semi-dark room. A young man walked towards her from behind the counter.

"Can I help you?"

"Margret Dolmer," she said, holding out her hand.

Jason fetched a chair. As he put it down, he nervously looked at her.

"Please sit down. Tom is not here. He came in and left his violin. Said he had to go to work. He looked very smart. He said he would come in later to do his practice. Would you like to stay? Would you like a glass of water? Anything?"

"Thank you, a glass of water would be most agreeable. It is rather hot today."

When she had finished her drink, she told Jason about Tom's job, about his successful studies and his responsibilities as the owner of an engineering company. Then she got up, thanked him for his kindness and asked him to give Tom a message.

"Tell my son that he can practise his violin at home. There's no need to do it in your shop. Thank you."

She gave him a quick smile and turned to the door.

Jason stared, confused, at her. He only managed a quick, "Oh he will like that very much!" before she took hold of the door handle.

With a Bling of the door bell she was out in the street.

What could she do next? Home did not appeal. Home seemed at the moment to be a sad place. She walked down the busy street and found a café and ordered lunch. This was her first outing on her own since Theo's death. Having picked a table by the window she could watch the world pass by without being involved.

She thought of Tom and his love for music. She felt she had to learn to accept the situation. She could not understand why it created such deep anger in her. Did she not love it once? Oh, if she only could remember.

The scenes on the street outside began to blur as Margret focussed inside herself. No matter how hard she tried, the vision of her memory would not go any further than to the day she met Theo. That was the time her life began. With Theo and his parents, happiness and security arrived in her life. The life before was a blur. She did remember her father. She did like him. Where did he disappear to? Then there was a rather uncompromisingly hard woman she called mother. Then she remembered the convent school where she spent all of her childhood days.

Margret shuddered, blinked her eyes and started to focus on the life around her. The waitress took her plate and the empty cup, wiped the table and made her aware that it was almost four in the afternoon. They were closing soon.

Margret got up slowly. Her hip hurt from sitting on an uncomfortable chair. She swayed a little but caught herself. Then she paid and with a thank you and sorry, she left the café.

As she walked past the music shop, she saw Tom inside. He was clutching his violin case with both arms, a broad smile brightening up his face. Jason had his arms stretched out in readiness to hug both Tom and the violin. Margret could feel the great joy between the two friends. She smiled and walked home.

She let herself into the flat and then heard Tom's key in the lock. Hastily Margret took off her hat and rushed into the kitchen where she sat down, pretending to prepare dinner. She did not know how to approach her own son. How to congratulate him for having taken over his father's position.

He stood in the door of the kitchen, his whole being filled with excitement, clutching his violin to his chest like a baby.

"Mother, in front of you stands the new Managing Director of Dolmer's Engineering! I feel that I managed well in that meeting. Though I must say Douglas was a great help. He knew how to encourage me."

He tapped the violin case.

"And then this!"

In his excitement, he walked towards his mother. He wanted to give her a hug, but she shrank back. For quite a while mother and son stared at each other. Tom put the violin on the table, stretched out his arms and gently placed them on Margret's shoulders.

"Thank you for accepting my music making."

He shyly looked at her and smiled.

"I must get dinner ready," she said, turning back towards the table.

After the meal, Tom suggested that they should go out somewhere to celebrate the beginning of his life as a Director. The start of something new!

Margret could not see a new beginning. It was a continuation. It was as it should be, where the son takes over from father, who took over from his father.

Tom shook her out of her thoughts.

"What do you think? Will you celebrate with me?"

She agreed. Yes, she would.

"I will order a table at Sissi. Do you mind if I bring Jason and his friend, Clara?"

His friends! Margret thought of Rubin, the little rude man.

"I suppose it would be nice to be surrounded by young people. But Sissi is terribly expensive!"

She looked at Tom who had settled in his father's chair. He cheekily smiled at her.

"Well, Madame Dolmer, you will be treated to the best meal you have had for a long time."

There was no reply from Margret. She got up and went to the kitchen to make them, as every evening before bed, a hot chocolate.

NINE

Tom and Margret's taxi picked up Jason and Clara. Clara was absolutely thrilled to be taken out by Tom. When she saw the taxi arrive, she fooled about on the footpath, her wide pink skirt swirling around her. A broad belt showed off her small waist. Her unruly hair fell over a small black blouse. She wore no high heels. Her long, well-shaped legs did not need high heels. Then she saw Margret in the front seat looking hard at her and she stopped showing off. Jason took her arm and ushered her to the door of the taxi.

A winding road took them through the beautiful, spring-fresh beech forest. The late afternoon sun just touched the new leaves and made them shine rusty-red. Now and then there was a break in the forest, and they could see the old part of the town hugging the river. Opposite, on the other side of the river, large, modern, square glass buildings: the modern business centre.

Tom had ordered a table at a window. He did think of sitting outside, but the evenings were still cold. The view was breathtaking. After having settled his mother at the table, he took Jason and Clara out onto the terrace.

"See there," he pointed.

"See what?" Clara looked at him.

By taking them from landmark to landmark, Tom made them follow his finger through the old town and downstream.

"There! Can you see that long brown building next to the river with a taller addition attached to it?"

"No!" Clara did not have the patience for a silly find a building game.

"Yes, yes. There. Got it! Well, what is so special about that building?" Jason had found it.

Tom looked at his two friends.

"That is where I work."

"You work in a factory? No wonder you want to switch to music!" Clara looked at Tom with a sarcastic smile." Let's go in and have a drink. Look at your poor mother sitting there all on her own."

"I can get you a drink. What would you like?"

The change in Tom scared Clara. The smart clothes; his whole attitude. This seemingly insecure, shy, quiet man suddenly behaving so formidably. She walked into the restaurant and poured herself a drink.

Margret looked disapprovingly at her.

"Tom asked us to wait. He has ordered Champagne," she said.

Defiantly, Clara returned Margret's stare and kept on filling her glass with some very nice red wine. She was not going to be told what to do, especially by this strange lady wearing those old-fashioned clothes. They were probably very smart last century. And look at that hat!

Sipping her wine, she ran her imagination over Margret and Tom's life. 'He probably got a raise at work, or maybe he won some money. This is a very expensive place; we are all invited! He is suddenly so pompous. Yes, the sudden arrival of money makes people feel so important, so horribly overbearing. Typical of the middle class!'

Tom walked in, tall and handsome, his curly hair looking a bit wild from the wind outside. He had his arm around Jason. They were both laughing. Clara could not help but stare. Tom raised his arm and clicked his fingers. With a smile, he thought, 'I have always wanted to do that'.

"Champagne, please!"

One of the waiters appeared, pushing a little trolley. On it a silver bucket filled with ice. In it a bottle of French champagne covered in a cloth. Waving his arms about he walked to the waiter and announced,

"Please open the bottle with a bang! It is a celebration!"

The waiter looked searchingly at Tom. Then he picked up the bottle and started to ease the cork, making sure he would not hit one of the ornaments. There were plenty of those in Restaurant Sissi!

Pop! went the cork. A second waiter had appeared with a glass that he swiftly held under the bottle to catch the escaping fluid. Everyone cheered.

Except for Margret. She had been daydreaming. Letting her mind wander back to the past. Watching the daylight fade from the landscape made her think of Theo's last days and how his life diminished. She thought of his illness, the long slow dying. Just like the light of the day he slowly faded, and then he left. The lights of the city were now sparkling and twinkling. Maybe that is how it will be now. Just a confusion of little lights calling, calling. But where to? She longed to be with her beloved Theo. They could dance and sing and laugh together. Mingle with the lights, with the stars.

The noise of the cork leaving the bottle shook her awake.

"Mother, a drink to our new life."

Tom held a glass in front of her. Everyone was standing, looking at her. There was a smirk on Clara's face.

Suddenly Margret stood up, determination in her whole body. She stood up tall and straight.

"To you Tom! You are a fine engineer, a good businessman; but my pride goes to the side of you that shows what a good human being you are. And I am sure one day you will make your violin sing!"

She put her glass on the table, walked to Tom and gave him a big, warm hug. For a short second, the world around them disappeared.

From another table came a loud cheer and enthusiastic clapping.

"Cheers to you both!" a man called. "You are absolutely right, Margret."

She turned and stared, then smiled delightedly.

"Douglas! Come and join us. Are you on your own?"

The waiter brought another chair. Laid another place.

Douglas shook Tom and Margret's hands and introduced himself to Tom's two young friends.

"My wife is at a Bridge tournament. She will be coming later. We also wanted to celebrate Tom's inauguration into the firm. You should be proud of that boy of yours!"

Another bottle of champagne arrived. This time no loud bang, just a sheepish fizz.

The bubbles had gone to Clara's head. She was not used to being an outsider. She wanted to be outrageous. To show off. To be the centre of the party. She pushed her hair behind her ear and snappishly asked what sort of important job Tom was doing. She got everyone's attention.

Douglas stood up and raised his glass.

"To the third generation running Dolmer's Engineering. To you, Tom. It will be as much of an honour working for you as it was working for your father. And cheers to you Margret. You have a fine son!"

Clara did not like being pushed aside.

"And who is he?"

Tom did not know how to deal with the situation, how to manoeuvre the aggression back to some sort of calmness. He started to feel his happy mood slip away.

"He is our manager!"

Margret had slowly walked up to Clara.

"He is the other half of our firm!" Lifting her little finger, she continued, "This man you call he has more knowledge in his little finger then you will ever have in your whole body.

It is knowledge gained out of experience, young Clara. It is knowledge life teaches you!"

"So? You have a clever manager…"

Margret stood straight and tall in front of Clara.

"Grow up, young woman!"

With that Margret sat down and continued sipping her champagne.

Hastily, Jason lifted his glass.

"Cheers to new experiences, to growing up!"

The waiters had removed the little bowls of hors d'oeuvres and were setting the table for the first course. Tom tasted the wine. He felt flustered. Clara's behaviour unsettled him. Why did she conduct herself like that? What is she trying to prove? Mock him and his mother, his life?

Clara looked at him as he tasted the wine. Tom did not react, just nodded at the waiter. He blamed her behaviour on too much alcohol and asked Jason to control his girlfriend.

After the meal Tom went outside. He lit a cigarette and looked down on the city lights. How different the old town looked to the new. No pattern in the one; uniform straight lights and lit-up boxes in the other. He could make out the dark stripe of the unlit river with its bridges like chains of pearls. He thought of the evening and felt it went well except for Clara; but she soon had fallen into silence.

He felt his mother's eyes upon him and turned around. She was looking at him. Her face soft in the candlelight.

'Oh mother,' he thought. 'What makes you so bitter? If I just could dig deep into your soul and find the reason for the darkness; the reason why you are so without cheer. If only.'

He saw Clara slumped in her chair, her head on Jason's shoulder. He turned back to the twinkling lights of the city. Where would Ruben's light be? Should he have invited him too?

He would need a few more days at the factory to organise his work times and to meet all his staff. Then in the days off he would be able to slip into the skin of his dream. His dream. Music!

He suddenly felt frightened. There is such great pleasure in dreaming, in planning. But again, he asked himself; would the reality be as good, as sweet as the dream? If the dream turned into reality would it create a disappointment? Oh Esther, what to do! Where are you?

But there was nothing. No music in his head; no feeling of having Esther close. Only the still night. The stars and the twinkling town.

Someone placed a gentle hand on his shoulder. Douglas came closer and held Tom.

"Don't worry about Clara. She had quite a bit to drink. Your mother wants to go home. I had a phone call from my wife. She is not coming. Shall I call a taxi?"

Finding an ashtray, Tom ground the cigarette stub into the sand and looked out into the dark.

"You know, you can always talk to me when life becomes too difficult," Douglas said as he gently led Tom back into the restaurant.

The drive back down the hill was not as jovial as the ascent. Tom was squashed between Douglas and Jason, who had Clara on his lap. He suddenly felt empty, tired and spent.

TEN

Margret picked up the phone. It was Clara apologising for her behaviour.

"You should apologise to Tom, not me. He is at work. Why don't you ring him there?"

Joyce answered the phone.

"Miss Clara Gilles on the line for you, Tom. Can you take the call?"

Tom met Clara outside the front door of the factory. They went to one of the smaller, more intimate cafés where the waiter knew Tom.

"Mr Dolmer, where would you like to sit?"

"Over there," Clara said, pointing at a very private table in a small alcove.

Tom decided to have a small lunch, Clara just a coffee. The situation was awkward. Clara stirred her coffee far too long. Tom was leaving the start of the conversation to her. She looked at him. He wore his tie loose, a blue shirt, light-grey jacket, matching trousers. He knows how to dress, she thought. The colours suit him. It all goes well with his blond hair and his blue eyes.

"I have one hour, then I have to go back," he said.

The waiter had taken his plate.

"Coffee, Mr Dolmer? Another coffee for the lady?"

Clara just shook her head.

Sipping his coffee, he looked at Clara, wondering when she was going to talk. She felt just like a little girl who had broken something expensive. Tom had to laugh. He leant back in his chair.

"Why did you want to see me?"

"Well, I just wanted to apologise for last night. I behaved badly."

"Yes, you did. Apology accepted."

Tom waved to the waiter and paid.

"I need to go."

Clara did not move. Never had she been treated in such a backhanded manner. She thought Tom was pompous and arrogant.

He stood in front of her straightening his tie, buttoning his jacket.

"Sorry, but I have to go back to work. Is there anything else you would like to say, Clara?"

All she could do was stare. There was something in Tom she found appealing, yet at that moment she disliked him immensely.

He held out his hand towards her.

"I must go. I have a meeting. I will no doubt one day bump into you at Rubin's. And thank you for your apology."

ELEVEN

Sitting in the kitchen very quietly working away cutting vegetables for dinner, Margret waited for the sound of Tom's violin.

He was sitting on his bed, leaning up against the wall, holding his bent legs tightly to his chest, his chin on his knees. Next to him the violin still confined in its case. He was waiting for a sign from Esther. Something. A little sound maybe. He slowly released an arm and touched the case; stroking it he still waited for a sign. Nothing.

He stretched his legs and placed the case on them. His fingers found the latches and opened the lid. His beloved violin lay wrapped in the silk cloth. He slowly removed the silk and there she was: his love, music.

He gently ran his fingers along the strings. The strange sound was mesmerising. A tingle went through his whole body.

He released one of the bows from its delicate latch, took it out, and tightened the hair by turning the adjuster. Tom covered his arm with the silk cloth and gently, using only the weight of the bow, let it drop onto the cloth to test the tension of the hairs. Then he took the block of well-used grooved resin out of its little hiding place in the case and tenderly, lovingly ran the tight hairs of the bow over it. The smoothness excited him. He took the violin out of its cozy home and softly plucked the strings. A terrible fear came over him and he put the instrument back.

In big black writing he saw the words on his wall DISAPPOINTMENT = PAIN. The words he feared the most of all the words in his dictionary.

"Oh Esther, come and play for me!"

He looked at his gleaming instrument.

"I will call you, Esther. Maybe together we can make music. I will do my best to make you sing!"

He ran his fingers up and down the strings, just along the fingerboard. The other part, between the fingerboard and the bridge belonged to the bow. A sharp electric pulse went through his body, all the way to his groin. Tom got off the bed, picked up the violin, put it under his chin. Gently and slowly he stroked the strings, one after another with the tight hairs of the bow.

In the kitchen, Margret smiled. Tom had closed his door and had placed the mute on the violin's bridge. Margret sat very still. She had stopped cleaning the vegetables. She did not make any noise that could disturb the sound escaping from Tom's room. She leant back in her chair, closed her eyes and tears began to trickle down her cheeks.

When Tom placed the violin under his chin he immediately became one with the instrument, at one with Esther. With each stroke, he released a perfect, clear sound. The deep G-string made him slightly bend his knees. When he got to the E-string the high bell-like note made him straighten up, tall; tall with his body slightly bent back. Like a clamp, one of his fingers pushed down on a string and another and another. A strange but clear tune unfolded. Higher and higher Tom allowed his fingers to march up until he ran out of string. Slowly he descended back to the lowest note. Back to the part where he had started. He took the mute off. He wanted to hear the real song of Esther, clear and loud. Tom lifted the bow.

He could not play. Something held him back. He thought of his mother. Did she really want him to fill the house with music? Or would she wish to turn the sound off, as she did with the radio when he was a child? Tom put the instrument back into its case, covered with the silken cloth and closed the lid.

In the kitchen Margret sat in silence. The music stirring a memory deep inside her.

TWELVE

Whilst outside Rubin's flat, waiting for Clara to finish her lesson, Tom watched the little bird and her mate fly backwards and forwards with little tit-bits in their beaks. They had picked a good spot to raise their young. Below were the tables of the café. They could find a lot of crumbs from Mrs Hawelka's cakes. The babies in the greenery erupted with loud, excited noises when one of the parents arrived with a beak full of food.

The music inside Rubin's flat stopped. Tom could hear footsteps coming down the hall; then the door opened. Clara looked at him without expression, pushed passed him and ran downstairs. The spiral staircase swallowed her up and all he could hear were her shoes clicking on the stone steps.

Tom turned towards Rubin's dark corridor and entered.

"Let's hear how well you can scratch your instrument."

Rubin seemed to be in a bad mood.

"Do I need to get my ear-muffs? You see my ears are very sensitive. Let's start the torture!"

Tom took out his violin and gently plucked the strings.

"Give it to me. She is slightly out of tune."

Tom held on to his instrument, "Teach me how to tune — please."

"You are quite sure you can hear the slight nuances, the slight difference between a flat and a tuned string?"

"Try me!"

Rubin sat down at the piano and struck a note.

"G," he said. "All yours."

And with that, pointing at the G-note, Rubin let Tom sit by the piano. He walked away and sat down in a large, dark, comfortable armchair amongst piles of papers. With a bored yawn he settled into the chair, picked up a sheet of paper from the top of one of the piles, and started reading.

Tom found the high E on the piano, struck it, and managed to get the string in tune. Then he slowly worked his way down to the G-string.

All the time Tom was humming. He did not use the piano. Bent over the instrument, almost touching it with his face, he worked his way from one string to the next, humming the note of each string.

When he finished and looked up Rubin was staring at him. He stroked his beard.

"How — where — when? Tom, you tuned by ear! You have done that before! Now just tell me you can play one part of Bach's double concerto! The only mistake you made is, that we first, always first, tune the A-string . A-string first, then the rest."

"I am sorry, Rubin," Tom looked puzzled, "Does one have to use the piano? Did I do something wrong? Is she not in tune? I just remembered the sound of the notes. They are in my head. Is that OK?"

"It is very OK," his teacher said.

He got up and motioned to Tom.

"Let me hear your practice strokes."

Tom put one finger on the strings. He stroked them one after another. The sweet sound filled his chest. The more he let his bow run over the strings the sweeter the sound became.

"Please play louder, harder. You are not at home now. You can make as much noise as you like. Loud and harder on the strings. But please without scratching noises."

Rubin sat in his big, old chair holding his hands in readiness to cover his ears.

"Like that?"

Tom had played all the strings.

"Look, Tom, tell me, have you played before?"

"Only in my mind. Yes, I have played in my mind since I was nine. Since I met Esther. But I have never held the instrument, not until a few days ago. I have had her for two years now but never touched her. I was frightened of making a noise!"

Why did Rubin not believe him? Believe him that the music was in his head. That he could memorise the sounds.

"Rubin, you must believe me! I am able to remember tunes. I have always been able to remember."

Rubin got up and walked towards Tom.

"You just completely astonish me. The whole of you! You are an enigma to me. Please, Tom, tell me who you are, tell me a bit about yourself?"

"Where do you want me to begin?"

"At the beginning. Let's say after you heard Esther play."

"When I was a boy there was always on Saturday after lunch an hour of light classical music on the radio. My father and I used to enjoy listening to it. My mother did not. She would turn the radio off. I liked the violin the best and soon learned a number of tunes. I could then whistle those tunes on the way to school or when alone in my room. When I heard Esther play at the market something strange happened inside me.

It was like my chest was filled with peace and sunlight. I knew the tune from the radio and started to sing. I found myself picking up a phantom violin and mimicking Esther's movements. She turned and smiled at me. I did not remember the whole tune. Maybe my mother had turned off the radio and I never heard it. I stopped singing, but still played my phantom violin. That's when I fell in love with Esther and her violin, with her eyes and her hair and her bewitching scent!

I never saw her again, but her spirit was around me a lot; it put tunes into my head; it made my heart ache.

When I was fifteen, after high school, I started to work in my dad's factory, learning the ins and outs of our company. Then I began university. There was no time for music, for Esther. Two years ago, my father died, and I had to take over the company. I was still studying. My manager had to take over the running of the firm. I bought my Steiner and for two years I just looked at it; dreaming. Then one day, Jason introduced me to you. So here I am hoping that at long last I will be able to play.

I do not want to become a virtuoso, I just want to play. Play well; make my violin sing like Esther did."

Tom stood still holding his violin, looking at Rubin.

"Rubin, will you help me?"

Rubin had been sitting intently, listening. The paper he was reading had fallen out of his hand.

"And no one in your family is a musician?"

"No. Does that matter?"

Rubin got up.

"Well, what are you waiting for? Let's start. Tune your instrument please and let's get on with it!"

He dug some sheet music from the pile of papers next to him.

"Can you read this?"

Tom walked to him, picked up the sheet, nodded, and started to turn the notes into song.

"Do you know this piece? Did you hear it on the radio, or are you reading the notes?"

Rubin looked at Tom with astonishment.

Tom shook his head and kept on humming. When he came to the end of the page, he looked at Rubin and said.

"I learnt to read music in the University Choir. I enjoyed learning to read music. It came to me as easily as mathematics."

"So, why don't you take up singing? You have a great voice."

"I love the violin. I love the way one can make it sing. I love the way this small instrument can create drama. I want to learn to play the violin!"

Rubin bowed and waved his arm towards the violin.

"Maestro, let's begin. And please, Tom, you will have to accept the way I teach; the way I treat you. The way I am. Please bow your instrument. Slowly, please."

Tom thought he had done well when practising his bowing at home, but Rubin was not satisfied. He walked about the room ruffling his thin, white hair. With a frustrated, "No, no, no", he adjusted Tom's fingers; showed him how to stand; how to hold his shoulder; how to keep his bow flat on the strings.

"Oh Tom, this is hard work. Why are you so tall? I can hardly reach your hands."

He picked up his own violin, checked its tuning, and showed Tom how to hold the bow; how to hold himself; and how to relax whilst doing all that. He showed how horrid scratching noises happened, grimacing all the while. He played sweet sounds whilst smiling and swaying.

Tom copied every move. He had put aside the romantic swaying and bending of his body. He was in total concentration.

Then came Rubin's verdict.

"Well done, Tom. That's enough for today, Next time we start with scales. If you like you can practise putting fingers on the strings, like hammers, hard and precise. No scratchings!"

They made an appointment for the next lesson.

THIRTEEN

Tom sat on what he regarded as his bench in the park. The sound of a yard broom shook him out of his thoughts. A street cleaner was walking towards him, pushing a large broom and whistling. His tool-stacked cart was standing by the fountain.

Tom realised that the water had been turned off. He felt the silence. Lifting his legs to let the broom sweep under the bench he asked the man why the fountain was out of action.

"Oh, the little ducks have hatched and like to go in the water. The council always turns the fountain off so that the little ones do not get sucked into the pump. They don't care so much for the little ones. More for the damage it does to the pump."

The broom had removed the small amount of debris from under the bench. Tom could put his feet back on the path.

"How do they get out of the water? The sides are rather high for little ducks," Tom asked.

"There is a little plank on the other side. Mother knows how to get out. They actually nest at the back of those bushes. There's a drain there, a little waterway. Look, here they come. They must have heard us talk. They know that humans will feed them. She has hatched a nice clutch this spring. First mum, then the littlies and last, dad. He has a green head. I better go over and give them some food."

He leaned his broom on the trunk of the tree next to Tom. Digging deep into his overalls he pulled out a fistful of seeds and scattered them on the path. The little family came quacking and peeping towards him. He scattered another handful.

"That'll do, kids, for today. Go and find some worms."

With a happy smile under his enormous mousey-grey moustache and a twinkle in his eyes he walked back to his broom. Noticing the violin case, he pointed at it.

"Musician?"

"No," Tom answered. "Learning."

The old street sweeper picked up his broom and with a jolly whistle continued his job. There was a slight vibrato in his whistle. He swept and made little mounds of fallen leaves, flowers and bits of paper. Then he went back to his cart, touching his cap with a little bow as he passed Tom. He swept the little mounds onto a long-handled shovel and tipped the debris into his cart. All the while whistling his tune.

Tom watched him rhythmically working his way down the path. He seemed to be fulfilled with his simple job, sweeping clean the path, feeding the ducks, working in this beautiful park.

He probably goes home in the evening to his family, telling them about the ducks, about the beauty of the gardens, the people he met. Maybe complaining a bit about the rubbish people leave lying around. But then Tom thought that a person with music in his head would not be the type to complain.

'I have music in my head. Yes, somewhere. I just have to find it!'

Tom looked at his violin. He opened the case, took the instrument out and held it up.

"Oh Esther, where are you?"

"Well, sir, give us a tune then!"

The old man stood in front of him. He had changed out of his work clothes, wearing now a well-used but clean suit. A swish-looking hat sat cheekily sideways on his almost bare head, He had combed his bushy moustache and it looked as if he had used a bit of spit, twirling the ends.

Tom was about to put the violin back.

"I can't."

"Yes, you can!"

The old man started whistling.

"Just make it up. Much more fun making up your own music. Come on, Give it a try! You'll never know if you don't try. Come on!"

And the old man whistled his tune, his beard twitching, his little eyes shining.

Tom put the instrument under his chin, remembering all Rubin's instructions: how to hold his bow and how to move it flat and straight over the strings. He thought of Esther and stroked the first string.

"That's it sir. That's great. There is the start of your music."

Tom put a finger on the fingerboard, hard and precise. Another and another.

"There you go, sir." And the old man whistled with the most amazing vibrato. Together they created music. The world around them disappeared. People passing laughed and some threw coins into Tom's violin case.

The old man stopped whistling.

"Well sir. That's me done. I'll have to whet my whistle. Would you like a beer? You might just have earned enough money for a beer! Look at that. Look at all those coins! There might even be enough for two?"

Tom laughed, packed up his instrument and together they went to the old man's local.

They found a table and the barman brought them two beers.

"On me." Tom pointed at his violin case. "What is your name? I am Tom, Tom Dolmer."

"My mother called me Arnold, terrible name. But I became Jack. You see, I have always been a small one, able to get about without being seen, popping up here and there. So, my mates called me Jack., You know like the Jack-in-the-box? During the last war, it was very convenient to be small, to be a Jack-in-the-box."

He sucked the foam from the beer leaving a white rim on his moustache.

"I did know a Theo Dolmer once. Relation?"

Tom did not know how to react. Should he tell him who he was or was it better to stay incognito. Tom was far too honest. He could not pretend to be someone else.

"Yes, I am Theo's son."

There was a long silence. Jack studied his beer and then looked up.

"I knew you when you were a little nipper. How's your dad and your mum? Was it Margret? And what are you doing sitting in my park brooding like a rainy day with your violin? You would not believe it! I am having a beer with Theo Dolmer's son and making bloody good music with him. Mother of God!..."

They ordered another beer and Tom told him the whole story. About his father's death, about his love of music and how much he enjoyed his work as an engineer.

"Well Tom, you do have a lot on your plate, a lot to think about. No wonder you feel as if your life is a bit of a mess. Look, son, you know where to find me. If you need an ear or a whistler, come and see me. But now I have to get home. My wife will kill me. She has a mouth like all the kitchen knives in the whole of our world and sometimes more. See you around, Tom. Take care and don't forget the music is in you!"

Jack walked out of the pub.

The light of the day had almost gone. The windows of the house across the road started to light up. People were settling down for the evening. Margret walked into the living room and closed the heavy curtains, then switched on the standard lamp. Tom sat in his father's armchair, smoking. His mother walked over to him and turned on the lamp on the little side table close to him. She could see that he was occupied with his thoughts.

"I met a strange man in the park today. He seems to have the job of keeping the park clean. Could he ever whistle! We made music together, him whistling away, me making up tunes on the fiddle. Passers-by thought we were busking and dropped money in my violin case. We got enough to have a couple of beers. When I introduced myself to him, he said that he knew dad.

He was a little old man, with an enormous moustache, which made him look like a walrus. He had cheeky little eyes, all wrinkled up from smiling. His name was Arnold, but he said most people called him Jack, Jack-in-the-box. He knew me as a little boy. Do you remember him, Mum?"

Margret had just settled down with her knitting.

"Yes, I remember Jack. He was our gardener at the factory. Very proud of his work. Dad always gave him a bonus at Christmas and a couple of bottles of beer. You and I did visit the factory often. I worked part time in the office. Oh yes, he would have known you. The two of you playing in the grounds. In the winter you helped him shovel the snow from the paths. He sort of looked after you when I worked. Goodness me, old Jack. Amazing he is still alive. He has always been old, and he has always had that amazing moustache."

She settled back in her chair with a slight smile, knitting in her lap, her eyes absent. She let go a quiet sigh, picked up the knitting, pushing the memory aside.

Tom sat up and looked at his mother.

"You never said that you worked with dad. When was that?"

"Oh, before you went to primary school. By the time you went to High school your father had got himself a very reliable secretary and then Douglas had finished his apprenticeship and started helping your dad. Granddad had passed when your dad was in his mid-forties. Now and then I would go to the office and help out.

So, old Jack is still around. You know, he taught you to whistle. I wonder if his wife is still alive? She was a beautiful woman. Then things changed. I never went back to the factory. I looked after Theo's mother before she passed. Yes, yes, well."

Margret was clenching her knitting needles, the wool cutting into her fingers. Her face had closed up. It looked like a mask.

Tom wanted to know more but her armour was well in place. He took a deep drag from his cigarette to calm his anger. Or was it sadness?

Releasing the wool from her almost white finger, Margret put the knitting back in the basket.

"I'll make us a cup of something."

With that, she got up and went into the kitchen.

Margret Dolmer had made herself a strong cup of black tea, sweet with a squeeze of lemon. Not a soothing drink. She was not tired. The past was stirring in her. She liked to remember the days just after she met Theo. How he had freed her and taken her away into a new, happy world. She smiled, sipping her tea, dreaming, remembering. Why did it have to stop? Why? And when? And HOW? She could not remember. Or did she not want to remember?

Tom had gone to his room and she could hear the muffled, gentle, quiet music. He was practising his bowing. Margret got up, turned off the lights and opened one of the windows to let some of the fresh, cool evening air into the room. She could see into the flat across the road. Light and music streamed out of the window, people laughing.

"How long since I have been able to laugh?" she thought.

FOURTEEN

On the writing pad next to the telephone were two messages; one to ring Jason, the other to get in contact with Clara; the telephone numbers, written very clearly in his mother's strong hand.

Jason wanted to see him in his shop. There was something he would like to show Tom. Clara could wait, he thought. Even though he felt attracted to her, Tom did not particularly like her superficial, sometimes shallow attitude.

With excitement Jason took Tom to the back of the shop. He pushed him into a small cabin-like glass box and invited him to sit on the stool provided. He closed the door. Tom could hear nothing. All the outside noises had been locked out. Suddenly the sound of the most beautifully singing violin filled his ears, then his head, then the whole of his body. He felt his heart beat against his chest. His whole body was electrified. He could feel a light pulse in his solar plexus. The world disappeared. Nothing existed.

A sharp, uninvited knock on the glass made Tom turn his head. Jason was pressing a record cover against the glass, on it in large lettering the words: *The Lark Ascending*. Tom turned away from Jason, away from the real world. He closed his eyes and floated away, away with the lark into the golden landscape.

Suddenly the music stopped. Jason opened the door of the cubicle.

"Well. What do you think?"

Tom's eyes were still vacant. He could not answer. Then he said slowly,

"What beautiful playing; what beautiful music!"

"No. Not the music! The new equipment!" Jason held Tom by the shoulders, "This is a new device for listening to records. I am going to sell records. Not just any record, the best! Only the best!"

"So, I can come here and listen to your excellent collection of music?"

"No, you have to buy the record."

"I don't have anything I can play a record on."

"I can get you a record-player. The best of course!" Jason looked proudly at Tom.

"OK, but I have to ask my mother. Then I can get, The Lark Ascending?"

"Yes, I also can get you headphones. Then your mother will not be disturbed. What do you think? I can organize them for you. Hey Tom, then you can listen to all the best violin music available."

With excitement he pulled at Tom's sleeve. Tom shook himself loose and stepped out of the music shop. He looked up into the blue late spring sky. The street noises disappeared. All he could hear was a violin singing. Closing his eyes, he felt the music enter his body and soul.

"Oh, Esther," he whispered.

A young man running across the road dodging cars almost ran Tom down. Suddenly Tom was back, standing in the city noise, his body filled with confusion. The dream and the reality had collided with him. He reached into his pocket to find the cigarette case. It was not there. He must have left it at home.

Jason touched Tom's shoulder. "Are you OK? You look like you've seen a ghost! Come let's have a drink. Clara is waiting for me in the wine bar. Come on."

The wine bar was crowded and noisy. Tom wanted a quiet place so he could sort out his thoughts, his feelings. Work out his confusions. Clara sat in the back, waiting. In front of her a fancy-looking drink. All sorts of decorations were poking out of the fluted glass. Tom did not like mixed drinks. His girlfriend at university made him try all sorts of strange concoctions.

"She always picks a dark corner," Jason said.

Before she could protest Jason took Clara's drink and walked through the back door. A very small courtyard opened up to them with a colourful collection of tables and chairs. Lots of pot plants with flowering shrubs stood around the edges of the garden. On each table an old-fashioned cup with a little plant growing in it. On one of the brick walls hung strange paintings.

Jason picked a table and put Clara's drink down. She followed angrily.

"What would you like, Tom?"

"A whisky. No ice, no water. Just straight. Irish, if they have it."

Tom reached for his wallet.

"And please some cigarettes."

"My shout," Jason said as he walked back into the wine bar.

Tom got up and looked at the paintings. They were lacquered to withstand the weather. He was not sure what to make of them.

"Modern Art," Clara said, stirring her drink with a little stick. It had an olive attached to it. "You like it, or you hate it. It leaves me cold. Jason said I don't understand modern paintings. What is there to understand? Either you like them, or you don't."

She was looking at Tom, stirring her drink.

"You never rang me!"

"Well, here I am, in person."

She looked at him angrily. He could not help but think her beautiful. Her hair roughly rolled up and fastened with a large comb on the back of her head. Some of the strands of hair had escaped and framed her face. But there always seemed to be anger in her face, tension on her brow.

He tried to start a conversation.

"How are your studies going?"

She ignored his question.

"I wanted to see you alone. Without Jason! He is such a busybody, so tiring. Maybe we could go for a walk somewhere quiet?"

Jason came with the drinks on a round tray. There was another one for Clara as well.

"Cheers!" he said as he sat down.

He turned to Clara and told her about Tom's new purchase. Her face became darker.

"If you were able to, you would sell your grandmother!"

Tom felt an argument brewing,

"Then I will be able to listen to the best violin music!"

"You should make your own music!"

Clara turned towards Tom. She wanted a fight.

"Yes Clara, but when I listened to *The Lark Ascending* ...Well I cannot describe the feeling. If there is a heaven, I would say it was heavenly."

There was a change in her face. She looked long into Tom's eyes. He thought he detected some sort of softness. She bent her head and picked up her drink. The sun hit her escaped strand of blonde hair. It had a slight red sheen. When she got to the end of her drink she kept on sucking on the straw. It made a gurgling noise. She looked at Tom and let go a little giggle. Then she ate the olive and started to stir her second drink. She knew that Tom was watching her.

"Sure you don't want any ice in your drink, Tom?"

Jason had broken the magic moment. Just as he did when Tom was listening to the music. Yes, he would like to spend time with Clara, get to know her better.

Butting out his cigarette in the little tin provided, Tom held up his glass and looked at the remaining golden liquid, smiled, mumbled something, drank the last of his whisky and got up.

"I'd better get home. Mother will have dinner ready and tomorrow I have a big day at the office."

He looked at Jason.

"Looking forward to getting my record player with the headphones and especially the record!"

He turned to Clara,

"Thanks for leaving your number. I'll ring in the next few days."

She pointed at his glass.

"What did you say to your drink?"

Tom langhed.

"You would not understand. It is in dialect. It's something I picked up from my father, a goodbye to your last drop of drink."

Clara went to say something, but Tom had turned and was walking away.

He had to bend slightly to get under a decorative arbor. As he walked into the wine bar, he could hear Jason and Clara arguing.

Arriving at the flat his mother called from the kitchen,

"Just in time for dinner."

They ate in silence. Tom had decided to talk to his mother about the stereo after their meal, maybe soften her up with a small port.

As always, Margret closed the curtains before switching on the lamp. The beautiful spring evening light covered; shut out. Tom had been watching the sun climb up the wall of the house across the road. Some of the open windows caught the sun and shone golden. One of the windows had not been fastened properly. Swaying back and forth it seemed to send him little messages with its golden flicker. Then the curtains went across and it was all gone. Then there only was the living room and his mother with her knitting.

Margret held up her new project, asking him what he thought.

"I love it. You are very clever. How you can create a garment with two sticks. Who ever invented knitting was a genius!"

With a smile he leant back in his seat.

"That calls for a drink. A little port maybe?"

Margret looked at Tom with a satisfied smile.

"Why not!"

Having set the glasses on the little table Tom filled them to the brim.

"Are you trying to make me tiddly?"

Tom smiled as he handed her the glass.

"Yes. There are two things I'd like to discuss with you. I need your approval."

He lit a cigarette and settled back in his chair.

"Cheers, Mum. To the future!"

She looked hard at him. Anxiety had crept into her. She did not like change. Gingerly she picked up her glass.

The room filled with tension.

"What's the occasion? To what future am I drinking?"

Margret took a small sip and then put her glass down. She picked up her knitting.

"I would like you to join us at work. We could do with an extra experienced hand in the office. I have talked to Douglas. He is very excited. We will take it to the board meeting tomorrow. What do you think? You are after all a shareholder! You should have a say in the business affairs. Come to the next meeting, the one after tomorrow. Please!"

The knitting fell into Margret's lap. She fiddled with her dress, rubbing it between her fingers as if she was trying to dry them.

In the dark room Tom could not read her face. The light was only falling on her slender hands and the contorted fingers.

"Think about it. Don't worry about deciding. Mother, drink to the future; our future."

With that he got up and topped up her glass.

"You are really trying to get me tiddly!"

"Yes, I have something else to tell you. I would like to buy a record player. If you don't mind, we could have it here in the living room. You might like to listen to something. You never know. If you don't I can use headphones. Jason can get some for me. I hope you will listen with me to the most heavenly music. You can listen and knit. Drink up, Mum."

Tom had crouched down in front of Margret.

"And yes, I would love to see you a little tiddly, Mrs Margret Dolmer!"

He put his hands on his mother's. Was there another crack appearing in her amour? She smiled and looked at her son.

"So, you are going to be my boss? How much will you pay me?"

He laughed and pressed her hands gently.

"Yes, looking forward to it. Wages have not been decided, but there will be plenty of free coffee."

She freed her hands and held his head. Tom thought of the beautiful music he heard this day. Oh, if she could feel the music as he could.

She released his face. He picked up his glass, finished his drink and went back to his father's chair. The room fell back into its usual silence. Margret resumed her slow knitting, thinking of herself going back into the world after two years hiding inside herself, inside this flat. Going back into the workforce after almost twenty years! She was not sure what to do.

She sighed, got up, and went to the kitchen; returning with their hot chocolate, as she did every evening.

FIFTEEN

Nervously Clara entered Dolmer's Engineering. She was a little early. She hated to be late. The receptionist's desk was unattended. She found a seat in a dark corner of the entrance hall where she felt safe. Tom had invited her to dinner. He had asked her to wear something for outdoors. All afternoon she tried to work out what he meant by outdoors. In the end Clara settled for a pair of white trousers, a light-green shirt and white jacket. It showed off her blonde hair and silken skin. Clara sat in the dark corner shining.

There was a lot of activity. A group of young men came running down the circular stairs. They disappeared into a door leading to the factory floor, busily talking. Clara was convinced they were talking about her. The thought of being looked at as Mr Dolmer's girlfriend made her cringe.

Then she noticed Tom looking down from upstairs, leaning over the ornate balustrade, searching for someone. He obviously did not see her and went back to his office. There was loud laughter. A rather good-looking woman came down the stairs.

'She is a bit too short and far too old for Tom,' Clara thought, feeling a slight jealousy creeping into her.

Tom followed her down, laughing, loosening his tie, removing his jacket. As he caught up with the young woman, he handed her his tie, jacket and his briefcase.

On top of the stairs, an older man called, "We'll knock it on the head tomorrow. Give my love to Margret. Have a good evening."

Tom waved to him, then looked over and discovered Clara.

"Hello," he said. "Have you been waiting for a long time? Sorry! Here I am now. Are you OK walking?"

They walked out into the beautiful late spring afternoon, into the fresh, green world.

There was no road, just a little path. They had cut through the factory gardens towards the river.

"Do you mind wading a bit? The water is not deep. We can take a short cut and I'll show you my tree. Or we can walk along the road?"

Clara was not sure. She chose the river which was in flood; brown and uninviting. Tom took off his expensive, shiny work shoes and his ironed sox, rolled up his trousers, and started walking on the little path along the river. In places the river lapped over the walkway. Clara looked at him. He was just like an overgrown boy. She took her pumps off, rolled her white trousers up to her knees, and followed. The water was freezing. She made little complaining noises but had to admit to herself that she quite liked this surprising and adventurous walk along the river.

"Snow-melt," Tom called out to her. "The water comes from the Alps and it's freezing!"

He turned around and watched Clara gingerly walking through the water. She was holding on to the top of her trousers like a little girl, as if she was wearing a dress. Carefully she walked like a ballerina, putting her toes first in the water. She looked up.

"Are you laughing at me?"

"No, just watching that you make it without falling into the water. I can always carry you? Or we can walk along the road? But you are doing great!"

"I am fine. How far to your special tree?"

Tom held up a thick curtain of wispy branches. Behind it was an enormous willow.

"Here we are. Just follow me. Take care of the roots. Some are still under water."

He walked to the other side of the tree. An enormous root had created a broad seat. Some obstacle a long time ago had pushed it sideways along the trunk.

"There, a perfect seat for a very brave Clara." Tom pretended to clean the top of the root for Clara to sit on. He made a gallant movement with his arm: "Voila, mademoiselle!"

"You are making fun of me?"

Clara's eyes were dark and angry.

"Not at all. Please, sit down. Would you like a drink?"

Tom dug deep into his pocket and produced a flask.

"Sorry, no umbrellas or olives on little sticks."

"You're doing it again, making fun of me."

Tom thought for a moment.

"You're right. I am sorry. I'll stop."

He removed the bottom part of the flask. It was a cup.

They sipped their drink, surrounded by the drooping branches of the old willow. Behind them the roar of the swollen river.

Clara looked at Tom.

"Did you come here as a boy?"

"Oh yes, a lot. Once I had to climb the tree. An unexpected flood came down the river. It can happen very suddenly. They came and rescued me with a boat. Did I ever get an ear-bashing from our gardener, Jack! He was supposed to look after me. My dad was away; my mother was looking after my gran, so fortunately they never knew about it. I had to promise never to come back when the river was in flood and here I am again."

He looked at her. "I'd clean forgotten about it until the other day when I met Jack again, for the first time in years."

He laughed and put the cup back on the flask and like magic it all disappeared back in his pockets.

"We'd better go if we want to get something to eat."

They carried on along the river until they came to an earthen flood bank. Behind it stood a small wooden building. Smoke was coming out of its chimney.

"There is no electricity here," he said. "We will be eating by candlelight. Our dinner will be cooked on a wood stove. All very romantic."

Clara stood staring. The little wooden house was built on stilts. It had a deck looking out on the river with simple wooden tables and benches. Smoke was curling out of its chimney. It could have come straight out of a fairytale.

"Can we sit outside?" she whispered.

"We can until the mosquitos drive us in. The fish will be from the river. Zita grows what she can. It is all very fresh, very uncomplicated and very delicious."

On the deck Clara picked a seat close to the river. She was totally spellbound.

"We never go to places like this."

Tom ordered the house wine. It arrived in a glass jug. A woman in her early thirties served them. She nodded at Tom and smiled.

"Would you like some bread with it?"

She had a slight accent.

"Please, those little rolls you make would be great."

Tom poured the wine. He settled back and let go a long sigh. "This is the life. I wonder how the other half lives."

"Bad day?"

Clara looked at him over the rim of her glass.

"No, not at all. Just complicated."

"Want to talk about it?"

Tom looked at Clara and started laughing.

"Hey, you sound like a good wife enquiring about my day!"

Tom smiled. "Sorry, I should not have said that. But I did. I want to hear about your day. How was your day?"

"Oh darling, absolutely awful! You know with the girls at the hairdresser, you know what I mean." She put her escaped hair behind her ear and sheepishly looked at Tom.

"Now who is making fun of who?"

They laughed together.

A basket arrived with little bread rolls. They looked fresh and crusty. Putting the basket on the table the young woman looked at Clara with her gentle black eyes and smiled. Her shining blue-black hair was tied back with a simple piece of string; her complexion was dark and exotic. There was an air of mystery about her.

"Kira," she said, holding out her hand; standing straight and proud. Her handshake was firm and short. Before Clara could tell her name, Kira had turned back into the little restaurant.

"They are very private people." Tom said to Clara. "Now, tell me, what made you want to play the violin? Why have you chosen this instrument?"

It took a while for Clara to answer.

"My parents both play so I play. My grandmother and her sister were very accomplished on the violin. No, that was not quite the reason. There is a long story behind that. Interested?"

Tom, munching on his bread roll, nodded.

"When I was a little girl my grandmother put on a celebration in memory of St. Lucia. It was some time in December. I was about four years old, dressed in a long white flowing dress. I had to walk on stage playing the violin. I must add that my grandmother, on my mother's side, was from Norway, where they celebrate this day. There was another girl, I forget her name, but I remember that she was tall and beautiful with straight, long blonde hair. She carried the ring with four burning candles on her head. The four candles symbolising the four Sundays of Advent."

Tom had settled back leaning against the balustrade of the decking.

"Am I boring you?"

"No, not at all. I have never heard of St Lucia. Please carry on."

"Anyway, I could not play the violin at that stage. My mother got an old bow and covered the hairs thickly with soap. Sort of using soap instead of resin. I was so proud walking out onto the little stage in my grandmother's house, running the bow theatrically over my little violin. My mother was playing behind

79

the stage. Behind me walked the beautiful, tall, pale-skinned girl in her white long dress. The ring with the four candles on her head. Oh, how I envied her hair."

Clara ran her hands through her unruly locks, trying to tuck some of it behind her ears. Tom filled her glass.

"I just felt as if I was the centre of the universe, slowly walking across the stage, pretending to play the beautiful hymn, behind me, lighting up the surrounds, alluring, holy looking, whatever her name was. We walked slowly, slowly across the stage until the music finished."

Clara's eyes refocused on Tom.

"So, I wanted to learn to play the violin. My parents were delighted. I am not too sure if I made the right choice."

She looked up, her expression changing.

"I am starving and so are the mosquitoes! Can we go inside?"

Before Tom could answer she had picked up her glass and was walking into the little building. She stopped in the doorway, turned and looked back at him.

"This is tiny!"

In the one room were a few simple wooden tables. Only one was covered with a starched white cloth. Upon it a glass jug of wine, cutlery, and a lit candle. Tom showed Clara to the table and pulled out a chair.

Clara noticed a gas lamp lighting up what seemed to be the kitchen. A woman stood in front of the wood stove jiggling a rather large pan. She only wore underpants and a large apron. Clara could see her bare back, brown and strong. The woman lifted her hand and called over the noise of the spitting dish.

"Good evening, Tom. Dinner will just be a minute!"

She had a very strong accent.

Clara looked at Tom.

"Do you take all your girlfriends along the river to the tall tree and then for a fish meal at this little, strange place?"

Tom laughed.

"No, I usually come here on my own. Look at Zita, slaving away on the hot stove. She cooks the best fish. She catches them in one of the side arms of the river."

Zita carried a large plate of fish from the kitchen. When the light caught her face Clara could see the dark skin. It looked like crumpled up leather, glistening with sweat. On her head she wore a cloth to keep her hair together. She looked at Clara, her eyes black and shiny.

"Enjoy! Please eat. Start."

Clara looked at her meal. The skin of the fish was covered in some burnt red herb. Fresh parsley was sprinkled over the whole plate.

Zita returned with Tom's meal. It was a different fish but prepared the same way. Her daughter, Kira, put a jug of gravy on the table.

"Do you have some salad?" Clara asked.

"No salad today, sorry."

Tom thanked Zita and started to dissect his fish. His method fascinated Clara. He used two forks. He took the skin off and laid it out on half the plate. Carefully he peeled half the flesh off the backbone, starting at the tail. Then he gently removed the backbone and put it on a spare plate. He poured a little gravy over one half of the meal.

"There! Would you like me to do yours? Better still, you can have mine." He exchanged the plates. "Be careful with the gravy, it's spicy! By the way, you eat the flesh with the skin."

"What kind of fish is it?"

Clara was carefully taking a small piece.

Tom waved to Zita and asked.

Zita had taken off her apron and now wore a long thin simple dress.

"Oh, just a fish from the river. Did not ask his name." A cough followed her deep laughter. She was standing with her back to the stove, smoking.

"You should stop smoking," Tom called to her

"You can talk, mister! Eat your food while hot!"

They ate and drank in silence. Zita hummed a foreign tune. The room filled with the sweet smell of her cigarette. The candle was only a little stump. It was time to leave.

"Zita, could you ring for a taxi, please?"

They walked to the main road, sat down on a bench, and waited for the taxi.

Clara had been quiet during their meal. She was overwhelmed. Never had she met a person like Zita. Never had she experienced such a tasty meal.

"Where is Zita from? What is her history?"

The arrival of the taxi stopped the possibility of her finding out.

"I will tell you some other time. If there is another time."

Tom opened the door to the taxi and smiled at her.

SIXTEEN

Margret Dolmer was walking up and down the kitchen, up and down the corridor. She straightened things. She moved ornaments. Everything was clean, dusted. Everything was orderly. Only Margret was in disorder. Walking did not help! She had walked to the shops but could not think of what to get. The only thing she could think about was Tom's offer to join the firm again. Be part of Dolmer's Engineering. He wanted her to come tomorrow and sit in on a meeting so she would get the feel of the place again. To meet the workers. What would she wear?

She remembered Clara sniggering at her about her outfit when they went out for dinner. She went into her room and looked through her clothes. She found a suit and laid it on the bed, stood back and looked at the dark-blue-grey linen garment with deep green trim. Not bad, she thought. She decided on a light blue blouse. In the drawer she found a pair of nylon stockings. She put a pair of tan shoes with little heels on the floor. Looking at her outfit she shook her head and started again to walk about her room.

Suddenly Tom stood in front of her looking bewildered.

"It's almost midnight! What are you doing up so late?"

Margret looked at her son, pointed at the clothes on the bed. Tom stopped her by putting his hand on her shoulder. She looked sternly at her son, her voice was angry.

"You and your great ideas. Why did you ask me to rejoin the company? My life was fine as it was. I don't need change! I just want to be left alone!"

Tom ran his fingers over the material of the suit.

"This is beautiful. What noble colours and that little touch of green trim. Is it new? Matching shoes and handbag." He looked at his mother. "Where did you get it? Are you going somewhere?"

"Yes, with you, tomorrow, to work! And where have you been? It is almost midnight. We are having a big day tomorrow. Better get to bed!"

Before he could answer she had stormed out of her room and disappeared into the bathroom.

She never noticed that Tom was barefoot and had his trousers rolled up to his knees.

There was a lot of noise in the boardroom. Joyce and one of the apprentices had brought in extra chairs. Almost everyone was going to be present at this meeting. Douglas was waiting downstairs for Tom and his mother. He walked nervously up and down. When the taxi stopped at the front door, he half-ran to open it for Margret.

She stepped out in her tailored suit, her make-up fresh, discreet and natural. Her hair elegant. She smiled at Douglas.

He went to greet her but suddenly his smooth words failed him. In his mind he tried, 'You look stunning!' and, 'You look so young!'

"You look wonderful, Margret. Not a day older," he at last managed to croak.

"Thank you, Douglas," she said as he took her hand.

The noise from the boardroom spilled down the spiral staircase. Margret smiled, remembering the days when she used to run up and down those stairs, chased by Theo. Of course, only after everyone had gone home. During work, one had to behave like a lady. Her father-in-law was an austere man. Such noise, as the staff displayed today, would have never been accepted.

Joyce tried in vain to organise everyone. But then Tom walked in and called,

"Good morning all! Please find yourself a seat."

In the silence he walked to his chair at the end of the table. Margret came and stood next to him.

"I would like to introduce you to a new member of staff. Mrs Dolmer will be working in the office."

A murmur went through the room. Tom pulled the chair out and offered his mother a seat.

Margret could not follow the discussion. Tom should have given her the minutes of the last meeting; she would have been better informed. She panicked like a little girl attending her first school day. She looked around the oval table. Across her, on the wall, the portrait of Theo, slightly smiling at her. She had always liked that portrait. He seemed to tell her that all would be fine.

There was a mixed bunch sitting around the table. In her father-in-law's days there would have never been a person in a boiler suit in his boardroom. Never would he have mixed with the apprentices. Talking to the factory workers would have been the task of the shop-floor manager. Margret's thoughts moved into the past. The talk became muffled. She looked at the portrait of her late husband.

'This place is full of ghosts. Full of you, Theo, and all the others who've passed or retired.'

She could almost see and feel the people of her time sitting around the table. There was Theo's secretary. She felt the past so vividly. She did not understand the present.

One of the young men stood up and started talking about a problem he was facing. How could an apprentice be asked about the workings in the machine room? She looked at her son, who was listening. When the boy had finished, Tom got up and spoke to Douglas. Then he shook the young man's hand and gave him a pat on the back.

"Well done, we'll look into it! Yes, well spotted!"

This would have never happened in her time. She straightened up and looked at Theo's portrait, then at Tom as he returned to his seat. He took her hand and gave it a light squeeze. With a smile, he whispered: "We'll soon be done."

They left the building. Margret walked between Tom and Douglas. The men seemed to be very happy with the outcome of the meeting. They were on their way to lunch.

Margret just ordered a cup of tea. Tom tried to talk her into getting something to eat.

Douglas looked up from the menu.

"How did you enjoy revisiting your workplace? Do you remember when you joined the company? How old were you? Eighteen? You were a breath of fresh air to us all. We were only men and this old, sour receptionist-cum-secretary. Old Mr Dolmer was such a tight old man. We all were scared of him. But you, Margret..."

But Margret's mood had shifted on the walk to the café. Her face was dark as she looked at him.

"One thing that never happened in those days was any of us attending a board meeting uninformed. My father-in–law, Alexander Dolmer, would have sacked you. And here I was sitting totally uninformed! I felt such a fool, so out of place."

To her son she said, "And you, Tom, should have known that. You should have informed me instead of gallivanting about with your new girlfriend!"

A waiter placed a glass of wine in front of her together with a plate of biscuits, and a bowl of dip decorated with a prawn and a little parsley. She looked at him.

"And what is that supposed to be? I would like some tea, please."

Tom winced. He felt like a little boy being told off.

"Anyone mind if I have a smoke?"

He looked at his mother.

"Yes!" she replied.

Douglas looked at them.

"Oh, please stop it, you two! You sound like a married couple.

Margret, we will make sure you are completely informed next time. The invitation to this particular meeting was meant to let you see how things are conducted under your son's reign."

"Well, I think Alexander Dolmer was turning around in his grave! What was it all about anyway?"

She picked up her wine glass and sipped.

Douglas smiled.

"It wasn't really what one could call a business meeting. Once a month every member of staff can come to the table if they have any complaints or ideas. We've found running the business on a democratic principle has created a happier workplace and, with it, the quality of work has increased. Yes, things have changed a bit, but we have to go with the times."

Douglas lifted his glass and clinked it against Margret's.

"You know," he continued, "you look smashing, fabulous, amazing! You really do. Maybe a woman of your stature will keep the young apprentices in check? They will show respect towards you, I know!"

Margret smiled. She picked up a biscuit, dipped it in the bowl, and nibbled it, pushing the prawn aside.

Tom sat back and watched Douglas charm his mother.

Douglas couldn't take his eyes off her. He would have loved her as his own back then, but she was married to the boss's son. Oh, how she brought light and fun into the dreary factory. She even managed to charm the old man.

What had made her so dark and unhappy? He knew that she was not happy when she expected her child after so many years of marriage. He did not understand why. His wife was overjoyed at the arrival of their first son.

"Do you want your prawn, mother?"

Margret shook her head. Watching her son slowly nibbling on the prawn, she thought of her husband. Theo also changed the running of the factory. He gave the workers the canteen and lovely seats outside. He created a garden, employed a gardener.

Then he built the extension, proper toilets, and the lovely airy upstairs offices. She remembered the fight between Theo and his father. Old Mr Dolmer just did not want to spend the money on such things.

She waved to the waiter.

"I'll have another glass of wine, please. And what do you offer for lunch?"

Tom looked at Douglas with a smile full of thanks.

SEVENTEEN

In the middle of the Dolmer's living room stood a new piece of furniture. Margret walked around and around it, wondering what to do. Where to put it. She recognised the radio and, lifting the top of the cabinet, she discovered the record player. She did not dare touch any of it. But she liked the simple design of the cabinet. She ran her hand over the wood. It felt silky.

"The wood is teak."

Tom walked into the room carrying a box of records.

"Beautiful. Very sexy."

"How can wood be sexy? Oh, really Tom! Where did you get that expression from?"

"Look, mother," he put the heavy box down. "It's just a figure of speech, a new phrase. The young people use it all the time! It does not mean that I will throw myself onto the cabinet!"

He tried to give her a hug. She moved away.

"I don't understand you anymore. It must be the company you are keeping. Anyway, what do we do now with this, this …. thing?"

"We work out where to put it. Then we plug it in and try it out. So, we have to choose a spot with a power point."

Margret did not like change.

"We should put it where the radio is at the moment," he continued. "Then it is in the middle of the wall, away from the window. When sitting in our chairs we can both admire it. You must admit it is a beautiful piece of workmanship."

He started removing the ornaments from the radio and placing them out of harm's way on the coffee table.

Margret had retreated into the kitchen. How old she suddenly felt! Why did he need another radio, a record player? Why did he not make his own music now he had bought himself a violin? Oh, why can life not just go on without all this change? She put the kettle on. She could hear Tom trying to shift the new cabinet.

"Mum please, give me a hand. I can't move this cabinet without upsetting the rug and I don't want to scratch the floor."

The old radio stood on the floor, the little table next to it.

"What are we going to do with the old radio and the little table? The table belonged to Theo's mother. She'll turn around in her grave! And your dad bought this radio. There is nothing wrong with it!"

"I'll think of something. Now let's just put this into place."

The device was plugged in. Margret went to attend to the whistling kettle. Tom opened the box and removed the records.

"I got you a record of dancing tunes from your younger days, Mum, and one with music by Johann Strauss."

"Tea or coffee?" Margret called from the kitchen. But Tom had his headphones on and a record playing. He could not hear his mother.

Margret stood in the doorway holding the teapot, looking at her living room in disarray. Tom had pushed his armchair closer to the record player so that the headphones cord would reach. The floor was littered with records. The little table and the old radio stood discarded in the middle of the room. Tom was half-lying, half-sitting in his big chair, eyes closed, his hands on his chest.

She tried again.

"Tea or coffee?"

She suddenly felt deserted and terribly alone; her space invaded, her home violated.

She went back into the kitchen and sat down at the table, her head buried in her hands. Only a few days ago her life was ordered; one day after another the same. There was a comfortable, safe routine. Then the offer to go back to work. For her, it had been quite enough to just go to the shops; sometimes to town to see the doctor; and her monthly trip to the cemetery to keep Theo's grave in order. That and household chores was quite enough for her.

With a big sigh she got up and turned the gas up to reheat the kettle.

The violin was mimicking the lark ascending. Tom's skin tingled. His clasped hands were trying to hold the trembling feeling in his chest. Nothing around him existed. There was not a thought in his head, just feeling, just music. It filled his whole body. The high, trembling notes would send a sharp, stabbing feeling all the way to his groin. When the orchestra started to accompany the violin, he wished them to leave, to just allow the violin to sing and soar, as the bird would have done. Tom floated, he was living his dream or was he dreaming his life?

Someone was tapping on his headphones. He looked up and saw his mother holding the teapot, mouthing something. The spell was broken. He took the music from his ears.

"Tea or coffee?" she hissed. And again.

"Well? Tea or coffee?"

Tom felt like someone he loved had been torn from his body. The music was gone. The bird had fallen out of the sky. He felt like crying. Should he just put the music back into his ears, go back to the dream or decide on what to drink? His mother's face was both pleading and confused. He pulled the speaker cord out of its socket and the beautiful singing violin filled the living room.

"Scotch, thank you! Scotch to celebrate my new purchase!" he said.

She stood stock-still in the doorway. The hand with the teapot started to droop towards the floor. Tom jumped up from his chair and saved the lid as it started to leave the teapot.

He took the teapot and put it on the little coffee table.

"Turn this racket off!" she yelled. "Turn it off! Why do we suddenly need all this change? I just cannot understand! Did your father and I not give you everything any young man would want, would need in life? It's those new friends of yours. Filling your head with all that! I am not interested in dancing music or Johann Strauss and I am certainly not interested in wailing violins. And then wanting whisky at this time of the day!

Your new friends have probably introduced you to those new drugs young people smoke! I heard all about that at the hairdresser from a poor mother whose son has, what did she call it, yes, blown his brain. Whatever that is. …And do something about this mess!"

She stormed back into the kitchen.

"And where is my teapot?"

Tom turned the music off, picked up the teapot from the coffee table and took it to his mother in the kitchen. She sat by the table staring out the window. He poured her a cup of tea. He added a sugar cube and a squeeze of lemon. He poured himself a whisky, lit a cigarette, and sat down opposite his mother.

She looked right through him. She did not touch her tea. He slowly sipped his drink. When he had finished the cigarette, he returned to the living room and started to put things back into place.

By moving the new cabinet closer to his chair, he managed to get the headphones close enough to listen to the music without his mother having to get upset. He put all the records in the compartment provided, placed the ornaments upon the cabinet, found a spot in the room for the little table, and took the old radio to his room.

Back in the kitchen he found his mother still sitting as before. She had not touched her tea. He put his hand gently on her shoulder.

"What do you know!" she whispered. "What do you know!"

She pushed his hand off her shoulder.

He stood for a while behind his mother feeling anger creep into his body. How could he know anything when she never talked? Never opened up.

He turned around, walked to the phone and ordered a taxi.

Without saying a word, he walked out of the flat into a spring afternoon.

The taxi stopped outside Dolmer's Engineering, but Tom did not go to work. He walked along the river to his tree. The water had receded. He did not have to take his shoes off. The roots of the tree were out of the water. He sat down and looked at the soothingly flowing water. Now and then some debris floated past. He wondered where it was going. He wanted to be able to go with it, visiting new and strange places.

He settled comfortably into the tree and grasped his knees tight and buried his forehead into them. He could only hear the gentle rustle of the willow leaves as the breeze travelled through them. All his frustrations, his doubt of not knowing how to handle his mother, his fear of disappointing his father, all rose up and then were slowly washed away by the river's flow. He fell into a deep meditation, soothed by the sounds of nature.

The crack of a branch brought him back to reality. He felt sore, stiff and itchy all over. The mosquitoes had been feasting while he travelled to a world beyond. To relieve the bites, he washed his itchy arms. He decided to continue along the river to the little fish restaurant.

"Sorry, no fish. You not ring!"

Zita brought a jug of wine. She joined him at the table. They both drank and smoked in silence. Putting her harsh, dark but caring hands on Tom's, Zita looked at him.

"What's wrong, my darling?"

Tom spilled out all his anxiety, all his confusion about his mother and how he could not understand her; how he wanted her to open up, to let him in, to let him help her.

"I have met your mother a number of times. That was when your father was still alive. You know, they helped us a lot after we had to flee. I could see in her eyes that she had a very difficult past. Something happened in her younger years. One day, maybe, you will know. Please be kind to her."

Zita relit her homemade cigarette. It filled the room with the most beautiful smell. She smiled at Tom, her black eyes sparkling.

"I have a lot to thank your mother. She probably saved our lives."

Tom watched the smoke of her cigarette hit the late afternoon sun.

"How did you meet my mother? Where did you flee from?"

Filling up their glasses with wine, Zita bent over the table and looked hard at him, her eyes becoming slits.

"We are Romani; Gypsies. My race has always had to move on; we have never had a country. Not until your mother offered us to make camp here on the river. Actually, it was a little man called Jack who found us. We were walking along the river. Suddenly the flood came. There was river all around us, and the water was rising. This Jack fellow saved us. He was in a little boat. He plucked us out of the water and using his oar steered the boat to dry land. He then pointed to a high spot telling us to go there and wait. He told us he was looking for a boy. His boss's son had walked off and he was afraid he might have got caught by the sudden flooding. My husband went with him and they found you up that big, old willow.

Oh, Tom, we were all so happy. Jack brought Vano back to us on our little hump of an island and creeping along the river's edge he took you back to where you came from. We spent all night sitting on our island. Yes, we called it our island. Kira was not well. She was coughing all night and Vano was not too good either. Jack came back the next day. Your dad was with him. The river had dropped, and we were able to wade to dry land. Jack showed us the way. We walked up-river until we got to the factory. Your mother had found some dry clothes for us and had made us a big pot of thick soup."

Her eyes were slightly shiny. Embarrassed, Zita ran her flat hand over her tightly bound black hair. She lit the candle on the table, looked at Tom and continued.

"Your grandfather was not happy in having us Romani stay so close to the factory. Clever little Jack, could he ever whistle that little man, found a safe spot along the river, where we could camp. And that is where we are now. Vano got very sick. He had pneumonia. He suffered terribly. He built this little hut with the help of Jack, who found lots of old timber, windows, doors and a wonderful wood stove. When it all was done, I cooked a fish dinner for your parents; the Romani way. I caught the fish, prepared it with herbs and spices and cooked it on this stove all those years ago.

After Vano's death, your mother called in, oh, at least once a week. She brought little presents for Kira and made sure we were well and had what we needed. She loved Kira. I think she would have liked to have a girl. When she lost her beloved Theo, she closed up completely. She stopped visiting us.

You know, darling Tom, it is very, what is the word, despairing, when you lose your life's partner. The tearing apart leaves a big wound. It takes a long time to heal, if it ever does."

She picked up the candle and lit her cigarette.

"Oh, darling Tom, I owe your mother so much and yet I have neglected her. Please, Tom, be kind to your mother. She good woman, hiding in her sorrow."

A long silence filled the almost dark room. His eyes swept around the walls. It was such a small place, kitchen, bedroom and restaurant, all in one.

"Where is Kira?"

Tom was searching in the dark.

"Oh, Kira is married. She live in town with husband. She just come and help out when I have guests."

With that, she got up and walked over to Tom.

"Time for you to go home."

Tom stood up and gave her a big hug and kissed her on the forehead. Her body felt like skin and bone. She laughed.

"Long time since a man hugged me. Now off you go. I'll ring for a taxi."

When Tom got home his mother greeted him with a warm meal. Then they went into the living room. She picked up her knitting, he chose a record, put the headphones on, and lost himself in music.

EIGHTEEN

M ost days after work, when everyone had gone home, Tom went to the machine room with his violin case under his arm. Here amongst the uncomplaining machines he felt that he could relax and be one with his beloved instrument. Here he could run his bow across the strings with enthusiasm, making as much noise as he pleased. Tom would smile and greet the machines, open his case and walk with his violin to the very middle of the room where the four lathes stood. He would stand there, look at each of them in turn, take a little bow, put the instrument on his chin and start his practice.

He had graduated from just running his bow over the strings to scales. He could hear Rubin telling him what to do. Slow, precise sounds of a violin filled the space. The acoustic was wonderful. He would practise scales for half an hour, then he allowed himself the freedom of making music. His own music! Often, he would sing along in harmony. Good days, bad days all his different moods would be turned into music. At the end of practice he would try to hit the high singing note of the lark. He could get the note right, but nothing like a lark up in the sky slowly, slowly disappearing. His sound was shrill, more like a cry.

The finale was running through his scales, faster and faster, always finishing on an up-stroke on a high C. With a flourish, Tom would remove the bow and bow deeply to all four lathes. Looking up at the industrial ceiling he would sigh,

"Oh Esther, will I ever be able to make my violin sing?"

At home, dinner would be waiting.

Every day Tom gave his mother a duplicate copy of all the

happenings at the office. She still had not decided if she would join the firm.

Usually, after dinner, she picked up her knitting or mending while Tom, with headphones on his curly head, listened to music.

One evening Tom did not get the stereo going. He needed to discuss business with Margret.

Douglas had asked Tom if one of his sons could join the workforce. Eighteen year old Angus had finished high school and had shown great interest in engineering. He did not want to go to university, but to learn the trade of engineering starting as an apprentice, on the very bottom of the ladder, and working his way up, as his father did.

Margret looked long at Tom.

"What do you want me to do about it?"

"Help me to decide, maybe."

She picked up her knitting and continued studying the pattern of the jumper. She showed no interest.

"Mother, please! What do you think? And do you at all look at the information Joyce so kindly copies for you? The ones advising you of the affairs at the office. In three weeks, we will have a meeting of the office staff. Yes, the floor manager will be there as well. We all would like you to come. Poor Joyce has been run off her feet since the receptionist left to have her baby."

Margret mouthed the numbers from the knitting pattern, then she quickly looked up at Tom.

"I will let you know in time. Why don't you listen to your music?"

Frustrated Tom walked up and down the room. He looked at his mother who by now was totally engrossed in her knitting. He walked out of the living room and into his room and sat on the bed. Frustrated he ran his fingers through his curly hair. Slowly he pulled his knees up to his chest, held them tight with his arms, and put his forehead on his knees.

He heard Zita telling him to be kind to his mother.

Several days later Margret eyed the small stack of neatly typed sheets of paper lying on the kitchen table. She picked them up and moved them onto the sideboard where she placed them with the rest of the information from the office. She took a quick glance at them, picked up the kettle, filled it and put it on the stove. Having placed two cups on the table she walked back to the sideboard, took the top sheet and started reading it. The kettle whistled and shook her out of her concentration. Margret made two cups of hot chocolate, took one to Tom and then sat down at the table. Reading about all the happenings at work, she suddenly got the feeling of actually being there. A slight excitement crept into her. She thought of the day when she got ready to go to the last meeting. Finding a suitable dress, putting on a little make-up, going to the hairdresser. It all made her feel alive, breaking the monotony of everyday life. Then Douglas told her that she was still young. Was she? Sipping her drink, she stared into nothing, the pattern on the curtain becoming blurred.

'What a silly idea. Still young. Really!'

She took her empty cup to the sink, rinsed it and put it on the draining board.

"Good try Douglas," she said to herself.

There was a little slit between the curtains where she saw the reflection of a drab-looking person with an unruly mop of curly grey hair, dressed in an old blouse and cardigan. A face with squinting eyes and a tight slit of a mouth.

Margret ran her hands through her hair.

'Maybe if I dyed it slightly darker?'

She turned sideways and regarded herself.

'I'm not that old, am I?'

She bent over the sink and closed the curtains, then returned to the table and the papers.

Tom walked into the kitchen with his empty cup and saw his mother bent over the papers.

"Come and sit here," she said. "Help me go through this stuff."

He sat beside her. She had marked passages she did not understand. Line after line they read the pages. Tom explained as they went.

After a while she looked at him, her eyes tired.

"I am just too tired to take any more in. Can we please continue tomorrow?"

She slowly got up, cursing her hips, and walked into the bathroom. Tom poured himself a small drink, fell into the big armchair, and with a happy smile started humming a tune from one of his records. The tune reminded him of something. Had he listened to it on the radio when his father was alive?

NINETEEN

The early summer grass had not yet been cut. In amongst the high grass a multitude of flowers were stretching their heads up towards the sun. Close to the playground was a small picnic ground and a circle of trees. There the grass was trimmed into a soft carpet. Tom was lying in the high grass, hidden from the world. He listened to the sound of the playing children. Now and then a child cried. Did it fall off one of the swings or was it frightened of going on the big slide? He just lay there and tried to work out the noises, what they could mean and where they came from. The birds had disappeared into the forest to escape the hot sun. Often the sounds mingled with his thoughts. Tom had come here to one of his favourite spots to let go of the week's events; to let go of all the conflicts in his mind.

He could not relax. He could not enjoy the peaceful surrounds of nature. He got up and walked through the high grass towards the circle of trees. When he passed the playground, he could see a couple of families sitting on blankets having a picnic. The children running about playing and laughing, some on swings, some hiding in the play-castle. A little boy ran over to Tom. For a long time, the child looked at him.

"Where are your children?" he asked.

Tom looked down at the boy.

"Oh, I don't have any children yet."

"Why not? You are big enough!"

"I will have children later."

Smiling, Tom ruffled up the boy's hair.

"Why do big people always ruffle up my hair? I am not a dog!"

Crouching down on his haunches, Tom shook his head.

"That is an excellent question. I don't know. I must think about that."

A young man got up and came to fetch the boy.

"Sorry about that. Thomas is always a bit forward. I hope he did not upset you?"

"Well, well," Tom ruffled up the boy's hair again. "Your name is Thomas? So is mine. Just that I am called Tom."

Little Thomas stretched out his tiny hand; Tom took it in his big one. They shook hands.

"Dad, can I show Tom my tree? My tree is a hazelnut. What is yours?"

"I don't know."

Taking the child's hand in his, they slowly walked to the ring of trees. Tom had to bend down a little to be able to hold the boy's hand. Thomas chatted all the way, telling Tom about his baby sister and how she cried a lot, keeping them all awake.

When they got close to the trees Thomas let go and ran down the small embankment to a perfectly flat circle surrounded by trees. Then, skipping along the circular gravel path, he suddenly stopped.

"There!" he said, "My hazelnut tree!"

Walking up to the tree, he gently touched the leaves.

"What is your tree, Tom?"

Tom pulled a folded brochure out of his pocket.

"Now let's see, how does this work. I need to find my birthday and that will tell me…. Oh, there it is. I am a linden tree. Let's go and find it. Here is the map of the trees."

Stepping sideways Thomas pointed at the very large tree next to his.

"There, this is the linden tree. We are neighbours!"

In front of each tree was a grey box displaying a label where one could find the months of birth, next to it a button and a small speaker.

"You can hear the words by pressing this button."

Tom showed the boy.

Thomas looked up, his expression deeply sad.

"It did not work last time! Read it to me, please."

Tom pressed the button and out of a tiny speaker a voice spoke.

Hazelnut born people always inspire their fellow human beings through their openness, honesty and directness.

Hazelnuts judge sharply, but remain tolerant through their intelligence as well as their intuitive talent.

The best Hazelnut People are those who do not by my fruit all ready, peeled and roasted, but they pick me at the edge of the forest, then look for a stone and strike me carefully to reveal my fruit.

The little boy did not move. He was totally enchanted by the voice coming from the speaker.

"Is there someone in there? Or maybe underneath? Oh, she did talk to me. Can we hear her again, oh please?"

And with that, he pressed the button again. The lady started talking all over again.

A voice calling Thomas to come stopped the boy from pressing the button a third time

"I think your mum is calling."

On the way back to the playground Tom tried to explain where the voice was coming from. He had no experience with children and his careful, technical clarification did not make an impression on the boy.

"Mummy, the tree was talking to me! Tom made it talk. Shall we try to make yours talk?"

The small family had packed up their picnic rug and basket. The little girl was crying.

"Next time, Thomas! Now thank Tom and say good-bye."

Tom crouched down and little Thomas gave him a big hug. He buried his head in the large shoulder and whispered: "Thank you." Then he let go and ran off in front of his parents to the car park.

"Thank you, Tom," the mother held out her hand. "You are good with children."

Thomas had found the car and was calling impatiently.

Tom turned and strolled back to the tree circle. The child had made him restless. He sat down in the centre of the circle and ran his hands gently over the tops of the high grass. Suddenly a deep resentment burst into Tom's body.

'Why, oh why did I meet Esther? She made me want to become music. To fill myself with the sound of a singing violin! To be just like that lark ascending. Higher and higher. To play this magic high note and let it spiral down my body!'

His thoughts went back to the little chap he had just met.

'I could have a small family, as well as listening to the music I like so much. Leave the dream of becoming music as a dream. My love could be directed to my children, my wife!'

He saw himself with a beautiful, gentle, understanding, caring woman. She would love music the way he did. They would have children just like little Thomas, inquisitive, intelligent. A perfect, happy life.

A gentle wind made the grass stir. With the wind came the music. Tom turned to see where from. It was everywhere, all around him, wrapping up his body tighter and tighter, then moving inside him. His body filled with the sound, pushing away his thoughts of little Thomas. He looked around in confusion. Nothing stirred, only the air and the grass around him. Sitting in the middle of the circle of trees, he had pulled his knees up, burying his head between them.

'Oh, Esther!'

With the feeling of music inside him, Tom walked to look at his tree. He pressed the button:

"The Linden Tree: If you are born between the 11th and 20th of March or the 13th to 22nd of September you are a Linden Tree.

You are gentle, indulgent and versatile. Linden are antennas of communication.

Linden-born people stand in the field of tension between dream and reality. They always strive for the realisation of their dreams and for perfection, this in the knowledge of their imperfection.

Linden man, you are balanced and peaceful. You can be a true, urgent help for your troubled fellow human beings. Realise your many dreams, my dear Linden man. Add to your imagination the energy to action. You can do it!"

Tom gently touched its leaves and whispered, "I will follow my dream, I will travel with Esther. I will make music. I will become music."

There were three piles of clothes on her bed. The wardrobe doors were wide open. Margret was taking everything out of the closet, sorting out her clothes. Every time she journeyed from wardrobe to the bed, she had to pass her dressing table and its large mirror. She smiled at her new image.

She'd had her hair cut and coloured a little darker. The hairdresser had wondered if her son Tom was getting married.

"No, I'm going back to work."

"At your age?" someone said from the back of the room.

"And what age would that be?" the young hairdresser answered into the mirror. She looked at Margaret. "We are going to make you look smashing, Mrs Dolmer! A bit of colour and a smart haircut will soon turn your boss's head."

Margret smiled at that thought.

On her way home she looked at the boutiques. Most of her clothes were twenty years old, but all in good condition and of excellent quality. Before Margret was going to spend money on a new outfit, she needed to see what she had to wear at home.

Every piece of clothing had a memory. Margret sorted her memories into the three piles: Keep, maybe keep, not keep.

Tom walked slowly up the many stairs to their apartment on the top floor. Still hearing little Thomas laugh, feeling his small arms around his neck. How he wished for a child. Then the music came and Esther's enticing scent. With it the longing to hold his violin, to make it sing. Slowly Esther pushed the thought of a life with children from his mind.

Was there a way to have both?

He opened the door. The table was laid in the dining room. There was a bunch of flowers on it. Margret called cheerfully from the kitchen.

"Have a drink. Dinner will be ready soon."

On the side board stood the bottle of Scotch and his favourite glass. Bewildered, Tom looked at the scene wondering if he should step into this situation with care.

"Could you please pour the wine?" she called.

Margret walked into the room carrying a plate laden with two large schnitzels and an array of vegetables. Putting it on the table she impatiently nodded towards the chair and asked Tom to start eating. She looked at him expectantly. It heightened his unease.

"I went up to the circle of trees," he said. He told her about Thomas. She did not seem to listen, just touching her hair, looking at him.

He realised she was wearing a beautifully-cut grey dress. He'd seen it before.

"You look different," he said.

"It still fits," she said.

He noticed the darkened hair. She wore a little make-up on.

"There is something different about your hair. Did you get it cut?"

She glared at him, sat down, and started pushing the food around her plate. Hastily, he said,

"You look great! But do eat your food. It is very delicious. Lovely wine too. Are we celebrating something? Cheers to whatever it is. And truly, you look great."

Taking her plate, Margret walked back into the kitchen. She reappeared with a small bowl of pudding covered in lashings of cream and put it in front of Tom.

Standing there she said,

"I am celebrating my decision to rejoin Dolmer's Engineering. I am celebrating working with my son, just like I worked with my husband, his father."

She ran her hands over her body to show him, make him aware of the new Mrs Dolmer. Then she walked out.

After he cleared the table and washed the dishes, he went in search of her.

He found her in the living room, in her cardigan and old skirt, settled down with her knitting, stabbing the needles into the garment. Irritated for not having been noticed.

The room was filled with anger.

He went to his room and opened the window. Attracted by the noise of laughing and singing he looked down into the courtyard. A group of young people sat on the grass under the big trees. The two couples had their arms around each other.

He decided to ring Clara in the morning.

He would fetch his father's car from the garage at the factory. Maybe she'd like to go for a drive. A picnic?

TWENTY

Tom pulled the dust-sheet off the three-year-old, grey Mercedes-Benz. Running his hands over the beautiful duco Tom could feel his dad next to him. They did have a car before this one. It had belonged to his grandfather. But his dad had always dreamed of owning the 'Ponton' model. "They are so much safer," he used to say.

Tom liked his grandfather's car. As a 14-year-old he was allowed to bring it out of its garage, drive it to the front entrance of the factory, and pretend he was his granddad's chauffeur. Hopping out of the driver's seat he would hold the door open for the old man and bow. Granddad would thank him and push a little coin into his hand. That car was black and had much softer lines, but it was not as powerful as the new one.

Tom had no use for it in town. There was no parking to be found close to the flat and he never went anywhere special. But now?

"Hello, anyone in there?"

Clara walked into the garage. She wore her light green summer jacket and loose white trousers. Her flat shoes gave her a bouncy walk. She felt full of confidence. Running a finger along the car's side she remarked,

"Oh, very nice. Somehow I expected you to own a VW Beatle!"

With an embarrassed smile he pointed at the picnic basket.

"I brought some food and wine, but we can always go out to eat. There are plenty of little places dotted throughout the countryside. Where would you like to go?"

Clara pulled up her shoulders and made a strange face. She

looks just like a little girl, Tom thought. One who can't make up her mind.

"Good, you are wearing some practical clothes," he said. "We can either go up in the hills or along the river. Maybe drive upstream? We can go into the wilderness or stay in civilisation. You decide."

With a determined movement, Clara pushed the strand of escaped hair behind her ear.

"Wild sounds good. And water would be great."

Tom put the basket of food and the bottle of wine in the boot.

"Wow, look at the size of the boot! You could live in there." Clara laughed. "Oh good, you have a blanket. I would not want to sit on the ground. You see, I am delicate!"

She looked at Tom flirtatiously. He tried to ignore her look.

"Let's hope the car starts. It's not been used in months. No, don't worry, one of my workers is a mechanic. He keeps an eye on it in case I plan to take one of my girlfriends for a picnic in the woods!"

He laughed and turned the key. The engine growled and then settled into a contented purr.

"Off we go. There is a radio if you'd like some music."

Clara snuggled into the comfortable seat. Her attitude towards Tom had changed. She looked at him.

"I hoped we'd be on our own. All quiet and alone."

"Don't worry we will be."

Out of the town Tom turned off the highway and drove on a narrow dirt road towards the river.

"There!"

He pointed at a punt coming across the water towards them.

"No one will follow us now."

He parked by the little boat landing.

The boatman helped them with the basket. She looked at the tiny boat with uncertainty. Tom gave her his hand and helped her step into the wooden craft. Clara sat down on one of the bench seats and held on tight. She was frightened of big expanses of water. She was frightened of small boats.

The ferryman took his seat. There was no engine and the owner did not row. But they moved. Clara was very worried.

"How come we are moving?"

The man smiled.

"We are being pulled across by the current of the river."

"So why don't we just float away downstream?"

Clara was puzzled and held on even tighter.

"Oh sorry, we are attached to a very strong metal cable."

She just shook her head.

Arriving on the other side she saw there was no landing pier. She would have to jump. The river looked very fast under the boat. She began to panic.

"I can't do that!"

The ferryman waded into the water and gently lifted her onto the gravelled bank. He smiled at her.

"This is the good part of my job. Are you OK, Miss?"

They all laughed. Tom gave the man some money.

"Just call me when you want to come back. Or shall we make a time?"

"Yes, maybe that would be a good idea. Let's say four pm?"

"See you then, sir."

He tipped his hat to them and off he went.

Clara looked at Tom who was already walking off.

"Come," he called back. "We will have to do a little walking to get to my spot."

They came to a large gravel beach. He spread out the blanket on a small, grassed area and gestured for her to be seated.

"Would you like a drink, mademoiselle? Coffee or wine."

"You've got coffee? I'd love some."

Tom produced a thermos and two cups.

"Sorry, no milk, but I have some sugar."

Digging about in the basket he pulled out a packet of biscuits covered in dark chocolate.

"How does that boat-thing work? Tom, you are an engineer. You should know."

He walked towards the water to demonstrate.

Clara called after him "Don't bother; it worked, I don't need to know how. As long as we get back again!"

The river was wide and here the water flowed slowly along the shore,

Tom had taken his shoes off. He waded into the water.

"Gee, it's cold," he said. "Still, a swim would be nice."

"You can't swim in that!"

She was not happy getting too close to the edge and moved farther away from the river.

"I used to come here with my dad when I was a child," he said. "The river flows slowly on this side and it is quite shallow. On the other side of the bend, she flows very fast. There is no beach and the river is very deep. It is quite safe to swim here. If you put your head under the water, you can hear the river sing. My father told me it was the song of the river maidens. You should try to listen to it."

Clara was hugging herself. She shuddered at the thought of it.

"I think I'll pass!"

Tom ignored her and continued his story.

"The river maidens live in the deep part of the river. They will grab you and pull you under. Very scary! Never swim in the deep part of the river, my dad said. But then, of course, there is always logic; a scientific explanation to kill the magic. The music is made by the pebbles in the river rolling over each other. It is a beautiful sound."

He walked back to Clara and sat next to her.

"I did swim across the river as a student. We started quite a way upstream and arrived here. I avoided that deep part over there.

Could not help but think of my dad's story. I still get a creepy feeling when I look across."

Looking out over the river he quietly said, "Oh, I miss you, Dad."

"Do you mind if I go for a swim? I did not bring any bathers, so I'll have to go in my jocks. Do you mind? I'll go up the river a bit."

Before Clara could say anything, he was off. She poured some more coffee into her cup and dug a biscuit out of its packing.

'Well,' she thought, 'I did want to go to some water, but this is scary water. The way it flows so fast. Never would I go in. Never! Not even to hear the music of the river maidens. No thank you.'

She looked at the peacefully flowing water. Suddenly she saw a person floating past. Tom waved, and then he was gone. Clara started to panic. How is he going to get back to his clothes? How far is the river going to take him? Should she get his clothes and run after him?

Clara sat there on the verge of hysterics and did nothing.

Then she saw Tom swimming close to the shore upstream. His curly, blond hair flat on his head. Slowly he swam to the little beach, where he stood up. Clara could see how he braced himself against the flow of the water. Tom shook the water out of his hair, making it stand up like a mop. She noticed his strong, muscular body. The yellow, curly hairs on his chest looked like they had escaped from his head. His face was full of enjoyment, just like a little boy's face. Clara smiled and waved. She thought,

'Were you in a swimming pool with still, blue water and edges all around, I would be in there with you Tom Dolmer. I love water, I love swimming, but this is scary.'

Tom appeared from behind the bushes that grew on one side of the little beach.

"What about some lunch?" he asked. "I am starving!"

Clara went to get the basket. She could hardly lift it.

"What have you got in there? Are we going to have gold sandwiches?"

Laughing, Tom opened the lid.

"No, only lots of great food. Can you spread out this cloth, please? Now I must say, I can take no compliments for the choice of food. The wine, yes. The food I got from our local restaurant. I just ordered a picnic for two."

He blushed slightly.

"The plates and anything else we need are strapped in the lid. The glasses are wrapped up in serviettes. There should be a board for the cheese and a plate for the meat. I have no idea what else there is."

Clara made herself busy creating a wonderful-looking picnic spread.

He stood back and admired her work.

"A feast fit for a king and his queen. Let's eat!"

The beautiful picnic had been totally destroyed. The cloth was littered with empty containers. Bits of food still in some of them. A few ants had started to arrive. There was a bee humming around a piece of quince paste.

Tom and Clara were sitting on the blanket drinking and laughing. Clara was telling a story about her little sister. Tom was filling their glasses with the last of the wine. He did not really listen to her, just watched her face, the excitement in her eyes, and how she tried to control the escaped strands of hair by putting them behind her ears.

"I hate that hair, it always gets in the way! I think I might just get it cut off. Have a short modern haircut."

Tom bent over towards her and removed the large comb holding her hair into the untidy bun on the back of her head, letting it fall over her shoulders.

"No, you must not cut it. It would really be a shame if you did."

He ran his fingers through it.

"No, you must not cut it!"

He pulled his hands away in embarrassment:

"Sorry, I did not mean to tell you what to do. Sorry."

He gave her back the strange, large comb. As Clara gathered her hair together by twisting it, she told him that the comb had belonged to her great-aunt. Sadly, she had never met her.

"My grandmother's sister collected such combs. I liked this one. It is quite old. I think about 1900. She left lots of them behind when she left. Apparently, I inherited her hair."

She rolled the long hair into its untidy bun and held it in place on the back of her head with the comb.

"There," she said, looking at Tom.

She kept on looking at him. "Have you ever had a girlfriend?"

"Why?"

"Oh, I just thought…"

He looked at her. Her face was going beetroot red. She wriggled about, not knowing where to look.

"Yes, I had a girlfriend. It was during my years studying engineering. We were together, I guess, over two years. She was nice, a few years older than me. Very clever and good looking.

My parents did not know that we lived together for almost eighteen months. She was very sporty and ambitious. Always had to win. My mother liked her very much. I suppose she thought having another engineer in the family would be of great benefit.

I'd also been very much in love with a girl during my last year at high school but had no time to take her out. You see I started to work at the factory at the age of fifteen. That and school! My Grandfather wanted me to start work as an apprentice. My dad wanted me to have an education. So, every day from school I went to the factory. You can see, there has been very little time for girlfriends."

"What happened to your girlfriend? Why did you split up?"

"It did not work. She became very pushy and bossy and then I could not stand her taste in music."

Playing with her hair she quietly said,

"I'd better be on my best behaviour."

She blushed again. Her next question caught him off-guard.

"What did your dad die of?"

He stood up. He looked down at Clara. He sounded annoyed.

"What does it matter what he died of! I could tell you anything. I am always asked that question as if it made any difference. He died! He died slowly! He suffered. That was bad. Sorry, but I don't like talking about it. He was my best friend. I miss him more than you can imagine."

She stood up and gave him a big hug.

"I am so sorry. I don't know what it is like to lose someone. I am truly sorry!"

Tom gently pushed her away.

"Time to pack up. We'll soon have to walk back to the ferry."

There was a little bench by the pick-up point. They sat next to each other looking out on the river, watching the punt slowly cross. Tom put his arm around Clara's shoulder.

"I like you, Clara. I like you very much. It is just, well, my life at the moment is in a bit of a mess. I need to sort things out. I need to get my world in order. I would like to be your friend."

Clara gave Tom a kiss on his cheek.

"Yes, I'd like that," she whispered.

TWENTY-ONE

Margret was nervously walking about the flat. Every time she passed the hall mirror, she looked at herself.

"Mother you look great and no, you do not need a coat. It is quite warm out there. It is almost summer, Mum."

"Where is my bag? Do I need a hat?"

Tom held the door open.

"You are holding your bag and you are wearing a very smart hat. You look great. Now let's go!"

Margret walked up to her son and straightened his already straight tie. She noticed the violin under his arm.

"Are you going to play at the office? And why do you not carry the case on its handle?"

"Please, can we go now?"

He pushed his mother out the door. Halfway down the flight of steps she suddenly stopped.

"I forgot to make lunch."

"Please, Mother go! We can buy lunch!"

There was a taxi waiting for them.

"A taxi? Why? We could get the tram."

"Oh no, Mother! So you can change your mind halfway to the office! Please hop in."

As Tom closed the car door, Margret was talking to the driver.

"You know this is a one-way street? You have to go to the next main road. There you turn right. And watch out it is a very busy road!"

"Thank you, ma'am. I know. I will safely get you to your destination."

Margret settled back in her seat, holding her handbag tightly on her lap with both hands.

"What about morning coffee? I did not bring anything!"

She looked unhappily at Tom.

"We do have a small kitchen upstairs in the office, and there are very nice biscuits. Joyce always makes sure there are some."

"I know there is a kitchen in the office. I designed it when your father started talking about extending. Men don't think of things like that. And a toilet! I made them put in one of those as well."

And so she talked all the way to the factory.

Douglas helped her out of the car.

"Welcome back, Margret. Good to have you back."

Tom excused himself. "I need to see how the new apprentice is settling."

Mostly though, he needed a rest from his nervous mother.

Douglas and Margret were already sitting at the boardroom table when Tom entered. Margret was sipping her tea, looking at her husband's portrait.

Joyce was fussing about with a plate of biscuits. She offered them to everyone. No one showed any interest. Tom seated himself in his father's chair, Joyce next to him. Margret stared at her son occupying Theo's seat. She suddenly got up and walked out of the room.

Douglas hurried after her. He found her leaning against the cupboard in the kitchen corner.

"I cannot do this. There is my son sitting in his father's chair. No, I cannot do this! Is he going to be my boss? Or what! Oh my God, Douglas, how am I going to be able to work here, a place full of ghosts! I can see and feel Theo all around, everywhere! No sorry, thanks for the thought, but no."

Douglas stood next to Margret.

"What about, if we all go to the café and talk. You will have to talk to Tom and Joyce about that. You go and freshen up and I will get the other two." He took her hand, gave it a gentle squeeze and smiled. "Yes?"

Margret nodded and walked uncertainly to the small bathroom.

For a long time, she looked at herself in the mirror. She touched her newly done hair, pulled the collar of her blouse. Stepping back, she saw her whole self.

"You can do it!" she said to the image. "Yes, you can do it!"

She stepped back into the boardroom and looked at her son.

"Maybe Tom, just for today you could sit somewhere else?"

"Sorry, mother," he said. "Of course."

He shifted. Theo's chair sat empty. They all looked at Tom expectantly. He looked at his mother.

"I would like you to call me Tom and please do not for one moment think that I am your boss! There is no boss in this company. Things are very different now. Douglas and I share all the responsibilities. At the moment Douglas is the one who carries most of the weight. But I'm catching up. Gary, the factory manager, comes to me or to Douglas, with his problems. If we cannot solve them, we have a meeting and discuss the situation.

But first of all we have to discuss you, mother, Margret. What shall I call you in front of the staff? What would you like me to call you?"

Margret took a long look at her son. 'How grown-up he is.' she thought.

"Margret," she said. "Yes, I'd like you to call me Margret. I'd like all of you to call me Margret. I am comfortable with that. Yes, Margret."

After the meeting Tom walked along the river to the town. Being too early for his violin lesson, he took the long way through the park and relaxed a while on the grass. Life was good. Putting his hand on the violin case Tom smiled.

"You and I. We get on. I just put the bow on your strings, and you sing for me!"

Tom entered Rubin's tower and sat on the old steps outside the flat. He looked out of the open window. It was so small that he only could see the ivy on the house next door, a green square in the grey of the town. He thought of this morning. Are all women so complicated? All that fuss! Maybe his mother could communicate better with a woman. Joyce and Margret seemed to get on really well. He looked at the green window and smiled.

He could hear noises behind the door. Rubin was coming down the hallway.

"Come in, come in."

He waved to Tom.

"Today you are going to play with Clara."

Tom felt the blood rising into his head.

"Oh, how nice," he said, following Rubin into his flat.

Clara smiled at him.

"I have found some little pieces for you to play. Simple harmony."

Rubin sweetly looked at her.

She studied the music and scowled.

"This is just child's play!"

Rubin ignored her and, looking at Tom, he said sternly,

"Tom, you need to learn discipline! You are far too romantic. Clara can teach you that. Maybe you can practise together now and then. So, let's begin. You first Clara. Please!"

Clara plucked the strings of her very beautiful violin to check the tuning. Her playing was precise and sharp. Every note clear! She looked magnificent. Tom found himself staring. Clara did not seem to hold the instrument. It seemed to float under her chin. She stood statue-like, swaying, her legs parted with her back straight, her head slightly bent back. And that strand of hair which always seemed to escape. When she finished she held the violin by its scroll. It just hung there between her long fingers. It reminded him of someone. Pushing her hair behind her ear, Clara looked at Rubin.

"Is that fine, like that?"

Rubin put another sheet of music on the music stand.

Tom looked at the notes dancing on their lines. He could sing them, but could he play them? In front of Clara?

"Can I please take this home and practise it first? I have never played this before."

The look Rubin gave him said everything. Tom tuned his violin. Then he sang the piece.

"You have a beautiful voice, why don't you take up singing?" Clara said mockingly.

Tom started playing. First hesitantly. Soon the music took over. He let the instrument, his love, sing. It was a simple tune, a children's song. Tom put all his feeling into it. When he finished, he tucked the violin under his arm and looked at Rubin.

"Beautiful, Tom." Rubin looked at Clara. "Beautifully played, with lots of feeling. You too played beautifully. Technically precise, everything exactly as it was written, but with no feeling!"

He walked about the room making stirring motions.

"If I could mix the two of you together. One with faultless technical knowledge, and the other who plays with emotion and romance. Well, it would be poetry in music."

Waving at Clara, Rubin told her, that her lesson was over. With an angry movement she put her instrument away in its case.

'No feeling', she thought. 'There is plenty of feeling in my playing! And every note is right. Sharp and precise. Really, no feeling!'

With an irritated movement she pushed the strand of hair behind her ear and walked out of the room.

"Shall we meet in the café after my lesson?" he called

"Maybe!"

And she disappeared into the dark hallway and out the door.

"Coffee Tom?" Mr Havelka offered as Tom walked into the café.

Clara was sitting by the window, the light shining on her reddish-blond hair.

"No, thank you. I have had more than enough coffee for one day. A glass of water would be great."

"May I sit with you?" he asked her.

She looked at Tom with thunder in her eyes.

"If you must."

He drank his water, paid for Clara's coffee and got up.

"Would you like to walk with me to the park?"

She picked up her violin and followed him out the door.

Tom put his arm around her shoulder. They walked slowly through the old part of the inner city towards the park. Tom steered her straight to the bench by the fountain.

She sat for a moment and then burst out.

"How dare he make me play a children's song! How dare he criticise my playing! I held my first violin when I was four years old. By the time I was ten I could play music by composers you would have never heard of when you were twenty! When I was fourteen, I played with my parents and we started the Gilles Quartet!"

She took his arm from her shoulder.

"Is Rubin trying to get us two to go out together? Maybe he thinks I will fall in love with you by teaching you discipline. By playing a stupid children's song."

Playing with her hair she started to laugh.

"Don't misunderstand me, Tom. I do like you. I like you, because you take me away from music. You make me feel relaxed. You give me the feeling of a different world. A world without music."

She got up.

"Goodbye, for now," she said.

"Can I take you home?"

"Thank you, no," she replied. "I know where I live. You can ring me."

Tom watched her walk out of the park, through the large iron gates.

TWENTY-TWO

The kitchen table was laid. There was still a little evening light trying to cheer up the dark room.

'The days are getting longer,' Margret thought as she put the meal in the oven to keep warm.

She'd managed to rustle up some dinner after coming home from her first day at the office. She was tired and had not yet changed. Taking her apron off, Margret walked into the living room and fell exhausted into her chair.

The flat was in darkness and completely silent when Tom got home. He smelt burning dinner. Turning on the hall light he saw his mother's handbag and hat hanging on the hall-stand.

Anxiously he called her name.

There was no answer. All he could hear was the oven hissing and spitting. He began to panic.

He found her fast asleep in her chair. In the kitchen he saw the table laid, but no food, and a little smoke escaping the oven door.

He tried to gently wake his mother. She blinked awake.

"Dinner!" she shouted.

Margret jumped up, cursing her hips, and limped into the kitchen. She turned the oven off.

"What time is it?" she asked with despair. "Oh no, dinner is completely spoiled."

With anger she looked at Tom.

"Don't worry, Mum," he smiled. "We can have bread and cheese and pickles and there is already a salad on the table."

He tried to put his arm around her. She pushed him hard away. He almost fell over.

"Where have you been?" she shouted. "Look what you've done! You spoiled the dinner!"

'Patience', he could hear Jack say

He stopped Margret from gathering up the plates. He took her gently by the arm and led her to one of the chairs.

"Sit. Please sit."

He opened the refrigerator and got out the cheese, pickles, and butter and placed them on a wooden board. He cut some slices of bread, which he put in a little basket.

"Anything else you would like? I am not too sure what you have in the fridge."

Before he sat down he poured two glasses of wine, then offered her some bread.

"Where have I been? Oh, Mum, you would never believe me! Have some bread. We can call this a late-night-snack."

Tom buttered his bread.

"Now tell me, how was your day at the office? Do I have a new member of staff?"

She ignored his question.

"Well, where have you been?"

The thought crossed his mind that he was over twenty-one and did not have to tell her anything. But he felt someone poking him in his back.

'Be nice!'

"You eat something and then I'll tell you where I've been and then you can tell me about your day. OK?"

Again, he offered her a slice of bread. She took it and put it on her plate.

"Salad, Mum?"

She looked at him searchingly. She began to smile.

"I think something special happened to you today."

"Yes," Tom answered. "Yes, indeed."

He told her about the lesson and how Rubin wanted him to learn to play with Clara. He told her how impressed he was when listening to Clara play.

"You know Mum, I felt she reminded me of someone. I don't know who, but she did. I've seen someone else hold the violin the way she did. Most performers tuck the instrument under their armpit. She held it between her fingers on the scroll. Very strange. I quite like Clara even though she's so difficult and moody."

He pointed at Margret's plate.

"Now, eat! Please."

Tom lifted his glass:

"And now to you Mrs Margret Dolmer. How was the office?"

"Fine, thank you."

"Is that all? Come on Mum, what did you do all day?"

She carefully buttered her bread and cut a small piece of cheese.

"Douglas took me out for lunch. Then I spent the afternoon working with Joyce. I answered the phone. I relearnt this and that about the bookkeeping.

I like Joyce. She took me all over the place. Introduced me to all the workers. You know, she never ever mentioned, that I am your mother. They all will call me Margret. No one knows I am the boss's mother."

She quietly giggled, then embarrassed turned it into a cough.

"When I got home, I cooked dinner. Oh my God, dinner! I'd better clean up the mess in the oven!"

"Leave it, mum, we'll do it tomorrow morning."

"Tom there is a lady on the phone for you. Can you take it?"

Joyce knew that Tom had Angus in the office with him. They were discussing his work program.

"Who is it?"

"Clara Gilles."

"I'd better take that. Thank you, Joyce. How is Margret doing?"

"Oh, great! She's almost ready to go home."

"I'll be a while. Can you please order her a taxi? I don't want her to go home on the tram. And tell her I might not be home for dinner. I'll ring her."

"Will do."

And with a click, Clara's voice was on the phone.

"Hi, Tom. Are you too busy to talk?"

He looked at Angus waiting for him.

"No," he lied. "Just hang on a minute."

He asked Angus to come back in half an hour.

"I'm back. Sorry about that. How are things with you? How was your week?"

"Oh, sort of OK." He heard her hesitate. "I wonder if we could go to Zita for dinner tonight? I can come to your work. I am not very far away."

He could hear traffic. She was obviously in a telephone box, not calling from home.

"It's probably too short notice to get any food at Zita's. She'd have to catch the fish and it's almost five."

"Oh," she said.

She sounded disappointed.

"Look, I'll give her a ring now. I'll let you know as soon as I can. Where are you? Are you not at home? How can I reach you?"

Tom knew that he would not get away before six-thirty. Friday was always a busy day.

"I'm not far from your work," she said impatiently.

"Can you come to the factory? You will have to wait for me downstairs."

They walked along the river. The wild, youthful waters of spring had turned into a smooth stream flowing towards its destination, through towns and fields, past mountain ranges. Many little rivers would join it. All kinds of boats would travel on it. Here and there a small waterwheel made the passing water work.

"Watching the flowing water always makes me restless. I so much would like to go with it. See foreign countries, meet new people, hear different music," he said. Clara looked at him, not quite understanding his yearning.

They sat down beneath the big willow, now in full leaf, the branches creating a green curtain. He had his arm around Clara's shoulder.

"When I was a little boy my father gave me an atlas. We used to follow rivers, pretending our fingers were boats or fish. We travelled to exotic lands neither of us knew anything about. He told me stories, I have no idea if they were true or if he made them up, somehow it did not matter.

One day, I promised myself, I will see these places with my own eyes."

With glazed eyes he watched the green-grey water through the curtain of willow.

Clara studied him.

"You're different today," she said. "You're different when you come out of your office too; so much older feeling. That's the you I don't like. The you with the Mr Dolmer feel about him."

Tom laughed.

"Yes, well, He is not my favourite person either. But I do like my job. And the people I work with have been my family. Some of them I have known all my life. I don't know many people outside of work. You know, I literally grew up in that place, playing about the machines! If it wasn't for my dad, I would have turned into a machine."

He got up and walked around the tree like a robot, pretending to fall over the exposed roots. Suddenly he was a boy again playing with his dad, being silly.

Clara laughed so much tears were rolling over her peachy cheeks. With a jiggery, clumsy, robot-movement Tom pulled his newly ironed handkerchief out of his pocket, gave it a slow shake and handed it to her.

"Mademoiselle!"

Walking to the edge of the river, he watched the water flow by. Quietly, almost as if he was talking to himself, he whispered, "And then I fell in love with the song of the violin."

She watched him and felt that he had slipped into a different world.

"I loved my dad. I loved him very much and I miss him."

"What about your mother? Don't you love your mother?"

"My dad took me away from machines and numbers and learning. Together we explored the river and the forest. My mother wanted me to be clean and tidy and clever. Oh, she was a good mother. She looked after my needs and my dad's. But there was no deep love in her, no affection. There still isn't.

I promised my dad to look after her. I do my best, but it isn't easy. She has high expectations for me, and I do not want to disappoint her."

He reached into his pocket and got his cigarettes, lit one and took a deep drag, turned around and looked at Clara.

"Enough of me. What about your parents?"

"Oh, they are OK."

"Just OK. Surely, they must be more than just OK? What do they do?"

"My dad is a medical specialist. A very important man in the hospital. My mum is at home. She is quite involved in music and clubs. I have a younger sister. She also wants to become a medico. My dad is also very sporty, and my mum isn't."

Clara started to play with her hair. After a long pause she suddenly said.

"Oh Tom, I am so unhappy!"

Quietly she started to cry.

"I have had a terrible argument with my dad! He wants me to stop seeing you. I got a bad mark in one of my subjects and he thinks it is your influence. I don't think it is your fault at all. I don't see you that often, do I?"

Slowly he started to stroke her hair. Then he brushed away the tears. The temptation to kiss her was stirring in him. But he just held her until she started to calm; until she stopped crying.

She looked at him with her tear-stained eyes.

"Well, you see, I thought, maybe you could come and meet my parents. I told them that Rubin told us to practise together. So we could help each other.

I thought maybe you could come tomorrow for afternoon coffee? And bring your violin? That might just convince my dad that you are not a bad influence on me. What do you say?"

He stood up and looked at her. He was astonished.

Hadn't she got terribly upset when they played together?

He needed time to think about her suggestion.

"Which subject did you not manage?" he asked.

She ignored his question.

"Well, what do you think? Did you practise the piece?"

He nodded. He'd practised nothing but it! How he had worked on playing it as technically precisely as absolutely possible. They had not played together since the fiasco the previous Monday.

Now he felt confused.

"I'm not sure," he said.

"Please, I need to know, so I can talk to my mother about it. You'd like my mother. Please come!"

"Let's walk. I can think better when I'm walking."

Arm in arm they walked in silence along the river towards Zita's house. After a while he turned to her.

"Yes, I would love to meet your parents."

She squeezed his arm.

The light was fading when they arrived at Zita's little house. There was a slight chill in the air. They decided to sit inside. The table was laid, a candle burning. Zita was standing at the stove. Beautiful smells filled the little room.

"No fish, darling. Just some kind of one pot meal. A kind of a stew."

TWENTY-THREE

Tom stood by his wardrobe wondering what he should wear. He heard the phone ring.

"It's Clara!" his mother called. "She says, 'Bring your bathers. It is quite hot, and you can go for a swim in their pool. They have plenty of towels.'"

He smiled. He felt good that he'd told her about visiting Clara's family. Even better, that his mother was pleased. He chose a light blue shirt, light grey trousers, a thin jacket. He decided against wearing a tie.

"Let me look at you."

Margret stood in the hallway waiting for Tom.

"No tie?"

He touched his throat and shook his head.

"Now you make sure that you are on your best behaviour when you see Clara's parents. Don't forget to ask if you can smoke and do stick to coffee. Don't start drinking Scotch, even if they offer it. Oh, I am so happy for you. Such a lovely girl, pretty and so…"

He kissed her cheek and was gone.

"Don't forget the flowers!" she called after him.

They'd been to the cemetery that morning. Their routine was always the same. The flowers at the gate, the setting up of the little chair for Margret. Tom removing the dead flowers and getting fresh water. His mother arranging the new ones, putting them next to Theo's name. It was a family grave. One day Tom would end up here, back with his dad. He found comfort in the thought.

He'd told his mother about the visit. She was pleased for him. At long last, he had a girlfriend.

'Maybe a little young', she thought. 'But, then, young is not such a problem. She can always be taught. And this romantic idea of becoming a musician might pass. Well, who knows?'

She'd smiled to herself. Aloud she said,

"Should you not take some flowers? One always takes something when invited. Chocolates or flowers. You choose."

Clara was nervously getting ready. She wanted everything and everyone to be completely natural. She certainly did not want to give Tom the feeling that she had been up since early morning running about, making a lot of noise, waking her father up on his day off. Living in the attic room Clara was running up and down on the wooden stairs. She could not decide what to wear, eventually settling on a floral summer dress.

Her mother was in the kitchen preparing a late Sunday breakfast. The smell of coffee slowly engulfing the whole house, drawing the family members out of their rooms.

Clara was on her way up to her room again when she met her father, only a towel thrown over his shoulder.

"Dad, you are going to wear something when Tom comes! Please be nice to him, please!"

Dr. Michael Gilles was on his way to the backyard swimming pool. He was a good-looking man in his early fifties. From his brown skin, one could see that he liked the outdoors. He was tall and slight in build. Being Sunday, Michael had not shaved. He never shaved on his days off. He also never dressed up. Days off should be celebrated with sloppiness and relaxation, with doing nothing of importance.

Gently he slid into the cool water. The pool was not large enough for serious swimming. Michael just rolled about in the water. He loved the feeling of weightlessness and the water all around him.

When he emerged from the bottom of his pool, he noticed Clara waving her arms and making signs. His ears were blocked; he could not properly hear what she was saying. When she came close enough to the edge, he sprayed her with water, making her scream and cry. He went under again, thinking about his day off. Gudrun could take care of the girls today.

Clara's howling brought her mother to the kitchen window.

"Daddy splashed me. Look at me! And it took me so long to decide on this dress!"

"It will dry in no time, darling. Come up, breakfast is on the table. Tell Dad. Susanna is already eating. You'll miss out on all the good bits. It's hours before Tom comes."

Clara got the big table in the garden ready for an afternoon meal. Being placed under a very large old walnut tree they would be sitting in the shade. She made sure that the lights in the lanterns hanging from the tree were working. She washed the seats, polished the glasses, and generally fussed about.

"Who's coming? Some prince?"

Her younger sister, Susanna, was standing on the upstairs verandah.

"Why don't you come down and help? You could get the garden chairs out of the little shed."

"No sorry, I have to study!"

Michael came down from upstairs via a cast iron spiral staircase. He went into the downstairs part of the building and got a wicker reclining seat.

"Come and sit with me, Clara. Get yourself a seat and tell me all about the young man who is making my girl go all funny."

He only wore a pair of shorts.

"Will you wear a shirt?" she said, dragging a chair along the lawn.

"No, it is Sunday."

He lit a cigarette, relaxed into his seat and looked at his daughter.

"Well?"

"Why do you think I invited him, Daddy? I invited him to find out more about him. I like him, but I don't really know much about him."

"It takes a lifetime to know a person. Should you be able to find out what he is like in one afternoon, you will be bored with him in a month!"

"I just want all of us to make a good impression on him."

"All of us? I'd better leave then. I just want to be me! It is Sunday! Well, tell me how old he is, what he does. Surely you must know that. And why he plays the violin."

She told him that he loved music — especially the violin. Then she told him about Tom's working situation and, finally, his age. That's when Michael turned and looked at her. He looked at his daughter for a long time. Then he shook his head.

"My dear, sweet girl! Don't you think he is a bit old for you? I was married at that age. You are only twenty!"

"Almost twenty-one!"

"Oh, please don't give me that twenty and so many months and so many days and hours and so on. You are twenty until your twenty-first birthday!"

Getting up he looked down at Clara.

"Well, now he is coming. We will just have to wait and see. Maybe he is underdeveloped or something like that. And what am I going to talk about with an engineer? All that on my day off!"

With that, Michael took off his shorts and jumped into the pool.

Tom preferred to take the bus. One did not see the surrounds when taking the underground. It took much longer going above ground. The bus went all over the town, stopping at every station, even if there was no one to get on or off.

Tom was the only passenger. He sat up front, close to the driver. As a little boy, he loved sitting in the front, pretending to be the driver taking the bus to exiting foreign places, strange people and the best music there was. He smiled at himself sitting there with his violin and holding the sad bunch of flowers.

"Going to see your girl?"

The bus driver looked at him through the rear vision mirror. Tom just smiled and nodded.

When he got off at the end station, Tom realised that he was far too early. He decided to have a good look at the neighbourhood. His father always wanted to buy a house here, but grandfather could not see any reason to do so. The flat was big and so much closer to work. Also, who would have time to look after a garden? Every house here was two-storied and had quite a large garden. He spent quite some time admiring them.

Clara's house was almost at the end of the street, opposite a wild-looking park. The house seemed to be quite old and in great need of some repair. He walked along a fence with ornate iron bars until he got to a solid-looking gate. There were a number of bell buttons. He pressed the one saying Fam.Gilles. Immediately a dog barked. The gate opened with a buzz.

Clara came running along the side of the house. She was wrapped in a towel. Her hair was wet.

"Oh, you brought me some flowers. How romantic!"

"No, they are for your mother."

"My mother has a garden full of flowers! Nothing for me?"

Pulling one of the flowers out of the bunch, Tom held it for a while, then put it behind her ear. Clara smiled and blushed.

He followed her along a narrow gravel path. The shrubbery growing next to the fence was thick and uncut. At the end of the path a beautifully-tended garden opened up. The cut lawn was surrounded by all kinds of shrubs. Garden beds in a myriad of colours intruded into the lawn.

The wall of trees and shrubs cut out the houses next door and gave complete privacy. A little garden shed, the door just hanging on its hinges, was overgrown by an enormous rosebush displaying masses of flowers. Close to the house, Tom noticed a very large, old walnut tree, with lanterns hanging from its lower branches. The tree was still laden with green nuts. Under the tree was a round table covered with a simple cloth, plates, glasses and other items needed for a festive meal, waiting for the party to begin.

Clara's mother climbed quickly out of the pool and covered her tall, slim body in a robe.

"Tom!"

She walked towards him, arm outstretched for a greeting. She had a firm handshake.

"I am Gudrun. Nice to meet you, Tom. Just put your things over there. They will be safe."

Holding out the bunch of flowers, Tom bowed slightly.

"You have a beautiful garden, Mrs Gilles, "My little bunch feels quite forlorn in it."

She laughed

"Thank you, Tom. That is very kind of you."

It had taken a while for Tom to notice the man sitting in a large chair, the newspaper almost covering his entire reclining figure. Clara nervously danced around him, trying to make him aware that they had a visitor. There was a lot of smoke coming from behind the paper.

"Daddy, Tom is here. Are you not going to say hello?"

Tom walked up to the chair, waiting until daddy had finished the article he was reading. When the paper eventually was laid aside, Michael looked at Tom over his glasses.

"So, that is the Tom Clara keeps on talking about. Has anyone given the lad a drink? What would you like? I am having a Scotch."

Dr. Michael Gilles was totally relaxed.

"Please call me Michael. None of that Doctor thing. For God's sake someone get that boy a drink!"

Michael's stern face suddenly cracked into a laugh.

"I have three women in the house and not one of them knows how to behave towards a visitor. Come on, lad!"

With ease he swung himself out of the chair and pushed Tom in front of him towards the downstairs flat.

"My father's old surgery. I would never work from home. You look like a straight Scotch man to me. Or do I have to water it down with ice or even worse with water? Or would you like a beer?"

They went back out in the garden, where the three women were busy getting the food from upstairs to the table under the tree.

Michael grabbed another garden seat and put it next to his. Offering Tom a cigarette he started to ask questions.

"Now tell me, Tom, why the violin? I thought you were an engineer? I suppose a good balance to go from numbers and machines to some sort of arty relaxation. I myself like the mountains. Yes, walking in the mountains. Preferably on my own. I can't stand chatty groups of people disturbing the silence of nature. The mountains clear my head, get me away from the responsibility of my work. Thank God my three women don't seem to be too fond of mountain climbing. So, I get a bit of respite from them too. Now tell me, why do you have to play with Clara?"

Tom started with the reason why Rubin had suggested the two of them play together. He did not tell Michael why he played. He just agreed that using music as a change from working was relaxing. That brought him to his work and his responsibility since his father's death.

He did enjoy the company of the Gilles family. They seemed to argue a lot, but it was a kind of teasing. When things got out of hand with his girls or the discussion became boring, Michael would slap his hands together and roar: "Enough!" Everyone stopped. Only the scruffy little dog started barking, thinking a game was about to happen.

The afternoon coffee Tom had expected turned out to be a late lunch. A large assortment of cheeses and cold meats, a number of salads, pickles and a basket filled with small bread rolls and slices of rye bread filled the table. Clara fussed arranging it all. Susanna watched her.

The two sisters were completely different. Susanna was very serious. She was about two years younger than Clara. She was doing her last year at high school and needed the highest marks possible to get into university. She wanted to follow in her father's and grandfather's footsteps. Immediately after the meal she excused herself and went to get on with her studies.

Gudrun arranged Tom's flowers in a vase in the middle of the table. Tom watched how she gently touched them — as she might when arranging her hair.

"There," she said, "lovely."

Tom smiled. She felt so serene, so very much in control, and somehow so very sincere. She had given him the feeling that she really thought the flowers he had brought were lovely. Her garden was full of much more vibrant flowers. Yes, Tom thought, a great deal more alive.

The flowers he bought were meant for the dead. Gudrun treated them as if they were jewels. He thought she was beautiful; everything about her was beautiful. Clara had inherited her hair, which was always escaping the big knot on the back of her head. Neither of the children looked like her. Their features came from their father.

The lanterns were dancing in the light breeze, their little lights trying to compete with the afternoon light. Michael lit a cigarette. They talked about their lives. Tom found out that Gudrun had Scandinavian parents. She was totally engrossed in music, played in a small private orchestra, was a member of a women's music club and looked after her family. Little stories were told. Tom talked about some of the adventures he had with his dad. He could not get himself to mention his mother. They never played their violins or went for a swim.

TWENTY-FOUR

A s Tom walked past the receptionist's desk on his way to the shop floor, he noticed Margret answering the telephone, a smile on her face. She connected the caller with someone in the building and then walked into her small office.

After having been working for two weeks Margret was starting to be at ease with her situation. 'If she only could act that charming at home', Tom thought. 'It feels as if she was leaving all her smiles and delightful moods at work. Maybe securely locked up in the safe?'

When he opened the door to the shop floor the noise of the machines made Margret come back to her desk. Seeing Tom disappear behind the door, she wondered what he was doing down there amongst the workers. This would have never happened in Theo's days. He would have sent his personal secretary.

The door opened again. She saw Tom walking out with one of the new apprentices.

Young Angus Henshall, the son of Douglas, nodded at her, "Mrs Margret."

She smiled back at him,

"Good morning, Angus"

'He is a pleasant boy, just like his father,' she thought. 'I wonder what Tom wants from him?'

As Angus, on his return from Tom's office, walked past Margret she was wondering what they had talked about. The boy looked deep in thought. He did not look at her, or nod, or smile as he always did. She liked him and was worried. It upset

her, making her feel on edge the whole morning. She must talk
to Tom about it over lunch.

When she and Tom sat on one of the benches by the river
eating their lunches, she asked him,

"What was that all about with Angus this morning? Has he
done something wrong?"

"Eat your lunch, Mum. Everything's fine with Angus."

But when looking at her, Tom saw her concern. Unwrapping
his sandwiches, he slowly said,

"I told him that I was very happy with his progress. I said he's
learnt very fast how to handle all the workings on the shop floor.
And I said that both his father and I feel that he should do a
business course. Also, he needs to learn more about engineering.

I feel that one day he could be able to step into his father's
shoes and take over the role of manager."

"Oh, that is wonderful."

Margret let go of her lunch and just like a child clapped her
hands together. "Oh, what a good idea. Yes, he is a clever young
man. That job will then stay in the Henshall family. Oh, Tom,
that is wonderful!"

"Now Mother, please eat your lunch."

Before she did, though, she asked another question.

"How is Clara? There has been very little talk about her. Did
your visit not turn out? Did the parents not like you?"

"Clara has to study, and her father is keeping her away from
anything, that could distract her. She has not been to her violin
lessons for ages. Rubin is not happy at all. He has been having
tantrums."

"So, you have Mr Rubin to yourself? How is that? I did not
like him at all. Why did you decide to go to him? There must be
other teachers."

"He is the best and I want the best!"

Tom could feel his mother's sudden agitation.

"Would you like something to drink? I can bring you a cup of tea," he said.

He got up, lit a cigarette and walked back to the office. There was a small kitchen for the workers downstairs.

She watched him go. She could not bring herself to like his friends. They were all peculiar. Not liking his friends meant that she did not have to communicate with them. She felt not liking his friends would keep him by her side.

He chatted with some of the men as he slowly made the tea for his mother.

'Maybe', he thought 'the river will calm her and bring her some good thoughts. Give her tranquility'.

He was mistaken. By the time he arrived with the two cups, Margret was boiling over. She took her cup and spilled some of the tea on her skirt

"Look what you have done now!" she snapped.

But Tom's thoughts were with his music. Ignoring his mother's aggressive tone, he started humming the first piece he had learned from the crisp new pages of *Kreutzer's Etudes for Solo Violin*. He felt like he was back at school when carrying his new book. He loved to open the pages and see the black dots walking on the five lines. There were forty-two Etudes to learn and he had just started on the first one.

"Must you hum? Look at my skirt! How am I going to go back to work with stains on my dress? Tom, I am talking to you!"

Looking at the flowing water he took the handkerchief she had ironed that morning out of his pocket and handed it to her.

"I am sure no one will notice. You have not touched your lunch. Is your tea OK?"

"There you go again. OK. OK, what kind of word is that? Your friends probably use it all the time."

"Mother, what is the matter with you?"

"Me?" Margret said. "Me? There is nothing wrong with ME!"

Tom walked away, downstream to his tree, where he sat for

a long time. 'Be kind' Zita had said. 'Be patient', was the advice from Jack.

"I am trying my best!" Tom shouted at the river.

When he arrived back at work, Margret was sitting behind her desk with a smile, talking on the phone. She ignored him.

Back in the office, he rang Clara, but her mother answered. No, he could not talk to Clara, she was studying. Gudrun could hear in Tom's voice that there was something amiss.

"Are you OK? You sound strange."

"No, I am not OK."

"If you need a chat, well, I'm available," she said.

TWENTY-FIVE

The café was very crowded. It was filled with the clatter of cups and the chatter of people. He saw Gudrun waving to him.

Her genuine concern made Tom open up. He told her all his sorrows, his dreams and all about his mother. He never mentioned Esther.

She looked at him for a long time across the table

"You are quite sure that your mother is not ill? Pain can be a trigger for aggression."

Had he noticed any physical problems? Yes, she did complain about her hip when getting up. But otherwise, Tom could not think of anything.

"You know Tom," she continued. "It does not have to be a physical pain. It can be a psychological one. A pain from the deep past. A pain that, when triggered, creates aggression. Would your mother see a doctor? I think that would be the only way to help her and you."

Tom put the cigarette packet on the table.

"This will kill you!"

With her beautiful hands she pointed at the packet and then looked sternly at him.

He was puzzled. "But Michael?"

"Yes, he smokes, and I do not like it. He cannot be told. I just learnt to live with it. Some things one just has to accept! Accepting creates a happy relationship, a happy family. Michael never smokes inside. That I would not tolerate."

She smiled, then looked hard at Tom and continued,

"My dear Tom, have you ever thought of getting away, having

a holiday? You could take your car and just go away somewhere. It would do you the world of good to get away and, who knows, your mother might just see what it is like to be without you."

"Where would I go? I would not know where to go?"

"Oh, anywhere! Up along the river, down the river, across the river, maybe away from the river. Anywhere!"

Tom took a cigarette out of its packet, then rolled it slowly in his fingers and tapped its end on the table. He was taking his time; he did not know what to say.

"Tom?"

Gudrun made him look up.

"Listen, would you like to come with us on a Music Holiday? Every year some of the members of my small orchestra and their children have a ten day holiday in the mountains. We get together and make music. And this time we will be celebrating Clara's twenty-first birthday. Why don't you come?"

He put the cigarette back in the pack and stared at her.

"Ten days in the mountains?" he said.

He shook his head reluctantly.

"I could not spare the time from work."

"Well, come for a few days, then. Clara would like to see you there to celebrate her birthday. Rubin will be there. It's in a little, isolated mountain village. It's another world."

Again he shook his head.

"Mother," he said.

The next evening, when everyone had left the factory, Tom took his violin and walked into the machine room. He bowed to his mechanical audience and started practising his scales.

No matter how hard he tried his fingers did not want to obey. The sound filling the room shocked him. This had never happened before. He tried again. Still, there was no music. Just appalling noises. Holding the violin up to his face he started to talk to it.

"What is the matter with us? Together we should be soaring away from everything. Leaving this plane, moving to another. We should be singing together. Not these terrible scratchings. Let's try again."

And so Tom tried again, but with the same result.

"Esther!" he called.

There was no answer.

Tom placed the instrument back in its case, covered it with the silk cloth and closed the lid. On the door hung his jacket. He took it off the hook and walked out of the room.

"Maybe the river will soothe my mind, my body; our spirit."

The phone in his office was ringing. Racing up the spiral staircase he just got it in time. It was Clara.

"I need to see you!" Her voice sounded hesitant, there was a little sniffle. "Please, can I see you? I rang you at home. Your mother told me that you might still be at work. I have been ringing and ringing! I so much want to see you."

"But what about your studies, your father? You cannot just leave without his permission."

She assured him that she was allowed to go out for a short time. Her father was at a conference and her mother did not mind as long as she was not out too long.

"I'm just about to go down to my tree at the river. My practice today has been terrible. Terrible."

"I'll come to you and we can sit by the river for a while and just watch it flow past us."

The evening light danced along the water.

He took his violin out of its case, ran his fingers over the string to see if they were still in tune. After having a stern word to her, he put the instrument under his chin and started playing. Now the notes came. She sang with the river, she trilled with the little waves. The evening light and the music danced on the water together.

Someone was touching his shoulder. He felt a soft, warm mouth on his neck. It made his body quiver, merge with the vibration of his music making. Still holding his instrument, Tom turned around. A strand of hair brushed his face. He just managed to put his violin down before Clara put her arms around his neck.

"I did not think that I would ever miss someone that much. Oh, I missed you, I missed you so much!"

He gently undid her embrace and got up from the seat. Tenderly he pushed the strand of hair behind her ear. Tears were slowly running down Clara's cheeks. He took her face in both of his hands and kissed her. She responded and pressed her body against his, her tears running freely. He could taste their saltiness.

With a loud sniff, she pulled away.

"I am so sorry! I did not mean to do that! Your music was so beautiful, and I stopped it. You know, I have been standing there listening for quite a while. Then the sun shone on your neck and your curly hair and I could not help myself."

Tom pulled her back towards him. Clara put her face against his neck and started sobbing.

"I have worked so hard. I passed the subject I had failed in. Boring History. And I am determined to pass the rest. In two weeks I have my final exam. Then I just have to submit my composition and play. And then I am free. Free forever. I just could not wait until then to see you."

She started sobbing again.

"I am not good with words. It is hard for me to talk about my feelings. Everything is a muddle. Oh, such a muddle."

Tom lifted her head and kissed her eyes.

"You must have fallen in love with someone. Who is the lucky fellow?"

Pulling back, Clara started to gently hit Tom with her fists.

"You are such a tease!"

Tom turned Clara towards the river. He put his arm around her waist. The sun was low, their shadows long, almost dipping in the water. He released her and got up.

"I'll get the car and drive you home," he said as he turned to walk back to the factory.

She was running after him, carrying his violin.

"You left your violin behind. You did not even put it in its case! What were you thinking! How could you."

Tom was shocked by his action. Yes, how could he! Holding the instrument tight under his arm he turned towards Clara and kissed her.

She gently pushed him away and mumbled:

"I'd better get home."

Clara forgot her house keys and had to ring the bell.

Her sister opened the door, looked at Tom, and shouted into the house,

"She's brought her boyfriend, Mum."

And with that short announcement, Susanna ran back up the stairs.

"Do come in, Tom," Gudrun called from the living room.

She was sitting at the end of a large, comfortable-looking sofa, legs curled underneath her, reading a book. She was holding it up to catch the last light of the day from the large windows.

"Please sit down, Tom. I just would like to finish reading this chapter."

Tom looked around the large room. At one end was a grand piano covered in a beautiful woven cloth. By one of the windows, a chair and small table with books scattered around it. Above the sofa, a very large painting. At the other end of the room covering both sides of the corner, more books. The room had a wonderfully lived-in feeling.

"Can I get you a drink?"

Gudrun had got up and stood in front of him. She wore loose white trousers and a flowing floral shirt. Her hair was just like Clara's, out of control.

Tom had to smile. Mother and daughter were so much alike.

"Clara please get Tom a Scotch. We'll go into the garden to enjoy the last of the day's light."

They all settled down at the table under the walnut tree. Tom sipped his drink and with Gudrun's permission smoked a cigarette.

"My first," Tom said. nodding at Gudrun.

Turning to Tom she asked if he had thought about the holiday in the mountains.

"I do need more information. When it is and how long for. You must understand that I have a job. Unfortunately, I cannot come and go as I please. I am really sorry. I do hope you understand. And then there is my mother."

Tom lit another cigarette. He got up and walked into the garden.

Clara wanted to run after him, but her mother held her back.

"We understand, Tom. I can write down the dates for you and you can then see how it will fit in with your work."

Picking up the board with the rest of the food, Gudrun asked Clara and Tom to bring the dishes up into the kitchen.

How different this kitchen was to his mother's! Much smaller, very well-lit and totally cluttered up. The window was overgrown with pot plants. A big basket of fruit stood on the bench in a corner. He saw a braid of garlic hanging on the wall, some onions, and dried leaves. There was a long shelf filled with little jars full of different coloured powders. Gudrun put the kettle on to make them all a cup of coffee.

Tom drove back to the factory. For a long time he looked out the office window watching the lights dance on the water. He could still feel Clara's kiss on his neck, her body pressing against his. Was she just unhappy not being free, caged up with her books? Or did she truly like him? Her life was so different to his.

He did love her family and their big, sprawling, lived-in house and its beautiful rambling garden. Their open, uncomplicated ways. Was that what attracted him to Clara? The attraction of opposites?

TWENTY-SIX

With deep concentration Margret counted her stitches. The standard lamp shone on her curly, steel-grey hair. Most of the colouring had disappeared. She had decided to leave her hair as it was. What was the use of spending money on outside beauty? She was old and there was nothing that would change that. Working made her tired. But on the other hand, it brightened up her life. She enjoyed communicating with strangers over the phone. The contact was distant and not confronting.

She stopped knitting and looked at her son. He had stepped into his father's shoes with surprising ease. The firm was doing well. Margret could see that when doing the books. She smiled. What would she do without him? Slouched in his chair, headphones on, waving his arms about as if he was the conductor of the famous orchestra he was listening to.

'How will the friendship with Clara work out?' Margret thought. 'She is so young.'

Suddenly noticing his mother staring at him, Tom turned the volume down and removed his headphones. He had bought a new record and was listening to a violin concerto by Max Bruch. The Adagio almost made him cry.

"Mother, did you want me?"

"Are you enjoying your new record? You seem to be!"

He blinked in astonishment. Was she interested in his music?

"It is beautiful! I am astounded how the soloist remembers all the notes. There must be millions of them! It's like learning all the words of a novel by heart. You cannot make a mistake! It would upset the other players. I am not sure if I ever will be able to do that. Maybe that is why I like to make up my own music?"

Margret did not reply. The room fell into its accustomed quietness. With some apprehension, Tom broke the silence.

"Mum, in a few weeks Clara has her twenty-first birthday."

Margret looked up. He had not called her mum for a long time.

"Is she that young?"

"I've been invited to her party. It is going to be held in a small village in the mountains. They will be combining the birthday with a ten day holiday. If I get time off work I would like to go, at least for the weekend. Do you mind?"

She got up and turned towards the kitchen.

"Mother please, don't just walk away!"

"You are old enough to make your own decisions."

With a loud slam Margret closed the door behind her. Tom was just about to go back to his music when the phone rang. A high-pitched scream from the other end made him hastily pull the receiver away from his ear.

"I passed! I passed all my exams! All of them. Even boring History!"

It was Clara. He could feel her dancing down the phone line.

"You must come and celebrate! I am so relieved."

"Congratulation Clara! What about if I arrange a dinner at Zita's? For all of us to celebrate your achievement. It's time we all got together. How about it?"

Tom felt the joy and happiness move down the telephone line and fill the gloomy room.

"I love you, I love you." Clara sang into his ear.

She hung up. He felt the room fill with the most beautiful aroma; a gentle music floated around him. He realised that Esther also was celebrating.

TWENTY-SEVEN

On Saturday afternoon the taxi pulled into the Dolmer's Engineering carpark. Tom paid the driver and got out and opened the door for his mother. She stepped out stiffly, wincing at the pain in her hip.

A little canary-yellow Citroen was already in the carpark. Clara was sitting on the bonnet making the little car rock. Tom noticed Gudrun standing by the river looking out over the water. Susanna was still sitting in the car. There was no sign of Michael.

"Daddy will be a little late. He was called up this morning. Something happened at work. I have not seen him today."

Tom felt disappointed.

"We'll wait a little longer for him." Gudrun called from the river. "This is a beautiful spot. So peaceful." She walked to Margret. "Mrs Dolmer, so good to meet you. I am Gudrun, Gudrun Gilles."

Clara jumped off the car, signalling to Susanna to come out of the Citroen. They introduced themselves nervously. Both were on their best behaviour. Margret was working hard to appear relaxed.

The awkwardness was broken by the arrival of a red MG. Michael jumped out. He took off his jacket and tie, throwing them onto the seat in his car. Then he stretched and stamped his feet.

"What a morning! I've been standing in one spot for hours. My whole body is asleep! This must be your mother, Tom."

Michael took her hand in both of his.

"So good to meet you, Mrs Dolmer. Please call me Michael.

I am not working now. I am just an ordinary person. My God, what a morning!"

He looked at the building and read the name.

"Dolmer's Engineering! Is that you Tom? This place has a great reputation. Well, well my daughter is going out with Tom Dolmer."

Margret had drawn her hands out of Michael's and stepped back. She felt like leaving.

"I wanted us to meet here so we can walk along the river to the restaurant," Tom explained. "You will see my favourite tree, also I feel it is the best way to approach this wonderful little restaurant."

"I can't possibly walk all that way," Margret said. "My hip."

"That can be so painful," Gudrun said. "Let me drive you and the others can walk."

Margret stared at her sourly and nodded.

Michael had already started towards the river.

"Upstream or down?"

Tom pointed downstream.

Clara held Tom back and when the others had disappeared, she gave him a big hug.

"Thank you for doing this. It will be good to meet your mother. Last time was a bit of a disaster."

They caught up with Michael and Susanna by the big tree.

"What a magnificent monster this is. And look there are very convenient seats everywhere."

Michael sat down on a root overlooking the river.

"This is the life. You are a lucky bugger, Tom, having this so close to work."

Clara was getting restless.

"We should go! Mummy and Tom's mother are probably already there."

Tom led the way along the riverbank, beside the quietly flowing water.

When the little house came into view, Michael stopped.

"What an absolutely charming place. No, not charming, romantic! How did you find this, Tom?"

The table looked beautiful with its white plates, simple wooden-handled cutlery, glasses, and jugs of wine. Zita had placed little bowls filled with her homemade mosquito repellant and citronella candles on the table. The smells coming out of the kitchen were magic.

Tom showed his guests to the table. Margret refused to sit between Michael and Gudrun. 'Oh please, Mother don't make a scene!' Tom thought.

Michael saved the difficult situation with a gallant movement of his hand, offering Margret his seat at the end of the table.

Little bread rolls and little bowls of dips were brought out by Old Jack, wearing one of Zita's embroidered aprons. When he came to serve Margret, he gave her a little squeeze on the shoulder and whispered in her ear,

"Do you remember Old Jack the gardener?"

She spun around, almost spilling the wine.

"Goodness me, Jack! What are you doing here?"

"Working, Mrs Dolmer. Enjoy your dinner. Enjoy everything!"

Jack winked at Tom. Tom smile at him. 'Oh, you funny little man.' he thought.

Michael raised his glass and stood up.

"I would have never dreamt that such a place existed. It is like out of a fairy tale. Thank you, Tom, for bringing us here. I would also like to raise my glass to you, may I call you Margret, for having such a wonderful son. I also would like to drink to my daughters for having passed their exams with amazingly good results. Love you all. Again, thank you. This place is like nectar to me. Now my glass is empty. Is there any more wine?"

Jack was playing an excellent waiter. He filled Michael's glass and stepped back. Tom had to laugh. Jack had put something on his moustache. It was blacker, and the ends looked like little spears. There the little man stood, straight as a soldier, wearing an apron, watching the glasses like a hawk.

Kira came out of the house with a large oval dish. Across a bed of parsley lay an array of small fish. They were crisp and covered in some red spice and surrounded by small potatoes. Jack's wife brought a bowl of steamed vegetables and another dish piled up with little dumplings. Then Zita's spicy sauce arrived.

Kira looked at Margret.

"May I help you with the fish?"

Margret stared at her in astonishment.

"Kira? It's you?"

"Yes, Margret. Very much so. Now may I help you?"

Margret's eyes moistened as Kira took her plate and filleted one of the fish for her.

"Yes Margret, I am Kira. All grown-up and married. You must eat the fish with the skin. We will chat after dinner."

Kira showed everyone how to fillet the fish.

The only noise was the clatter of cutlery. A sign that the meal was being enjoyed. A platter with more fish was brought out.

"Where can I find the creator of this food! Never have I tasted fish like this," Michael said.

Before anyone could stop him, Michael was in the little house. There he was confronted by a dark-skinned lady wearing nothing more than underpants and an apron. She was standing in front of her wood stove frying more fish. He could see the muscles on her back moving as she lifted the heavy iron pan off the stove. She turned around and he was confronted by her leathery face. Was she old? Her black eyes shone. They seemed to be young and lively.

"Oh hello, I am Zita. Please excuse me, darling."

She put the blackened iron pan on a thick piece of wood on the bench.

"Everything all right?" she said as she put the spitting fish on some paper. When she had moved away from the hot pan Michael walked up to her and kissed her on both cheeks.

"You are a genius. I have never tasted fish like that. Where do you get the fish?"

"I catch it in river. That lot I had to net. I needed to get fish that were about same size. I usually catch with line."

He noticed an accent.

"Where are you from?"

"Oh, from nowhere. I am Romani, Gypsy. But I live nowhere, many years, long story. You better have some more fish, while it is still hot. We talk after dinner over coffee and cigarette. Yes?"

With that she turned back to the fire.

Zita had wiped her hands on the apron and Michael could see her legs; strong, muscular and young-looking. 'This lady has an old-looking head on a young body.' Michael thought. He wondered what happened to her face.

The taste of the fish took Margret back to a time long gone. She used to come here with Theo. Together they went fishing and then cooked the catch on an open fire. They had wonderful evenings together. Kira used to look after Tom. They would go down to the river and float things on the water. There was also Jack, but he did not have a wife then. Not that she could remember. Oh, how much she liked little Kira, how much she would have liked a little girl. But there was just Tom; well, he was a surprise packet. She did love her son, but a daughter would have been — well...

A big sigh escaped her.

"Are you all right, Mum?"

"Yes, yes, just reminiscing."

Michael turned to her.

"May we join your journey into the past?"

"No!"

Michael smiled at her.

"I do understand, the past is private. It belongs to us alone."

He offered Tom a cigarette. Tom looked at Gudrun as he took one. She just smiled at him and waved her hand.

The table was cleared. The candles lit. Kira refilled the little bowls with mosquito repellent water. Jack brought some more chairs and small coffee cups. Then Zita came out of the house. She wore a simple, colourful summer dress and was carrying a big coffee pot.

"Sorry, no milk. Forgot to buy milk."

She filled the little cups with the black liquid.

"That's it. No sweets in this house, darlings."

Kira, Jack and his wife joined them.

The conversation started to flow. Most of the stories came from the deep past. Even Margret opened up and started telling stories from the time when they met Zita and her family. It was the day Tom got lost and the river was in flood.

"I heard about that story some years later." Margret looked at Jack. "Oh Jack, I don't know what I would have done to you if we had not found that fine young son of mine. Look at him…" and there Margret stopped talking.

"A very handsome, caring young man with a big load on his shoulders." Gudrun finished her sentence.

"Oh please, can we talk about someone else?"

Tom was getting embarrassed.

"This coffee is deliciously different to any coffee I have ever had!"

Michael almost licked his cup.

"It is something my people picked up when traveling through Turkey. Strong and sweet, with a little freshly-ground cardamom. You boil the water in the pot and throw the coffee in. Then the cardamom. Boil it up once, then scare it with a little cold water. That will help settle the coffee grains. Wait a bit. Serve. Simple!"

Zita looked at Michael with her black sparkling eyes. He had the feeling she could read his mind.

"Thank you, Zita, for the best meal I have had for a long time! Would there be a chance of getting another cup of coffee?"

Margret was restless. She found Michael's charming ways

sickening. She could never trust such a sweet-talking man. She looked at Tom who had his arm around Clara.

"I'd like to go home, Tom."

"Something wrong, Mother? Aren't you having a good time?"

"Thank you, I had a very good time. Now I'd like to go home."

She got up, cursing her hips. She could hardly walk. Michael was quickly at her side, helping her.

"You should have that seen to, Margret."

Michael's whole persona changed. The way he held her, the way he spoke. He had slipped into the role of a doctor.

"I can find the best help for you, the best specialist. There is no need these days to live with pain and unease. Maybe Gudrun will drive you home? If you like?"

"I will be better when I start to move. Thank you for the offer, but I would like Tom to take me home."

With that Margret started to walk towards the little hut.

Tom asked Kira to ring for a taxi.

"Please don't go. I'll be back in half an hour."

"More coffee?" Zita asked.

"Oh yes, please!"

As he stepped out of the taxi on his return, Tom could hear the chatting and laughter coming from the little deck by the river.

He walked over the flood embankment, around the house and looked at the joyful picture of his friends in the candlelight.

"Welcome back, Tom!" Michael called.

He stood up and for a minute it looked like he was going to make another speech.

Kira filled the wine jugs. Zita made another pot of coffee. Laughter and good, happy conversation spilled out into the night, towards the river and from there with the flow of the water into foreign countries.

TWENTY-EIGHT

"What are you reading?"
"Oh, just some music I have to learn."

It was evening. Even though there was some of the day left Margret had drawn the living room curtains. She was always concerned that the people across the road would look into their lives. Tom's concentration had been disturbed. He looked at his mother.

"Why don't we use the room facing the courtyard again? It would make such a great living room. We would have no one looking in. Also, the view over the trees is so soothing. Isn't that the reason why granddad bought this flat on the top floor?"

Margret shifted about in her chair. She straightened out the supporting cushions and let go a little sound of pain.

"Have you thought of Michael's offer of getting some help for you? Is it not better to know what the matter is with your hips?"

"Oh, Tom, please! All those changes you want to make. It all makes me tense and unsettled. I thought our life was fine, just as it was!"

Slowly she got up and shifted the pillows, then she walked out of the room, trying hard not to limp. Tom continued to read, humming the notes as his finger followed the lines. Then, closing his eyes, he tried to sing the notes from memory.

"Do you have to hum? It is such an annoying grunting noise!"

Margret had brought a bedroom pillow to make herself comfortable. Picking up her knitting, she continued working on Tom's jumper. But she just could not get comfortable. Tom watched her. He had put the sheet of music aside.

"Mother?"

"Not now, Tom, I am counting. This is a difficult part of the pattern."

Walking across the room, Tom opened the window, lit a cigarette and watched the fading light on the house across the road. Lights were turned on. He could look into the lives of his neighbours. What kind of life did they have? Hardly any of the windows were covered with curtains. It gave him the feeling of being invited into their homes. He could hear laughter, the clinking of crockery. There was some fighting going on somewhere.

"Mother, we must talk. Please."

"About what?"

She looked up at her son.

"Is there a problem? At work? Have you had an argument with Clara?"

Tom pulled up a chair and sat down next her.

"About you!"

"Me? Why?"

"Have you thought about Michael's offer to help you to have those hips looked at? It must be terrible being in pain all the time."

"I have known worse!"

Margret put the knitting aside, moved about in her seat, and looked at Tom.

"Quite honestly, the less I have to do with Michael and his lot the better. I have nothing in common with that family. No, thank you, I am fine!"

He sat back. It was as if she had smacked him in the face.

"Sometimes, Mother, I have the feeling that you do not like me!"

"What gives you that idea?"

"So, you did not enjoy the evening at Zita's?"

Long did she stare at her hands, then at Tom.

"I would have preferred it without the Gilles family. And then I am not that fond of fish and spices. It was great to see Jack again. And little Kira, all grown-up. Yes, it would have been so much better just with them."

Margret smiled, picked up her knitting but did not start to knit.

"Would you like to go back, just for a chat and a coffee or tea? We could go after work. The days are long now. Zita might be able to contact Jack. He could come too. And maybe we can get Kira to come?"

Slowly she nodded.

Tom picked up the sheets of music and walked out of the living room.

In his room, he turned on the reading light. He sat on his bed, the light shining only on the sheet of music; the rest of the room in darkness. It was his way of focusing on the work he had to learn.

But Tom found himself looking out of the window to the tops of the trees in the courtyard and beyond to the lights of the town. And somewhere was the river. He could not see it but the feeling of it was there. Very seductive, calling, calling.

Looking back down on the paper with the black dots dancing on the five lines, he smiled and started singing while his finger moved from note to note.

It was Monday afternoon. Tom sat on his bench in the park reading the music he had to play.

To get this very difficult piece right was very important to Tom. Rubin had given him a folder of music by a man called Kreuzer. *Forty-two Etudes for Solo Violin*, it said on the cover.

"Number six!" That's all Rubin said. "Learn it!"

Tom had shown the music to Clara. She said that Rubin had lost his mind. This was far too hard for a beginner. But then, everything was hard at the moment! Tom had stopped visiting the river fearing he might want to jump in and float away. Away from his mother and Kreuzer's music!

Taking his violin out of its case he started fingering the notes as he sang. In his head, he could hear Rubin stamp and shout. Tom just could not cope with another upset person.

"Excuse me, you are not allowed to play music in this park! Move on, please. You can go and busk in the streets, not in a park!"

An officious-looking man stood in front of Tom. The violin case was next to him on the bench. It was open, and he noticed some coins in it.

"No, I am not busking. I am just quietly practising, doing my homework."

"Well, my dear young man, do your homework at home, not in the park. I am sure that's why it is called homework."

The inspector laughed at his own joke.

Putting his violin back into its case, Tom looked at the laughing man.

"Am I allowed to read my music? Maybe a little humming? Very quietly? Or maybe I could whistle? Is that OK? Is that permitted in our park?"

Without saying anything the inspector walked away, Tom continued reading and learning one of the difficult passages. He kept his case closed.

Sitting on the old, well-worn stone steps outside Rubin's door Tom could hear shouting. The door flew open and Clara, her eyes teary, looked at Tom.

From inside the flat Rubin was calling for him to come in. Clara gave Tom a quick hug and nodding her head towards the flat she whispered,

"He is a monster today. See you for coffee?"

"Come in, come in, my boy. Let's hear your scales. All of them."

Tom tuned his instrument and started.

"Very good. Now to your new piece."

Horrified Tom looked at Ruben. Gingerly he started. Tripping over passages, repeating others. Tom wiped his sweaty hand on his trousers. It took him the whole lesson to scramble his way through the piece. He knew all the notes but getting them right and keeping the tempo he could not manage. And so, he expected Rubin to have one of his tantrums.

Rubin sat in his big old chair and smiled at Tom.

"Not bad, not bad at all. Let's go and cheer Clara up. I need a coffee."

Tom stared at Rubin. 'Not bad?' he thought. 'This was shocking, sounded terrible.'

The old man gave him a little punch on his chest.

"Tom, I never asked you to play the Kreuzer! I asked you just look at it. Learning to read it. The piece you were supposed to play is this one." Rubin took a sheet of music and gave it to Tom. It was amongst the forty-two etudes."You played this one, the sixth, the one I asked you to look at. Amazing! Quite amazing the way you managed! Let's have a coffee."

Clara was sitting by the window, her eyes still wet. He tried to comfort her by putting his arm around her shoulder. Rubin discretely walked into the kitchen and talked to the Halwelka's.

He came back with the coffee.

Red-eyed Clara looked at Rubin.

"I hate you!" Another stream of tears escaped her eyes. "Oh, how I hate you!"

Rubin took a crumpled, old handkerchief from his pocket and held it out towards Clara. She screwed up her face.

"No, thank you."

Tom handed her his, new, clean and ironed one.

"Thank you," she kept on sniffing and crying.

"You might hate me today," Rubin slowly said to Clara, "but I tell you, when the crunch comes, and you do well, then you will love me. Yes, I am strict. Yes, I am horrid. Yes, you hate me today!"

Turning to Tom he continued.

"I'd better explain. The situation is such: Clara's family have a quartet, but only three of them are playing. Susanna does not play an instrument. The lady who plays the first violin is getting married and then she will be away for weeks. Three people are not a quartet! So, for the next performance, I am the first violin. I will not tolerate imperfection! Only the best will do. And Clara can do much better than she is doing at the moment. Hence the tantrums."

Looking again at Clara he continued,

"You can hate me as much as you like, as long as you get the best out of your beautiful instrument. Good playing never outstays its welcome, my darling, bad playing is not invited!"

Tom looked at Clara.

"You play in a quartet? How lucky you are! Who are the others?"

After she had blown her nose and wiped her eyes, Clara told Tom that her mother played the 'cello, her father the viola, she the second violin and Rubin the first. They were getting ready for a house concert in two weeks.

"Will you come, Tom?"

"Of course, he will come. Just you wait, Clara. Give that young man of yours a few years and he will be part of the Gilles Quartet. You will by then be playing first violin and I will drive you all crazy by being your very strict teacher and critic if you have not put me in my grave by then."

The word grave shook Tom. He thought of his mother, his difficult mother. He jumped up.

"I must go. Sorry, but my mother is waiting for me at work. No, sorry Clara, you cannot come. I am taking my mother for a chat to Zita."

"Who is Zita? I thought I knew everyone!" Rubin asked Tom.

"You tell him Clara, I must be off."

TWENTY-NINE

Pacing up and down in the entrance hall of Dolmer's Engineering, Margret's mood became darker and darker. She started to regret having agreed to meet Zita for a catch-up. She was not one who enjoyed revelling in the past. What good does it do to bring the past back into her life?

'I am where I am, and nothing will change that. I am fine where I am. I feel safe, I do not need change and I do not need to be confronted by the past. I just want to be left alone!'

Up and down she walked, talking to herself. Her hands in tight fists. She turned around and walked to the entrance. She was going home.

They almost collided. Tom, out of breath, felt his mother's anger. He knew that in a situation like this talk was of no use. Making a stop sign with his hands, he managed to make her stay put.

"I'll get the car and drive you," he said.

Slowly she ran her finger along the top of the bonnet of the car.

"Your father was very proud of this car. There never was a speck of dust on it. It was always clean!"

She waited for him to open the door. Tom took his time walking around the car, then helped his mother into the front seat.

She checked the dashboard for dust and showed Tom her finger. He smiled, got into the car, and slowly drove off. Inside he was boiling.

During the short drive to Zita's, Tom was showered with abuse. He finally stopped the car, looked long and hard at his mother, then, trying to keep a calm voice, asked her,

"Why do you hate me so much? What have I done to you?"

Margret looked at him. Slowly she said, in a low voice: "What do you know! What do you know!"

"Yes, I know absolutely nothing. How can I when you do not talk to me. I am not a child anymore! It sometimes feels as if I am living with a brick wall!"

He put his foot hard on the accelerator. The powerful car took off with a squeal.

Outside Zita's, Margret decided that she did not want to come in. Tom left her in the car and walked slowly to the little house. The table was set on the deck.

"My mother's in the car. She is all yours," he said, and kept on walking towards the river, then upstream to his tree.

Being in the safety of his tree, hidden behind the green curtain, Tom smiled to himself. Alone at last! He felt his dad next to him. Such a comforting feeling. Leaning against the large trunk he started talking.

"Read me a story, Dad. Take me away with your imagination."

Tom closed his eyes and waited.

The touch of a gentle hand made him look up. Kira was smiling at him.

"Thought I find you here, move over."

Kira was a few years older than Tom. They were very close when younger. She was his Gypsy girlfriend; he, her little blond prince. Kira used to come to the factory and lure him away from Jack's watchful eyes. Together they would sneak to their big tree and climb up into its green foliage. It became their castle, their fantasy world.

She snuggled up to Tom, her small, thin body almost disappearing.

"Once upon a time there was a little boy with very curly blond hair..." and so she told Tom the story how the little boy grew up into a big man.

When she had finished Tom told her about his love for music, the confusion it had brought into his life, the conflict it had created between him and his mother.

He put his arm around his little, dark Gypsy childhood friend.

"Kira, I do not think I can carry on living like this. I have a very good plan that could help me to escape, but I have promised my dad to look after my mother. She could live for another twenty or thirty years!"

She got up and took his hands.

"Come, together we will work out what to do. Sitting here wishing and dreaming will not change your situation. Come and let us talk!"

Tom did not move. He took out a cigarette and lit it.

"See the flow of the water, Kira? Look how smooth it runs. Smooth and constant."

"Do you think this river's life has always been smooth and constant, Tom? Wake up! You cannot just look at the now! This river has been through all sorts of difficulties. Just think of its beginning. All the turmoil, all the hardship it went through. Then people regulating it! Making the water go where they want it to go! Do you think this river has ever had a free will? This part of the river you see is old. Yes, sometimes it shows its wilful strength. But mostly it is calm and old. You will be like that one day. But now we must talk and work things out. Please, Tom, come."

Kira pulled Tom's arm. Slowly he got up. How was he going to face his mother?

When the little house came into view, Tom froze. He could just see his mother sitting outside on the deck. Jack was there, holding what looked like a teapot. Zita was sitting on the top rung of the balustrade, smoking. No noise drifted across to him. The scene looked like a photograph, an event frozen in time.

"No, I cannot meet her. I cannot talk with her. Sorry."

Jack had noticed Tom and Kira. He waved and pointed at the teapot. Then he put the pot down and did a little comic jump. Kira laughed.

"Oh, our funny Jack-in-the-box. Such a comic little man. Come, Tom, we have a very good friend there waiting for us. Let's go."

Tom lifted Kira onto the deck, then he climbed over the railing. Zita poured him a cup of coffee.

"Please sit, Tom."

He did not move. Neither did Margret.

Tom put the car keys on the table and said,

"There must be somebody here who can drive. Whoever it is can take my mother home. Just leave the car outside the factory. I will put it away later."

Tom drank his coffee, thanked Zita and just as he was about to climb over the balustrade, Jack slammed his flat hand on the table, making the cups jump.

"Sit down, Tom. Behave like a grown-up!"

All heads, even Margret's, turned towards Tom, who seemed to become paralysed.

"Sit down, please."

Jack walked over to Tom, took his arm and led him to a chair almost opposite Margret. Tom could not look at her as he spoke.

"Quite honestly, I do not know what I am doing here. I am the unwanted child. I am the destroyer of her life. She has made it quite clear how she hates everything about me. Yes, a good mother she has been, but there is no love, no love whatsoever. There has never been a good word, a hug, a kiss, nothing. I will keep my promise to my dad who I loved and who loved me. I am not sure how I will manage, but I will keep my promise. I will take care of her!"

Tom lifted his head and looked at his mother, his blue eyes hard and determined. He started to get up.

"Sit!" Jack pushed him back in his seat. "Thank you, Tom, for your words."

"You know nothing!" Margret shouted at her son. "Nothing!"

"How can I? You never talk. You just criticise!"

Tom lit a cigarette. He needed to get up and walk. Walk off his anger. How he disliked being so angry. But Jack held him down.

"What do you know!" Margret whispered. Her son's deep anger frightened her.

"Tell me what I don't know!"

Zita sat next to Margret. Putting her hand on Margret's she quietly said, "Do tell him, darling. It is better coming from you than from me."

"What do you know?" Margret shrugged away from Zita.

"Enough to make peace between you two."

"I am not well, I would like to go home. Please call a taxi."

Tom pushed the car keys across the table and looked at his mother.

Zita turned Margret towards her.

"Will you tell, or shall I?"

"What do you know, you Gypsy witch!" Margret said with a hiss.

"No, darling, I am not a witch. You have told me enough. Long time ago. Long time ago, when sitting by campfire cooking fish. Tom and Kira playing in some puddle getting all muddy. Theo was working. You had the afternoon off. It was springtime and not long after my husband's death. You told me about your unhappy life. No, darling, no Gypsy magic! So, who will tell?"

There was a long silence. Tom looked at Zita. Her face, leathery and wrinkled was kind; her eyes black and sharp. He wanted to go and hug her.

Margret looked at Zita. She could not tell the story of her past. How could she ever have called her a witch? Margret felt deeply embarrassed.

"You tell them what you know, please. I could not possibly talk about my life."

All eyes went to Zita.

"First, I think, we all need a drink. And maybe a little to eat?"

Kira jumped up and fetched some wine, glasses and some little bread rolls. Zita lit one of her cigarettes. She had climbed back onto the balustrade, her feet on one of the chairs. Behind her the green of the shrubs growing along the river. Her face was lit by the harsh light of the low sun, emphasising her deep wrinkles and putting a dark blue shine into her black hair. And so, she started.

"Once upon a time there was a tall, handsome man who fell in love with a beautiful, delicate woman. He was a successful businessman. She loved art, music and entertaining. But the children she carried did not want to come alive into this world. Then one day their loving created a child that decided to stay with them. The mother became very weak after the birth and could not look after the child. The father loved his little girl. They called her Margret."

Slowly Zita turned her head to Margret, whose face was turned down towards her hands. Margret shook her head. She did not utter a word. Zita looked at Tom. The big blue eyes of his father looked back at her. His lips were slightly parted.

Zita continued.

"Her health deteriorated and when Margret was almost four years old her mother passed away. That is when the sister of Margret's father stepped in to help. She was childless and fell in love with the little girl. The decision was made that the child was going to move in with her aunt."

Zita bend forward and touched Margret's arm.

"Do you want me to continue?"

Without looking up Margret nodded.

"Two years later, at the age of six, Margret was sent to a boarding school in the country. It was a Catholic convent of the strictest variety. There was no singing outsid of church. No laughing, no dancing, no running. Margret was pushed into a mould, her free spirit destroyed, and she learned to hate.

During holidays her aunt would come and see her, but never take her home. Now and then her father would visit.

Margret stayed in the convent until she was fifteen, then, returning to her aunt, was used as a housekeeper.

I believe that at the age of sixteen she met Theo and they married when she was eighteen. After that she never kept up contact with her family."

Margret's body had slowly sunk towards her hands. Her head was almost touching the table.

"The rest of your life, my dear friend, is for you to tell your son."

Zita touched Margret's shoulder, making her straighten up.

Long and hard Margret looked at her.

"My dear friend. My dear friend, you are telling someone else's story. That was not my life! My mother never held me, never loved me. My mother did not want me! Often was I told by her, that I was a mistake, or something like that. I was not wanted! It was my mother who sent me away to that school! Never will I forget that place. We were supposed to love a man called Jesus. We were taught through learning to hate and constantly threatened with hell! For years I lived in fear of being taken by the devil into the flames of the inferno! No, no my mother never loved me, never! You are wrong, my friend!"

Smiling at Margret, Zita continued.

"Yes, you are my friend. I always will remain so. Margret, we have choices in life, to be well or unwell; to be happy or not, to look at the good sides of life or the bad ones. To remember the good or the bad. You have the choice! You my dear friend, have chosen to only remember the part of your childhood filled with misery."

Throughout the talk Tom held Kira's hand, his good friend from childhood. Kira suddenly let go. She could not understand Margret's denial of her past, of her childhood. Quietly she started crying.

"When I was a little girl and we were building our little house with Jack and Theo's help, when Tom was four or five, I remember you being so happy. Reserved, very private, yes, but happy! Where has that Margret gone?"

Silently the tears were running down Kira's cheeks. She sniffed but made no attempt to brush them away.

Margret turned towards the young woman. Oh, how much she would have liked to have had a daughter. With deep affection she said,

"Oh, my dear, dear child, I do not know!"

Kira picked up a serviette and blew her nose.

"Maybe we need to see if we can find her? Would you like me to help you?"

Margret dug her hands into her thighs. She sat rigid as she let go a quiet moan. Her whole body was in pain. Margret looked away from Kira. With cold eyes she turned back to Zita: "Where did you get this fairy tale from?"

She tried to get up, but Jack held her gently down. Margret looked at Jack. Through her clenched teeth she hissed at him,

"Let me go. Let go of me!"

THIRTY

As the night gave way to the first glimmer of daylight Tom found himself parked outside the Gilles house. Someone was tapping on the car window.

After the get-together with Zita he'd decided to drive up to the circle of trees to find peace of mind. It was such a dark night he could not find the way to his favourite spot. Tom sat in the carpark looking down on his town. Deep sadness fell over him. Up and down he walked. His head was filled with the question Why! Why his mother was so bitter. If he only knew.

Tom decided to talk to his father. Ask him if he would release him from his promise. To free him! Unclip the leash he was on! He drove to the cemetery, but it was locked.

Gudrun's worried face looked at him through the car window.

"Tom! What are you doing here? Have you been here all night?"

She was taking their little dog for a morning walk.

Opening the car door she invited Tom to join her.

"Come, let's walk."

Tom was very tired and deeply confused. 'A walk will do me good,' he thought.

They went across the road and into the wilderness of the park. Neither of them spoke, only the little dog barked. Gudrun walked briskly down a small hill towards a lake where the dog was yapping at the ducks on the water. With long, decisive steps, Gudrun followed the path which took them around the lake and then back up again towards the road.

He stood watching her.

Back in the house she made him a strong cup of coffee. They

took their coffee out into the garden. The sun was just touching the tops of the trees.

"Six-thirty," she said, looking up into the foliage. "Come, Tom, sit with me. Tell me why you were sleeping in your car."

He walked about in the garden. It felt so fresh, green and peaceful. Gudrun watched him. She did not push for an answer. Eventually, he sat down.

"I love your place. It calms me. It makes me feel safe."

Slowly he told her about the evening at Zita's."

"I just don't understand why she will not accept me. Why she hates me so much. Why is she hurting me? Now mum knows of her past. She knows that she was a wanted child. That her mother loved her!"

He got up and started walking again: up and down in front of Gudrun.

"Why does she not believe Zita? Why!"

Gudrun looked at Tom and patted the chair, inviting him to sit down.

"Maybe she needs written proof. Some people just do not believe what they hear. And, my dear Tom, I think there is much more to your mother's problems."

The sun has touched the trees and is now almost shining on the shrubs. It is close to eight and I have to make breakfast for my family. You can help me. We will eat in the dining room."

He shook his head.

"I'd rather not. It would be difficult for me to explain. And I have a staff meeting this morning. It is our monthly meeting and I cannot be late for that."

Throughout the meeting and throughout the whole day, Margret ignored her son. Tom did not mind. He had nothing to say to her. On the drive to work, he had forged a plan for his future. All he needed now was the courage to bring it about.

On his desk lay a small pile of personal letters, amongst them an envelope containing a very formal invitation card to the musical evening at the Gilles. Tom took the card and stood it up against the foot of his desk lamp. This was the first ornament to decorate his desk. His office was without any ornaments, as his father left it.

He sat back in his chair and looked around the room. It did not feel at all like his office. It still belonged to his father. The bookshelf filled with out-of-date engineering books and old technical journals. The wooden panelled walls were bare. The desk was parallel to the wall, facing the door.

"This is the first day of the rest of my life," he said to himself.

He got up and pushed the desk across to one of the corners. He could now look at his beloved river instead of at the door. He felt much more private. He got a large box from the storeroom and put most of the books in it.

To get the impression of his office, Tom went to the door to take a look at his handy work. A few personal items and the room would be his.

He phoned Clara. She sounded very tired and irritable.

"We have been rehearsing all afternoon. Oh, I hate Rubin. What can I do for you?"

Tom hesitantly said. "I was going to ask you a favour. You see, I am rearranging my office, sort of putting my own mark on it. I think I need some help. Sort of putting the feminine touch to this austere room. Would you have the time to come and give me some advice?"

Clara let out a little squeal.

"Oh yes, this is just so exciting! Can't wait. I cannot come today. We are having a rehearsal with daddy. See you tomorrow at nine?"

"I told you, the picture was not big enough!"

Clara was removing the wrapping from the framed print. "You know Tom, I would have thought you'd go for a romantic kind of painting. Miro is very modern."

Tom had fetched a nail and hammer.

"I like it. I think it fits perfectly into an engineering business."

He held the print up.

"You are right, it is too small."

There was a knock on the door. Tom quickly turned the framed print against the wall. He could not take his mother's criticism. But it was Joyce. She noticed the picture.

"Tom, there's a picture rail up there and I can get you some proper hangers. No need to put a nail in the beautiful wooden panelling. Show me; what did you get?"

Turning the print around he apologetically explained that he could not afford an original painting.

"An original Miro!" Joyce laughed. "That would be quite something. We would have to increase our insurance!"

She looked at it: "I like it. Very playful! Very engineering! It will certainly brighten up the office. But it is not big enough for this wall. What is the title?"

Clara laughed. "The Melancholic Singer."

"Oh, very you, Tom!" Joyce smiled at Clara and left the room.

"Lunch?" Tom suggested to Clara "Then I have to do some work."

After deciding to go back to the park they bought some sandwiches. Sitting on the grass, Tom leaned against one of the old trees. The bed of roses was in full bloom. A sweet perfume filled the air. Clara walked over to the flowers. She meandered around them, stroking their heads. She looked beautiful with her unruly reddish blonde hair and her light summer dress. As she ran her fingers over the flower petals, a shadowy silhouette seemed to follow her, copying her every move. Then she turned around and the apparition disappeared. She saw him watching her.

"What are you staring at?"

"You, of course! Your hair, your tall slender self. The roses, the grass, the sky. Come and sit with me!"

He put his arm around her.

"Last night I made a big decision," he said.

She turned to him.

"Just across the road from work is a small block of flats. They've been there forever. The company owns one.

It's not a big flat and it is on the ground floor, but there is a door out into a little garden. I am going to move into it."

She stared at him. She began to smile.

"Will you help me choose furniture? I have a small bed, a desk and a bookshelf. And a big map my dad gave me."

She leaned to him and gave him a long kiss. She pushed him over and they tumbled and rolled on the grass.

Back in his office he was staring out the window when Joyce walked in, carrying a very lush-looking pot plant. She placed it close to the window, where Tom had placed the armchairs and coffee table.

"There! Now all you need is books on the shelves. Maybe a nice glass ashtray on the table. Glass is very popular at the moment. It looks like you are now becoming the boss of this business. Making yourself at home at long last. Welcome."

Tom got up, stretching out his hand as he walked towards Joyce. He would have loved to give her a hug. He just took her hand in both of his and thanked her.

"Now it is my office!"

He smiled at Joyce.

She stepped back and studied him and smiled.

"You might want to get the grass and leaves out of your hair," she said, and left.

Tom sat in his room that evening deciding what to take — both for his new office and for his new flat. Some of his technical books for work, plus the atlas, and one of the dictionaries. Maybe a few little items he had picked up when walking with his dad. A picture of them when they were at the river. Yes, it would be comforting in having a bit of his dad in his office.

And then, how would he furnish his new home?

"Tom, dinner is ready!" she called.

He got up. He was suddenly nervous. How could he tell her?

The kitchen table was not laid. An envelope, looking very much like the one he had received from the Gilles, addressed to Margret, was the only thing on it. He picked it up and took it into the dining-room.

"I believe this is yours?"

He held the letter out towards his mother.

"No, I don't think so."

Pointing at the table, she continued, "I have cooked chicken with roast potatoes. I thought we should start eating in the dining room again. And I would like to open up the middle room and turn it into our sitting room. We will be able to watch the sunset over the city. Also, no neighbours! We will be able to keep the curtains open. You will have to help me move the furniture. I will look for someone to take away granddad's old bed and some of his furniture. Make the room ours, so to speak."

Still holding the letter towards his mother, Tom stared at her. For the last twelve months he had suggested to do that. To use granddad's old room, the room where he had lain sick for months. The room where he died. With this announcement, she had turned his decision to start his own life totally upside down. How could he broach the subject now?

He watched his mother cut up the chicken and put a large portion on his plate, next to it golden roasted potatoes. He knew he had to reconsider his plans.

He put the letter next to Margret's plate and sat down.

"They must have made a mistake with the address," she said and gave the letter back to him.

"I have already got my invitation. Why don't you open it and have a look what it is all about?"

Margret tried to look civil. "I am not going out. Not to the Gilles. Not anywhere. I am too tired in the evenings. Take someone else."

She started cutting up her small portion of chicken breast. "Salad, Tom?"

She took a few leaves.

"Mother you will have to answer!"

"I'll give it to Joyce. She can do that for me."

Suddenly the atmosphere was destroyed. The food tasted ordinary. The golden-brown potatoes had lost their beauty. Tom watched his mother eat, slowly dissecting her food into small pieces, then pecking at it like a little bird.

'Peck, peck,' he thought. 'At your food, at my life, at my friends!'

"I am going to be very busy. So, I am not too sure when I can help you move the furniture, rearrange the flat," he said.

"Yes, I hear you are changing the interior of your office. Removing you father. Yes, I suppose that will keep you busy for quite a while."

Tom swallowed his anger and smiled at his mother, who was still pecking at her food.

"This was a great meal. Thank you, Mum, can I help you later with the dishes? I need to talk to you."

"Talk away, I am all ears."

She settled back in her chair. He took a deep breath.

"I'm going to move into the company flat across from the factory."

"You're what? But that flat is rented out. You can't just make people leave!"

Margret was outraged.

"The lease runs out in two months. I won't renew their contract. I'll get the place painted out and in about three months I will be moving in."

"And the girl will move in with you, I suppose. People like that have no morals!"

Margret got up and started clearing the table.

Ignoring her sneering remark, he continued,

"Please sit down and hear me out! In two weeks, the Gilles

family and Rubin will be giving a small house concert. If you have a look at the card you can find out what they are going to play. I have offered to help them set up chairs and get ready for the concert. So, I will be busy that weekend.

Two weeks after that I am going for a ten day holiday in the mountains. It will be Clara's birthday."

He waited for a reaction from his mother. Her expression did not change.

"The main reason I am moving out, is the way you conduct yourself towards me. It will be better for both of us to separate."

"And here I am rearranging this flat the way you always wanted it! And now you tell me this!" she hissed at Tom.

He stayed calm.

"Have you ever hugged me? Said that you loved me? I am your son, your blood. Your son created in love with my wonderful father. You did love him? Did you?"

"How dare you bring your dad into that! And what about your promise to the father you love so much? The promise to look after me?"

"I am not going to the moon, Mother. I will just be a phone call away. And then we will see each other at work. Sit together, eat lunch by the river. You must see that our relationship does not work."

"And who is going to look after your clothes, cook for you and all that!"

"Maybe it's about time I learnt to look after myself?"

Getting up he pointed at the letter from the Gilles family to Margret.

"You should answer personally. Don't use my secretary! I shall ask Kira to come with me."

He walked out of the dining room and back into his domain where he sat on the bed hugging his knees, thinking of his future.

THIRTY-ONE

When Tom and Kira pulled up across the road from the Gilles house for the concert they were met by young Susanna, who was standing at the front door, still buttoning her dress.

"Who is going to help Oma up the stairs? Where is a strong man when there's a need for one?" she called, nodding to the taxi that had just arrived and was trying to park amongst the ranked cars of other concert-goers.

The taxi driver was trying to help a very regal-looking lady out of the car.

"It's my grandmother," Susanna said. "My Oma, Mrs Gilles, my dad's mother."

Tom hurried over to help.

The old lady looked at him and smiled. She pushed the fumbling driver away.

"Leave me. I'd rather this handsome young man help me, thank you." She let Tom try to lift her to her feet. He felt her look past him.

"What a stunning girlfriend you have," she said, trying to get her feet out of the back of the car.

Kira blushed under her dark skin. Tom turn and looked at his friend. The small amount of make-up had transfigured her. Her dark gypsy eyes seemed larger, the black hair had a blue sheen. She had used some lipstick to show her full lips. Kira had always just been Kira, his playmate, his gypsy-queen, his good friend. Never had he seen the beautiful woman in her.

"Are you going to help me, young man?" Oma Gilles said, still struggling to get out of the car.

Kira gently pushed Tom aside, leaned into the car, took the old lady's legs, gently swung them around and then holding her arm helped her to get out of the taxi. She waved to Tom to take Mrs Gilles other arm and together they walked her to the front doorsteps.

"Well done, well done!" Susanna said, as she slipped on a pair of flat shoes. "How are you, Oma? Mummy and Daddy are very busy, so you will have to do with me."

"Who is this tall, strong man?" Mrs Gilles asked her granddaughter.

"Oh, that's just Tom. He's my sister's boyfriend."

"How many girlfriends does he have?" she asked her granddaughter as she helped her into the living room.

Tom was amazed at the changes in the room. In front of the grand piano was the circular seating for the musicians. There were about twenty seats awaiting the guests and a special chair for the old lady.

Rubin was fussing about arranging the sheets of music and turning on the lights on each of the stands.

Watching his teacher scurry about made Tom realise that he was overdressed for the occasion. Rubin just wore a tight silk vest over his starched white shirt. The trousers had seen better days, but the shine of his shoes could blind one. Tom took off his bow tie and opened his shirt. It was quite warm in the room. Since he wore a dressy vest, he felt that he could remove his jacket. He envied the girls in their thin, flowing summer dresses.

Just before the first guests arrived, Susanna came and asked him to fasten the clasp of a beautifully-beaded necklace.

"Better wear it, Oma gave it to me. Can you please help me with the arrival of the people? I am on my own. The rest of the family is busy getting ready to perform. They're all nervous wrecks!"

"What can I do?"

"You can entertain your latest conquest, my grandmother."

The room was filling. Tom saw Jason. Otherwise, he knew

nobody. Susanna and Kira handed out the programs. Rubin had disappeared.

The sound of instruments being tuned could be faintly heard.

Tom was completely engrossed in the atmosphere. The chatting of the old lady, the tuning of the instruments, the hum of people talking; all the different new smells took Tom away.

The chair next to him was empty in readiness for Kira. But Tom felt a slight, humming breeze and a sweet smell. Tom knew the unmistakable scent. He did not dare say her name. Putting his hand on the empty chair, the thought of Esther became so intense he did not feel Kira taking his hand.

"Is this seat for me? Or is it occupied?"

Applause removed the dreaminess from Tom's eyes. Rubin had strutted into the room to introduce the first part of the program. He spoke at great length about the piece by Bedrich Smetana. He had chosen No. 1 in E minor, *From My Life,* to show the talent of the quartet. Starting with himself, first violin, he then introduced the others: second violin, Clara Gilles; viola, Michael Gilles; and 'cello Gudrun Gilles.

Tom could not take his eyes off Clara as she walked in straight, tall and full of confidence. She wore a long, sleeveless light blue silk dress with a slight green sheen to it, cut to fit her figure. Her hair was tightly rolled into a bun on the back of her head. Just one strand was allowed to hang beside her face. Her eyes were directed towards the floor; or was she checking the music?

Gudrun had the same dress. She looked relaxed. One could see that Michael was not very comfortable in his outfit. He wore the same as Rubin, except he did not wear a tie, his trousers were new and well-fitting. They all bowed, took their places and the music started.

Tom's eyes never left Clara. He was fascinated to see how she communicated with Rubin with her whole body. Only now and then would she glance at the music in front of her. Rubin had his eyes on every member of the group. He had no sheet music in front of him. He was playing from memory.

Suddenly the extravert teacher turned into Tom's idol. There he was playing from memory, making sure that his young protégé could follow the difficult piece. Gudrun, sitting next to Clara, didn't look at her music either. Tom felt her sending helping energies to her daughter. Michael was completely in his element. He moved and swayed to the music, letting his beautiful instrument sing.

Looking back at Clara Tom felt she was completely wrapped up in the music. He fell totally in love with her. She was beautiful. She was clever. But most of all she was music.

Suddenly the fourth movement finished. Total silence filled the room. Then the roar of applause and cries of "Bravo!"

The four musicians stood, bowed and walked out.

Tom felt as if something had been ripped out of him. He wanted to run after Clara; tell her how much he loved her; but no one moved. Just shuffling of seats and some coughing. Sitting in the front row next to old Mrs Gilles made it impossible for him to get up and walk out and he needed to walk.

Mrs Gilles took his hand. "I am so proud of my family. Did your girlfriend enjoy the music? This was a difficult piece." "Kira is not my girlfriend, just an old family friend I've known nearly all my life. No, actually, I'm going out with Clara. I met her through our music teacher, Rubin."

Mr Gilles looked long and hard at Tom.

"Oh, you will make a charming couple. Both playing violin. Very charming."

With that she smiled. Tom could see where Michael got his smile from.

"Is it OK to get up?" he asked her.

"Of course, of course, my dear man. You no doubt wish to smoke."

As he got up, he noticed Jason waving at him. They both

walked out into the street. Tom lit a cigarette. Jason pushed his hands deep into his pocket. He looked at Tom, then quietly said,

"Isn't Clara to fall in love with? God, she is so lovely. But she won't have me! She just plays around with me. Sort of flirts and then laughs and off she goes. Infuriating. I have known her for years. But no luck!"

Tom walked up and down outside the house, starting to get his inner balance back. He did not hear a word Jason was saying.

They heard applause begin and rushed back inside.

Rubin was introducing the next piece. He stared at late-comer Tom.

"We will now play Mozart's String Quartet No.19 K.465, *The Dissonance.*"

Everyone clapped.

Rubin bowed to Mrs Gilles but kept looking at Tom. He had noticed the enchantment in him during their playing. He had a feeling that this concert would create many changes in Tom.

Everyone loved the Mozart, including the musicians. Tom could not understand why the piece was called *The Dissonance.* There was harmony in both the music and amongst the players.

Again the applause brought Tom back to reality. No one moved. The clapping got louder, and the room filled with the calles of Bravo. A chorus of, "Encore, Encore!" began to swell.

"You want more? What about you Mrs Gilles?" Rubin slightly bowed towards the old lady. "Any request?"

She threw her arms in the air and laughed.

"What about some Joseph Haydn? Maybe just a bit of Haydn, if you are not too tired?"

"Haydn String Quartet no. 68, Third Movement, and then a little something for you Mrs Gilles."

It was a jolly piece. Tom liked it. He moved his body to the music. The old lady turned her head and smiled at him. After the short piece, Rubin stood up and urged the audience to stand. He waved to Mrs Gilles, advising her to stay seated.

With gusto and joy, they played *Happy Birthday*. Everyone sang. Some, including Tom, in harmony. Then loud clapping and lots of "Hurrahs!". Susanna gave her grandmother a beautiful bunch of summer flowers.

"Happy birthday Oma and many more!"

"Oh yes my child, there will be many more. Where is that strong young man? I would like to sit on the sofa. In the middle with my two grandchildren on either side"

Susanna asked Tom and Kira for help to move the chairs into a semicircle. They removed the music stands. Then the doors into the dining room were opened and the most beautiful table laden with food confronted them.

Tom helped Oma to the table, helped her choose some food and then escorted her to the sofa.

Seeing Gudrun, he took her hand in both of his to congratulate her. She turned and hugged him. But her face was serious and she leaned close to him.

"Clara will need someone to talk to. You might just be the one. She always feels depressed and lonely after a performance. Today she was brilliant. Rubin worked her so hard. I was very cross with him. And she now will be very depleted of energy. Go to her. I think she needs you."

He found her in the kitchen, crying. He took her in his arms.

"I love you," he said. "You are so beautiful, so amazing."

Melting into his body Clara slowly calmed. At the same time, he could sense that other sweet, familiar scent.

"Don't cry," he said. "Why do you cry?"

"I don't know. I am not sad. But I am so tired, so tired. And I feel so empty! I feel like I'm falling down, down; tumbling and falling down, down. Oh Tom, it is so very frightening. Please hold me, stop me from falling!"

Holding her close he could feel her body shiver. He did not know what to do.

"You were wonderful. Oh, how proud I am to be in love with you. You just played, well you almost played like…"

He could not bring himself to mention Esther's name.

"Your gran will be looking for you," he said.

With a big sniff, she straightened up and eased herself from Tom's embrace.

"I'll just freshen up! You go and have something to eat."

Tom found Gudrun.

"Clara will be with us soon," he said. "She is fine, just freshening up. By the way, your mother-in-law is amazing. How old is she today?"

A pair of arms wrapped themselves around his waist.

"Ninety," Clara said, "And you know what? She likes you, that is quite something."

Kira joined them. She gave Clara a big hug. "A wonderful concert. You were wonderful. I like Smetana. Never have I heard one of his quartets. I did not know he wrote any. Clara, you played superbly. Not a note out of place. Thank you. And thank you, Tom, for bringing me. Mother would have enjoyed this performance. Maybe I can bring her next time?"

They could hear Oma Gilles calling. She wanted her grandchildren close by and that handsome young man and the beautiful, exotic Gypsy girl.

"Where are they! Where are my young people! The sofa is empty! And could I please have a glass of that champagne. I might be old, but, thank God, I still have a loud voice. Come, children, sit with me! I need your young energy about me!"

Michael had joined them at the table. He had changed into something comfortable. He pointed at the next room.

"You better go before she screams the place down."

When everyone had left Michael pulled the armchairs and the coffee table back into place. Rubin joined them. Gudrun made coffee.

"Anyone for some Schnapps?"

Michael was already getting up to fetch the bottle and glasses.

Rubin looked at Michael, "Yours?"

Michael smiled and nodded.

"I made it last year from green walnut husks."

Rubin held out his small glass.

Tom only wanted a sip of the strange drink.

"I have to drive Kira home," he said.

"Fill it up! Fill it up!" Kira said. "I can take a taxi. We can take a taxi. This is delicious. My mother makes Schnapps from forest berries. We go every year and collect them in the woods."

Grandmother Gilles looked at Kira.

"Where are you from, my child? Dark skin, black eyes, and hair, but fine-featured face and body. Where were you born?"

Bending forward to be able to look across Susanna, Kira laughed.

"I come from nowhere. Gypsies have no homeland. But now I live here in the city with my husband."

She held out her glass for some more.

Michael told her how strong the drink was, but Kira just laughed.

"No one has ever drunk me under the table!"

Clara's head sank onto Tom's shoulder. She was fast asleep. He looked around the room, taking in the atmosphere. There was such a comfortable feeling; a lived-in feeling, a feeling of belonging. This is how he wanted to live.

Tom felt Gudrun look at him. She smiled. Michael was filling glasses with his strong drink. Rubin looked at Tom. He seemed so much smaller. All his buoyancy had vanished. He seemed deep in thought. Their eyes met. Without a change of expression, Rubin kept on looking into his eyes. Then his eyes moved to Clara. Tom noticed Rubin's moisten. The old man's thought had wandered into his deep past.

Suddenly he got up and walked to the window and looked out into the black night. Tom very gently placed Clara's head on her grandmother's shoulder and walked over to his teacher. He put his arm around the little man's shoulder. Together they looked out into the black nothing.

"Esther?" Tom said quietly into the dark.

"Yes, Esther." He pushed Tom's arm away. "Yes Esther, the bitch. I wonder where she is! She should have been here. She belongs here!"

His anger was frightening! Gudrun came over and told Tom to leave them. She led Rubin into the dining room and closed the door.

The party had been broken up. A taxi was ordered for Kira. Tom was to stay in the cellar guest room. Clara was to share the room with her sister, Rubin to sleep in Clara's loft room. Grandmother Gilles had a room made up on the same floor, the old maid's room next to the kitchen.

While everyone got ready for bed Oma stayed sitting on the sofa. She called Tom to her side.

"Do you go to the opera?"

"I've never been," he said. "And this, this was my first concert."

"We must go. I must introduce you to the opera. Yes, and we take Clara. This little town does not have an opera house or, for that matter a concert hall. We need to go to the city and stay the night, I will take you both. I like you, Tom. You will be a good steady influence on lovely Clara. I am very excited by the thought of taking you two. Now, please, could you help me up. My legs are not very obedient."

THIRTY-TWO

The bedside lamp showed Tom a small, cozy room with a window high up, almost touching the ceiling. It was open and the warm summer's air with a smell of garden entered.

Tom lay back and found his thoughts drifting to Rubin. Their playing had been so intense. Rubin's focus had been on Clara for weeks, preparing her, carrying her along. How it must have drained the old man. And then the memory, the longing for Esther. Tom knew that she had been sitting next to him before the concert. Was she also with Rubin?

The lampshade created a circle on the ceiling. The light was attracting a myriad of small insects. Tom watched them flap, contained in the ring of light. Then he noticed a shimmer of light on the floor. Someone was opening the door.

It was Clara.

"Move over!" and she slid into his bed.

She cuddled up to him like a kitten, soft and warm. Tom slightly moved away.

"I haven't got any..."

"I have."

Clara slid a small package into his hand.

Their lovemaking took them to a faraway realm. For a long time, they lay linked together, only feeling each other. The room disappeared. Nothing existed. Just Tom and Clara. Later they lay on the single bed watching the window showing some of the first daylight.

"Must go," she whispered.

Tom watched her in the dim light, looking for her nightdress.

He could see it on the chair by the window. He remembered how she had struggled out of it as she lay in bed.

He did not tell her where it was. He enjoyed seeing her naked body, slim and youthful. Then she found it, pulled it over her head and was gone. He stayed in bed and watched the day arrive.

A pair of legs walked past the little window of the cellar room, behind them a dog, yapping; wanting to play. Tom had a quick shower in the tiny bathroom, got dressed and found Gudrun playing with the dog. Rubin was also up. He was wearing a dark brown dressing gown. His hair was standing up in all directions. He wore no shoes. Noticing the old wrinkled toes, Tom realised how old Rubin was. He had never thought of him being old.

"Coffee?" Gudrun pointed at a little table by the stairs. Tom went to help himself. He felt they all knew about him and Clara. He felt he must be showing it on his face. Showing his happiness. He took his coffee and stood in the shade of one of the trees.

"Did you sleep all right in that small bed?"

Gudrun threw the ball for the yapping dog.

"Thank you, very well."

No one seemed to notice his happiness. He relaxed. Clara came down the spiral staircase in her nightdress. The sun was shining on her face, making her squint. She shaded her face with her hand. Her hair was everywhere. Tom noticed Rubin staring at her. He realised she had not yet seen him.

"Where is Tom? Maybe I need to get him out of bed? He might like a coffee. Anyone know how he likes his coffee?"

"Just black." Tom answered.

She jumped the last of the steps and ran over to him. Giving him a big hug he could feel her naked body under her thin garment. It made him remember.

"Did you sleep well? That bed is terribly small for such a big man."

"Thank you," he answered. "There was a slight interruption during the night, but I soon sorted that out."

They both laughed knowingly.

THIRTY-THREE

Standing in the kitchen of his mother's apartment Tom waited for his toast to brown. He was quietly singing a part of the music he'd heard the night before. Closing his eyes, he could see Clara playing her violin. Or was it Esther? They two melting together then separating again.

"Your toast is burning!"

Margret stood behind him. Her loud voice made Tom jump. "Do you want to burn the house down?"

"We need to talk," she said.

"About what?"

"It is the flat situation I want to talk about. I will have to be there when you talk to Douglas about it. I am part owner of the company and I am senior to you. Please let me know when you will meet him. A short phone call will do."

She started to walk into the hallway. She turned back to him.

"Well? Are you coming to work with me?"

"No, thank you, Mother, I'll walk when I'm ready. See you at work."

The front door closed with a loud bang. Tom took the toast and threw it in the bin. Then he cut some more bread, put the slices in the toaster, this time watching not to burn it.

When he walked into the office building, he could see his mother behind the reception desk, talking on the phone. Margret seemed to have a happy, joking conversation. She did not look up. Taking two steps at a time Tom walked up the spiral staircase and into his office. Minutes after him Joyce came in with his private mail. Tom noticed that Joyce had hung the picture. It was slightly to one side of the wall. The empty wall space was filled with the pot plant. She had rearranged the seating corner. On the table stood a very handsome glass ashtray.

"Coffee?"

Tom walked up to her and gave her a gentle kiss on the cheek.

"Thank you, Joyce, this looks wonderful. So very clever the way you have arranged my office. Give me half an hour and then I would like to see Douglas. Later I need to see his son, Angus. This afternoon I am out, violin lesson."

"You sound very chirpy! Very happy! You feel different, Tom, something special happened?"

Tom took the letters, made a coy face and smiled.

"Yes, Joyce, lots has happened."

He sat down in one of the armchairs, lit a cigarette and started to open the mail. Finding nothing of great urgency, he leant back and looked out of the window, looking at the slow, lazy flowing river.

"Yes, my dear river. I think I am starting to travel. I am starting to go somewhere."

A knock on the door made him turn. Douglas stood in the doorway. Joyce came with two cups of coffee. Tom was using the new glass ashtray. Joyce smiled and winked.

After asking how he was, how the family was, Tom went straight to the point of their meeting. He told Douglas about his plans to take over the small flat.

There was a knock on the door. Margret came in. Behind her Joyce followed with a cup of tea and some biscuits.

The two men got up and Tom fetched the chair from his desk, offering his mother one of the armchairs. She shook her head.

"This won't take long," she said. "I'm senior partner in this firm. It's me who decides whether or not we evict that poor old couple from their home. I consulted our solicitor and he agrees with me."

She took a breath and glared at Tom.

"You have no right to throw those poor, old people out in the street just so you can have a place where you can carry on with your girlfriend.

Honestly, the morals of that little bitch! Who does she think she is!"

Both Tom and Douglas were speechless.

Douglas took Margret's arm and led her to one of the chairs.

"Please Margret, sit down. Please!"

Tom got up as she sat down. He gestured to his desk and pointed at the chair.

"Mother, you are welcome to run the place. I offer you my desk, my office, and my job. The income I get from my shares will keep me alive. I do not need much. I just would like my new painting and the car. I am sure you can work that out with our solicitor."

He walked towards the door. Before he opened it, he turned back to her.

"Angus is due here in a little while. You'll have to work out how to organise and finance his studies. And then there are quite a lot of workers on the floor ill. Some kind of tummy wog going around. You might have to help out. Work has to go on!"

Douglas stepped in front of Tom and forced him to sit down.

"Please you two, will you stop behaving like children! Both of you, sit down!"

Tom glared at his manager.

"I will gladly talk about the situation, about any situation. But my dear mother has decided to absolutely despise me. I am twenty-six years old! I need to live. My father was married at twenty-six! I have had no life. Just work and study and now sitting evening after evening in that cold flat watching my mother knit.

Am I not allowed to fall in love! To have friends? To have a girlfriend? Why does she not feel happy for me? Why is she not a little proud of me? Why does she hate me? What have I done?"

Tom started pulling at his blond curls. Suddenly stopping, he looked at Margret:

"The ball is in your court. You decide!"

Douglas knew what it meant when Tom slowly combed his fingers through his hair. His father did the same. It meant decision time.

Tom picked up the phone.

"Joyce? Would you please come to the office now?"

"I'll be with you as soon as I can get away from this desk," she said.

Angrily, he shouted into the telephone:

"Well, find someone who can sit at the desk for a short time! There must be somebody in this place who can answer the telephone and take a message! I need you now!"

Margret turned towards her son. She had detected the manner of her father-in-law; short-fused and demanding. The way he slammed the receiver down. The way he lit a cigarette. The way he leant both his hands on the top of his desk. He did not look at her, just stared at the desk until Joyce came into the room.

Joyce felt the atmosphere and took on the role of an obedient secretary.

"You called? What can I do for you?"

"I need you to make an appointment with our solicitor some time tomorrow. I would like him to come to the office for a meeting. Then, please Joyce, reschedule my appointment with Angus for tomorrow. I will be out all afternoon. Thank you. That is all."

He started to sort out his personal mail. Looking at Margret and Douglas he nodded.

"Meeting's over," he said.

They both tiptoed out.

Tom went through all the legal documents of the flat.

A knock at the door and Gary, the floor manager, entered.

"This gastric stomach problem has taken another worker. We are now four people down and struggling getting the work out."

Tom looked at him and nodded.

"I'm very busy today, Gary. I must go out on business. But

tomorrow I have just one meeting and then on with my overalls and I'm all yours!"

Tom was not going to miss his violin lesson and dinner with Clara.

When Gary left Tom opened the window. Beautiful fresh summer air was entering the room. He watched the river. Steady and silently it was moving. In his mind, he could feel the boat, his vessel of freedom, tied to the shore in readiness; waiting for him to begin his life's journey.

THIRTY-FOUR

It was 7.30 the next morning when Margret entered her kitchen, Tom was not around. She noticed the coffee pot on the sideboard and touched it. It was warm. So she knew that he had been home for the night. He must have left early. What was he up to?

At work, Tom went straight into the machine room, put on his overalls, and found Gary.

"What have you got for me to do?" he asked.

Gary looked at him and then showed him a blueprint.

"Can you machine that, boss?"

Tom studied the drawing and traced it with his finger. He nodded and set it down beside a lathe. Gary watched him setting the machine up. Tom's fingers were sure and precise on the dials.

Some of the workers were already busy. They nodded at him with respect.

A phone call eventually took Tom away from his work in the machine room. In his overalls, he walked into the boardroom where his mother, Joyce, Douglas and the old solicitor, advisor to his father, were waiting.

Tom excused his outfit and asked them to please wait while he changed and washed his hands.

He returned in a light summer suit, sat down in his father's seat and put a bundle of documents on the table.

"Joyce, please take notes.

Thank you all for coming. We all know what this meeting is about, and I hope we can resolve the problem smoothly and with satisfaction."

He put the first document on the table and asked the solicitor to read it carefully.

"My mother, Mrs Dolmer, approached you recently about the legal situation of the small flat belonging to the business. Yesterday I visited the leaseholders to look into their situation. The elderly couple told me that they are trying to get into a retirement home. According to him, Mr Huber, they both find it hard to look after themselves. I have offered to help, which delighted them. Please read the document and the contract, if possible now, and give me your verdict."

Margret looked at her son. Never had she seen him so professional, so calm, so calculating.

"Since Mr Henshall is financially involved in this firm, I felt he also should be present at this meeting. Your input, Douglas, would be appreciated."

Shuffling the papers he put the next document on the table.

Tom looked at the solicitor. "You should have this document in your file. It needs upgrading. My father's passing would have created a few changes."

Looking at Joyce he asked for some coffee and an ashtray.

The solicitor looked puzzled. He spoke nervously.

"I am sorry, but Mrs Dolmer has not been in contact with me recently. Neither by phone nor personally. Maybe she saw or rang my clerk? I am really sorry, but I do not know what this meeting is all about!"

Very slowly Tom reached for his cigarettes. As he lit one, he looked hard at his mother. She would not meet his eyes.

'You lied? How dare you!' he thought.

Tom stood up and started pacing up and down behind his chair. Eventually, he sat down again.

"So then, let us start at the beginning. The firm owns a small flat nearby.

My question to you is this.

Who in this firm has the power to decide what can be done

with the flat? Does it need to bring in rental money? Can I occupy it? Then I would like to know, who, since my father's death, is in charge of Dolmer's Engineering?"

As he spoke, Tom looked at his mother. His blue eyes had become dark and angry. His persona remained calm. The solicitor pushed the documents into the middle of the table.

"I cannot do anything until I have seen Mr Theodore Dolmer's last will. He was the owner of this company. I will need to see what is written in the will."

Jumping out of his seat, Tom leaned over the table towards the solicitor.

"You wrote his will. You should know!"

"Sorry, Mr Dolmer, but I need the document in front of me before I can answer your questions. The legal system works differently to engineering. Make an appointment with my secretary. I will have a documented, written answer for you in a few days. Good day to you all."

With that, he walked out of the room. Joyce also got up. She went to make the appointment. The rest of the company sat in silence. Tom walked to his mother and slammed his hand on the table in front of her. He said nothing. He left and put his overalls back on and returned to the machine room.

Margret slumped behind the desk at reception. The young woman who looked after the phone while she was at the meeting smiled at her, Margret did not notice. She felt extremely tired. Her whole body ached and felt clammy. All she wished was to be in the safety of her home. Why did everything suddenly change! Margret just wished that all went back to the way it was.

Someone dumped a parcel on the counter.

"Anyone there? I need a signature! Hello-o-ho!"

Margret stood up and signed the paper. She did not attend to the parcel or see who it was for. It sat there until a worker from the machine room noticed it.

"Oh Christ, how long has this been sitting here. We need that part badly!"

Picking it up he ran back.

The phone rang, but Margret did not notice. Joyce came running down the stairs and picked up the receiver.

"For you, Margret. Are you OK? Can I bring you a cup of tea? It is Kira on the phone. Will you take it?"

Margret slowly lifted her head. Her face was grey, her eyes dull.

Joyce told Kira that Margret was busy. She would ring back. She hung up and looked over to Margret.

Margret was slumped forward in her chair, arms tightly wrapped around her chest. Her face was grey and her eyes dull and unfocused. Her breathing was almost inaudible.

Joyce ran to get Tom from his lathe.

"I think Margret's had a stroke," she said.

Tom stared at her. The thought crossed his mind that she was just putting it on.

But when he saw her there, grey and suddenly wizened he rang for an ambulance.

THIRTY-FIVE

As soon as Clara walked into Tom's family flat she felt the cold welcome of the dark interior. Opening the window to let the warm summer night air enter the unhappy atmosphere, she noticed a couple across the road leaning out of their window waving to someone in the street. They noticed her and waved. She answered their greeting. Clara could feel the warmth and happiness stream into the whole flat. Quietly, she started humming.

She had spent the afternoon at Dolmer's Engineering's reception desk, answering the phone while Tom — still in his factory floor overalls — was at the hospital, anxiously waiting for news of his mother. She had quite enjoyed the role of receptionist.

Turning on the lights she could hear Tom emerge from the bathroom.

"Will your mother be all right?" she asked him anxiously.

"Michael tells me it's a heart attack. She's stable and they'll monitor her tonight and there'll be more tests tomorrow."

He sighed.

"She gave us all a terrible scare," he said.

He slowly led her away from the room he disliked so much.

"Look at this view," he said when they entered his room.

The lights of the town were twinkling at them.

"Would you like a Scotch? I found the bottle and the one glass. Do you only have one glass?"

He gave a short laugh.

"There are some more in the cupboard. I am the only one drinking, so there is only one glass out."

Tom put his arm around Clara.

"You are amazing. Thoughtful, kind, beautiful; and on top of all that you play the violin like an angel. No, no Scotch for me. I have you! Oh yes, I have you!"

He sat on his small single bed, leaning up against the wall. His body felt like lead. Before he knew it his head drooped and he was asleep.

Clara tried to make him comfortable but could not budge him. There was just enough room on the bed for her. She got undressed. On the chair she found a woollen blanket. She laid it over Tom and then climbed into the remaining space in the small bed.

"Good morning."

Tom stood in front of the bed holding two cups. He wore only a shirt. Clara stared at him.

"Oh, am I embarrassing you?" Tom laughed. He turned around and walked out of the room.

Clara did not know what to say. There was never any embarrassment in her house. Her dad liked walking around in his birthday suit, as he called it. Clara sat up in bed, pulled the blanket up to her shoulder and looked around the room. There were lots of books and a desk, all very neat. What caught her eye was a big map. Most of the rivers had been traced with a dark blue pencil. There was a cross on one of the larger rivers, next to it a boat. Little papers with pictures on them were dotted along many of the dark blue lines. There was a small poster of a violin and on the desk a picture of a man and a boy with a fishing rod.

Tom walked back into the room wearing his mother's apron.

"Coffee, mademoiselle? What would you like for breakfast?"

Clara slid back into the bed and started laughing. Tom put the cups down and slipped under the covers with her. Their lovemaking was long and sweet. Outside the sun was starting to touch the tops of the houses and churches of the town. It was still very early.

They walked to work together. The town was waking up. They

reached the office just after seven. Tom could already hear the clanking of the machines. He ran up the stairs to his office where he changed into a pair of crisp, new overalls. Joyce must have brought them in. A note on his desk told him that she had gone to the hospital to see Margret. She would be back by eight. Clara took Margret's place at the reception desk.

In the machine room Tom saw Angus and his dad with Gary, the foreman, and one other worker. Gary asked Tom to get the storeroom into some order. They needed more steel and there were some orders which had to be shipped out. At eight one of the apprentices came and that was the whole workforce for the day. The rest were ill.

Michael rang. Tom went to his office where it was not so noisy to take the call.

"How is she? Is she awake?"

"She's resting, Tom. She's a lot calmer and had a good night. But there is a heart problem. Irregular heart beat, blood pressure way too high. She doesn't like me being in her room so I've put her in the hands of a very good specialist, a woman.

And she's asking for you. In fact she's quite anxious about how you're handling it all. You should come and see her."

"I'll be there as soon as I can."

"Good, I'll let her know. And, by the way, who is the girl with the charming manner on your switchboard now?"

They both laughed.

Tom took off his overalls and washed his hands. Looking at himself in the mirror he quietly told himself that nothing now could change his life's direction. He noticed a shadowy figure behind him. She looked like Clara. He turned around but found himself alone in the room. There she was again in the mirror, moving all the time. He could feel the breeze she created around him. There was quiet humming. It sounded like Clara. He turned around again. No one was there. Tom filled the basin and washed his face, then ran some of the water through his curly hair. The apparition had white hair. He could see a strand of it swaying.

"Esther!"

The figure stopped moving, they looked into each other's eyes and she was gone.

THIRTY-SIX

The hospital room was spacious and friendly. The curtains were partially drawn to keep the sun off the bed. His mother was sitting up supported by a number of large cushions. A nurse fussed with the bedding. Michael was there with a woman a little older than himself, looking at Margret's medical record.

"Tom, this is Dr Ries, the cardiologist."

They shook hands. As Dr Ries and Michael left he said,

"Drop in to my office when you've seen your mother."

Before Tom sat down next to his mother, he took her face in both his hands and kissed her forehead.

"How are you? You look so much better. Goodness me, you gave us a fright!"

The nurse asked Tom if he would like a coffee or tea, but Margret quickly answered.

"Coffee, black and strong. That's how he likes it."

When the nurse had left, Margret started complaining about the food and the state of the tea. Tom tried to cheer her up.

"Lovely view you have. And look at those beautiful flowers."

Tom thought that the flowers in the vase on the little table by the bed came from Gudrun's garden.

Margret enquired about work and how they were managing.

"We are another man down. I quite enjoy being a worker again. Gary bosses me about. Today I worked in the storeroom. Lots of ordering to do, parcelling up and sending off. Yesterday I worked on the lathe. I really enjoyed that. Been a long time, but I can still turn steel!"

The nurse brought a cup of coffee on a little tray. She smiled at Tom and put it on the bedside table. He took a sip.

"Thank you. A perfect cup of coffee. Black and strong."

She smiled at him and quietly left the room.

"And you, Tom? Are you looking after yourself? How about food? Did you find the bread and butter?"

"I ordered dinner for the whole work force from the little cafe down the road and I got some breakfast on the way to work. I was at work before seven. The machine room was already in full swing. Joyce came to see you before work. I would not know what to do without her. She is a marvel!"

"What about the reception? Who is answering the telephone?"

"Oh, we take it in turns," he lied.

"Well, it looks like you can all do without me!"

He smiled at her.

"Only with great difficulty."

"What about your girlfriend? I suppose, now that I am out of the way, she will move into the flat with you! I know that kind of person. No morals, No morals. Free love and all that kind of thing. They talk a lot about that at the hairdresser!"

Her voice became louder and more shrill.

The nurse came in.

"Mrs Dolmer, don't excite yourself! Sir, can you step outside while I do her Obs. and meds, thank you?"

"Can you direct me to Dr Gilles office, thanks?" he asked her.

"Sit down, sit down." Michael pointed at one of the chairs. "Your mother seems determined to be a difficult patient! We do need to do more tests, so I think it better that she stays with us.

Margret will have to go to the Rehab Ward for a few weeks. The heart muscle will need at least three months to repair itself.

I hear some of your workers are down with a stomach problem? Something the workers ate? Or is it a virus? You better see me if you feel unwell. And how is the new receptionist? She seems to enjoy it.

Your mother is also undernourished for her body size and the hip problem comes from too little movements, and I think also from being so tense all the time. The tenseness comes from the high blood pressure.

Dr Ries is taking over. So from now on, she will communicate with you. Take care. Maybe you have time to visit us again?"

Michael shook Tom's hand and walked him to the door. There he took Tom by the shoulders and looked at him hard.

"Don't you hurt or upset my dear daughter!"

Tom looked into Michael's eyes.

"Never!"

Margret was asleep when Tom returned to her room. He snuck to the bed and kissed her on the forehead.

"Don't you worry," he whispered. "I will not break my promise. Neither to my dad nor to myself. I will come and see you tomorrow. Sleep well."

Outside the hospital Tom found a bench under a group of trees. He lit a cigarette and tried to shake his mother out of his psyche. Why was she so unfriendly? No nicety, no thank you! No love!

'Oh, Dad, what to do?'

"Smoking will kill us!" Dr Ries sat down next to him. Tom offered her a cigarette. She accepted it gratefully.

"You have a very difficult mother! We can do nothing right for her. We will keep her for some days, then she will go to Rehab. Is there anything she likes doing to keep her busy? She does not like reading; hates magazines! I would be grateful if there was anything she could do to keep her occupied."

"Knitting," Tom said. "She is knitting a jumper for me. I can bring it in."

They both sat quietly with their own thoughts.

Dr Ries turned to Tom.

"She is very unfit. Losing her breath and tiring that fast is not a good sign. In Rehab she will have to do some physical exercise."

Tom laughed, "I wish you the best of luck. My mother only exercises if it is of any importance in getting on in life. Not hers, just life in general. I will bring the knitting later."

THIRTY-SEVEN

Tom paced restlessly around the apartment. Its quietness made him edgy. All the windows were shut. Clara's perfume had been wiped out by the stale odours of old. The kitchen, the living room, and everything else in this space where he had lived all his life was neat and tidy. Tom paused at the closed door to his grandfather's room.

For the first time since his Grandfather's passing Tom opened the old man's room. It was as it had always been. A sturdy empty desk; clean and bare. A large bed covered with a dark blanket. A bedside table with a reading lamp and a clock. By the window granddad's big, dark, bulky, well-used armchair. Next to it a table and a lamp. There was a book on the table.

He sat down in the armchair and opened the book. It was a travel log with black and white pictures of African people. There was an inscription from his grandmother. *Enjoy your travels through Africa. With fondest love, B.*

Thumbing through the book he came across an old photograph of a young woman. He turned the photograph over but there was nothing to indicate who this mysterious person was. He closed the book and took it with him when he left the room.

He collected his mother's knitting basket, put the book into his briefcase, fetched his violin, left the flat and went back to the office.

Dolmer's Engineering greeted him in silence. Never had he heard the factory so quiet. Tom went up to his office and aimlessly walked up and down. He felt restless and without purpose. Sitting down in one of the armchairs by the window he lit a cigarette and tried to relax. Outside the river was calling.

With his grandfather's book Tom went to sit under his big willow by the river. Did the old man ever travel? His father never said so. Flipping slowly through the pages he found a number of chapters marked in pencil. They were all about journeys throughout Africa.

He settled back against the big trunk of the tree and lit a cigarette. The wind caught the smoke and made it drift along with the water of the river. Did his grandfather dream of travel too? He never gave Tom the impression of being a dreamer. He was such an austere person. There was nothing romantic about him. Oh, how he wished he knew more about his family, his origin; who his ancestors were? Who Margret's mother was?

Again, he looked at the photo. Maybe it was his grandmother when she was young?

He'd only known her when she was a sick and old woman. They had lived in the little flat Tom was now anxious to inhabit. Margret had been looking after her then. He was at school; granddad and dad at the factory.

No matter how hard Tom tried he could find no more memories of his grandparents. He would have to ask his mother.

The thought of his mother made him think of their dismal, cold, gloomy apartment. The events and confusions of the last few weeks now seemed to crush him. His deep love for Clara; the confusion of feelings towards his mother.

He knew he could not go back to a life that slowly squeezed all happiness out of him.

The river gently moved along, calling, calling.

He needed to get away.

What had Gudrun said?

'Just drive! Up river, down river, away from the river. Anywhere!'

Back at the office he picked up his briefcase with the book in it, his violin and got the car.

He left his mother's knitting at the hospital. He did not go to see her. He tossed a coin and it told him to drive inland towards the hills; away from the river.

THIRTY-EIGHT

Tom liked the little guesthouse. It looked half forgotten sitting on the hillside overlooking a valley.

He decided to stay. It was Friday late afternoon and he was the only guest. He booked in for three nights, all meals provided. He asked for a room looking over the valley. Tom was told that the rooms did not have en suite. Bathroom and toilet were at the end of the corridor. Would he like some refreshments now? They could prepare some afternoon tea. Would he like to have it in the dining room or upstairs?

The old couple was trying to be helpful by carrying his luggage.

"Thank you," Tom said, holding on to his briefcase and violin.

"Musician?" the old man asked.

"No, no. I am learning. May I do my practice? I will be as quiet as I can, so as not to upset the other guests."

"What other guests. You are the first one we've had in ages!" the old woman replied.

"Do you take a cheque?" Tom was worried they might not. He never thought of bringing enough cash

They both enthusiastically nodded.

The room was small but comfortable, with a door leading out onto a balcony. Red geraniums hung in pots off the balustrade. The bed was big and covered with a puffed up eiderdown blanket. In a corner, Tom noticed a small washbasin with a mirror above it.

"Wardrobe, bedside table, reading lamp." Tom said to himself. "What more does a man want!"

He took the one chair outside onto the balcony and sat down

looking over the green valley with its small creek. Beyond the stream the steep grassland led to a wood and on to high mountains.

"Clara would love this," he thought. That thought reminded him of his dinner date with the Gilles. He must ring and tell them he could not come. There was a knock on the door.

"Where would you like your afternoon tea?" the old lady asked.

"I'll come down, and please can I have coffee, not tea?"

On a tray were some little cakes, cream, jam, a coffee pot and a cup and saucer.

"Would you like to sit outside? It is such a beautiful day."

Tom picked up the tray and followed the old couple out into the backyard.

"This is just what I needed!" he said.

"My name is Peter," the old man said. "And where are you from?"

"Oh," Tom laughed. "I've run away from home, but just for three days. I'm from the small town by the river. My name is Tom."

The conversation was easy, uninvolved and had nothing to do with Tom's life and his problems. Nature and weather were their main subjects. The couple told Tom about their simple life. She had hens, sold their eggs and the odd bird.

"Would you like chicken for dinner?" she asked.

There was no problem in catching one of the birds. As soon as they saw the old lady they came running from all directions. She just had to bend down and pick one up.

"Yes, this one is a young one. We don't want to break our dentures eating tough meat, do we?"

She looked at her husband and they both giggled, sharing a quiet joke.

Tucking the hen under her arm she walked to a chopping block, talking quietly to the bird all the time. Before the animal knew its head was off and, headless, it flew about the yard.

Shocked, Tom stepped back. He had never seen an animal killed before.

"Don't worry she does not feel a thing without her head!"

And again the two of them giggled.

The meal was delicious. Never had Tom tasted such a chicken. It was served with potatoes and cabbage out of the garden.

The old lady had introduced herself as Edwina.

"A terrible name. My folks thought by giving me a posh name I would marry posh, get away from the farm and become genteel! Look at me."

Again, they giggled. With a smile Peter told Tom that love changed her situation of becoming posh. Edwina blushed.

They were sitting in the large kitchen. Pots and pans, strings of onions and garlic, dried flowers and strange herbs hung on the walls. The dresser was filled with all sorts of cups. Plates neatly standing behind them. Nothing matched. Next to the wood stove a tin pot with an array of wooden spoons, on it a black kettle, steam coming out of its spout. In the oven a pudding, its aroma filling the air.

After dinner Peter gave Tom a glass of Schnapps made from mountain berries. Then a different one, a herb Schnapps. There were now about five bottles on the table to be tasted. Tom offered Peter a cigarette and the two men sat at the table drinking and laughing and chatting.

Edwina sang as she cleared up and did the dishes. Tom could not remember ever having been so relaxed and happy.

He fell into his soft bed with the fluffy eiderdown and slept until the strange noise of a rooster crowing woke him up. The smell of coffee filled the house.

Edwina was standing at the wood stove when Tom entered the kitchen.

"What would you like for breakfast, Mr Tom?"

"Whatever you have," Tom replied.

"Oh, are you sure? Peter starts his day with a large cup of

strong, sweet white coffee, a raw whipped egg in it. With it, he usually has a good hunk of bread with butter and jam. He likes to start the day with sweet things. I like a salty start to the day. Eggs, bread, and butter. That sort of thing. Then coffee with lots of milk."

"I think I'll go for the savoury variety. Can I help?"

Edwina pointed towards the table and asked Tom to sit down.

"Men just get in the way!"

After a very hearty breakfast, Tom went to call Clara. The phone was in the hallway, which gave him some privacy. He was glad that Gudrun picked up the phone. Telling her that he would not be able to come to dinner that evening made her ask where he was.

"I don't know where I am. Truly, I do not know. Taking your advice, I just picked a road and drove. It took me inland and I am now in the most charming little guesthouse in a valley somewhere. It does not matter where I am. On Monday morning I will follow the road back and hopefully, having had a good rest, will be able to undo all the knots from last week. Please tell Clara it has nothing to do with her. I will ring her on Monday."

In the background he could hear Clara.

"Is this Tom? Where is he! I want to talk to him! Don't hang up! I'll take the phone in daddy's study. Don't hang up!"

Tom waited for the click in the line. Clara started asking questions he did not want to answer at this point. All he wanted was to be surrounded by the silence of the valley.

"I do love you, Clara. I do. I do. It has nothing to do with you. Honest! No, I don't know where I am. Truly! Yes, I am alone. Just an old couple and a lot of chickens. Well, the idea is to do as little as possible. Just walk and such. Yes, I have the violin with me. Yes, I will practise my scales. I must go. Big hug. Love you. Truly."

Forlorn, Tom stood in the small, dark space. The front door opened, and Peter walked in. With him cold air and sunshine.

"Want to go catch a trout for dinner?" Peter asked.

"Sounds great. My dad and I used to go fishing in the river. Yes, fishing would be great."

"Oh, not that kind of fishing. Ever tickled a trout before, son? Let's have coffee first!"

They took their coffee and sat on the front verandah. The little guest house had been bathed in sun since early morning. The other side of the valley was still dark and asleep. The first rays of sunshine were running over the steaming creek. Here and there the brook was in shade, which gave it a strange cut-up feeling. Tom watched the light walk into the bottom of the soft valley.

"See!" Peter pointed towards the creek. "When the water stops steaming, we can go and get us a trout."

In front of the house grew an old, very large oak tree. Tom went to sit under it. His thought strayed away from the landscape to Clara. She would love it here and he would love having her with him, sitting under this majestic tree, putting his arm around her shoulder, smelling her hair, making love to her under the big, fluffy eiderdown. He should go back and get her.

The thought of Clara made the memory of the last week creep into his mind. He felt tension in his body. The problems at work, his mother, the flat.

'Never will I live in that flat again. Never! Not one night. I can rent a room somewhere until the small flat is vacant. Yes, I will rent a room. Then I collect my desk, my books, the photo of dad and me and the map. I don't even want the stereogram. I will make my own music!'

The sun was now shining on the creek. Peter tapped Tom on the shoulder and pointed down into the valley. He did not carry a fishing rod or a bucket. They walked along a little well-trodden path, taking them through the high grass full of wildflowers.

Peter walked slowly along the edge of the stream. He asked Tom to stay a few metres behind him. The old man's body became agile as he turned into a hunter. He knelt down quietly, sedately. Slowly he inserted his hand and arm into the water and after a while with great speed pulled a fish out and threw it on the bank.

Tom jumped back.

"Kick it away from the water!" Peter shouted, "Quick before it jumps back in!"

Having cleaned the catch, Peter decided that the fish was not big enough for the three of them.

"We must now go upstream," he said.

Tom wanted to know how he managed to catch the fish. Peter explained the science of trout tickling as they walked.

"You know trout tickling is not allowed. Yes, it is a crime to tickle trout!"

Peter giggled, stopped, made a sign for Tom to stay behind and started to sneak along the stream's edge.

Looking at the water Tom could see a big fish in the middle of the brook. It was facing upstream, its fins and tail slowly moving to stay put. The water was crystal clear, and he could see the beautiful colours of the trout. Peter kept on sneaking upstream. Tom was mesmerised watching the fish. Suddenly it darted away to hide under the overhang of the creek's edges. At the same time a yell from Peter who was lying on the ground by the water's edge. Tom saw a fish fly through the air and into the high grass.

On Sunday morning Tom went with Peter to help feed the animals at the neighbour's farm. They took the cows out into the fields, fed the chickens and the pig. In exchange, Peter got some milk and a piece of roasting pork.

"For the young man," the wife said. "We killed a pig a few days ago. You, Peter and Edwina, will have to come over tomorrow and help us make the sausages. Later in the week we'll stoke up the smoke oven."

"I wish I could stay longer," Tom told her.

She looked at him.

"You must come back one day and taste my bacon. It is the best in the valley."

Walking back Peter laughed.

"Whatever she does, is the best in the valley. She is a good sort, though. Her husband had a nasty accident. He broke his hip. So, I help them out. Bit of this, bit of that. The only thing I wouldn't do is milking. No way!"

Early Monday morning Tom sat with Peter and Edwina in the kitchen where she had prepared an enormous breakfast and packed him some lunch.

"Edwina, I'm so glad that your posh name did not help you get into genteel company. I would have never met you. I would so much like to thank you both. You have no idea how wonderful my stay with you was.

Thank you, Peter, for your lesson on trout tickling. But I think I will leave that to you.

Not that I can ever pay you enough for your kindness, but here is my cheque."

Tom handed Peter an envelope. Then he drank the last of his coffee, said goodbye to the cozy kitchen and his new friends, picked up his two pieces of luggage and walked out. The valley was still shrouded in darkness when Tom started the car and turned down towards the town on the river.

Peter opened the envelope to look at the payment. He ran out the front door. Waving the piece of paper, he called after the car,

"Tom, this is far too much!"

Edwina read the name on the bottom of the cheque. *Tom Dolmer. Dolmer's Engineering.* And underneath, *Director.*

THIRTY-NINE

At seven on Monday morning Tom was back in his office. He felt strong and was looking forward to solving all his problems. When Joyce arrived, he asked her to organise a meeting with all the staff and then another one just between him and Douglas.

"I would like to thank you all for coming in this morning. I can see that you have got over your health problems. Now you all know that a week of not working means a week of falling behind. Anyone who is able to stay for a few hours after work will be paid double time. Thank you."

Someone asked how his mother was.

"Thank you for asking. My mother suffered a heart attack and they tell me she will not be able to come back for another six months. I haven't seen her for three days; but when I did, she was driving the hospital staff around the bend."

After the meeting Tom asked Douglas to stay on.

"We need to find a receptionist as soon as absolutely possible. I cannot spare Joyce. Do you know of someone, even if it is only until we find a permanent replacement, for my mother?"

"So, Margret will not be coming back? Is she that ill? I must go and see her."

"I think it's too premature to make plans for her at the moment."

He turned away from Douglas to the window and looked at the river. Was his little brook joining his beloved river?

After Douglas had gone Tom rang old Mr Hubert at the flat. He asked after their health and well being and renewed his promise to help them find a place in a Home. He would stay in touch.

At lunchtime Tom took Edwina's lunch packet out of his briefcase. It was quite a large parcel. He went to the bench by the river. Untying the bow of the string holding the paper together made him smile. So much care and love; he could almost feel it vibrating from the package. There was the large hunk of bread with lashings of butter on it. Separately packed was some of yesterday's dinner; a beautiful piece of pork. There was cheese and a few pickles. And again, separately packed, a slice of cake. Tom laid the feast out on the bench. Would he ever find the road that took him to the valley? It was dark when he came back home.

FORTY

Tom saw his mother sitting on a bench in the hospital's well-kept garden. As he drew closer, he noticed her fingers tightly knitted together. She was staring into nothingness and did not notice his approach. Having thought of her previous reaction to his visit, Tom had not brought her anything. No flowers, no fruit. Standing in front of her, he bent down to give her a kiss on the forehead. She moved her head away.

"Oh, it's you! Where have you been and when can I go home? This place is getting me down. They are talking about sending me to rehab. Whatever that is. I just want to go home. You can help me rehab at home."

Tom sat down next to her. "I'm only an engineer. I know nothing about the human body. You have to get that kind of information from Dr Ries."

"They also want to do a mental assessment. She said it was routine. There is nothing wrong with my mind!"

She kept staring straight ahead, her hands almost white from tension.

"You know what it is like when they get you into a hospital. They check every little bit of you. They did the same with dad. Just let them get on with it. The more co-operative you are the sooner you will be out of here. I can't do a thing."

Tom looked at Margret and laughed.

"Well, maybe I could stage a kidnapping and get you out that way!"

She stared at her son.

"Are you completely mad?"

Tom put his hands gently on his mother's.

"I hope not."

They sat in silence, Margret wringing her hands, Tom trying to enjoy the surrounding.

"Lovely park."

"Yes."

"Do you mind, if I smoke?"

"If you must."

Tom noticed a café.

"Would you like a drink of some sorts? I would love a coffee. We could go and sit and chat at the café over there?"

"If you like."

Helping Margret up he felt how unsteady she was on her feet. None of her brisk, hurried walk. He had to hold and steady her. Slowly they started to walk. Every bench they passed he asked if she would like to sit down, but her stubborn personality would not let her rest.

Each step Margret took with great concentration. Holding on to his stable arm, she could feel his strong supporting body. They fell into a steady, slow, rhythmic walk across the park

'Why can't I tell him that he is such a good young man?' Margret thought. 'What stops me from doing so?'

Tom felt his mother grasp his arm as hard as she could.

'She is so frail!' he thought. 'Why can't she show me a tiny bit of compassion? Why does she dislike me so much?'

At least in the café she found the tea to her liking.

"That stuff in the hospital is terrible!" she said. "This is proper tea."

"Would you like to have lunch here tomorrow with me?"

She looked around apprehensively. She nodded.

"Yes, that would be nice. What day is it?"

"It's Monday and I do need to get back to work. I shall go and talk to the doctors on my way out. Shall I take you back now?"

"The nurse will pick me up in a wheelchair if you take me back to the bench."

Tom was thinking about Clara and her birthday. He would be away for three days. How would Margret take that?

Just as Tom was going to walk out of the hospital, he met Michael.

"Long time, no see!"

He shook Tom's hand enthusiastically.

"When are you coming to see us again?"

Tom told Michael that he was coming after work to pick up Clara. He was going to take her out to dinner.

Clara was outside her house when Tom drove up. She looked upset. Before he was out of the car she snapped at him.

"Where were you all weekend? Rubin is furious because you didn't come today! And..."

He gave her a big hug and finished her sentence.

"And I love you, too!"

She wore her deep green dress with the matching little jacket Tom liked so much. Her hair had been tamed with a large comb on the back of her head. She had put on a little eye makeup, but no lipstick.

"You look beautiful."

Clara pulled a face.

"You do! You do!"

"And you look scruffy. You do! You do!"

She wiggled out of his embrace and pranced into the house.

Tom followed after her. Michael greeted him from the living room.

"Have you got time for a small drink? And a chat?"

Clara put her arm around Tom's waist and pulled him close.

"Daddy, this evening he is mine. I will not be sharing!"

Tom felt the blood shoot into his face. He put his arm around her shoulder and kissed her on her forehead.

"Just one drink and a little chat, please?"

Michael had already poured two glasses of Scotch.

"I need to talk to Tom about his mother."

Tom sat down and picked up his glass. He was suddenly nervous.

Michael took a sip and then said,

"We are worried about your mother. Margret does not want to get out of bed and walk. She'll become weak in her legs. She seems to have given up her will to live. She refuses to do any exercises and sends the physiotherapist out of the room! Every five minutes she calls for a nurse for something or another. She will not go to the bathroom.

I think she is severely depressed. She sees the psychologist soon. I can only hope that will help her."

Tom got up and walked to the window. After a long silence he turned around and looked at Michael.

"I don't know how one can help my mother. I promised my father to take care of her and I will. I'll make sure she has what she needs. I'll make sure she has someone to take care of her when she gets home.

But I cannot, after the way she recently treated me, live with her.

That is why I went away for the weekend and, while I was away, I made the decision to move out as soon as possible. I just have to find placement in a decent home for the old couple living in the company's small flat."

With great passion he continued,

"I will not go back to that flat to live! It is full of unpleasant thoughts. It gives me shivers all over. It sucks all the happiness out of me! Until I get into the small flat, I will stay in a hotel close to work!"

Michael put his arm around Tom's shoulder.

"I'll help you find a place for the couple in the flat. Now you go and relax with Clara and let me sort it out."

"Where are we going?"

Clara had applied more eye makeup and organised her hair some more while Tom and Michael had been talking. Tom took her arm as they stepped into the street.

"I found a little place not far from here. Or do you want to go to a restaurant in town?"

They fell into a rhythmic gait. Tom started to whistle. Clara shyly hummed. Together they made up a tune. A gentle wind wound itself around Tom's face and neck. With it the smell of Esther.

"I could have walked on like that forever," Clara said as they sat in the empty garden at the rear of the restaurant. It was Monday and they were the only customers. Tom ordered a bottle of wine.

"Where did you go last weekend?" she asked him

"I really do not know. I just took the first road away from the river and carried on. Then took a smaller one that led me into a beautiful valley. I stopped at the first guest house. It was perfect. Everything was perfect. For two days I existed in a kind of magic bubble. I did not think of work, of my mother. I did not practise my violin. I did, though, wish you were with me in this Arcadian world. I have no idea if I ever will find it again!"

The waiter brought the menu. Tom ordered schnitzel with a mixture of salads. Clara decided to have the same.

"Tell me all about that magic valley."

Tom told her about Peter and Edwina. How Edwina came to have such a posh name. He told her about catching the chicken but left out the beheading of it. He talked about the trout tickling. About helping to take the cows to their pasture. He told her about the lunch Edwina had packed for him. So much love, he said. So much caring! And he told her how much he missed her under the big fluffy eiderdown.

"We must go there. We must find the way!" Clara said excitedly.

"Maybe, one day," Tom said dreamily.

When he farewelled Clara at her door on their return Michael called out to him.

"A small Schnapps?"

Michael's head appeared around the door. Tom shook his head.

"No, I have to drive."

"Pity. But I think I've found a choice of homes for your couple."

He looked triumphantly at Tom.

"At this time of the night? Where?"

Michael tapped the side of his nose.

"Connections, Tom, connections. I've narrowed it down to two. One is private. One is government. Probably the latter. I'll look into it tomorrow. You have a good night."

Back in the Mercedes Tom looked in the mirror and smiled at his reflection. His plan was falling into place.

FORTY-ONE

Joyce found Tom standing by the window in his office. Without turning around, he said.

"I've moved out of our flat. I'm staying at a hotel close by. I'll give you the phone number in case I need to be contacted."

She stared at him.

"Why?"

"Because I cannot live in a space that is soaked with hate, that's why. She has managed to destroy all the feelings of love and care my dad left in the flat. Even his chair has lost his vibrations!

No, I cannot go back. I'd rather stay in a miserable little, charmless hotel. Anything, Joyce, anything, but that joyless flat!"

Only one little bedside lamp lit up the small hotel room. Tom had carefully hung his clothes in the wardrobe. On the inside of the door a notice from the management showed the rules of the house. *No Smoking* in big letters. He sat down on the bed that was covered with a golden brown, fluffy blanket. Opposite, on a small table, he had put his violin. Above it was a mirror with ornate edges. He looked at himself in the mirror. The edges were twinkling at him as he moved.

Tom felt his eyes moisten. Slowly tears ran down his cheeks, over his stubble and down his neck, emptying all his tension, all his sorrow, life's pressures and expectations. He stretched out his arm and touched his violin case.

"Oh, my love, oh my love I have neglected you."

Opening the case, he slowly and gently ran his fingers over the strings. The violin reacted with a beautiful whisper. He closed his eyes and started to move from side to side. With the gentle breeze came the sweet smell and the music. In the mirror the out- of-focus visage of a woman. She was slowly swaying.

"Esther. Help me!"

The breeze embraced him, held him. The fragrance of the gentle wind made him feel faint and he sat down.

When he woke, he found himself fully dressed on the bed. The violin was back in its case; the case on the table under the mirror. He turned off the lamp. There was a slight shimmer outside the window. His view was the grey wall of an airshaft.

Sitting up he started to laugh. It was the most miserable room he had ever been in. And Clara wanted to come up and stay with him!

He watched the grey wall getting lighter and lighter. He went to have a shower, then got a clean shirt. Breakfast was going to be served from six onwards. He had ordered a full breakfast and just hoped it would be better than the dinner.

He stepped out into the early morning street, towards work, towards another lunch with Margret; towards the many challenges life suddenly had put in front of him. The ever-moving river called. He sat on the bench near it, watching the water flow by, thinking of nothing. His mind was empty, only his ears hearing the slight whisper of the water; hoping for a sign of Esther and her music

A gentle tap on the shoulder brought him back. It was Joyce.

"Are you all right, Tom?"

"Yes, yes. I am fine, thank you."

She smiled at him.

"There's a phone call for you from Mr Goldmark!"

Back in the office Tom was connected with his teacher who immediately launched into a voluble tirade.

"Where have you been? I know what is going on with your mother. No excuse, no excuse. Practice comes first. Always.

I just need to know if you are going to the country with the Gilles this coming weekend? You offered me a lift and I've made a booking in a charming guesthouse for us both. Single rooms, of course. There will be only you and me, no youngsters making noises all night. They serve an excellent breakfast. So, please tell me what…?"

Tom smiled. He could picture Rubin's agitation.

"Yes, Rubin, I am going. I am…"

"Can we go on Friday evening? It's a three-hour drive. Probably two, the way you young people drive! The days are long now. Will you come and get me? I can get a taxi and come to you! Yes, I come to you! That's arranged. What about five?"

And with that Rubin hung up.

FORTY-TWO

A small suitcase, his violin, and briefcase were sitting in Tom's office in readiness for the weekend. The working day was not quite finished. He still had a few things to talk over with Joyce. And he was nervous about leaving his mother. Had she accepted his story about him going away for a break alone?

"You wanted to see me?"

Joyce stood by the door.

Tom handed her the phone number of the guesthouse where he was going to stay.

"If Margret calls, this is where I will be. Just give her the number, that's all. No details. And thank you, Joyce. Thank you very much."

The phone rang. It was the new girl, Christine, from reception.

"There is a young lady here waiting for you. Her name is Clara."

Tom asked Christine to send her up.

He went back to his desk. He was dead tired. All he wanted was to sleep.

"You look terrible!"

Clara walked behind his chair and put her arms around his neck and held him. Tom could feel her warm, soothing hands on his chest. He laid the back of his head against her breasts and closed his eyes.

The phone rang again.

"There is a Mr Goldmark in reception. Shall I send him up? Oh, sorry he is already on his way upstairs. Sorry."

Looking out his door, Tom saw Rubin opening door after door trying to find the right one.

"I am here, Rubin. Come in!"

"Why so many doors! I have my instruments sitting downstairs. Are they safe there? What kind of car have you got? Is it safe? I dislike cars. They are so dangerous. Are you ready? I am! So, let's go!"

Taking Rubin to the armchairs by the window he asked him to sit down. He was early and Tom still had a few things to attend to. Clara joined Rubin and they quietly talked about the upcoming weekend. They were both looking forward to the yearly meeting with their musical friends.

"Wonder if the quality of playing has improved?" Rubin said sarcastically. "You young people never practice your scales!"

He scratched his ears.

"Ten days of amateur music. Will my ears survive?"

Joyce came in and asked if they would like a coffee or maybe tea? Tom introduced her to Rubin, who mockingly remarked,

"Secretary? Well, well. Nice meeting you, Miss Joyce. No coffee for me, thank you."

Tom cleared his desk.

"Let's go!"

The car was waiting at the front entrance. Clara slid behind the wheel.

"I'll drive. You can sleep! No arguments, please. I'm the one who knows the way."

"I don't like women drivers!" Rubin snapped.

Tom was too tired to protest.

"Well, you'd better stay behind," she said sweetly to him in the mirror.

Soon the quiet hum of the engine made Tom relax and fall asleep. Rubin, in the back seat, arranged the pillow he had brought. He seemed to forget the dangers of female drivers and also nodded off.

A change in speed woke Tom. The headlights showed they were driving up a winding road. The dashboard clock showed it was after nine. He bent over to Clara and gave her a quick kiss on her cheek.

"Would you like me to drive?"

She nodded and they both started looking for a safe place to stop. He pointed to a spot.

"Are we here?" The stop had woken Rubin. "Where are we? It's so black! This looks like nowhere! Did you take us to heaven, Clara?"

Tom took over the driving. The road straightened up. Clara opened the window and let the wind ruffle her hair. Tom could hear the sound of rushing water.

"In daytime you'd see a whole carpet of yellow buttercups! Up above is a small waterfall. Its water spreads out through the forest. Take care. Somewhere here the water will run over the road."

She bent forward to see better.

"There, watch out, slow down!"

He slowed. He could see the water gleaming black across the road. There was a hiss as the car drove through it. Clara put her hand on his leg.

"When I cross that water I always know that I am entering paradise," she said. "Now the forest will finish, and we snake down into the valley where the village is. Not far now."

Driving into the village Clara guided Tom to their accommodation. There was one house in the village square with the outside lights on. As soon as they stopped a tall elderly man came out. He had to bend to get through the low door. Everything of the two-storied building seemed to be small.

"Welcome, welcome. Can I help you with the luggage?"

Tom helped Rubin out of the car. He looked rather stiff after the long drive. Clara had opened the boot and was helping to get the cases and instruments.

They climbed up the narrow stairs to the upper floor.

"I'll have the room with the single bed," Rubin said, and walked to one of the doors. He had obviously been here before.

"The other room is for Tom. You never know, he might just end up with some company."

He looked at Tom coyly. Then at their host.

"Any chance for some supper? And maybe a drink, Ernst?"

Tom and Clara opened the door to the second room. It had the most enormous bed in it. Both of them felt embarrassed.

"You have done it, haven't you? I mean slept together?" Rubin called to them, climbing down the old stairs. They looked at each other and rolled their eyes.

Ernst, the landlord, took them into the kitchen where his wife had prepared a hearty supper.

"Drink?" he inquired.

"Would you have a beer?" Tom asked.

Looking at Tom in disgust Rubin said: "Beer? Really Tom in these parts one only drinks Schnapps! I'll have one of those, Ernst; one of yours!"

Clara looked at Rubin and asked for beer as well.

Rubin started to pile up some of the food onto his wooden board. With the sharp knife supplied he cut everything up into little pieces. Then with the point of the knife, he started to spear some of the food and put it into his mouth.

"That's how we eat in the country!" he said, smiling at Tom,

Ernst came in with the beer and Schnapps. He laughed.

"Just eat any way you like, Mr Tom. There is a fork next to your board."

Rubin looked at Clara. With a cheeky smile he asked her,

"Where are you staying, my dear? Are you booked in at the hotel? Your parents always are staying at the hotel. It will probably be closed by now. Will you sleep in the car?"

"Oh, Rubin, stop teasing! I'll stay here tonight. With Tom! So!"

The cry of an owl woke Tom. He lifted Clara's arm gently and moved to face her. He could feel her hair. In the darkness he found her mouth and gently kissed it. With a little moaning noise, Clara turned over and onto his arm. Moving her long hair aside he kissed her neck and shoulder. She turned on her back, stretched her arms and legs, but did not wake up. He tenderly kissed her shoulders, her breasts. It was completely dark. He could not see her. Just feel and smell. Clara put her arms around Tom's neck. Tenderly he made love to her.

When he woke up it was barely light. Clara was curled up against his chest, lying on his arm. Carefully he pulled it from under her and got up.

Rubin was already in the kitchen.

On the table a coffee pot and cups. The fire in the wood stove was lit; upon it a large pot of water. The lid was joyously jumping, telling everyone that the water was boiling.

"Coffee?" Rubin asked. Tom nodded.

They sipped their drinks quietly. Suddenly Rubin got up and started pacing. He stopped in front of Tom who, in his mind, was still with Clara, feeling her, smelling her. Rubin put his hands on Tom's shoulders.

With a slow, serious voice Rubin said,

"Tom, I do like you. You are reliable and honest. You are considerate, unlike me!

Clara is very special to me. She's told me how much she loves you.

Tom, never, never ever hurt that young woman. She is special. Yes, she is special to me. If you ever hurt her, I will personally come and destroy you! That is a promise, Tom!"

They locked eyes.

'Never ever could I hurt Clara', he thought but he did not say it.

He took his cup and walked out into the village square, into the cool, fresh alpine air. Without warning the music came and the sweet smell. He felt it wrapping around his body.

Clara had snuck up behind him. She slowly turned him around and gave him a passionate kiss.

From the doorway behind them Rubin called,

"Program for today:

After breakfast, we are going for a walk. Exercise will do us the world of good.

Then Clara and I will practice. It would not hurt Tom to do his too.

Then lunch.

Then resting.

Then walking.

Then practising.

Then free time.

Please do not object. It does not work with me. So, let's put on our walking shoes and do the round of the village. Oh yes, by the way, Sunday is a free day. Let's go!"

Rubin stuck to his program. Through the wall Tom could hear Clara play. Then he'd hear Rubin reprimand her. Patiently she'd repeat the passage. Eventually she'd get it right, move on, and the process would start again.

Tom rebelled. He didn't even open his violin case. He sneaked past the door behind which Clara struggled with her instrument and her tutor.

As he walked out into the square, he saw Gudrun's little Citroen and labouring with the luggage and the instruments. He went to help her.

"Thank you, Tom. Michael and Susanna are coming in the MG. Michael just loves the curvy road and Susanna hates my car. Some boy might see her in the old washboard car, as she calls it. Thank you. Be careful getting the 'cello out. I had to remove the back seats to fit everything in. Oh, what a rush everything was. And the traffic!"

Tom had never seen Gudrun so stressed. She looked extremely tired.

"Let's get all the luggage to your rooms and then what about a drink of some sort afterward?" he suggested.

Tom picked up the 'cello. Gudrun smiled and took it from him.

"This is my child number three. If you could take the cases, please."

With the viola in one hand and the 'cello in the other, she entered the hotel.

The owner greeted her by taking the instruments from her.

"I have carried your babies many time before, Mrs Gilles. Those in their boxes and the real ones. I believe Clara is already here with Rubin?"

Looking at Tom he smiled.

"This must be Clara's boyfriend. News travels fast in a small village. Welcome."

Gudrun had picked up a case and her handbag and started up the stairs.

"Same rooms?" she asked

It was a large, light and airy room with a door to a second bedroom. The room looked new, but it somehow had an old-world feel about it. The window faced into the backyard of the hotel. By the window were two armchairs and a small table.

Gudrun pointed at the seats.

"Please Tom, sit down. I am glad I have caught you alone. I need to talk to you."

She smiled at him, pointing to a chair. He sat down nervously on the edge of the seat and studied her. She frowned.

"It seems to me that Clara really loves you. The bad and the good. The easy and the hard. And she has changed. Become quieter, more focused. She wants to be with you all the time and is very excited about you getting your own flat. I have nothing against young people living together but, in this case, things are a bit complicated."

She took a breath and frowned in concentration.

"At a very young age, Clara showed extraordinary talent in music. Rubin said she was a 'Wunderkind and wanted to take her under his wings there and then. We'd had one very talented person in our family. Her life ended in tragedy. We did not want to push such a life onto an undeveloped child. I wanted Clara to grow up as all children do. School and a home life, sport. Just an ordinary child's life.

Now she's finished her education and we have handed her to Rubin. He is a hard taskmaster and will take no nonsense. There will be a great deal of work in front of Clara.

She dreams of becoming a solo performer and travelling the world. To get there she needs to focus on her playing.

Michael and I have nothing against her staying with you. She can help with decorating your new flat and buying furniture and such. But her full time living place will be with us until she has reached the standard Rubin wishes her to reach. Rubin is a strange, eccentric little man, but he is good, and he knows everyone in the world of music.

Just one more thing. Please be careful. A pregnancy would be the end of her musical career at this stage. There is plenty of time for children later."

How much Tom would like to have children with Clara. He could feel little Thomas's gentle arms around his neck. Then he did understand what music meant to Clara. Never would he destroy her dream. Yes, Tom thought, Clara is young and there is time for having children. He leaned forward and replied,

"Thank you for being open and honest. I will help Clara to reach her goal."

Gudrun smiled.

"Will you be back next weekend? There will be a number of performances by the children of my colleagues from our small women's orchestra. Also, it is Clara's twenty-first birthday and after her performance we will be having a party here in the hotel. Don't tell her, it is a surprise.

I know you cannot stay for the week. You also have your life to live, your responsibilities."

Bursting into the room Clara interrupted Gudrun's talk with Tom. She stopped when she saw Tom with her mother.

"Here you are! I have been looking for you all over the place. Do you want to have some lunch?"

"I have been sitting in the car for hours," Gudrun said. "I'd rather go walking. Any takers?"

They walked through the village and down towards the river. Tom let go of Clara's hand and started jumping onto large boulders in the middle of the foaming waters. The noise of the almost white water was tremendous. He loved the tension, the energy of the water.

Clara hung on to her mother's arm. Gudrun smiled at Tom's youthful joy.

"He is fine," she said soothingly to her daughter. "Water is the best cleanser for the soul. The youthful river brings out the young feelings in a person."

She walked on up the river, leaving her daughter watching Tom nervously. When he jumped back on shore she grabbed him.

"Tom, please don't ever do such a thing again!"

They followed Gudrun, who had stopped in the middle of a simple wooden bridge, enjoying the spray and the noise. She pointed upstream.

"The water comes from the glacier up there on the mountain."

They could just see a little of the white ice through the trees. They followed her along the little path into the fir tree forest until they heard the sound of falling water. The trees, the grass, the moss was wet, and the ground covered with little yellow flowers.

"There!" Clara pointed. She had a little yellow flower behind each ear and some in her hand. "There is the waterfall."

A fine mist surrounded the place where the water pounded into a small ditch of well-worn round stones. Clara ran through the mist and Tom saw her on the other side shrouded in a curtain of fog-like droplets. Her hair was coming down. She stood completely still, then she started slowly waving her arms up and down.

Looking at Tom she made mocking, ghostly noises. He thought he saw another ghostly image merging within Clara's.

"Esther," Tom whispered.

Gudrun glanced quickly at him.

"What did you say?"

He felt her anxiety.

"Oh, nothing," he replied.

Coming back through the misty spray Clara gave Tom a hug.

"You are all wet!"

"Mummy said water makes you feel youthful!"

With that she skipped back down the hill towards the river.

Watching her, feeling the mist upon his arm and smelling the fir trees all around, Tom sighed. Gudrun looked at him.

"If life could just stay like this forever," he said to her.

She nodded. Her eyes were moist.

FORTY-THREE

It was four o'clock Monday morning. Quietly he had crept out of the warm bed. He gave her a gentle kiss and got dressed in his office suit. In the kitchen the kettle was simmering on the wood stove. He made himself a strong cup of coffee.

He got into his car and found a small parcel on the passenger seat with a note attached. It just simply said: *Enjoy and I love you*. Opening the parcel he found a cardboard box filled with sandwiches and little yellow flowers. He looked up at the building and whispered,

"I love you too."

Tom drove out of the sleeping village, over the youthful river, through the forest. The tyres hissed as he drove through the water from the little waterfall. In the early morning light the carpet of yellow flowers seemed to whisper farewell to him.

The noise of the machines greeted him back to his other life. Standing in the entrance hall of Dolmer's Engineering he felt like a stranger. Christine at reception greeted him with a smile. Joyce was busy upstairs. Douglas was walking about the landing. It took Tom a few minutes to get his body, mind, and spirit back into this world.

"Hi, Tom! Did you have a good weekend?" Joyce asked. "There is a lady waiting for you in the office. I'll make you a good strong coffee. It looks like you need one!"

Puzzled, Tom entered his office and found Kira standing by the window. She heard him come in but did not turn around.

"I remember when your father had that wall built. You know the one stopping this place from being flooded."

She turned to Tom.

"You look like you've been up all night. I do like the unshaven look. Suits you. Honestly!"

He hugged her.

"Yes, I was up most of the night. I left at four this morning."

Joyce came in with the coffee. They sat down at the little table.

"What brings you so early to Dolmer's Engineering?" Tom filled the cups. "Milk? Sugar?"

"I took the morning off work to talk to you about Margret."

He felt a sharp stab in his chest.

"Do you mind if I smoke?" he asked.

Kira shook her head and continued.

"I went to see her on the weekend. She asked for you, but I did not know where you were. It made her agitated.

But that is not what I came to talk to you about."

She paused. He watched her closely.

"I found out where Margret's mother is buried. Her married name was Lamberg. Sophia Grete Lamberg. She is in a family grave with her husband and two stillborn children. I can take you there. They must have had money. It's an impressive grave. I also found out her maiden name. It was Gallas. She was a singer."

Tom stared at her.

"How? How did you find out? How?"

Kira laughed.

"Easy! There are government departments where you can find out about your ancestry. All you need is a name. I started with yours! The rest is just a bit of detective work.

Now I'm digging in music documents trying to find Miss Gallas, but I've had very little success. Maybe one of your musical friends can find out something about her?"

Tom was struggling to take this astonishing information in. He thought of Rubin. He was a walking musical encyclopaedia.

"I think I know someone who might be able to help."

Kira shifted in her seat.

"The question now is how do we convince Margret to accept her real past?"

"I'll talk to her doctor at the hospital. Would you come along if needed?"

She nodded. "Of course I'll come! But now I must go. I do like that bit of golden stubble on your face. It reminds me of the country. Come and have some dinner with us. Why not tomorrow?"

He watched her leave and then sat there, trying to digest this bolt from the blue.

"You look terrible!" was his mother's greeting. "What have you been doing the last two days? Gallivanting with your girlfriend? I bet she does not give you much time for anything. She looks that sort."

Margret was sitting on the bench in the hospital garden. Even though it was quite a hot day she wore a woollen jacket and hat.

"You did not shave very well this morning. Look there," she pointed at a spot on his neck.

She is certainly in good form, Tom thought.

"Thank you I am well. How are you Mother?" he said. "Lunch?"

Margret stood up and started walking towards the café.

"This place is closed on weekends," she said as she walked across the grass, ignoring the path. "It seems that people are not interested in making money. Or maybe they are just the lazy kind! Probably more likely the lazy kind!"

She ordered soup and bread. Tom had a big meal. It had been quite some time since he ate the carefully prepared sandwiches. He took Clara's note out of his breast pocket.

"What's that?" Margret asked.

"Shopping list," he replied, putting the note back.

"So, how was your weekend, Mother? Did you get any visitors? Did someone take you out for lunch?"

"Joyce came and took me out for lunch. I had a visit from Kira and Douglas on Sunday. No one seemed to know where you were."

"I drove up the river to a spot I know where there's a little ferry. I took it across and just lay by the water. Went for a few swims. On the way home, I found a guesthouse and spent the night and most of Sunday there. I walked in the woods and yes, I was alone."

He stared at her defiantly. She studied him, sensing he was holding something back.

"Clara and her family are in the mountains. It was too far to go just for a weekend. But if I take Friday off I can be at their closing concert. And it's Clara's twenty-first birthday on Saturday, to which I've been invited. It all depends on how the week pans out. Things are still in a bit of an upheaval."

After having had lunch with his mother, Tom took her back to the bench in the hospital park. She was going to wait for the nurse to come with the wheel chair. She told him that she had been moved to the rehabilitation wing. She thought it was a waste of time.

Margret watched her son walk towards the building. She clenched her hands into fists. Quietly she talked to herself: 'I will not let go of him! I had to let go of so much in my life. He is all I got left. No one will take him away from me.'

As if Tom could feel the tentacles of his mother, he turned around and waved to her before entering the building.

The waiting room was almost empty. Tom sat down. Putting his hand into his breast pocket he pulled out Clara's note. He kissed it. He felt that ghostly presence again. He pressed the note onto his chest.

"Esther? Clara?" He whispered. He closed his eyes. 'I am so tired, so tired,' he thought.

A tap on the shoulder brought him back to the hospital waiting room.

"I'm sorry I kept you waiting. Please come in."

Dr. Ries looked at Tom with concern. He swayed a little as he got up.

"Sorry, I must have fallen asleep. Had a very short night."

"So, how did you find your mother, Tom? She is off all medication except her blood pressure pills. Still working on the strength of those. And she is now in the Rehab building, which is far more comfortable than her previous room."

"She was in great form being her good old self. Criticising, abusive and generally nasty. I got a most charming welcome. How do you feel she is?"

"Physically or mentally?"

"Both!"

"Physically she seems to be quite good. They are still monitoring her heart. Mentally...? Well I think you should talk to our chief psychologist. Let me see if she's in."

The room was bright with the open window facing the garden. There was no desk, only comfortable armchairs and a table scattered with some notes. On the windowsill stood a deep green vase filled with summer field flowers. A bookshelf reaching up to the ceiling covered one of the walls. Some of the books had been removed and lay in a pile on the floor. Next to the books, a stool. There was no one waiting for him.

Tom was about to leave when a voice called from the depths of the corridor.

"How do you take your coffee, Mr Dolmer?"

He could hear the clicking of high heeled shoes.

A very short woman in very high heels entered, carrying a tray. She had thick, snow-white hair cut in a bob with a severe fringe just above her plucked eyebrows. The same modern cut as Susanna wore. Tom thought the cut did not suit her.

"Hello. I'm Andrea Coder," she said, as she placed the tray with the coffee on top of the papers on the table.

She smiled at Tom. Her eyes were intelligent and shrewd. She wore an expensive-looking suit.

"Please do sit down. Excuse the books everywhere and do you

mind if I have my lunch? I have just finished with a client. May I take my shoes off? They are extremely uncomfortable. That's what happens when one is short and lives amongst tall people. Vanity: my middle name."

She kicked the shoes off and walked to the window and bent to the flowers. Taking a deep breath, she sighed.

"You see, Mr Dolmer, each client leaves something behind in one's psyche and I somehow need to remove it. Flowers and fresh air do the trick for me. Could you pour the coffee, please."

She watched him pour. He sensed that she was evaluating him.

"Your mother is the most interesting case I have had for a long time. There are a lot of things going on underneath her unpleasant crust. She is actually a very nice person if one can push aside her disagreeable way of being."

She lifted the tray and pulled out a sheet of paper.

"How busy are you? And may I call you Tom? I do really have to talk to you about Margret. Do you have some more time? I can postpone my next client. I feel it is important that we talk."

Finding her phone behind the pile of books she spoke to reception. She did not excuse her actions. She just asked to keep the client waiting a half hour.

"Tom, I feel there is far more to Margret's past then she remembers. She fills up with hate when talking about her mother. No mother can be that horrid! Do you know anything from her youth?"

Slowly, at first hesitantly, Tom told her what he knew of his mother's past. Andrea listened without interrupting, occasionally nodding and smiling to encourage him to keep going. When he finished, she said,

"You know, Tom, your father's death has put a lot of fear into Margret. She is terrified of being left alone. She often talks about it and, you know, she does realise that you have to have a life. She talks a lot about you. How you are so very much like your father and grandfather; two men she loved and admired. She finds it intolerable that you are so much in love with music. She despises singing. It hurts her in her chest.

Oh, Tom, all this is fascinating. I might just, if I may, write a paper on your mother and you. You are an amazing young man. How do you manage with all the responsibilities you carry on your shoulders? You cannot be older than thirty?"

There was a knock on the door.

"Oh dear, the client! Our time is up."

She stood and eased her feet back into the shoes.

"We'll talk more next time. Please remember this conversation is between us, it is confidential. Here is my card. Make an appointment. See you soon."

Then she touched her hair and said,

"Is my hair all right? I had it cut today. It is the latest style. Do you like it? Oh dear, sorry...vanity."

She touched her hair again and smiled.

"Please come and see me soon. There is a lot to talk about. I visit Margret every day. I think we slowly are becoming friends."

I t was an impressive grave. Behind it a large old silver birch, it's long thin branches almost touching the monumental head-stone that was adorned with two angels, looking happy and playful. Under each angle a carved name. The silver plating of the letters had faded. They were hard to read. Tom got as close as he could without standing on the grave. Under one it said, *George,* under the other *Irene.* There was some decoration, but lichen had started to grow over it. The grave was well maintained. Tom noticed some wilted flowers in a ceramic vase. He removed them then went looking for a tap to fill the vase for the flowers he had brought. Having arranged his bunch and brushed leaves and bark off the white polished slab of marble he noticed writing on the stone. It was a poem. Since it was partially covered with lichen he could not make out what it said. He decided to come back with something to clean the surface. Tom wanted to be able to read it.

He sat down on the path in front of the grave. The headstone was also decorated. Big round patches of lichen covered most of the writing. He needed to read all the words. This was a memory to his Grandparents, his aunt, and uncle. Margret's real family!

Then it suddenly struck Tom. Who had brought the flowers? Who had cleaned the grave? He decided to come back. He had the feeling the flowers were for her. But then they could have been for his grandfather. He could have had a lover later in life. Maybe even more children. But why abandon Margret?

Tom looked at the names but could not get an answer. In his pocket diary, he noted down the birthdate of his grandmother,

Sophia Grete Lamberg. After a last look at his lost family, he started to walk through the vast city of graves filling the General Cemetery.

The next day over lunch Tom decided to tell his mother about her family and the grave.

"You'd never guess where I went yesterday?"

She looked up from her soup, showing a flicker of interest.

"Oh, and where would that have been?"

"I took some flowers to your mother's and father's grave. Your little brother and sister are also buried there. It was good to meet my other family. Your mother had a pretty name. Sophia Grete. I guess Margret was chosen from your mother's name?"

He kept his eyes on his plate, making a show of cheerfully eating.

He heard a loud clunk as Margret dropped her spoon into her soup bowl. He carried on talking.

"It is a beautiful grave, but I did not care much for the location. I think the place where dad and his family are is so much more beautiful. On a hill overlooking nature. By the way, next week we will have to go to dad's grave with new flowers. I'll take you in the car. I will be able to get the car quite close to dad. What about that?"

He looked at his mother. He knew that he had brutally jumped into deep water, hoping she would be able to digest the news without any health consequences.

He noticed her eyes watering, but she did not cry as such. Then, she started to shake.

"How, how did you find my family?" her voice was trembling. "How?"

"There is a government archive where one can track these things down if one has enough patience."

He did not mention Kira's part in it. He thought his mother would not like to know others had been delving into her past.

"Why did you go looking for them? You never met them. You did not know them! Why dig up the past!"

"Because they are my family. My grandmother, my grandfather, my aunt, and uncle! That's why! Even though I never met them, they are still my family!"

Her mouth became a slit. Her eyes cold. He pressed on.

"Would you like to go and see the grave? I will clean the stone so we can read the poem on it. The headstone also is quite overgrown with lichen. I need to find out how to get it off, so we can read the inscriptions. On top of the headstone are two little, chubby, happy-looking stone angels. They represent the two stillborn babies: George and Irene. They are really quite beautiful. Behind the grave is a silver birch. It must have been planted for your mother. It would be almost as old as you."

Very quickly Tom added,

"We can go next week when I am back from Clara's birthday in the mountains."

Margret kept on staring.

"Brother? Sister? I do not have any siblings! Never had!"

"We can bring her some flowers and maybe some little toys for the children."

"Where did you say the grave was?"

"The large Central Cemetery. The grave is in the old section."

"Oh," she said.

There was a long pause.

"I am so tired today. They have changed my medication. The doctor said it would help me to be less agitated. I don't quite know what she was talking about. Maybe you can find out what they mean by being agitated. I am just so tired. I would like to go back to my room now."

FORTY-FIVE

Next to him on the car seat wa a road map. It was a beautiful early spring morning. He was driving towards Clara, music, happiness and laughter. Leaving behind his mother. As the distant between them increased, his guilt at the way he had treated his mother began to ease.

Tom recognised the pine forest. The road had flattened out and started to descend into the next valley. There were the yellow flowers! Then the swooshing noise as he drove over the water on the road.

"Welcome to paradise," he heard Clara whisper.

He could feel his heart pounding, jumping about in his chest, sending a sweet, sharp pain down to his groin.

He left the Mercedes in the town square. Looking towards the guesthouse he wondered where Clara might be. He stood there, breathing in the crisp mountain air. He stretched and smiled and then, instead of going to the guesthouse, he followed the path down to the river.

He sat and watched the water flow. It was so much faster, so much more tumultuous than his river back in the town. It was a river like Clara herself. Young, vibrant, joyful.

He felt a presence behind him. Someone leant over him and hair brushed his cheek.

"Oh, I do love you, Tom Dolmer."

Bending down Clara kissed him.

He laughed and stood up and embraced her.

"Let's walk," she said. "I need to walk. You can tell me all about your week."

They walked upriver, the water foaming and splashing next to them. Tom was just about to cross the bridge when she led him further upstream.

The path entered the pine forest. For a while they walked in silence, feeling the softness of the ground covered in pine needles. The path became steeper. It veered away from the water and soon they could only hear the soft noise of the wind through the pine needles. Clara pointed to the left.

"We are going over there. Trust me, I have been here many times. We are going to my secret place. A place like your tree and your river."

The pine forest opened onto a stone platform. The vista that revealed itself to Tom was stunning. Below, in the valley, he could see the village; next to it the river, white and foaming. Clara found a spot and sat down against a pine tree.

"My spot! You must find yours! This is now our secret place. Is it not quite something? This spot knows all my sorrows, all my happiness. It knows all about you. I came up here during the week. I missed you so much. I had a good cry.

From up here I can shout at Rubin down there. He is such a fussy, hard taskmaster. I don't know who he thinks I am. Some sort of genius? I was so tired and sore from all the playing and walking! Somehow it was good you were not here. I would have been too exhausted to make love. But I did miss you and your hugs and your security; your strong arms. So I came up here, crying and shouting and then feeling better."

Tom put his arm around her and they both looked down onto the village.

With her head on his shoulder Clara asked: "How was your week? How is your mother? Did anything exciting happen?"

"Yes! Thanks to Kira I found my grandmother's grave. Next week I will go and start to remove the lichen, so I can read all the words on both the headstone and the large slab of white marble covering the grave. On the marble is a poem. I really would like to know what it says. In the grave also lie my grandfather and the two unborn babies; my uncle, and aunt."

She started to cry.

"It must be terrible to find your family all dead and gone? I could not imagine such a thing. How do you feel about it?"

"I actually feel very happy to have found them. With my father's family everything was laid out in front of me, I knew my grandparents, my father, my mother.

But my mother did not know any of her family. Her mother died when she was four years old. She does not know anything about her mother's love. She will not be able to love until she finds out. Until she can replace her imagined past with the real one. I am determined to help her! Maybe then she will start to love me."

Tom's eyes moistened. The landscape became soft and foggy.

"Meeting you, Clara, made me see the world with new eyes. I now know what real love is like."

Tom put his hand on his chest.

"When I first saw you, up there in Rubin's tower, I felt as if I had known you before. Everything about you was familiar."

He laughed.

"Maybe I met you in another time? Who knows?"

Clara looked at Tom.

"I would like to come and help you clean the gravestones. May I please?"

"That would be wonderful."

"I would like to help you make your mother happy. Help her find love. It must be terrible not to be able to love!"

She hugged Tom.

"I want to climb into you and stay there forever."

He gently pushed her away. Quietly he said just one word, "Rubin."

"Bloody Rubin!"

She jumped up and stomped off.

When Tom had caught up with her, he held her tight to him and whispered,

"Tonight, after your performance, we will climb into each other, we will be together all night! Now it is Bloody Rubin time."

Arriving back to the village square a shrill high voice called,

"Lunch is served! NOW! Or it will be spoiled!"

In the middle of the dining room, a very large table was laid. Sitting at the head of it was Oma, old Mrs Gilles. Next to her Gudrun. Rubin also was seated. On the other side of Clara's grandmother sat a man who Tom did not know.

Tom walked to old Mrs Gilles, took her hand in both of his and did a little bow. She laughed, took hold of his head with both of hers and kissed him on both cheeks. "Good to see you, Tom, meet my other son, Edward. He drove me. I came yesterday. So good to have you here, Clara has been impossible!"

"Yes, impossible," echoed Rubin.

Edward smiled at Tom and extended his hand. He had the slightly bemused air of a scholar.

Michael sitting opposite his mother stood up and lifted his glass.

"Let's drink to life, love, and music. Let's drink to our beautiful and talented women. Let's drink to all the handsome, clever men seated around this table. Let's drink to a successful weekend. Please charge your glasses. Cheers!"

Impatiently Rubin stood up. To Tom's surprise he clambered onto the chair he had just vacated. He started shouting,

"Enough, enough of compliments! Please listen carefully! I will only announce this once. The program for this weekend."

Everyone turned to him. Tom could see the little man swell with importance.

"Today at five the little ones, the children, will be holding their concert. Please attend to support them. It is important for them to have an audience.

Due to tomorrow's dance and its accompanying horrendous music, we will be holding our main concert this evening at eight.

Miss Clara Gilles, violin, will be accompanied by Mr Frank Gardel, on piano, playing a beautiful piece by Beethoven. This was the last sonata our great maestro gave us. It is the Violin Sonata op. 96.

Saturday morning the whole group of students will be performing an outdoor concert to thank the village citizens for their patients. The piece we are playing will be a surprise.

Just one more thing, no sorry, two:

I would like to thank Gudrun Gilles for her absolutely wonderful support and her inexhaustible help in organising all the events during the week. She has such a magnificently sublime way of getting on with young people, and with old."

Rubin bowed and smiled to Gudrun.

"The second is that I ask, no demand, of our two young performers to prepare themselves for tonight's concert. A two-hour meditative rest is recommended. Preferably alone!"

He looked hard at Clara, then at Tom.

"Now, just one more thing. Could someone help me off this chair. Thank you, that is all. Oh, by the way, there are programs available."

He looked at the people around the table. His eyes stopped at Gudrun, then Clara. How much they reminded him of his lost love. Tom had left his seat to help his teacher off the chair. He held his arm and as Rubin slowly found the floor with his foot, the two men were facing each other.

Tom and Rubin sat in the kitchen of the guesthouse. The clear tones of Clara's scales filled every corner of the old house. For all her talk of rebellion against her tutor's regime, when it came time to practice she buckled down.

Rubin nodded to Tom and gestured in the direction of the music.

"Thank you for the way you support her. She needs to stay in that space of music now until the concert. That way her concentration stays with the task at hand. But we can relax! What about a Schnapps?"

He poured the home brewed strong drink.

"Cheers, Rubin." Tom lifted his glass. "To a good concert!"

"Oh, don't you worry, she will be good. It is that young pianist I am concerned about. No, Clara will play faultlessly tonight."

"There's something I want to ask you," Tom said. "Something personal."

"What's on your mind?"

"I'm trying to find out who my mother's real mother was. I believe she was a musician, but I have very little to go on."

"Oh, good! A mystery. I love mysteries." Rubin leant forward. "What was her maiden name?"

"Sophia Grete Gallas."

"Sophia, Sophia? Sorry, I have to think about that. What instrument did she play?"

"She was a singer. Mostly Lieder. Mainly in small, private functions. Sort of like Hausmusik. She generally performed privately. It would have been in the later part of the nineteenth century."

"That long ago! That long ago, I have to think even harder. Sophia Gallas. Let's have another Schnapps. I might be thinking better. Landlord, where are you!"

The landlord replenished their glasses and brought out a board of cheese and rye bread.

Tom asked for a beer. He went and stood by the stove. There was a special warmth from a wood fire, he thought. The evenings were chilly here in the mountains.

"Come, sit down. Have some cheese. Sophia Gallas. She died, when? How old was she when she died? When did she stop singing?"

Tom resumed his seat.

"She died in 1908 at about the age of thirty-five to forty. I think she got married when she was between twenty-five and thirty. I found that much at the Registry Office. I think that after she married a Mr Lamberg she stopped singing."

Tom looked hard at Rubin.

"I need to convince my mother that the past she talks about is a past somewhat concocted in her imagination, not the real past."

Gudrun walked into the kitchen Clara's dress carefully draped over her arm.

"Sorry, am I disturbing something?"

"Nothing that cannot be continued later. Time to get changed. Tom, please get changed in my room. You did bring a suit?"

Rubin asked Tom not to disturb Clara.

"You will leave after us. There is a seat reserved for you in the tenth row, middle."

As Rubin left the room Tom heard him mutter,

"I just hope the piano is tuned."

He showed his ticket to one of the students working for the evening as an usher. Down at the front an elderly lady in a wheelchair waved and called him. It was Oma Gilles.

"Why so far away? Come and sit with us. You are practically part of the family. Oh, I like your shirt. You look very smart and handsome."

He had bought a new shirt with small decorative folds on the front. He wore it with a white bow tie and a very dark blue suit. He disliked black.

"Thank you," Tom replied with a slight bow. "I think Rubin did not want me to distract Clara and therefore put me out of sight."

"Don't you worry. Clara will be completely focused on her music. She gets so into the music. She becomes the piece she is playing. So, my dear boy, you will sit next to me. From this side, we will be able to see Clara."

On the podium, the grand piano was being tuned. Rubin was leaning into the piano waving his arm up and down to show the frustrated piano tuner how to turn his tuning tool. At long last the little man was satisfied and disappeared through a door at the back of the stage.

Tom glanced around. All the seats in the hall were occupied. He was surprised to see his old friend — and former rival for Clara's affection — Jason, sitting there. Jason smiled and waved to him. Tom felt a sudden stab of jealousy. Why was Jason here? Then he laughed at his reaction and waved back to Jason.

Slowly the lights were dimmed and a spotlight directed onto the piano. Rubin came back on stage and announced the piece to be played. He asked not to clap between the four movements. With a flamboyant gesture he pointed towards the door at the back of the stage. One of the spotlights followed the path of his arm.

First Clara then the pianist, Frank Gardel, came onto the stage. They bowed and took their places. The spotlight lost Clara and roamed about seeking her.

Oma Gilles patted Tom's arm. Bending down to him she whispered,

"This is all done by the students. It seems that the young person in charge of the spotlights is having some problems finding the star. I find all this very charming."

The spotlight found her and Clara laughed and turned to the audience.

"Ladies and gentlemen this little entry was very carefully rehearsed."

She took a deep bow. Everyone laughed and clapped.

"Let us now go to Beethoven."

She picked up her music stand and put it close to the piano. Rubin was going to turn the pages for Frank Gardel. There was complete silence in the hall. The two young musicians looked at each other, Clara nodded and started to play.

As soon as she put her violin under her chin her whole persona became music. Did Tom detect a shadow close to her? With an almost teasing attitude, the violin played the first bars. The piano answered. The two young performers never missed a note, never lost contact. Frank Gardel was a bit older than Clara. Neither of them seemed to be looking at the music. Rubin kept on turning the pages. Clara's music stand was in the dark. There was no way she could see the notes.

'She must be playing from memory,' Tom thought.

He was fascinated by the bond between the two musicians. Another twinge of jealousy went through him. It was hard for him to concentrate, to fully enjoy the music. He would have to get the record and listen to it. Clara was moving in and out of the light. Rubin turned another page. He suddenly looked up into the darkness of the audience. Tom thought he detected a smile. With a loud crescendo, the first movement came to an end. Rubin's attention was back on the sheet music.

During the second movement Tom closed his eyes. Clara had shifted closer to the piano. The music was slow and sweet. The union of the music reminded him of lovemaking. With his eyes shut he soon became totally taken in by the music's tenderness.

Applause, stamping of feet, Bravos! brought Tom back. Oma Gilles was pulling his arm.

"Could you please help me to stand Tom, please?"

He held her while she called *Brbavo*. He did not move. He just looked at Clara with her shining eyes and her hair and her smile. He could see she was looking for him but could not find him. The two musicians bowed. They were holding hands. Rubin stood in the background. A little girl walked on stage with an enormous bunch of flowers. It almost looked like a walking bouquet. As Clara took the flowers, she noticed Tom standing next to her grandmother. She kissed the girl on the cheek and smiled at Tom. Then she walked off the stage and was gone.

"You better go to her, Tom. Clara is always very emotional after a concert. Go and help her come down from where she is at the moment. Slow and gentle. Go. There are stairs over there to the back of the stage."

When he got into the shabby little back room he saw Gudrun comforting Clara. The flowers were lying on the floor. Tom gently put his arms around them both. Gudrun moved away and let Tom embrace Clara. She was shivering. He took off his jacket and put it over her bare shoulders. Holding her tight he started humming parts of the music he had just heard.

"I could not see you. You were not in row ten! I thought you had not come."

"I was here all the time, with you and Beethoven. What beautiful music you made. You have filled me with music!"

"They want me to go out again. Frank is already on stage. They want an encore! I am empty! I have no strength left!"

"Take some of mine!" Tom hugged her tight. They started breathing in unison. Clara stopped shaking.

Tom looked at her.

"What are you going to play?"

"Just a serenade by Franz Schubert."

"Darling Clara, you can do that in your sleep!" Tom laughed.

"How do you know what I can do in my sleep!"

Tom gave her a kiss and looked at her and whispered. "I know, I have slept with you!"

Taking his coat off she pushed Tom aside. She fastened her hair with the large comb and, almost falling over the flowers, picked up her violin. Rubin appeared out of the dark and opened the little door. The spotlight came on and Clara stepped into it. Rubin mimicked a kiss towards Tom and walked out behind her.

Tom heard the audience erupt with applause. Gudrun came up to him and gave him a big hug.

"You are a clever man."

"No," he shyly answered. "No, not at all."

Then the feeling of a presence was all around him. The familiar smell, the soft breeze. For a few seconds he closed his eyes to draw in the tenderness of Esther. He whispered a thank you, and turned towards the stage door where he could see Clara.

Clara put the violin under her chin, looked at her musical partner, nodded, and they started. Clara turned so she could look at Tom by the door. Tom felt she was playing the serenade for him. From deep down a memory filled his whole being. He had heard someone playing that sweetly, so full of emotion somewhere, a long time ago.

Clara turned back to the piano as they reached the end of the serenade. She took Frank's hand and they bowed together. Clara hurried off the stage. She walked up to Tom and whispered,

"Now you can show me what you can do in bed!"

Bed was still a few hours away. In the hotel, a light supper had been prepared for the Gilles family and their friends. The company around the table was noisy. The word success wove like a musical motif through the conversations. Michael stood up to make a speech. There was protest from the whole family.

"Just a very short one," Michael said convincingly. "I just would like to say how proud I am of my girls. One can create the most gastronomic delights, the other takes you to heaven with her music making. Well done girls, well done!"

Clara's head was on Tom's shoulder. Her eyes were shut. Gudrun noticed her head slowly drooping.

"Someone take Clara to her room. Poor girl, she is exhausted."

Getting up to help Clara, he noticed that her grip was getting tighter. Not sure where to take her, Tom looked around the table. He felt embarrassed. All eyes were on them. 'Which room?' he thought.

Rubin leaped up. "Oh for God's sake take her to bed, man!"

He pointed to the door leading to the square.

Slowly Clara started pulling Tom towards the front door. Once outside and away from prying eyes she turned towards him, pressed her body against his, and kissed him. Throwing her head back she started to laugh.

"Maybe I should become an actress!"

Pulling Tom behind her she skipped across the square to the guesthouse and the upstairs room.

Next to the bed stood a small table with a bottle of champagne in an ice bucket.

"What time is it?" she asked him.

"Almost midnight!"

"How close?"

"Not quite five minutes."

"Well, you'd better unzip my dress."

He did so, at first hesitantly. But then he kissed her back and shoulders and the dress fell to the floor.

"What is the time now?"

"Two minutes to midnight."

Tom was getting a bit annoyed.

"Undo my bra, take off the rest!"

Naked, she turned to him.

"And now you!"

She undid his shirt and reached for his belt. Embarrassed, he finished the job for her.

"Now open the champagne and pour some."

He did as he was asked.

"Cheers."

She lifted her glass.

"Happy birthday to me. I wanted you to be the first one to give me a birthday kiss. Today I am twenty-one!"

The glasses clinked. Tom took hers and put them both down. Then he picked her up and kissed her.

He carried her to the bed and she sank into the fluffy eiderdown. Out of the depth of feathers and cloth, Tom could hear her laugh. She stretched her hands out towards him and, finding his arm, pulled him hard down onto her.

FORTY-SIX

Everything was so quiet and still that Clara could hear Tom's heart as she lay against his chest. They were still lying on top of the bed cover. In the dark she could make out the shape of the window. Everything else was black. Only wanting to feel and hear, she closed her eyes. There was Tom's even breath, the slow beating of his heart, and there was a humming sound in her ear. She felt her own heartbeat and Tom's warm body against hers. Her hands found his chest and she let her fingers play with the short hair.

Softly she felt the end of his rib cage. She put her hand on the solar plexus and made a wish, forever mine. She found the navel and gently, carefully, outlined it. Round and round. Tom started moving. She moved her hand further down his body; it stayed lightly between his legs. Tom moaned and Clara opened her eyes. The window had become lighter. She could just see outlines of the landscape outside.

"Oh, please do not let this night ever end. Do not ever let us grow old. Do not ever make us take each other for granted, or fight, or be apart.

Please make us love each other forever, forever!"

The window grew lighter. Time moved on. The outside world woke up. A rooster crowed, the birds started to sing. She could hear a door open into the backyard. Somewhere a dog was barking and the owner answered. Tom turned towards her and pulled her close.

"Happy birthday," he said. "There is a present for you under the bed."

Clara started to wriggle, but Tom held her firm.

"Please, can I have it now! I promise I will be back in your arms straight away after I have seen what you got me. Promise!"

Tom let her go and watched her pull the flat parcel from under the bed. She ran her hands over it.

"It is a picture! Am I right?"

"Yes, and it has glass on the top. So be careful."

Ripping the paper, the picture appeared. She almost squealed in excitement.

"The Fiddler on the Roof!"

She started singing the song.

Tom knelt beside her on the floor.

"Actually, it is just called, The Fiddler. The art dealer told me that Marc Chagall likes to make his subjects fly about. There was another one I liked where an entwined couple fly over a village. I thought that could have been us. But you liked this one and then I thought this print is very appropriate."

He pointed at a little figure in the background. He felt it could be their lucky angel. Deep down he had called it Esther.

"Look," Clara pointed at a snow covered roof. "Someone has been walking on the roof. Yes, I like the idea to have our own little lucky angel."

She picked up the picture and stood it against the wall. Putting on her oversized jumper she started to collect the clothes they had left on the floor.

"Lovely shirt," she said as she carefully folded it. "I am really very hungry. Let's have some breakfast and then go for a walk. Maybe to the river?"

The kitchen was lovely and warm. Rubin had opened the little stove door and was feeding it small pieces of wood. He watched the flames take hold. The wood crackled and spat. Sparks flew out the stove door. Embers smoked on the floor.

Tom and Clara entered the kitchen to a shower of golden sparks and the smell of burning embers.

Tom slammed the little stove door shut. Rubin looked up.

"Oh, I do enjoy a little fireworks," he said.

Clara brushed sparks off his trousers.

"Are you trying to burn the house down?" she almost shouted at him.

He laughed.

"Happy birthday, my dear. I knew you would not let me burn. Happy birthday!"

He pointed at the table in the corner. It was covered with flowers. In the middle was a pyramid of food. On top, a candle. There was an unruly charm about the decoration. It was not created by a woman's hand.

"Happy birthday, my dear, dear child. Now I have known you for twenty-one years. Now that you are twenty-one I am at long last allowed to take you on as my full time pupil."

He bowed to her.

"And the honour is all mine, my dear."

"Now, let us eat. The plates are somewhere under the decorations. Everyone for coffee? Tom would you please light the candle? It is quite safe up there."

They picked food from the mound. There were cheeses and different meats, pickles and fruit. The base was made of slices of bread. Little balls of butter rolled out of the jumble. Everything was cut into bite-size pieces. As they ate from the pile two clumsily-wrapped parcels emerged, held together with household string.

"Your real present." Rubin smiled. "And you cannot exchange it!"

She brushed the remaining food away and carefully removed the candle. She did not want the light to go out. Clara took the bigger parcel first. It contained a set of the best violin strings one could own. She tried to look excited. The smaller one was a long old-looking box. It had a little button on the side.

"You push the little button in and then you can open the lid," Rubin said, trying not to sound excited.

Clara pushed the button and the lid sprung open.

The most beautiful necklace looked up at Clara.

"For me?"

"Yes, my dear, for you. It was my mother's. You are my most precious child. Now it is yours. The stones will mirror your sparkling eyes. It will look beautiful on your skin."

Clara took the jewellery out of the box and draped it over her hand.

"It must be terribly valuable."

"Money has nothing to do with it. Just enjoy it and maybe one day you will have a daughter. Then you can give it to her.

Now, who would like some more coffee. Soon I have to get ready for the concert in the square. Maybe you two can help with the seats? And I need a word with Tom, alone."

Clara put the necklace back in its box and stood up.

"I leave you to your men's business," she said as she left the room.

Rubin filled his and Tom's coffee cups and settled back in his chair.

"My dear boy, you are probably wondering why the musical guardianship is now handed over to me. As you know I have known Clara all her life. At a very early age, she showed an incredible talent in music. She could read music and knew which black dot, as she called them, belonged to which part of the piano. Her grandmother, Gudrun's mother, taught her. Together they played games on the piano. Clara would sing the notes played for her and when she got bored with that she would dance to her grandma's tunes."

Rubin got up and paced about the kitchen.

"I knew Grandma Asplin very well. She was the sister of a very good friend of mine."

He stopped and looked at Tom, long and hard. Suddenly he shook his head and resumed pacing.

"We all could see the talent in the little toddler and I wanted to take Clara on as a student there and then. But Gudrun stepped in and refused. She wanted her daughter to grow up without being treated like a Wunderkind.

Gudrun said that I could take her as a full time student on her twenty-first birthday. Maybe they all thought I might not be living then! Clara has been my part time student all her life. I stuck to my promise and treated her like any other child."

Rubin suddenly changed. He looked at Tom, worried.

"Just look at her! How she behaves after a concert. She plays like an angel. She soars into a different sphere! She seems to become a different person. But after she has been up there, filled with music, she has a hard time getting back down. You did a wonderful job the way you managed to calm her. I just panicked. Maybe I am too emotional. I do not know if I can take on the responsibility of teaching her to become a concert performer."

He stretched his arms to Tom.

"Would you help me? I feel she loves you very much."

Tom had been taking it all in. Now he nodded.

"Yes, yes, of course I will. But Rubin it is you who will be with her most of the time. You must not push her so hard! You must never get her to the point where she starts to cry or becomes angry. You must show her your love for her. Make her play for you because you love her. Not push her to fame! Music should become fun for her once again. Let her perform! Clara loves to show off, to perform!"

Tom looked into his empty coffee cup.

"The way you handled her yesterday before the concert was wrong. You behaved like a sergeant major!"

Rubin stared at him.

"So, I need to change my teaching techniques?"

"Yes!"

Rubin walked up to Tom.

"If you were standing, my boy, I would give you a big hug. Thank you for that."

Tom slid along the bench behind the table and stood up. They hugged.

Rubin stepped back. His eyes were moist. He studied Tom again.

"By the way," he said. "When I was turning the pages for young Gardel I suddenly remembered something about the name, Gallas, your grandmother's name. It has a familiar ring. I will have a good look at my newspaper clippings and the programs from the last century. I am sure I have seen that name somewhere. Now I must go. My God why did they choose to play the Bolero? I just can't stand it! It is so boring!"

At the door he turned back to Tom.

"When will you come back and make some music? It is in you, my son, and it wants to come out. You will be one of those lucky people who will be able to play just for the love of it."

Clara almost ran Rubin over as she came storming back into the kitchen.

"Not one of them has remembered my big birthday! Not one. I got smiles and a good morning! Nothing more! Everyone is busy carrying chairs and giving me a smile and a well done, great concert. But no birthday wishes."

Pushing her gently aside Rubin laughed.

"Maybe you are not born yet. Maybe you were born after lunch?"

She stormed out again.

Tom found Clara lying on his bed, her face covered with her hair, her arms tightly folded across her chest. She had been crying. Now she was angrily murmuring to herself about how much she hated everyone. She could not understand how her family could have forgotten and ignored her.

Tom listened to the complaints coming from under the strands of hair. She had not noticed him. To make her aware of his presence he stomped on the floor. She opened her eyes and saw her blue dress with Tom's head above it.

"Your mother asked me to wear this. It does not fit. I guess it was meant for you? Everyone is waiting for you at the hotel. Lunch is being served."

"Get out of my dress, you idiot!" she snapped.

Never had he seen anyone get dressed so fast. She pulled the dress on and demanded he zip it. She quickly brushed her hair, rolled it up on the back of her head and held it in place with the big comb. She looked at herself in the little mirror. She sucked her lips, pulling the redness of the blood into them, looked at Tom, nodded and took his hand.

"Promise me that you will never forget me, Tom Dolmer!"

Kissing her he whispered, "Never!"

Crossing the square they could hear the music. She grabbed Tom's hand and ran to the hotel. Totally stunned she stopped in the doorway of the dining room.

A long, beautifully decorated table in blue and white greeted her. Deep blue cornflowers intermingled with white daisies stood in crystal vases. On the white tablecloth were dark blue napkins. Blue candles in shining silver holders created sparkling lights in the glittering, polished glasses. There was an array of cutlery showing the many courses to be served.

A table was set aside for the presents. Already parcels, each beautifully wrapped and tied with ribbons in Clara's favourite colour, had been put upon it.

At the end of the beautiful table sat Oma Gilles. Next to her was her scholarly son, Edward. Behind her Gudrun, Michael and Rubin were playing Happy Birthday on their violins. The candles lit the room with their warm, yellow, flickering light. Everything on the table sparkled. A waiter helped Oma Gilles to stand up.

"Happy birthday, my darling Clara. And many more! May the word happy be with you always," she said, smiling, and then slumped back into her seat.

Everyone started to sing. As he showed Clara to her seat Tom joined the chorus. His strong baritone voice singing along in harmony.

In the kitchen, the most amazing cake was being decorated with twenty-one candles. It was in the shape of a full size violin lying on a bed of marzipan with black lines and dots depicting music. Blue icing-flowers surrounded the cake.

The small group of family and friends left the dining room to retire to the sitting room where the cake was going to be presented.

As the song ended Gudrun pointed to the small table.

"And now, Clara, your presents."

Tom's eyes went to an old, battered violin case that lay beneath the table. He saw how Clara was immediately drawn to it. Gudrun picked the case up and handed it to her.

"This violin is an heirloom. It belonged to someone very special to us all. This instrument will help you to make your music sing. Please use it only on special occasions."

Tom desperately wanted to touch it. But he felt Rubin's hand on his arm signalling a sharp no!

Looking down on his teacher he saw his face was white as snow. Hanging on to Tom's arm Rubin muttered something about sitting down. As Tom helped him to a chair he whispered: "Do not touch that case or the instrument!"

Clara opened the case and took the violin out. No one noticed Rubin putting his face in his hands. She checked the tuning and then put the violin under her chin and started playing.

Rubin began to cry. Tom could see his body slightly shaking. The sound of the violin became softer. It felt as if it was a long way away. Then it was close; so close that it almost touched Tom's body. He could feel the sound, like a breeze. Was there a sweet smell in the breeze? It went round and round, tighter and tighter, almost suffocating him.

Clara stopped playing. Tom was free of the bond; the smell vanished; but Rubin was still crying.

"I think Rubin is not well," Tom said. "I'll take him back to the guesthouse and make sure he is fine. I will be back in no time."

"Thank you," Rubin said when they reached the guesthouse kitchen. Tom got him a glass of Schnapps and sat down next to him.

"You do know whose violin that is?"

Suddenly Tom knew.

"Esther?"

Rubin nodded. His eyes were wide.

"I cannot stand having Clara play it. You must help me stop her from playing that instrument. I cannot bear it, and neither can you! Please stay with me for a while. Please?"

"Esther's violin? But how? How did Gudrun come by it?"

Rubin waved his hand dismissively. Tom saw how it trembled.

"Should you be lying down?"

Rubin nodded. The colour had drained from his face again.

Tom took him upstairs and helped him undress and get into bed. Suddenly, Rubin had become an old, frail man. Tom sat with him, watching his eyes close and hearing his breathing deepen.

Tom didn't know what to do. Could he go back to the party? What about the violin? Did Gudrun find Esther and why? What did she have to do with the Gilles family? He was frightened but he was also curious. If it really was Esther's violin then he desperately wanted to hold it.

He went out into the summer air. It was still slightly light. He walked across the square, through the little laneway and down to the river. He found a large rock close to the water, took a cigarette out of its pack, lit it and pulled the smoke deep into his lungs.

"Must you?" he heard his mother say.

"You don't need that, you have me," Clara whispered.

"I need it!" Tom said.

He kept on smoking, feeling the effect of the nicotine. Slowly he calmed down. Slowly he felt his feet back on the ground. The river was just visible in the vanishing light. He could hear it though, feel its youthful splashes, its energy.

A very strong urge to push Esther out of his life filled his mind. She should go now, she must go! He needed a level head to take care of Clara and his mother and his work.

He was just about to shout out, "Goodbye Esther!" into the noise of the foaming water when a deep fear engulfed him. Would his love of music disappear? Would Esther take it with her? Would he just be *Mr Dolmer, Engineer*?

Did she not lead him to where he was at this very moment? Had she not been with him for a long time?

Getting up he could hear a lot of noise. And then he heard Clara calling him.

He saw the Town Hall lights came on. He'd forgotten that the celebrations were going to continue in the Hall with a dance organised by the young musicians.

Tom looked up at the sky. A few stars slowly appeared. The summer nights were getting shorter.

Clara called again. He could see the light of a torch.

"Tooo-oom! I know you are there somewhere. Tooo-ooom!"

He watched the beam of the light dance about but he did not call back.

He felt apprehensive about joining in. He could not dance. And he knew that all eyes would be upon him, along with little whispers about his and Clara's relationship. He suddenly understood his mother always wanting to be in the security of her ordinary little life, fearing or dreading the unusual, the new. Tom felt like that right now. Where would he like to be? In his room with his map, his violin, his dreams.

Clara called again.

"I know you are here somewhere!"

With that she shone the light in his face.

"You missed the cake and coffee? Why did you leave?"

"I had to take Rubin back. He was not well. Then I can't dance. I've never been to a dance."

"You've never been to a dance? You poor man! I'll teach you, even though I don't think you'll get much chance for dancing."

On stage was a small band. Susanna sat behind an array of drums. There was a boy with a double bass and another with a guitar. Jason was sitting on the edge of the stage, also strumming a guitar. Tom noticed Clara's violin case on the piano. Next to hers was his. Frank Gardel was sitting at the piano trying out a few chords. At the back of the hall were some tables and chairs, the rest cleared for dancing.

Clara dragged Tom to the stage, where only yesterday she had performed Beethoven. She introduced him to Frank and all the other musicians. A young girl walked up to him, playing her clarinet. She walked around him, making up a tune. It reminded him of the meeting with Jack in the park and how he teased him to play whilst he whistled. She seemed intent on provoking him. After she had circled him a few times, she let go a piercing tone, pointed the instrument at him, and walked over to Susanna who took on the challenge and started to softly caress the drums.

The bass player plucked his strings and suddenly some sort of tune emerged. Then the girl walked over to the piano and tried to tempt Frank into joining. Shyly he played a few chords. The clarinet pointed at the violins upon the piano. Making squealing and squeaking noises it pointed at the two cases.

Clara got Tom's violin out of its case and gave it to him. The girl with the clarinet started to skip about the stage playing a happy tune.

'This is a conspiracy,' Tom thought as he took the instrument from Clara. His hands were tingling. They wanted to play. He plucked the strings. They were in tune. Pointing his bow at Clara, he saw her face turn scarlet. He knew now that she was in the plot as well.

Jason laughed,

"Come on, Tom. You can do it. Come and play with Annie. Look how she's flirting with you!"

Annie could not have been more than thirteen. And yes, her music was flirting with him. Again she walked around Tom, playing a sweet and slow tune. Like the Pied Piper she made him follow her to join the bass and drums.

'Oh, why not!' he thought.

He put the violin under his chin and started to mimic Annie's tune. She let go a high squeak, looked at Tom, and started playing in earnest. They stood opposite each other and let fly. The top of her head hardly touched his shoulders. He wondered how such a small body could blow so hard. It looked like she did not breathe.

Susanna was hammering the drums as they all followed Annie's rhythm. Clara stood next to the piano, clapping to the beat.

From behind the hall someone joined in. The room was filling. Someone began to sing wordlessly. The atmosphere was electrifying. Someone called, "Bravo! Bravo!"

Someone else shouted, "Go, man, go!"

It broke the spell for Tom. He looked up and saw the hall full of people and he lost his nerve. He could hear them shouting, "More! More!" as he walked off the stage.

Clara found him at the back of the Town Hall, his violin under his arm.

"Come back and play," she said. "You sounded great!"

He shook his head.

"I'm not a performer. I just enjoy playing. I really just play for myself, for my own enjoyment. You, being a performer, probably can't understand."

He gave her his instrument.

"You'd better return her to her case."

She kissed him.

"Please try again. For me."

He put his arm around her and shook his head.

"Two performers in a relationship would not be good. It would end in professional jealousy.

You will be the performer. I will…well, sort of, just play about. Not that I don't take my playing seriously. Don't get me wrong. I'm just made differently. Now please, take her back and put her to bed. I'd like to stay here for a little while. Out here watching the day go to sleep. I have not much chance these days to watch the natural world."

Tom turned towards the sound of the river. Clara did not move.

"I'll stay here with you. It's a very beautiful night. But first I will put your second love to bed. The cool, damp air will only harm her."

"Thank you for understanding."

Sitting down on the back steps of the old building Tom suddenly felt old. From inside the hall he could hear dancing, music and the excited shouts of the young people. Clara should be in there with her friends dancing, laughing, having youthful fun. Suddenly he was not too sure if there was a future for them. Thinking back on his youth he had to admit there had been very little fun in his life.

Rubin was very quiet during breakfast. He picked at his food and eventually pushed it aside. Tom was occupied with the thoughts of the coming week, his work and his mother.

"Are you returning to town today?" Rubin asked him.

"I am. Why? Do you want to come?"

Rubin nodded. He was still pale.

"My work here is finished," he said.

"It's so quiet," someone said. "Is this a funeral?"

They looked up to see Clara standing there.

"Yum, I can smell a cooked breakfast. Must be Sunday. How are you two on this beautiful morning?"

"We two have decided to return to town today," Tom said.

He poured her a cup of coffee.

"Will you stay on?"

"Me? I am coming with you, of course." She looked at Rubin. "I think I still have one week's holiday left. Don't I, Rubin?"

"Yes, yes!" Rubin waved as if pushing her away. Clara shrugged and pulled a face.

"Are you OK?" she asked him.

"Yes, yes, I am fine. Maybe a bit of a hangover from last night's Schnapps. And then it has been quite a week. I am not that young anymore, you know."

He hesitated, then he added,

"Maybe, Clara, you should leave that old violin you got for your birthday with your mother. I do feel responsible for it. It's old and frail and quite valuable. You should concentrate on your professional instrument."

Clara was standing by the stove, helping herself to the food.

"I do love fried mashed potatoes. Yum, and maybe just one sausage and an egg? Yum!" She joined them at the table. "If I'm not careful I'll be as big as an opera diva!"

She looked at Rubin's and Tom's worried faces.

"Sure," she said. "Sure. I don't think the instrument liked me, anyway. It felt awkward in my hands."

Rubin brightened up.

"Maybe I will just eat a little. I believe fatty food is good for a hangover."

He pulled his plate back towards himself and started eating.

"When are we leaving?" Clara asked.

"When you've said your goodbyes."

Tom drove across the old wooden bridge. It clacked and groaned in farewell. They left the yellow flowers behind. Clara put her head on his shoulder and began to hum a tune. Tom tried his best to just enjoy the drive, the beautiful landscape, and Clara's touch and her scent.

But as they left the mountains behind and the road became busier with trucks and buses and the reminders of town life the harder he had to fight away thoughts of the week ahead.

FORTY-SEVEN

They had slept in his grandfather's big, solid bed. It had been a warm night, the houses of the town letting go the heat bestowed upon them by the summer sun during the day. Clara lay on top of the new linen. She was curled up like a kitten, back towards him. Tom's fingers followed the contour of her body to her shoulders where the soft line disappeared into an unruly tangle of wild blonde hair with a red tinge to it. He did not touch Clara. He did not want to wake her. The windows were wide open. There was no fresh mountain air entering to cool them. The rays of the morning light fell on her body and turned it silky. For a while he watched her breathe, slow and even.

Tom slid out of the high bed and got dressed. He needed to find an open shop and get some breakfast supplies and some coffee.

When he returned he found Clara rummaging through the kitchen cupboards. The pantry door was wide open. The kettle was screaming on the gas stove.

"I was going to surprise you with some breakfast. There is nothing! Not even a grain of coffee."

He put the bag on the table, turned the kettle off, and hugged her tight.

"Oh, I love you, my little Hausfrau."

"Make love to me," she replied. "I like it best before breakfast."

Tom carried her back into his grandfather's room and dropped her carefully on the bed.

"I don't think my grandfather would mind. He was that sort of man. As a child, I did notice him putting his hands on my grandmother's sizeable backside. Only later did I understand what it meant."

"I like your grandfather," Clara purred.

Tom told Clara his day's program over breakfast.

"I'm going to be very busy, but I'll do my best to get away after lunch with my mother. Then we can go out for dinner. There is a great little place not far from here. And you can stay here and practise your scales!"

He ducked as a bread roll came flying at him.

"Go! Off you go, Mr Dolmer. I'll be fine. I can always drop in on my other boyfriend — whinging Jason."

"Where is my hat and coat? My case? Miss Gilles?"

As she jumped up to get his case Tom grabbed her and hugged her tight.

The streets were busy. The tranquility of the soothing country landscape was long gone. As Tom walked he tried to organise his mind. He could hear his grandfather: 'One thought, one action at a time, my boy.' Then he would ruffle Tom's hair. 'Otherwise, my boy, everything ends in disorder.'

There was nothing in order in Tom's head. He tucked the briefcase under his arm. Clara had handed the case to him at his front door. It had felt wrong. It created confusion in his mind.

She was his lover, his friend; not his mother. Not the person wanting to look after him. He did not want anybody to look after him! He walked through a red light and created a cacophony of car horns and the odd bicycle bell. He bowed to the cars and thought of his grandfather.

Tom took a short cut out of the noisy streets to the river. The path along the wide, slow-flowing river was narrow, running along the back of industrial buildings. In his mind was a different river; young, splashing, cold and clean. It was new, straight from its source, unpolluted. Drifting along dreamily he almost fell over a pile of garbage.

He quietly thanked his grandfather for building his factory

outside of town. The building was on a flood plain, surrounded by trees. The wall cleverly constructed on the river's edge protected the factory from floodwaters. Jack had created a natural-looking garden that needed little maintenance. Tom remembered his grandmother's flowerbeds, carefully maintained by her until she was too ill to look after them. Now no one would ever know they were there.

"Make a list," he said to himself as he unlocked the door leading into the reception. He was glad to be early. It gave him time to adjust. He went up the staircase and into his stale and stuffy office, opened the window, and looked out onto the river.

'It will be a hot day today,' he thought as he walked to his desk.

He found a piece of paper for his list. But he could not think of what to write. Biting his pencil, he tried to push a new thought out of his head.

'Where did the Gilles family get Esther's violin from?'

He wanted to ask Rubin, but his teacher's reaction when he saw the instrument stopped Tom from doing so. And how did he know that it once belonged to Esther? It was like an electric shock had gone through his body when Clara took the violin out of its case?

'I was only ten years old when I met Esther!' he suddenly thought.

He put the pencil down, ran his fingers through his hair, loosened his tie and undid the first button on his shirt.

"I need a smoke!" he said out loud.

There was a knock on the door and Joyce came in with his morning coffee.

"I thought you had given up!" Joyce laughed. "Hard isn't it? How was your weekend? Tell me later. Clara is on the phone. I'll put her through."

It was only five minutes past eight. Clara knew that work at the factory started at eight. She knew that Tom would be there.

"I miss you already," she said. "I thought I could come over after your work and we could go for a swim. I can bring some food. We can have a picnic. What do you think? Isn't there a sidearm of the river just downstream from you? Might we be able to skinny-dip there? Wouldn't that be romantic? I'll bring something against mosquitos. Say yes, please!"

"Yes, yes, yes. But listen. I'll be with my mother at about one. That will take an hour. Then I must see her doctor and, all going well, I'll be able to take the rest of the day off. Come here about four. If anything comes up you might have to wait a bit. Bring a book. I'll get a bottle of wine."

He could hear a little squeal on the other end of the line. Clara was happy. "Love you. See you then."

Joyce returned with Tom's personal mail.

"Don't forget you have a meeting with the solicitor tomorrow," she said. "And please confirm with me when our next staff meeting is to be.

And, there is a Mr Goldmark on the phone. He sounded very impatient. Do you want to take the call?"

"Can we have the staff meeting this morning? And do you have time for a little private chat later? And ask Angus to bring the car around at twelve-thirty and please ask him to wait for me. I'd like a chat."

He was thumbing through the mail when the phone rang.

"Tom! Why do I have to wait so long before they put me on to you? I need to see you!"

"Good morning, Rubin, and how are you on this beautiful morning?"

"Beautiful, is it? Can you come and see me today?"

"I can't get away, Rubin. My day is already too full!"

"You have no time for your teacher! Your mentor!"

"I can come tomorrow. Morning coffee at nine? I can stay until eleven. How does that sound?"

There was a silence. Tom dropped another advertising brochure in the bin.

"Alright, then. That will have to do," Rubin said reluctantly. "I'll see you at Havelka's."

Returning to his mail Tom came across a handwritten letter addressed to him. He opened it. It puzzled him. A hand written letter. No company letterhead. The shaky writing was that of an old person.

"Dear Mr Dolmer,

I found your address in the Engineering section of the telephone book. I need somebody to come and fix the plumbing in my house where I live alone. Could you come?"

The letter went on in great detail about the serious problems the writer was having with their plumbing. It was signed, *A. Singer (Miss)*.

Tom scratched his head. On the one hand this had nothing to do with him. On the other...well, it would take his mind off his problems. And helping someone would make him feel a lot better. He found the address of a plumber he knew and whose work he was confident in. He smiled as he formulated a reply.

Back at his desk after the staff meeting he thought,

'List! What's next?'

The paper on his desk was blank. His head still full of Esther and her violin, of Clara and her family, and of the big question about his grandmother. He just wanted it all to go away. He hated secrets, unsolved situations.

"You wanted to see me?" Joyce broke his thoughts, standing in the doorway with a tray of coffee and cake. "If it's private, we might as well have a good time. Over by the window?"

Tom had started to chew on his pencil again.

"Hello Tom, I have cake!" she laughed. "Leave the pencil alone!"

They sat at the coffee table by the window, Tom smoking, Joyce sitting straight in the armchair. Her tight skirt did not allow her to lounge like Tom, who had stretched out his long legs.

"I'm sorry," he began, "As this will be work for you, but just with your finger in the telephone book.

I need to find a furniture removalist to move the Huber's out of their flat and into the Home. Then I need someone to remove the furniture left behind and someone to repaint the walls and, if necessary, re-polish the floors and whatever else needs doing. I'm hoping they can be relocated next week.

Today I'll see how mother is and then slowly work on a plan to get her settled back into one of the flats."

Joyce was taking notes.

"Is Clara going to live with you?"

Tom shook his head. "Only this week."

"Something wrong between you?"

Tom laughed.

"Everything is great! Oh, by the way, Joyce, do you know how to remove lichen from stone or marble?"

Puzzled she looked at him.

"Remove lichen? What for and where from and why?"

He looked at her with slight embarrassment.

"It's to do with my grandparents, my mother's people. I've finally discovered their burial place.

The stone is overgrown with lichen and I would very much like to see what is written on the large white marble slab on top of the grave. It looks like a poem. One can hardly read the names."

He hesitated. She could see his uncertainty as he continued.

"I want to take my mother to see it. She's never seen it before. She has agreed to come. But I'm worried that it might upset her.

Oh dear, my mother. I always get a strange feeling in my chest when I have to go and see her. She changes all the time. Sometimes I feel that I need to put on protective armour."

Tom got up and walked back to his desk.

"Thanks, Joyce. I must get on with work. I'd like to take the afternoon off. Maybe we can talk about all this tomorrow. I need to be in early."

Margret wore a floral summer dress. She'd had a haircut. Tom was late and she looked around anxiously. She had so much to tell him. And she wanted to know how his weekend was.

She shifted along the bench into the sun.

'I should have brought a cardigan,' she thought as she wrapped her arms around her chest. Then she heard his steps. Immediately she straightened up and unfolded her arms, looking nonchalantly around.

"You look lovely! I love that dress, and there's something different with your hair. Do they have hairdressers in the hospital? Sorry I'm late."

Sitting down next to her, Tom saw she was slightly shaking.

"Are you cold?"

She nodded.

"Well, let's go and get a cup of tea."

Margret removed the slice of lemon with her spoon. He noticed her hand shaking. A young nurse brought her a blanket and gently folded it over her thin body.

"Thank you," she said to the nurse with a smile. She turned back to Tom as the nurse left.

"She is a lovely young woman. You would never think that she has two children. Her husband also works in the hospital."

The marked change in her mood took Tom by surprise. He was unsure of how to react to it.

"Are you going to have some lunch?" she asked him.

He felt the nervousness in his stomach as he replied.

"I'm actually meeting Clara after work and we're going to have a picnic by the river."

"You should have brought her here with you and we could have had lunch together. Now please tell me how your weekend was?"

"The most relaxing part was the fresh air, the clean river, the slow pace. Maybe one day I can take you there."

Margret smiled.

"That would be nice. Dr Ries has found me a new counsellor; a lady only a bit younger than me. Someone who actually has lived and experienced life and does not talk like a textbook. She has taken me out of the group therapy sessions. We meet every day and talk about our lives and our families.

The young nurse who came is also lovely. She has shown me pictures of her children and I've told her about you. I did mention Clara, but I know so very little about her."

Margret picked up her cup with both hands.

"You know," she continued, "now that I've sorted out the staff, got rid of the ones I don't like, I quite enjoy being in Rehab. I have taken to watching the television in my room. But I do miss not having an aim in life. Life seems so pointless. I need to do things, be of use!"

"What about your knitting?"

Margret held up her shaking hands.

"There must be something they can do to stop the hands from shaking?"

"It is apparently old age," Margret answered.

"Old age? That's outrageous! You are not old! Yes old, but not really old, like grandpa was! I'll talk to Dr Ries about that."

Margret's lunch arrived. Tom ordered a sandwich. As she ate, he said,

"Shall we go and visit dad's grave this week?

We could go Wednesday morning and have lunch at the little café just below the creek?"

Margret nodded.

"I'll pick you up in the car. I'll be able to drive the car to the grave. You can get some flowers. I bring a chair for you. What do you say?"

Again, she nodded.

He could see that she was tiring.

"Shall I walk you back to your room?"

She pushed her plate away, sighed, and nodded again.

They walked slowly to the entrance where Tom took one of the wheelchairs. He wheeled her down the long corridor, all the way to the end of the Rehabilitation wing of the hospital. She was in her new room, overlooking the garden. He helped her back into her bed.

He walked out of the hospital deep in thought, wondering what had caused the change in her mood; wondering how permanent it might be. And then wondering how he could possibly handle it if she really had changed.

FORTY-EIGHT

The river was low; the swimming hole brown and muddy. Clara was not going to even put a toe into that water. Amongst a swarm of little flies she tried to arrange the picnic. She was determined to fulfil her promise to stage an outdoor dinner. But as soon as she put food on the plates the flies swarmed onto it. Desperately she waved serviettes over it. In the end she covered the whole spread with towels and went to sit in the car with the windows wound up.

Tom joined her and they sat in the car looking at their covered spread. Clara started to cry. Tom found the situation funny and started to laugh.

Clara attacked him.

"I tried! I tried!" she shouted. "I am just useless! Useless!"

Getting hold of her hammering fists he bent towards her and gave her a kiss.

"Oh, I love you when you are angry. Now, let's be brave and get out there amongst the wildlife, collect the food and then find another place to have our picnic. There's somewhere special I want to share with you."

He drove to the circle of trees. She looked at them in astonishment and then at him.

"Let's find your tree," he said.

It was the silver birch. Excited, she pressed the button and listened intently to the voice. She reminded him of young Thomas when he had listened. She listened twice. And then again. When the voice came to the line,

'You are a silver birch woman
I will give you your Latin name BETULA.
Full of melody is my green crown"

she smiled at Tom.

"I like that line," she said, holding him tight.

That evening sleep did not want to come to Tom. Looking over the soft contours of Clara's curled-up body against the slight light of the summer night shining through the window he, for the first time since she'd moved into his life, felt overwhelmed by her presence.

They had made his grandfather's room theirs. Clara did not belong to the rest of the flat. It was full of ghosts; especially his mother's. No matter how hard he tried his mother was always about the apartment. Tom could not ever see Clara being able to cope with her moods, her sarcasm, her heartless approach to everything.

He quietly got up and put on his shirt and sneaked into his old bedroom where he sat on his bed. Leaning up against the wall he pulled his legs up and clutched his knees. He tried to rock gently. That always used to help him relax.

The thoughts kept on coming, like a train with a different problem in each carriage. Mother, Rubin, Clara, Esther's violin, the grave, Grandmother Lamberg, work. He saw the little stone angels playing on top of the gravestone. He tried to visualise his delicate grandmother. Again he puzzled over his mother's apparently changed moods. Could he trust her to stay that way?

He paced up and down in his room. 'I must make a list! I must sort out all these situations and deal with them one at the time,' he told himself.

Stopping by the hardly visible map of the world he touched the words, Circumstance, and Disappointment.

How could he not disappoint any of his friends when circumstances got in the way? He ran his finger along a river and thought of his dad. He jabbed at the map. 'I will stick to my promise. I will make sure that mother is well looked after. But, Dad, I cannot live with her!'

Next week he would organise his life. Back to taking Monday off with lessons in the afternoon. Practice after work. Weekends with Clara. That sounded simple enough to him. It worked before. It would work again!

He made a cup of coffee and went into the dark living room. He turned on the standard lamp by his chair, chose a record, put his headphones on and started listening to his beloved music. He turned the light off to allow all his senses to be involved with the sounds of the violin. The window was closed but he could feel a slight breeze surround him. With the feeling of utter peace and the memory of Esther Tom fell asleep.

A gentle kiss woke him. He looked up in confusion, then he saw who it was.

"Hello," Clara said. "If you can't sleep you can talk to me."

"That is something I still have to learn," Tom answered.

FORTY-NINE

Sitting by the window in Havelka's café Rubin put a folder on the table. It was markedConcert Programs.

He pushed it towards Tom .

"Good that I'm a hoarder... No, a collector. I just do not throw away anything that involves music. There, have a look. I've removed the ones of no importance to you."

Tom stared at the well-thumbed folder, suddenly afraid to open it.

Rubin sipped his coffee and smiled.

"Did I have a good time reminiscing? What a life I've had! Wonderful. Wonderful. And filled with music and people I loved and still do."

His eyes grew vague as he wandered into his beautiful past.

'Oh, Esther he thought. You and I will have to make sure that this young man continues to love his music.'

Suddenly, with a loud crash, he put his flat hand, thin fingers splayed out, on the folder.

"Before I let you have a look at this card, I need you to give me your word, your absolute promise to stand by Clara. Next week her holidays are over. I've entered her in a competition for young violinists. She is not that young anymore, but she got in. Clara does not know yet.

From next week on she will have to practice every day. You have to help her be focused. You have the ability to do so. Please? Clara will have tantrums. She'll hate me, cry and generally behave like a spoiled little girl. I've seen it all before. Not with Clara, with someone else."

He studied Tom thoughtfully.

"Now, do you really want to dive into the past?"

"I thought that was the reason for this meeting?"

Rubin nodded at the folder.

Tom slowly opened it.

On the very top was an invitation to a house concert at the Honourable Vice Admiral Franz Benedict von Staden's private residence. The paper had yellowed and it was hard to decipher the brown writing. Tom could just read some of the songs to be performed. Tom picked it up cautiously. Silverfish had started to feast on the paper. He squinted to see better. Rubin noticed and handed him a magnifying glass. He came prepared.

There was a slightly foxed and faded photo. There was a name under the photo. Tom almost dropped the magnifying glass:

Sophia Grete Lamberg.

Tom stared at the name and then at Rubin.

Rubin smiled.

"My parents went. They had friends in high places. Keep on looking, there is quite a lot of information to be found."

But Tom had found what he was looking for.

"I need to make a copy of this. May I borrow it?"

"You can have it, my dear boy. It is part of your past. You have to take it! My parents will not mind, and I have already too much stuff. You have seen the piles of it in my room. Take it! I will find you a big envelope."

Rubin looked down on the bench seat.

"Oh, look I just happen to have one here. Things you find here at Havelka's!"

Tom smiled at Rubin, who was looking extremely pleased with himself. He placed the card very carefully into the large envelope and put it in one of his folders in his briefcase.

"What are you going to do with this information? Tell your mother?"

Tom laughed.

"If it were that easy. No, I will talk to her therapist and to Dr Ries. Then we will hatch a plan. But now I have to go. Duty calls."

Tom straightened up his tie and put on his jacket.

"Thank you, Rubin. Thank you so much! And I'll see you Monday at the usual time."

"Don't forget your fiddle," Rubin said in farewell.

Tom turned to leave and saw the phone sitting by the cash register where Mr Havelka stood. He pointed at it and indicated he wanted to make a call. Mr Havelka smiled and nodded and stepped away.

Tom dialled his home. It was odd to hear Clara answer.

"I hope you've been practising," he said.

She snorted.

"Are you with that monster who calls himself a teacher?"

"I'm just leaving. Can you meet me at my office?"

"Why? What's going on?"

"I'll show you. Come soon."

He dug in his pocket for a coin for the phone. Mr Havelka shook his head sternly.

Returning to his office Tom found a note on his desk:

For Mould and Mildew Stains
A clean bucket.
Hydrogen peroxide.
4 litres of water.
Protective gloves.
Soft bristled brush.
1 clean rag or cloth for cleaning.

Tom looked from the list to the bucket that stood next to his desk, in it all the necessary items for cleaning his grandparents' grave. He picked up his phone.

Joyce answered.

"Something wrong?"

"You are the best, the best, the best! Please come to my office."

She came in with her notebook and pencil.

"No, no, you will not need them. Please sit."

Tom pointed at the armchairs.

"Thank you so much for the information and for all the cleaning material. You are wonderful. Clara calls people like you a brick. I suppose it means solid and reliable. Where did you find this information?"

"In a book! I just went to the library and they handed me this book about all sorts of cleaning and other household information. How was your morning?"

He took the envelope from his briefcase and put it on the small table. Very carefully he removed the card.

"Can you read this?"

Joyce shook her head. "I'll need a magnifying glass."

Tom gently touched the photo.

"Sophia Grete Gallas. My grandmother."

Joyce touched it with reverence.

The door behind her opened. Clara stood there uncertainly.

"Are you having a meeting? I'll come back, but you did say to come quickly."

"No Clara. Come in. Have a look at this."

Clara touched the card with the same reverence as Joyce had shown.

"Sophia Grete Gallas. It has such a beautiful sound to it."

"This card is almost one hundred years old! I hope I can get it copied, maybe repaired. Something must be done to preserve it. Do you think we can get the picture enhanced? I wonder where I can go to get that done?"

"I'll find out," Joyce said quietly.

"You know," Tom continued, "my grandfather might have still been alive when I was a little boy. I wonder what happened between my mother and her parents?"

Clara touched Tom gently. She never had to struggle with such mysteries.

"We will find out. Yes, between all of us, we will find out," she said.

Tom sat down, suddenly exhausted.

Joyce put the card back into the envelope.

"I'll start making inquiries," she said. "And about moving the Huber's, I've got a removal van for next Wednesday. The painter and carpenter would like to have a meeting with you at the flat some time after that. Perhaps Friday?"

Tom nodded, his thoughts still with the photo of his grandmother.

Joyce smiled at Clara and left them alone.

"Oh Tom, how exciting!" Clara said. "You have a musician in your family tree. No wonder you love music so much. And your voice, you must have got that from your grandmother?"

He looked at her with moist eyes. It felt as if he was looking at her through a wet window. She looked beautiful. He felt he could see someone else in her image. Rubbing his eyes he said,

"Let's go for a walk. Maybe to my big tree?"

Without parting the curtain of willow branches Tom stepped into his beloved spot by the river. This time he did not sit down on the large root. He walked to the edge of the water, spread out his arms, and screamed,

"Take me away! Take me away!"

Clara did not know what to do. Never had she seen him like that. Her steadfast, reliable, balanced friend and lover. She buried her face in his back, feeling the tension there, and quietly mumbled,

"You can talk to me. I am your friend. I might be able to help?"

He turned around and put his arms around her.

"I'm not used to sharing my thought, troubles and fears."

"Let's start by sitting down and then just let go. Let go and speak as if you are making your music."

Leaning against the trunk of the age-old tree, the tree that had listened to him so often, Tom tried to let go of his troubled thoughts. But he did not know how. Patiently Clara waited. She put her head on his shoulder and started humming a tune. Like a gentle wind, the music wound itself around them, and then there was the elusive, wonderful smell.

'Esther likes us being together,' he thought.

The thought helped him begin to talk.

"How am I going to convince my mother that the memory of her childhood is complete fiction? What am I going to do with her and my life when she comes home? I cannot live with her. She sucks all happiness out of me! How can I manage to fit you, my dear, dear Clara into a life with my mother? I have promised my father that I will take care of her. I will not break my promise. Who can answer those questions? Can you?"

Looking through the hanging branches he watched the river, moving, moving, never stopping.

"My mother would like you to come and visit her," he added.

"Well, isn't that a good sign?"

Tom laughed: "As long as she's in a good mood! She was then. But she can be horribly vicious!"

"I can cope with that. Shall I come with you tomorrow?"

"Tomorrow we visit my father's grave and then, after lunch, I'm going to clean her parents' gravestones."

"I'm coming! I can meet both your mother and your father. If it doesn't work out, I'll just sneak away. Easily done in a cemetery."

FIFTY

Margret sat on the edge of her bed. She was both nervous and excited. Tom had said that Clara would be coming along. Why would she want to come to a cemetery? 'Strange girl,' she thought. From her first meeting with Clara, she remembered a very pretty, but giggly young girl.

'No, it will not last,' had been her first assessment. And now?

The nurse came in with a wheelchair and Margret's jacket.

"Just in case you get chilly. And I have put a small blanket on the chair.

I think I saw your son coming up the corridor with a most attractive young woman. They make a lovely couple."

Margret said nothing.

"Have a nice day, Mrs Dolmer," she said.

She stepped aside to let Tom and Clara enter the room.

Clara was shocked at the changes in Margret. She looked small, thin and brittle. Clara felt her heart go out to Tom's mother. She gently took Margret's arm.

"May I help you into the wheelchair?"

Margret hesitated and then whispered,

"Thank you, Clara."

Tom took hold of the wheelchair. He bent down and gave his mother a kiss on the forehead. "How are you today? You look lovely."

She did not answer him.

Margret did not know where to begin her silent conversation with her beloved Theo. Hands tightly knit together she sat there staring at the bunch of flowers Clara had bought.

'Oh Theo, help me! Oh, why did you leave me! I just wish I could be with you in the dark, the stillness forever and ever.'

Behind her, sitting on the bench under the tree, Tom was talking to his dad. He asked... No he begged for help to make Margret get better. To accept his life. To start loving him just a little.

Clara stood there uncertainly, feeling the tension. She did not understand how mother and son could coexist with such negative energies around them. She also talked to Theo.

'You do not know me. I will do my very best to help build a bridge between Tom and his mother. He needs her love. She needs to learn to unlock her heart. I promise!'

A sudden gust of wind blew their shade-giving umbrella over. Margret started. She called to Tom.

"I want to go!"

At the gate Clara bought another bunch of flowers.

"For your room," she said to Margret.

Outside the café they helped Margret into the wheelchair. The tall chestnut trees now in full leaf provided plenty of shade. Tom had a lot of trouble getting the wheelchair to roll over the gravel. Clara showed him how it was best done.

"My Oma is in a wheelchair," she smiled at Margret.

They found a table and Tom placed his mother's chair facing the door of the café.

"So, you are a musician?"

Margret looked expressionlessly at Clara.

"Well, actually I am a long way from being a musician. Yes, I have been playing all my life, but it takes more than that to be recognised as a musician. And next week, when my holidays are over, the hard work will start."

Margret looked at Tom.

"But Tom told me that you are very good?"

"Maybe?"

Clara looked at Tom with a frown.

"Yes, maybe. But there is so much more than just being good at playing. I now need to learn to perform under pressure; to perform to a concert hall full of strangers. I have the feeling that my next big hurdle will be to play in competitions."

Margret's hard eyes examined her.

"You seem to have grown up since I last met you."

Clara put her hand on Tom's shoulder.

"That is all his fault!"

Then she laughed. Tom blushed. Margret's expression did not change.

'She is very pretty and witty and clever.' Margret thought 'She better not hurt my boy. She better not take him away from me!'

"So, where would you say Tom will go with his music making?"

"I would put Tom in the category of a professional man who loves music. A bit like my father, and also my mother. They are very much involved in music. But it is not their whole life."

Clara had kept eye contact with Margret. She now understood Tom. These cold eyes could pull all happiness out of you.

Back at her room in the rehabilitation centre, Margret wanted to know when they would take her home.

"Dr Ries is back from her holidays on Monday. We'll decide then. I'll have to find some daycare for you. We'll see. Now have a rest. I'll see you tomorrow for lunch."

The nurse came and tucked her into bed. Margret watched Clara arrange the flowers in the vase. Satisfied with the arrangement she kissed Margret on both cheeks.

"Have a good rest."

Margret took Clara's hand in a hard grip and held onto it.

"Will you come tomorrow?"

Clara nodded.

FIFTY-ONE

They walked into the gates of the town's Central Cemetery, both wearing the overalls he'd brought from work. Clara carried a bunch of everlasting flowers. Tom carried the bucket with the cleaning material. In his pocket he had two small toys; a little car and a doll. No one had visited the grave since Tom had been there. Clara pointed at the two little angels.

"So sad. Oh, so sad. The whole situation is just so depressing. How? Why did Margret never know?"

She sat down on a bench in the shade.

Tom sat next to her and put his arm around her shoulder.

"You were wonderful this morning. Thank you. I am so proud of you. The way you handled my mother. I was on tenterhooks all the time. I think we are making progress."

"It is so sad! Your poor mother. Poor you!"

She stood up and started to cry. Then, with a loud sniff, she pointed at the grave.

"Let's start!"

She read the instructions on the bottle of hydrogen peroxide.

"This is terrible poisonous stuff! Can't we just scrape it off? Can I borrow your knife, please?"

She knelt down and gently scraped the knife under the lichen. It came off in a large slither. Then another and another.

"Look!" she said excitedly. "Look, it is a German word! It says something like *Schoene.*"

She stood up with excitement.

"Of course *Die Schoene Muellerin;* a song by Franz Schubert. I forgot who wrote the words. My mother has the record!"

"Who are you and why are you dressed like that!"

The caretaker stared angrily at them.

"We get a lot of strange-looking people here, but I've never seen someone in a boiler suit. Who are you? And please get off that grave!"

Tom smiled placatingly and stretched out his hand to the angry man.

"We are trying to get the lichen off so we can read the poem. This is the grave of my grandparents. I have only recently found it."

The man looked at them, and then at the bottle of peroxide

"Terrible stuff! Don't use that! I'll get you something better."

He returned with his bottle of something.

"This keeps the lichen away! This gravestone's been unattended for a long time but a week ago I noticed fresh flowers."

"That was me," Tom told him. "Has anyone else left any?"

The caretaker looked sheepish.

"Sometimes I do. I just love those little angels and, I must admit, I feel sorry for the couple. No one caring for them. All the other graves get flowers at least once a year. I hope you don't mind!"

Clara hugged him impulsively.

"What a caring man you are!"

Carefully the caretaker brushed his special solution onto the lichen. After a while, using a small scraper, he lifted a large flat piece off and Clara started to read.

THE BROOK'S LULLABY

Good night, good night!
Till all shall awaken
Sleep away your joy,
Sleep away your sorrow.

The full moon is rising,
The mist dispersing.
And the sky above,
How boundless it is!

She began to cry and went back to the bench. Tom tried to comfort her. She pushed him away.

"Leave me alone. Go away!"

The two men started on the headstone and soon the names were clearly visible:

Sophia Margarete Lamberg nee Gallas 1874-1904

Wolfgang Lamberg 1871-1952

And under the little angels:

George and Irene

Tom sat down beside Clara. He took out a cigarette and offered one to the caretaker, who shook his head. Tom looked at Clara who said nothing. Tears were running down her face and her eyes were all puffed up.

"I could have met my grandfather," Tom slowly said. "My mother's father. I could have learned so much about my family. Look at the mess his absence has left behind."

He turned to Clara.

"You will help me to solve this mystery?"

Sobbing she hugged him tight. He could hear a little, "Yes."

The caretaker had sneaked away. When he came back later to finish cleaning the lettering he saw two little toys — a car and a doll — sitting on the gravestone. He smiled and gently touched them.

FIFTY-TWO

Tom was late for his violin lesson and Rubin was angry.
"Have you done any practice at all?" was his greeting. "Or do I have to stuff something into my ears? You know, I have very sensitive ears!"

Tom shook his head guiltily. There had been no chance whatsoever to even look at his instrument.

"Come back when you at least have done your scales! And I mean every day! All of them! For at least half an hour!"

Ill-tempered, Rubin walked around his piles of papers, holding his hands over his ears. Then he he jabbed his finger at Tom.

"Why do you bother to come? Why do I bother trying to teach you? Oh, Tom, let's go and have a coffee."

In the cafe, Rubin said to him.

"I heard you play with that little girl at the dance party. You have the music in you, no doubt about that. But you have no discipline whatsoever. You just want to make music, any kind of music, your music. You will never make a real musician! I mean a real one."

"But, but I want to make my violin sing like…"

Angrily, Rubin cut him off.

"You will never play like her. She had the music in her and she had the discipline to play the notes in front of her. She grew up with music. Her parents loved music. Oh, Tom, it takes more than just wanting to be like her, play like her."

He got up and started pacing.

Tom patted the seat beside him.

"Come and sit down and let's talk about something else."

"NO!" Rubin shouted at Tom. "You asked me if I still want to teach you and the answer is, YES. I might be able to make you, sort of, play the way the dots on the paper tell you to."

"What is wrong, Rubin? Why are you so upset. Come and talk to me."

Rubin sat down. He stared around the room and then at Tom. "Is it too early for a glass of wine?"

Tom shook his head. Mr Hawelka brought two glasses of wine.

They quietly sat and sipped their drinks.

"I'm sorry, Tom," Rubin eventually said. "Managing Clara is so hard. I've got her into a competition. If she wins I lose her. She would have to continue with a teacher in the city. We might both lose her. I do want her to win and get on with her dream to become a concert violinist. She dreams of travelling the world, to play in the best concert halls. And she can do it. But I will lose her."

"We will never lose Clara, never. The city's only one and a half hours away from us. That's nothing!"

"Do you know what it is like to become a top musician these days? The regime is gruesome! They have to practice like athletes have to train! And you need the most ferocious memory. The competition is huge. Everyone wants to be famous! Oh yes, you wait, we will lose her!"

Rubin lifted his empty glass towards the kitchen door.

"I'll have another one, please."

"Her training will take years!" Tom said.

"That's the only consolation I have. I might be dead by the time she leaves. But then, I would love to see her on stage, hear her play in one of the big concert halls.

The Gilles have a flat in the city. Clara probably will move in there. Then she will meet a musical young man and puff she will be gone. Lost to us both!"

Tom shook his head.

"No, never. We have a very strong bond between us."

"Ha! That's what I thought with Esther! Suddenly she was gone! I still do not know why!"

Thick tears ran down Rubin's grey cheeks and disappeared into his carefully trimmed beard. He punched his fist into the air, then stretched out his fingers, and said,

"Puff, and she was gone!"

Tom offered him his handkerchief. Rubin ignored it and continued.

"Clara is the child Esther and I never had. I love her as if she was. I cannot bear the thought of losing her as well."

Tom looked hard at Rubin.

"Rubin, we cannot look into the future. We do not know what it will bring. Please do not dwell in such sad, negative thoughts. I love Clara, more than I ever have loved anyone before. If she should find her dream and maybe another love and be happy doing so, I can only join her in her happiness."

He took another cigarette out of the packet but did not light it.

"You told me once that you thought it was, as you put it, a waste of time to dwell in the past. You said we should fill our short lives with the thought of future. History, you said, was the past. It was the future we needed to look towards."

Rubin pointed at the cigarette.

"Are you going to light that? Go on, it'll kill you. Yes, death! I am an old man with lots of big words. There is a lot of past in my life. More so than future. I do live in the past now. What I told you were just big words. Big words that give me the air of looking clever.

But I am not clever. I am just a little old Jewish man on the doorstep of wherever we go when we die. They call it Passover. Pass over ...to where?"

He ran his beautifully sculpted old hands over his face, brushing away his tears. Then he looked long and hard at Tom.

"Yes, I will continue to teach you. You will never be very good, and I will keep on teaching you. That way you will never leave. We have a bond, you and I. No, we have two! Double strength!"

He put out his hands to Ton. Tom held them. They were cold. For a long time, they sat like that. Rubin gently gave Tom's hands a slight squeeze.

"Yes, two bonds. Clara and Esther!"

He let go of Tom's hands and got up.

"See you next Monday. Scales, every day, for at least one half hour!"

FIFTY-THREE

In the backyard of the Gilles property Tom could hear the sound of Clara's violin.

It faltered.

"Again, from the top," Gudrun said.

He heard Clara's angry screech of the bow across the strings. Then the study piece began again.

Michael came down the iron spiral staircase.

"Just a few more minutes and she'll be finished."

He pointed to the table under the big walnut tree and turned on the little lanterns hanging from its branches.

"Are you still playing?" Michael asked him.

"When I have the time. There is so much happening right now. And Rubin is beside himself with worry about losing Clara to the city."

"The silly old man! Clara will only be having three lessons a week there. The rest of the time she will be here and under his guidance. He is so dramatic. Gudrun is not going to allow her to be totally involved with her music. Clara is not stable enough. After every serious performance, she sinks into some sort of depression. I was told it happens to overstrung artists, whatever their art. Gudrun will not let her out of her sight until she can see that Clara can manage the pressure of performing."

Michael lit a cigarette, then continued,

"Apparently there was someone in her family who went slightly mad. It is some family secret. Very hush, hush. Well, I suppose one does not want to admit that there is a little madness in the family. Anyway, I leave that all to Gudrun."

He leaned back in his chair.

"I believe your mother is almost ready to go home. How are you going to handle that?"

Tom shrugged.

"Find some home help, I suppose? There was a suggestion of employing the young nurse from Rehab. My mother likes her."

"There are agencies for that sort of thing," Michael replied.

The music stopped.

"We'll talk about that later. Now we'd better join the ladies."

Clara came out of the house and stood at the top of the stairs. She wore shorts. A sudden breeze blew her hair back. It pressed her thin blouse onto her body. Tom found himself staring. Michael noticed.

"She looks like a Botticelli angel, doesn't she? This daughter of mine looks so much like her mother. God, I do love them all!"

"Who is Botticelli?" Tom looked puzzled at Michael.

"Oh, he was an Italian painter from the fifteen-hundreds. I will show you some of his pictures. I have a book upstairs."

Clara had joined them.

"Who are you talking about?"

"An Italian painter."

"Not Botticelli!" Clara interrupted Tom. Angrily she looked at Michael. "I am nothing like his stupid angels. I wish you'd allow me to just be me!"

She had moved her chair close to Tom and put her head on his shoulders. He pushed the strands of hair out of her face and gently kissed her.

"I think I will help Gudrun with the dinner," Michael said.

After dinner Michael put a large book on the coffee table and invited Tom to join him. On the dust jacket was a portrait of a young woman, her golden hair loose and windblown. The oval face tilted slightly to one side. Tom put his fingers over the figure's lips.

"Clara," he whispered. "The skin, the hair, the shape of the face and the eyes. But not the mouth. I see what you mean, Michael."

Clara saw them and shouted,

"Don't you show him the whole figure! I don't look like that! I think I will get my hair cut off, like Susanna! Then you can never call me a Botticelli angel again!"

Calmly Gudrun put the book back on the shelf with all the other art books.

"Anyone for fruit salad? Clara come and help me in the kitchen."

"Speaking of Susanna," Tom said. "Where is she?"

"She's still up in the mountains, working in the kitchen of the hotel. She's decided to take a year off before going to university. She wants to travel. For that she needs money."

Michael settled back in the armchair.

"What a day! The hospital is a nightmare at the moment. Summer holidays! Good for the ones who get time off!"

He turned to Tom.

"What is the problem in finding a nurse for your mother? As I mentioned before, there are agencies where you can apply for help. You can't just pluck a nurse out of the hospital."

Gudrun and Clara returned with the fruit salad.

Gudrun placed herself in front of Michael, hands on her hips.

"Margret has managed to upset most of the nurses in the hospital, not to mention her young therapist. Once back home she is Tom's responsibility, and I for one will not stand by and watch him struggle with this problem.

She likes Dr Ries and Andrea Coder. The three of us will help Tom as much as we can. You, in your capacity, can pull strings and make things happen. Our strategy is to be able to arrange for that young nurse who Margret likes to get some time off from her hospital duties."

She thumped a bowl of fruit in front of Michael.

"Tom has enough on his plate. For goodness sake can't you see that?"

The embarrassment was too much for Tom. He excused himself and went out in the garden. As he climbed down the spiral staircase he lit a cigarette. The little lanterns hanging from the walnut tree still shone into the dark foliage. Walking into the darkness of the garden, he could hear the argument between Gudrun and Michael drifting through the open window.

The sound of someone playing the violin filled the darkness. Clara leaned against the table under the big tree, the little lanterns slightly illuminating her. She was playing and crying out,

"Stop it! Stop it! Oh, please, stop fighting!"

Tom started singing to her music. She stopped playing and looked about for him. In her left hand, between her fingers, Clara held her instrument on the scroll. With her blonde hair undone she looked like Esther. He saw the tall slender woman with her white hair slightly undone, holding her violin between her fingers on the scroll. She was smiling at him. He felt a chill run through him.

Then Clara saw him and smiled.

"I hate it when Mummy gets angry! Now I try to heal them with my music but I don't think they can hear me over their shouting. Daddy can be such a beast!"

She stretched her arms towards Tom.

"Oh, Tom, come and give me a hug. I need your strength!"

"And I need you," he whispered. "Tomorrow I want to show you something and get your advice on it."

"What? What is it?"

He smiled and touched her lips. Her curiosity had driven out her anger.

"Tomorrow you will see."

After he left Tom did not go home. He drove instead, to the factory. He walked into the darkened machine room with his violin. The machinery loomed as dark shapes. In the darkness he bowed to them and started to make up a tune. Tom played until his fingers hurt, now and then calling for Esther to come and help him, to come and take him away. To explain!

He felt the slight breeze of her presence, and her beautiful aroma. But she did not take him away. She left him, and he found everything as it was before.

He thought of Rubin and how he cried after her. "I looked for her everywhere but could not find her!" How he warned him not to be bewitched by Esther's music.

'Why, oh why, does Esther manifest herself in Clara?' he thought. 'And why did Clara get her violin?'

Tom put his instrument back into its case and covered it with the silken cloth.

He went up to his office. He switched on the lights. There was an enlarged copy of his grandmother's invitation on his desk. Joyce had managed to find a photographic studio where they restored old photographs. The card was now twice as large, the image repaired to show a beautiful young woman with black, very curly hair. Across the bottom of the picture was a name or a signature.

'Maybe the photographer's?' he thought.

Then her name, *Sophia Gallas*, slightly on an angle in the right-hand corner, in old-fashioned writing.

The contents of the program Tom could guess. The Sch. could only mean Schubert and *Winterreise* was still quite easy to read. And then there were the names of the host, the date and address, partially eaten by silverfish, but still decipherable.

He kissed his finger and pressed it on the image of his grandmother. "What do I call you? Grandmother? Oma? Gran?" Stroking her curly black hair, he ran his fingers through his blond curls. "I will call you, Sophia!"

Next morning they stood outside, looking at the apartment building.

"This is it," he said to Clara. "My new home. Come on, let's go in."

Ceremoniously he inserted the key, stood back, and bowed her into the foyer.

"Downstairs flat with garden," he said. "But to the rear for privacy. The builders are ready to discuss the changes I want made. That's where I need your advice."

He unlocked the door to the flat and ushered her in.

"It's dark," she said, "and poky. Too many rooms. Too much dark wood. Too 1930s!"

"See, that's why I need your advice. How do we modernise it?"

He smiled as she looked around. She was in her element now.

She frowned at the tiny old gas stove on its cast iron legs.

She frowned at the rickety shower stall and the mildewed curtain.

She looked thoughtfully at the tiny living room and the window that showed them their small piece of garden.

"We'll put French doors in here," she said. "Open out onto the garden. That will be nice. We'll have winter sun."

"The floors are a real concern," he said.

He pressed his foot down and listened to the timbers move.

"We'll get it fixed!" she said, now laughing. "Oh, this is so much fun, Tom. Your own home at last! We'll knock out a few of these inside walls, open it up, let the light shine in!"

Then she grew thoughtful.

"Have you discussed it with Margret?"

He winced.

"No. Not really. That is the hard one."

She returned to the light coming through the living room window. She pirouetted, turning to him, arms outstretched.

"We need to make it truly ours," she said.

"How do we do that?"

Her smile grew mischievously lascivious.

"Now? Here?" he said.

She nodded and slowly slipped her feet from her shoes, watching him all the while.

FIFTY-FOUR

The three of them sat at what had become Margret's favourite table in the hospital cafe. Tom was watching his mother closely. She was smiling, but he could not read her mood. He could sense the old anger glinting behind her eyes.

"Cheers!" Clara lifted her glass. "Well Margret, soon we will be eating in your flat. I believe in two weeks you will be able to come home. Don't worry I will not be living with you. My daily regime at the moment is pretty hectic. Every morning mummy and I walk in the park, then at least half an hour scales. And all that before breakfast! Poor mummy works as hard as I do. Almost every day Rubin comes. So, cheers to your homecoming!"

Margret picked up her glass and stretched her smile further.

"It is a pity that you are not going to come and live with us."

He blinked at this. Was it really his mother speaking?

Suddenly she turned towards him.

"We will need to find someone to help me during the day. Mrs Andrea Coder told me that there are agencies where one can find help. It will not be easy for me to have another woman in my house, but if that is the only way they will allow me to come home, then so be it. I like Mrs Coder. She has helped me a lot. I would like to continue seeing her. If that is possible."

She had not finished her soup. Nervously she pushed the spoon back and forth in the bowl. Tom knew what that meant. He gently put his hand on hers.

"We all will do our best. It will be good to have you back home again.

I'll ask Mrs Colder to recommend somewhere and you and I will go together and interview possible candidates."

Helping his mother into the building they saw the nurse coming towards them with the wheelchair.

"I thought you might like to have a ride, Mrs Dolmer."

"Thank you, I would," she replied.

He kissed his mother on the forehead.

Margret gave him a tired smile, the nurse turned the wheelchair towards the long corridor, towards Margret's room. Tom and Clara watched them until they had disappeared. For a while they were both deep in their own thoughts.

"I should go and see her counsellor while I'm here," he said.

"I should go home and practice. Tomorrow is a special torture day for me. Mummy and I are taking the train to the city to meet my new teacher. I'll have to play for him and see if he will have me. After tomorrow we will see if I will end up being a musician or if I have to learn to be something else."

Clara gave a strange laugh. Tom could feel her nervous fear. He knew that she would have liked him to come with her.

He kissed her gently.

"Everything will be fine," he said.

She gave him her nervous, disbelieving smile and turned for the hospital gates. He watched her pass through them and then went in search of Andrea Coder.

"Ah, Tom!" she said when he stepped into her room. "Please, sit down. We have some serious talk in front of us."

She put a jug of water on the table, two glasses next to it. Tom noticed an ashtray. He smiled, she certainly knew him by now.

"Tom, your mother will never be well enough to be left by herself. And you my dear young man need to live your life. We certainly do not want you to fall off the rails."

She laughed and poured water in the glasses.

"I have a proposal. I do strongly feel that Margret needs to go into a Home. We have some very good establishments in this country. One of them right here on the other side of the river. You can actually see it from your work. It is the new, tall building sitting almost on the edge of the water. It is new, beautiful, has the best staff, but it is expensive. Everyone has his or her own little apartment with a balcony looking out on the river. She can bring her own furniture; set herself up as she pleases."

She looked questioningly at Tom.

"She will never agree!"

Tom looked for his cigarette packet. He put it on the table. "Money is no problem. My mother has her own money. She has shares and then the big flat. No, money is no problem. She will be the problem! No, she will never agree!"

He got up and started to pace the room.

"Please Tom, sit down. Have a smoke! But please stop pacing about like a caged animal. I cannot talk to you pacing about. Please sit!"

Tom ran his hands through his hair. Looking at Andrea he slowly said,

"I am so tired of everything. I cannot argue with my mother. I cannot make her do anything!" Tom sat down and lit a cigarette. "Give me a broken machine any day. But broken people? I do not know how to fix them! I cannot help them! I am trying but it does nothing. Nothing!

I will never be able to talk my mother into going to a Home. She would look upon it as a betrayal."

He took a long draw of his cigarette and pulled the smoke deep into his lungs.

"I have promised my father, whom I loved, to take care of my mother until her death. I cannot and will not break my promise!"

"Tom, dear Tom. Don't you see that the circumstances of your lives have changed? We are not machines! We are made of blood and flesh and feelings. Yes, Tom, feelings! Everything in your life has changed since your father's passing. Margret got ill, you found your love! Circumstances alter cases! Please, Tom, stop torturing yourself. Everything will work out!"

Tom started to get up again. Andrea pushed him back in his seat.

"Now listen. I will handle this. Leave it to me. I do not make promises. I will do my best. Now, do you have any questions?"

"Yes. What did you do to turn my mother into a person of understanding? How did you do that? She's been quite nice lately. And she likes Clara, I think. So, how did you do that?"

She smiled.

"It is called, learning to forgive. Margret has forgiven the mother in her imagination. She has put her away into the past, not allowing her to come and haunt her again. It is a technique I use with people who are surrounded and governed by hate. But with Margret the reality is still there, deep down. It is only put away. It could surface at any time. The death of her beloved Theo, your father, stirred up the memories of her childhood. She is still grieving for him, she always will. And that brings me to the visit to the cemetery. Yes, I still think we should do that. Was it to be this Sunday? I will visit my father's grave around eleven. But I might just see you before then."

Getting up she held out her hand, Tom took it in both of his and pulled her towards him.

"Thank you for all you have done for my mother and for me."

He bent down and kissed her bright red lips, leaving a slight red mark on his. Andrea gave him a tissue and pointed towards the mirror. She watched him in the reflection.

"No, Tom, I am not doing all that for you or Margret. By helping you I help myself. Everything new makes one grow into a bigger person."

FIFTY-FIVE

Tom sat in the dark in the living room. He knew his way in the dark. Had he not lived here all his life? Taking a glass and the bottle of Scotch from the cupboard, he walked to the armchair that once was his father's. After he had turned on the standard lamp he filled his glass with the golden liquid and lit a cigarette. 'My life is not from a storybook. It is as real as this,' and he lifted up his glass to take a sip of his drink. "Cheers Tom Dolmer, Director, Lover, Son!"

After his second glass, he started pacing. 'I must make a list, a plan. I need a filing cabinet, so I can file each situation. Then I can deal with them individually! One drawer for work, the other for Clara, music and loving. The largest one will be marked Mother'. I will then deal with each one separately. Yes, keep them apart in drawers and only open one at the time! Cheers Tom!'

His engineering brain was completely engaged. He saw his life in graphs, numbers, and percentages. Everyone in his life had been put in a box, labelled. After the third glass, he felt strong and capable. He had another.

He picked up the bottle and the ashtray and walked back to his room. His body felt light and free. He thought he had put every situation in the right drawer and that he was master of the drawers. He was the one who would decide which drawer was to be opened. 'No more circumstantial situations', Tom said to himself. 'I will be the controller! Yes, Tom Dolmer, the Controller!' He laughed and filled his glass again.

A slight breeze woke him up. He lay naked on his bed. He could feel it drift over his bare body, almost like long hair being gently brushed over his skin. With it came the sweet smell and the music. The room was totally dark. He sat up. The air movement slowly drifted around his body, touching his back, his hair and face.

"Esther!"

Tom tried to escape by crawling under his blanket. He put his head under his pillow. He still felt her. In amongst the music he detected someone laughing.

He shouted, "I cannot do this anymore! I need help! I need a friend who really and truly cares and can help."

A name came into his mind: Zita. Zita, the gypsy! She had always been honest with him.

Smoke was curling out of the metal chimney as Tom approached the little cottage/restaurant. Tom could see Zita sitting outside smoking. She felt him approach and turned and waved.

They hugged, then Zita pushed him away and frowned.

"Darling, your body feels all messed up. How shall I put it! You feel like you are covered in spiky prickles. You need a cleansing swim. You need water all around you. Let's go for a swim."

Embarrassed, he looked at her.

"Never you mind that. My body is not as beautiful as it once was, but you just don't look at it. Come, let's go. Let's get rid of all that mess and confusion in and on you."

She climbed over the railing of the deck and walked to the river's sidearm, where she kept her boat. She stripped off, leaving her clothes on the ground and, before Tom noticed, was in the water. He took off his cream-coloured linen suit and hung it carefully over the bushes.

"It's lovely, darling. Come on!"

Slightly embarrassed Tom held one hand over his private parts as he ran towards the water. Zita laughed.

"Come on, Tom, I have seen plenty of those male parts. Don't worry about me!"

They laughed and splashed each other like two children at play. At times Zita's black face would dive under to turn up quite a long way away. Then she disappeared under the water. Tom looked for her, turning this way and that, only to discover her almost dressed on dry land.

"This is not fair. Now please turn around, so I can come out!"

"Why darling? Is your body as old and dried up as mine? Something wrong with your body? I know, it is all white! I'll forgive you for that."

She kept on teasing him. Then she suddenly got up and walked away.

"Fish for breakfast!" she called over her shoulder.

They sat quietly sipping Zita's special coffee. Tom's plate was scraped clean.

"Well, darling, the water has washed most of that prickly feeling off you. So, what do you want to talk about?"

"I don't quite know where to begin. I feel, I feel that I cannot cope anymore. I seem to be surrounded by difficulties. Last night I got quite drunk at home by myself."

"Yes, darling, I can smell the drink on you. It totally disturbed the vibration of your natural body. Drink is great, but it does not solve problems, it only fogs them up."

"So, how am I going to cope with all these difficult situations I've been confronted with? I do love Clara and I truly want to be with her. My mother? Well, you know about the promise to my dad. Then there is work. Well, work can look after itself with Douglas taking care of it. But my mother? I do not trust her now that she is all lovely and understanding. I do not trust it. Her good old self will suddenly come back! That's why I feel it is important for her to know the truth about her past. Does she really like Clara? Is she putting all that loving and liking business on, so she can come home and give me hell?"

Tom filled his cup and lit a cigarette.

"Last night, before I got drunk, I made a filing cabinet in my mind and I put each of my problems in a different drawer. But this morning I know they're still there, waiting to get out. The last six months have been such a roller-coaster."

Zita put her arm on his shoulder.

"Darling, please, slow down. I love the filing cabinet! Not a bad idea at all!"

Tom looked at her.

"No darling, truly. So, Margret is in one, Clara is in another. Yes? So. Problems with Margret, open her drawer, take her out. Yes? Deal with her. You clever young man with lots of intuitive thinking. As long as you don't drink."

Suddenly Zita laughed out loud.

"Sorry darling, but I somehow cannot see Margret in same drawer as you and Clara. Sorry, naughty thought, but funny. Please excuse this old gypsy woman. So, Margret goes into her drawer when you are with Clara."

They both laughed. Zita kissed him on the cheek.

"Oh, my dear darling boy. What would we do without humour and love and forgiveness."

She looked at Tom.

"And truth! Yes, my darling, truth!"

For a long time they sat together looking out towards the river. The sun slowly crept over the bushes along its shores. The shadows started creeping down the little house and soon they both sat bathed by the summer sun.

Tom felt restless. Zita could feel it but said nothing. She knew that it was better for Tom to open up, to talk to her.

"Should I take my mother to her parents' grave? I do want so much for her to know her true past. I do not know what happened during her sessions with the counsellor. What made her suddenly so calm. I just fear that her anger is still there. Deep down. What do you think? What should I do?"

"Well, darling Tom, truth in the long run always wins. Still, I cannot tell you what you should do. You will find the right way.

I know you will. But please, without whisky. Drink is great, but not a problem solver!"

They got up and hugged.

"Thank you, Zita. You are a true friend."

"Oh, darling, what else could I be. I love you dearly, my boy."

FIFTY-SIX

The railway station only had four platforms. Tom looked for the arrival time and platform number of the commuter train from the city. He was early and decided to sit down on one of the benches. The noise and the smell of the small station made him think back to the times when he would come home from the university, his dad waiting for him. His father's first words would always be,

"Look at you, son. You've grown again. Soon you will be much taller than me. Let's go and have a coffee."

They would go to the little café across from the station. Dad would always take his bag and carry it for him as if he were still a little boy.

"So, how was your week? Still in love with that clever girl?"

Then he would start talking about his love, his only love, until they finished their coffee.

"Better get home to mum! She is looking forward to seeing you."

But his mother never came to fetch him from the station.

Tom watched the people coming out of the waiting room. The train must be arriving soon. He remembered his excitement when the train pulled into the station. He and his father would go up the river in the summer and play chess or cards in the colder weather. He could not remember his mother ever participating.

'I wonder what that clever ex-girlfriend of mine is doing? She probably married some other engineer and has children.'

He smiled to himself thinking about it.

'Yes, she was clever and extremely good-looking. She taught me all I know about lovemaking. But her taste in music!'

316

A shiver went through his body. 'She did not really want me, she was after becoming Mrs Dolmer, partner in Dolmer's Engineering.'

"What are you smiling about!" Clara was standing in front of him, clutching her violin case under her arm. She looked tired and irritable.

"Nothing in particular. I was just thinking of a beautiful girl I…"

She bent down and kissed him.

"You were thinking of me. Oh, I do love you. Let's get home. Mummy is waiting at the entrance of the station."

Still smiling Tom stood up. He took her in his arms.

"Yes, my most beautiful girl. It is so good to see you. Let's go."

Tom brought the car to the front entrance of the station. Gudrun was waiting, surrounded by a number of packages, instruments, and bags.

'All this for just one day away?' Tom thought as he loaded the luggage into the boot of the car.

"Where to, ladies?"

"Home!" they answered.

The dog was so pleased to see Gudrun he almost tripped Tom, who was carrying a number of the parcels and bags. Michael came down the steps to help him.

"The ladies have been out shopping! I hope there is something exciting for me, like a new tie or sox!"

"I love you too, Daddy. Good to see you!"

Michael put all the bags and parcels in the middle of the living room floor.

"So, which one is mine?"

Gudrun looked at him. "Any food in the house?"

"I could make you a drink? I thought we were going out for a meal!"

Letting herself fall into one of the armchairs she looked at her husband. She was extremely tired.

317

"Yes, a drink would be great. Thank you." She looked at Tom. "Would you like a drink? Are you OK? You look a bit pale."

Tom just wanted a glass of water. He still felt last night's drinking and the events of the day. All he wanted was to go to bed, to cuddle up with Clara and sleep. Sleep without dreaming, without having his thoughts keeping him awake.

"I will have some wine with my meal. It has been quite a day and I suppose quite a night too. I am just very tired. Sorry about not being good company."

Clara came in from the kitchen.

"What did you do last night?"

"I got drunk!"

"On your own?"

He did not answer.

"Go and help dad with the drinks. I'll have a Vermouth. Don't forget the slice of lemon. And maybe we have some nuts or some other nibbles."

Gudrun looked at Tom and continued, "Are you all right?"

"No!"

"Would you like to talk about it?"

"No, not now."

Tom settled back in the comfortable armchair and stretched out his long legs. Running his fingers through his hair he let go of a long sigh. Gudrun got up and kissed him on the forehead. Then she went into the kitchen. She returned with a glass of freshly-pressed orange juice.

"So, how was your day?"

Michael settled down next to Gudrun on the sofa.

"You know how much I dislike the city. The noise, the constant movements, the bad air. And all those people rushing, rushing! Other than that I feel our trip was successful. I personally did a lot of sitting and waiting. You should ask Clara about her day. While you're doing that I'll rustle something up for dinner."

Clara had sunk into her chair and was fast asleep.

Smiling, Tom got up.

"I think we are all tired."

In the kitchen he found Gudrun leaning on the table. The refrigerator door was open. Never had he seen her so listless and tired.

"Thank you for the offer of a meal. I will pass and go home to bed. Maybe we can get together over the weekend?"

He gave her a hug and walked out of the house.

The phone rang. Tom sat up, dazed. He looked around. He was back in his mother's apartment. He picked up the ringing phone.

"Why did you leave? I have not seen you forever!" Clara started to cry. "I am coming over!" Tom could hear an argument in the background. Suddenly Clara screamed: "I am twenty-one and can do as I like. I am going!"

It was close to eleven when Clara arrived. She still wore her city clothes. Her hair was in total disarray. Sobbing she fell onto Tom's chest.

"I hate daddy. He is always so domineering! He calls it being responsible! We all have to do what he wants!"

He closed the front door with his foot. Hugging Clara tightly Tom started slowly to rock. Gently he hummed. She started to relax. He felt his chest getting wet from her tears.

"Let's go in the living room."

But Clara slowly pushed him into the bedroom. Leaving her clothes lying on the floor she climbed into granddad's high bed. Tom picked up her dress, folded it up and put it on a chair. He sat on the edge of the bed and looked at her curled-up body. She was shaking and crying. Even though it was a warm night, Clara wrapped herself up tight with the summer cover. She was soon asleep. Tom went to get another blanket.

When he returned she was sitting up. She looked distraught.

"Hold me. Please hold me! I got such a fright when you were not there. Don't ever do that again. You could have woken me and told me that you were going! I was so lonely, so empty and you were not there."

She put her head on his chest and fell back asleep.

When he woke Tom could see the dawning sun over the rooftops. Clara lay on his arm with her face slightly bent backward. Her hair was wrapped around his arm. She looked peaceful. The demons from the night before had gone. Long did he look at her. 'What happened? What made her behave like that?' Tom kissed her, she stretched out pressing herself tightly to his body.

The sun was shining into the room when she woke up. Tom had made coffee and was sitting on the bed drinking it.

"I dreamed that you made love to me."

He just smiled at her, handing her a cup.

"Well, did you?"

"Tell me about your day."

She ignored his question.

"You know, Tom, deep down I am very frightened of the changes happening in my life. I want things to stay as they are. Like a lovely dream one never wants to end. But there is also this excitement growing in me. The wish of one day becoming a performer; to feel the music take me away; to hear the audience clap and call for more! When I was a little girl I used to pretend I was on a great stage making music.

But now that all this might come true, I am frightened of the change. I want to be here with you forever. Just here looking out into a new day with you. I am frightened that the new life will push you away, that you will slowly fade away into your life as I will into mine."

Tom did not know what to say. He knew what she meant. He often had the same thoughts. Deep down though he knew that he would always love her.

"We will have to wait and see what the future presents us with. It is useless to be frightened of situations that are written in the future. I love you, Clara. Whatever life brings, however the circumstances, I will always love you."

"You promise?"

"No, I will not promise. Now tell me about your day. Then we will go and have breakfast and then I will take you home."

"There is nothing much to tell. I don't really want to talk about it."

Clara turned away from Tom and looked out the window. Then she got up, dressed, and walked into the kitchen where she filled up her cup. She sat down at the table, her head in her hands.

"Soon your mother will be sitting here with you and I will be sitting at home without you. And so, the changes start."

"Not necessarily." Tom had dressed in a pair of light summer trousers and a light blue shirt. She turned around.

"You look so handsome in blue. What do you mean by, not necessarily?"

Telling her about the plans of trying to convince Margret to go and live in a Home brought all the sunshine back into Clara's face.

"Tell me more!"

"Not until you tell me about your day!"

They hugged and laughed

Over breakfast, Clara started slowly to talk about her experience.

"I do like the new teacher: Oskar Bulgakov. There is something familiar about him.

I'm sure I've met him before. He is tall, like you. He has grey-green eyes that looked straight at me when I spoke. I had the feeling that he took in and computed every word I said. He has beautiful hands and the whitest, softest hair I have ever seen. It fell down to his shoulders. I had the feeling that he knew mummy. It was just the way he smiled at her. He does know Rubin. He said that I had been in the hands of the best.

Then we talked about the pieces I like to play and then he

asked me to play one of them. Halfway through my playing, he joined me on his grand piano. He liked my playing, just thought I need to change the way I stand. I need to learn to relax. Then we talked a bit more and then Mummy and Oskar Bulgakov worked out my program. Well, then we had lunch, and then we went shopping."

Clara looked at Tom for a long time before she resumed speaking.

"On the train this fear of change crept into me. It just grew and grew the closer we came to the station. Then there you were telling me that you had been sitting on the bench thinking of me and my fear of losing what I hold so dear grew into a giant. Oh, Tom, always love me. Promise!"

Tom shook his head. He lifted her hands and kissed them.

"I have to go and see my mother," he said. "She'll be waiting for me at the café. Then I have a meeting with Andrea Coder."

"While you make plans for your mother, I could walk with her in the park and entertain her. Maybe I can see how she feels about her future?"

He looked at her sharply.

"Yes," Clara promised, "I will be careful in what I say! Don't worry."

FIFTY-SEVEN

As soon as Tom walked into Andrea Coder's office, she confronted him.

"Sit!"

She pointed at one of the armchairs.

"I need to talk to you about you! How do you manage to juggle all these different situations? There are two very difficult women in your life, plus your work; not to forget your love for music."

Tom did as he was told and started laughing.

"I have this wonderful invention. It is called a filing cabinet. I have told you about it. It works! A drawer for each problem."

"Yes, yes!" Andrea seemed agitated. "I had a word to Margret about the Home. She is absolutely not going! So, there you are. We need to find you some help. I can get in touch with an agency for you and find someone to look after her."

Tom looked sharply at her.

"Now please, you sit! She is my mother. I will do that. I am going to take three weeks off work. Hopefully, in that time, things will sort themselves out.

I would like to talk about Sunday. Is it still on? Has she been told? I don't want to spring the visit to her parents' grave on her on Sunday morning!"

Andrea shook her head.

"I am sorry Tom, I've been so occupied trying to convince Margret to go into the Home, I forgot about Sunday. Was it eleven? Yes, I'll be there."

Tom looked out the window into the hospital garden. His

mother and Clara were sitting on a bench in deep conversation. He smiled.

'Things will work out. They will have to work out!' he thought.

Andrea followed his gaze. She stood up.

"Session over!" she said. "You should join your ladies!"

When Tom joined them, Margret was having her tea with lemon.

"I've never had tea with lemon," Clara said to him, as she sipped her newly discovered drink. She smiled at Margret. "There is always something new to try in life."

Tom stretched out his long legs and folded his hands behind his head.

"That's the life. What a wonderful day. In a few days, we'll have the longest day of the year. How about we go up in the hills above the town and watch the sunset? There probably will be lots of bonfires along the river. We can go to Restaurant Sissi or I can pack a picnic. What do you think, ladies? After that, the days will be getting shorter and we will slide towards winter and Christmas."

Clara clapped her hands excitedly.

"Let's go out in style. Let's go to Sissi. I promise I will behave. But please just the three of us. No other guests."

Margret frowned at Tom.

"Yes, why not. You, Tom, will have to bring me a dress from home!"

Tom looked at her.

"Why don't we drive by our home and you pick your own dress? I wouldn't know what to choose and would probably make a terrible mess of the colour combinations. You know, being a man and all that!"

"Clara could help?"

Tom kicked Clara under the table.

"Oh, I don't know, Margret. I think you should choose."

He took his mother's hand.

"And I do want us to visit your parents' grave soon."

"Not that again," she said. "You are dreaming, my dear son. There is no grave. There were no dead babies. But if it makes you stop talking about it, if it makes you happy, I will come."

Tom felt Clara squeeze his leg. She looked at Margret.

"Why don't we go on Sunday? Maybe Tom can take us out to lunch? What if we pick you up on Sunday at ten?"

Margret nodded.

"Tomorrow I have to work on my music," Clara added.

Margret pulled up her shoulders and sighed.

"I am tired now. I need to rest."

She got up. She hooked her arms into Tom and Clara's. By the entrance, she stood on her toes and gave her son a kiss on his cheek, then turned towards Clara and kissed her as well.

FIFTY-EIGHT

Although they'd got there early the cemetery car park was nearly full. Everyone was trying to see their dead before the day got too hot.

Margret sat in the car watching the crowd queuing in front of the flowerseller. Clara had brought a bunch of flowers from her garden.

She couldn't understand why Tom had insisted on bringing her to this place. But she had agreed to go along with the charade for his sake.

'What a pretty girl' she thought, looking at Clara in her loose summer dress as she and Tom got the folding chair and sun umbrella from the car's boot.

Margret clambered out of the Mercedes and hooked herself into Clara's arm. Slowly they weaved their way through the cars towards the entrance.

As they approached the large, ornate iron gates it felt to Margret as if the crowd went into slow motion. She stopped and stared at the imposing ironwork. Tom had taken her other arm. Margret felt the gates grow larger. Or was she getting smaller? The chatting crowd became muffled and fuzzy. And the gates kept growing.

She looked at Tom.

"I am feeling faint. I need to sit down. Somewhere in the shade."

Clara held the umbrella over her as they passed through the menacing gates. Tom found a shady spot and sat her down on the folding chair. Clara went to get a glass of water.

"Thank you. That's better. It must have been the sun playing tricks on me. Thank you, I am fine."

They both looked worried. She smiled reassuringly for them.

"Let's go and see that grave and then we can have a cup of tea at the kiosk."

They walked along the wide path. Margret looked at the grand graves. For some reason she felt nervous and she covered it by talking.

"Not like our little graveyard. Still, your dad has a great view from his spot. This place is very imposing. A bit scary don't you think? And so well looked after! I feel uncomfortable leaving marks in the path."

Tom and Clara could feel her grip getting tighter on their arms. They turned into one of the side roads. Margret laughed and pointed at the sign on the corner. She stepped back to be able to read it.

"Lamberg Lane," she said. "I wonder who this Lamberg is?"

Then she stopped laughing and looked at Tom.

"That was my maiden name. How dare they call a path in a cemetery after me! Is this a joke or what!"

She tried to turn around and go back.

"I have changed my mind. I don't want to see that grave! I want a cup of tea! And maybe a cake, if they have anything decent in that kiosk."

But Tom and Clara did not move.

"We are almost there, Mum. Now we have come this far surely you can fulfil my wish? Please?"

Margret sighed and smiled to herself. 'Lamberg Lane, really!'

She let them lead her slowly on.

Tom could see Al pushing his trolley past his grandparents' last resting place. Al lifted an arm with a little wave. Just a little movement to say: 'I'm here, mate, if you need me.'

They stopped in front of the beautiful grave. The newly-polished white marble gleamed. He set up the chair. Clara removed the old flowers and arranged the new ones from her garden, leaning the little doll against the vase. Margret sat down.

Tom stood next to his mother, shading her with the umbrella. Clara was satisfied with the arrangement of the flowers and moved away.

For a long time they looked at the grave.

Eventually Margret took Tom's hand and looked up at him. She frowned, puzzled.

"I know this place. I have had dreams about this place. How can I? I have never been here before! But I know this place. I know it very well. Maybe I saw it on the television in the hospital."

She put her other hand on her chest.

"I know this place. In here! In my heart! Oh Tom, who are those people, why do they have my name? My mother's name was not Sophia and she died much, much later. I was well married when she died. Do you know, I cannot even remember her name? I suppose I called her Mum? It was not Sophia. Far too pretty for such a terrible person."

She kept on scanning the gravestone.

"It is a beautiful grave. Maybe it belongs to a different Lamberg family? There must be more about? Still, I know this place, in here!"

She pushed her hand harder onto her chest.

"Also, you know, I remember it being much bigger. Very imposing. I remember not liking it. Oh, Tom, I feel strange. I must have dreamed about this place or seen it on the television in my room. I would like to go now. I would like a cup of tea. Would you not like a cake? And maybe a juice? Maybe an ice cream? Yes, I would like an ice cream. Yes, ice cream in a waffle cone. Strawberry, my favourite."

Margret did not move. Tom held her hand and let her talk. Clara sat quietly on a bench in the shade, tears running down her flushed face.

"And who are George and Irene? They just have one year carved with their name. What does that mean? I do remember the little angels. I must have dreamt it! Can one dream about things that really exist but you haven't seen them?

328

But then Tom, I don't dream much and then I cannot remember my dreams. Theo and I used to laugh about that. I used to talk in my sleep. Theo could never remember what I said."

She looked back up at Tom.

"I'd like to go now. Where is Clara? Let's have a cup of tea!"

He helped her up. Turning around she saw Clara, tears streaming down her face.

"Darling, why are you crying?"

Margret sat down next to her. The white marble shone at her.

"Cemeteries make me sad," Clara said. "Sophia was barely thirty years old when she died, and she had two stillborn children. That is so sad."

Margret put her arm around Clara, trying to calm her.

"You know, Margret, I sometimes feel that I know places. My dad always laughs and tells me that we had visited that particular part of the world when I was little. Funny isn't it how things stick in your brain?"

"Just as well they do!" Tom continued the conversation. "If we would forget everything what would the sense of learning be? Let's go and have some tea."

The sun was high. The car park almost empty. They decided on a cool drink. Most people had scattered in search of a cool place. Tom could see Al standing chatting to the man in the kiosk.

"I want to go back," Margret suddenly said. "I'll be fine on my own. You stay here. Have some cake!"

Getting up she took the folding chair and walked through the gates. Clara ran after her with the umbrella.

"You sure you will be OK?"

Margret smiled and nodded and kept on purposefully walking.

Clara watched her walk down the main path, then turn into Lamberg Lane. Tom noticed that Al had disappeared. Nervously he lit a cigarette. Clara ordered a pot of coffee and a jug of water.

"Just leave her! She'll be fine. If anything happens, there are plenty of people to help. Drink your coffee and relax!"

Having put the chair close to the big slab of marble, Margret slowly started walking around the grave, her hand just touching the stone. She noticed the delicate writing. Tom could maybe sing the song for her. He can read notes, she thought. The writing was too small for her to read. She noticed the two toys and smiled. 'Silly boy,' she thought, 'leaving toys for dead children.' She kept on walking, touching the stone. 'Could one really remember things from a long time ago? Could Clara be right? But why would I have been at this grave site?'

"I would have been barely four years old!" she said loudly to the carved date of Sophia's death.

She sat down and opened up the umbrella. She felt tired. Her head would not stop. Memories churned around in it. She was just about to nod off when she heard a familiar, complaining voice.

"Oh, this stupid path! How can a woman walk on it in her heels? And the sun, so hot. You'd think the powers would organise a cooler day for this!"

'Andrea Coder,' Margret thought.

Andrea came out of a small side lane, stopped, and took off her shoes.

"Bugger men!" she said. "I'll never meet my prince here, anyway." She walked slowly, trying to avoid the stones.

"Who are you talking to, Margret? I've just had another argument, sorry Dad, discussion with my dad. He is resting over there. Well? Who are you talking to?"

"I don't know! Tom brought me here. Apparently, my mother is in here. My mother died after I was married! Sophia died in 1904! I was barely four years old!"

Margret pointed at the bench. "Let's sit down together. Over there? You look terribly uncomfortable."

"Vanity!" Andrea rolled her over-mascaraed eyes. "Tell me about this grave. It is exceptionally beautiful. There is, or was, money in that family, or fame. There are a lot of rich and famous people buried in this cemetery. My dad was famous for his wealth. That's about all he had going for him!

Anyway, what about those people?"

She looked closely at the big slab of marble.

"There was obviously music in the family. Looks like a song by Schubert. Yes, I know that one, but I cannot sing, nor can I read notes. It is *The Brook's Lullaby*. Sorry, I cannot read it. I am not wearing my glasses. Again, vanity!"

"Tell me, Andrea, can deep memories be brought up? Let's say by looking at something?"

"I'm not sure I understand you," Andrea lied. "Tell me more."

"When we walked towards the big entrance gates I had a distinct feeling that they were growing larger. It was very frightening. The people walking into the cemetery suddenly walked in slow motion and became sort of fuzzy, like out of focus. It was a very fearful experience. I thought I was going to faint. But as soon as we had walked through I felt fine.

Coming to the grave I had such a strong feeling that I had been here before. It was the whiteness of the stone. I must have seen this grave in a dream or on television, I thought. Even sitting here now, it feels so strongly familiar. Then Tom insists that Sophia was my mother. You see my mother's name was not Sophia. Yes, I must solve this with logic, not with silly feelings. There is no one alive to prove my ancestry."

Margret looked at Andrea.

"Do you think feelings mislead? Maybe you can help me solve this?"

"No Margret, feelings are not misleading. They very often open a door helping to understand situations. You must not be afraid of listening to your feelings. To your intuitions."

Al was pushing his cart down one of the sidewalks. Andrea called him over and asked him to get Tom and Clara.

"Yes, ma'am."

He touched his cap and bowed ever so slightly. Andrea laughed.

"Our cemetery philosopher."

Settling back on the bench Margret kept staring at the Lamberg grave, shaking her head, mumbling quietly.

Clara and Tom came running along the path.

"Are you all right, Mum?"

"Yes, yes!" Andrea said. She pointed to the writing and music on the stone. "Can you read this? Or better can you sing it?"

Walking to the grave Clara looked at Tom. "I am a terrible singer!"

"Who cares! Let's give it a try."

Good night, good night
Till all shall awake
Sleep away your joy, sleep away your sorrow

The full moon is rising
The mist dispersing
And the sky above, how boundless it is!

"Please sing it again," Andrea asked. "And maybe Clara could sing a little louder? I can hardly hear her. Please, Clara?"

After the first line, Tom started to sing very softly allowing Clara's voice to take the lead. After the word sorrow he stopped. Clara's voice filled the air and it filled Margret's heart.

"That was beautiful, Clara. Would you mind, just once more? Please?" Margret asked excitedly. "I know that tune. I know that song. Tom must have it on one of his records. Oh, please Clara, just once more?"

Andrea looked at Tom and smiled. She put her finger on her mouth, signalling him to be silent.

"Bravo, bravo Clara! You have a lovely voice. Truly you do!"

Margret got up and gave her a hug. "My boy is a lucky man!" She looked at Tom.

"Can we go and have some lunch? But please not at the kiosk. Will you join us, Andrea? Can we please find a quiet place?"

Margret looked at Andrea.

"And can I please come with you?"

Margret wanted to talk about her feelings, but how could she do that in Andrea's car. A little red soft-top sports car. The top was down. Noise and wind buffeted her even though Andrea drove slowly.

"Andrea, can I talk to you while you are driving?"

Laughing, Andrea invited Margret to talk on.

"I am only driving this slowly so we can talk."

"I want to talk about my feelings. They occupy my mind so much. It's been so long since I've allowed myself to have feelings. I don't like the feeling of feelings!"

Andrea pulled over and looked at Margret.

"Look, Margret, you have to decide for yourself if the truth is to come to the surface.

I'll help you wherever I can. But you have to want to find out. Look upon it as a mystery you need, no, you want to solve. Not only solve for yourself, but also for Tom, who is desperate to discover his family.

Young people do need the feeling of belonging. We all need to know where we belong, where we come from. Why do you think I go and visit my bad-tempered, grumpy, selfish dead father? Just like you, I did not know my real mother. I have no husband, no lover, no children. Just grumpy dad."

She started the car. Margret put her hand on Andrea's arm.

"Thank you."

Andrea drove faster. She felt Margret needed to be with her own thoughts and not with hers. 'Yes,' she thought as she put the foot harder on the accelerator. 'We all have to come to grips with our past.'

Tom had trouble finding the restaurant. They had ended up on the hilly side of town. The narrow streets of the outer suburb did not allow parking. Tom saw Andrea outside the large gate of an old house. She was waving and pointing towards a laneway where her red car was parked. From there they could walk into the backyard garden of the establishment.

Margret was not in the car. Andrea took Tom and Clara aside.

"She's inside, absorbing it all," Andrea whispered. "It's all there, rising up inside her. Please don't ask her about what happened today. Don't talk about her family. She now needs to digest and think about the events of the morning."

Margret hardly seemed to notice them when they entered. Andrea ordered a big platter of cheeses and cold meats and bread.

But Margret was too tired to join in. She just had a cup of tea. Tom tried to encourage her to eat, but Andrea waved her hand at him.

"I think I will take Margret back to her room. I'll see you tomorrow, Tom."

Andrea helped Margret up. Tom rose, too. For a while they stood looking at each other. Margret put her hands on Tom's cheeks, but she said nothing. The words did not want to come out. Quietly, Tom whispered,

"I love you." He felt his eyes prickle with moisture.

Margret let go of him and walked away with Andrea.

For quite a while Tom and Clara sat in silence.

"Do you really love her?" Clara asked.

Tom shook his head bemusedly.

"I don't know. She is a stranger to me. We have nothing in common. I can't talk to her about my life, my thoughts, my troubles. When I was a child she only criticised.

No, I do not know if I love my mother! I just feel if I say it often enough it might awaken between us."

She could feel him falling into himself. Tom pulled his feet tight towards his body. His arms were clenched around his chest. His head drooping. Clara freed one of his hands and kissed it.

"I love you! I really do. I have never felt that way before."

Lifting his head, he turned towards her.

"What is love?"

"You and me?"

Tom turned away, letting his head droop again.

Clara, still holding his hand, kept on kissing it.

"Oh Tom, if one could only measure love!"

She sat up straight.

"Maybe that's how we need took at love! Then one could say, I love my mother that much." She let go of his hand and pretended to create a size with her hands. "I could say, I love my dad that much, my sister so much, my dog, well just that much. But you," she strained stretching out her arms and fingers, "that much and more!"

"Why do you love me?" Tom asked.

Clara let her arm drop.

"Really do you need to ask! Ok. Let me think. You are very handsome and good in bed. I love your blue eyes and your curly hair. Oh, Tom, you know why I love you. We are part of each other. We need each other. I do not know why, but we do! So then, why do you love me? Is it because I look like a Botticelli angel?"

Clara got up and stood in front of Tom. Hair was hanging over her face. She was angry. Tom looked up and, pulling her face towards his, gave her a long passionate kiss.

"Oh, I love you when you are angry. I love your music making. I love your hair. I love your body. I love you because I have known you before. Somehow, I feel that you have been with me most of my life. You feel right to be with. I only feel half a person when you are not with me."

Tom got up and held her.

"Your way of measuring love is fantastic! Then I can say; Yes, I do love my mother. I love her so much."

Putting his arms in the air Tom said,

"I love you, Mother!"

In the restaurant, the waiter thought Tom was calling him and came over.

"Anything else you would like, sir?"

Looking sheepishly at Clara Tom said,

"Oh, I could do with a Scotch and a cigarette! May I, darling?"

Clara gave him a light punch in the chest, laughed and ordered a glass of wine.

Lifting his glass to Clara Tom laughed.

"Usually tension and pressure make me want to have a drink and a cigarette. This is a celebratory drink. I have the feeling that there is a change in the air!"

With his violin case under his arm, whistling a tune, Tom walked through the park towards Rubin and his lesson. He was feeling on top of things. He had dropped Clara off at the train station. She had another tutorial with her new teacher. He'd met with his manager, Douglas Henshall, and arranged to take three weeks off work to get his life in order. He'd ordered a table at Sissi for the summer solstice on Wednesday.

His little flat was ready. All it needed now was furniture.

He frowned as an unpleasant thought came up.

His mother had said nothing about their visit to the cemetery. And now he had to find someone to look after her as she would be coming home the following Monday. Home to live alone, for Tom would be in his new flat.

It was a beautiful summer's day. He put his violin case on one of the benches in the park, took off his tie and put it in his trouser pocket. He rolled up his shirt sleeves, stretched out his arms and fingers as wide as they would reach and whispered to the deep blue of the sky.

"I love you, Clara. I love you!"

He repeated it over and over. People were staring at him. He did not mind. Then the soft music came with the gentle wind and the enticing smell. Slowly it danced around him, almost making him feel faint.

"I love you too, Esther."

And he tried to stretch out his fingers further, but they stayed the same.

"My two big loves!"

Rubin was sitting in the café. With his snow-white hair, his grey face and black suit he looked like a black and white photograph. Tom could feel his depressed state of mind when looking at him through the window of the café.

"Let's sit outside," Tom suggested. "It is beautiful outside."

"There is nothing beautiful outside or inside!"

Rubin got up and walked to the entrance of the building he lived in and climbed the old stone spiral stairs, stopping now and then. The door to his flat was open.

Seated at last in his large armchair he asked quietly and authoritatively,

"Have you done your scales?"

"No, Rubin, I have not. But I have played my instrument. I need to make music. It helps me to stay sane in my insane life. I made music, my music."

Rubin smiled at the young man.

"Oh, Tom, I don't know why I keep on asking you? I know you do not practise the conventional way. I have no idea why I even invite to teach you. I cannot teach you anything. I need you though. What does a teacher do without a pupil? So, I suffer your playing!"

Tom crouched down in front of his teacher and took his cold hands.

"You have taught me a lot! How to hold the bow. How to stroke the bow over the strings without scratching. Most importantly, how to tune my instrument! And then would I have met Clara and fallen in love with her?"

Rubin pulled his hands away and snapped at Tom.

"Don't ever hurt that girl! Do you hear me? Never!"

The old man sank into himself. Tom picked up his violin, checked the tuning, put the instrument under his chin and started to play. He made up a tune, now and then accompanying himself by whistling or singing. Rubin sat up and stared at his pupil. Suddenly he clapped his hands and Tom stopped.

"Hold your bow like that! Oh, I must show you!"

He got up and got his violin.

"Like that! Have I not told you thousands of times? You are scratching. That is quite horrible, those scratchings. When you get excited you just scratch away. My poor ears! If you want to make that instrument sing, you must learn how to hold your bow! You see, my dear boy, that's why I ask you to do your scales first. Sort of warming-up exercise. You concentrate when you do your scales! When you know how to play, then you can go off and have fun."

Tom began playing scales: major and minor. Rubin beamed.

"Now you can play again! Go on, have fun. I quite enjoyed your improvised tune."

But Tom shook his head and put his violin back in its case.

"I cannot just switch my music on and off! I played to you because I felt you needed cheering up. It just came to me. I am not a performer! I don't do requests! But I do want to play well and I do want to make my instrument sing like….."

"Come on, say it!" Rubin walked towards Tom. "Say it! Say her name! I knew it! She got you! Oh, Tom, you must send her away. She could come between you and Clara. Oh Tom, don't you ever hurt that girl!"

Picking up a sheet of music, Rubin urged Tom to play it. As always, he sang the piece first and then tried to play it on his instrument. Slowly he worked his way through the short piece, making sure that no scratching noises escaped from his bow.

"Good! Now you take this home with you and play it every day until it becomes part of you."

He pushed one of his fingers into Tom's chest. With every word he gave his pupil a poke.

"You, my dear boy, need to learn the technical side of playing! Discipline!"

Then he laughed.

"And now we have a coffee down at Hawelka's. I want to talk about other things."

In the cafe Rubin launched into a speech.

"You might have noticed that I am not guiding Clara towards her first competition. With sadness I had to admit that she needed someone younger to look after her. So, I handed her to my good friend and ex-pupil, Oskar Bulgakov. He is a good man, an excellent pedagogue, and of course, well I was his teacher, a very skilled violinist."

Tom noticed Rubin's eyes moisten.

"For quite a while I was deeply depressed. I just wanted to die. Yes, truly. And I thought I was. I got this shake in my hands. I could not hold my violin. I decided that it would be good for everyone if I just left, joined my beloved Esther."

Rubin gave a little laugh.

"But Michael noticed, took me aside, talked to me, got me I little pill and here I am quite happy to be alive. Then I still have you? You need a lot of teaching my boy. And I will look after Clara and take her through all the preliminary stages. We somehow have to find out why she feels so down after a performance. Even Gudrun is at a loss. You are very good for her. I saw it after the last concert."

Tom looked at his watch.

"I have to pick Clara up at the station," he said. "And take her home."

"Good. I shall come, too."

Tom stared at him.

"Gudrun has prepared the cellar room for me. I'm staying there during the week."

He grimaced and got up and shrugged.

"They feel it is important to keep an eye on me!"

Susanna cooked them a beautiful, simple summer meal. Gudrun had stayed in the city. She was also taking lessons. Her women's orchestra was to hold a concert. Michael had settled with the newspapers in one of the cane lounges, smoke rising up from behind the paper. Now and then an arm appeared reaching towards his glass. Rubin had fallen asleep in the deck chair.

Clara and Tom sat on the ground, leaning up against the warm wall of the house. It was a beautiful summer's evening.

"How was your day?'

"How was yours?"

"Ladies first!"

Tom put his arm around Clara.

"I don't like going to the city on my own, but I know I have to get used to it.

Oskar is a great teacher. He is kind and not at all pushy like you know who! But he is strict. Everything has to be as it is written. You would love that!"

She laughed and gave him a kiss.

"I think he is in his mid-sixties. Maybe a little older than dad. At least as tall as you. He has beautiful shoulder-length, silver hair. But I just love his hands, strong and somewhat elegant. Can one have elegant hands?"

"Tell me, Clara, how do you feel after a concert? Why do you give me the feeling of being so frightened?"

"I don't want to talk about it. Not today, on such a beautiful evening. I'm too tired to talk about it."

"Please Clara, tell me. Maybe I can help?"

She was quiet, as if summoning up force, then she yelled, "I am frightened!"

Startled, Michael looked up from behind his papers.

"Have you ever fallen down from a great height?" she went on, more quietly. "Have you ever dreamt of falling, falling? Falling into a black hole with no bottom. A black hole swallowing you up? Have you ever felt all your strength being sucked out of you? Like the air going out of a balloon? With the result of ending up like a shrivelled nothing! Well, have you?"

She moved away and looked at him.

"When I play, I move into a different realm. A place one cannot touch. I do not know where and what it is. It is somehow like lovemaking. For a few seconds, I feel that I am not here. But when

I come back I have you there. Holding me. I feel you everywhere and I know that I am safe."

She started to cry.

"At the last concert, I could not see you in your seat. I was frightened to finish my playing without you catching me afterward. Then you were there and held me. You gave me my strength back. Then I could carry on and perform the encore."

She looked at him through her tears.

"How am I going to manage when you are not there?"

"I will always be there when you need me!"

"Will you stay with me tonight?"

"Rubin is staying in the cellar flat."

"No! In my room. High up under the roof. I have a big bed!"

FIFTY-NINE

A new bunch of flowers stood in the wide-open window of Andrea Coder's office. She had asked Tom to see her before he had lunch with his mother.

"Would you like some coffee?"

She pointed at the small table on which a coffee pot, two cups and a small plate of biscuits stood.

"Please sit. We need to talk."

She poured the coffee and handed Tom a cup.

"Black and strong, I believe? On our way back from the cemetery Margret and I had a long chat. Better said, Margret talked a lot. I feel very strongly that she had recollections of her childhood when visiting the grave. We now have to give her time to let her memories come to the surface. She is naturally frightened and worried. Please, Tom, do not talk about her past, or of the grave. It really shook her when Clara sang the song. I think she should hum it when in Margret's company. Maybe with an excuse that she just cannot get it out of her head. I feel that this song was one of her mother's favourite. Maybe you can buy a record of Schubert Lieder? Sophia might have been singing them when she was pregnant with Margret. An unborn child is very much aware of outside noises."

She refilled Tom's cup. Andrea had not touched hers.

"Please Tom, no more talk about Margret's past and please do NOT show her the invitation card. It might just be too much for her to accept.

And now to Margret's homecoming."

Andrea handed Tom a brochure.

"This is the place where you can find a professional carer. But they will only come during the day. The only live-in companion I could find is, well…you might not like the idea."

Shifting about in her seat she looked hard at Tom and continued.

"A very dear old friend, alas not with us anymore, had carers from the country. They were farmers' wives. They work in pairs. Each lady works for two weeks. That way they are only two weeks away from their home. The pair will stay with your mother until she cannot live in her flat anymore or dies. It will always be the same two women. They will do everything in the house.

My friend was very happy being looked after by these two ladies. She could die in her bed surrounded by her family. Think about it. Let me know soon before these two go to another job."

"I agree."

"You don't want to think about it?"

"I've spent weeks, months, thinking about it. Now I want action!"

He stood up and kissed Andrea on both cheeks.

"When can I meet the ladies? Show them the flat?"

"I'll get on to them immediately."

He walked across to the window and put his face into the bunch of flowers. Andrea smiled. Looking up, he saw Clara and his mother slowly walking towards the café

Tom watched them from the entrance to the courtyard garden. Oh, how wonderful it would be to have a new, a different, mother coming home! Or would she — at the arrival into her old flat — fall back into her old self? Was she going to accept having someone live with her in the flat? In her kitchen? Doing her shopping?

This week he would start to move his furniture into his newly renovated flat.

Clara noticed him and waved. Margret looked but did not react.

Lunch was as it always was. Margret drank her tea, pushed the food around her plate and said very little. Tom told her about having taken three weeks off work to help her settle into the new flat. He mentioned the carers but did not say that they were farmers' wives. She said nothing about them but leapt immediately into the fray with Tom's work.

"It would not take us three weeks to settle back into the flat! Your father and grandfather hardly ever took time off. You have every Monday off!"

"Look, mother, I am only a telephone call away. You can ring me if things are not satisfactory."

"What do you mean by satisfactory. There was nothing unsatisfactory before! Was there?"

Clara put her hand on Tom's knee and gave it a gentle squeeze.

"Are we going out tomorrow, it being the longest day of the year?" she asked. "I can come home straight after my lesson in the city. I'm sure Rubin will give me the afternoon off. Did you book a table at Sissi?"

He put his hand on top of Clara's and nodded.

Margret looked to Clara.

"I don't really want to go. I get far too tired in the evening. No, I do not think I will come. I'll just be in the way!"

Tom, who was already seething inside, wanted to get up but Clara held on to his knee. She smiled at Margret.

"What a pity. I think Tom has ordered a table on the edge of the decking, so we can see the bonfires up and down river and watch the fireworks. You would not want to miss that, Margret?"

"Well, you will just have to watch it on your own. Also, I have nothing to wear. Only this!" Margret pulled irritably at her dress. "No, Clara, you cannot talk me into coming!"

Tom lit a cigarette. Clara held hard on to his knee.

Taking a deep drag, Tom leaned back and looked at his mother. With a fake smile, he said,

"There is always next year, Mum."

Margret felt his anger. She knew him too well not to notice. Something deep down inside her, telling her that she should make an effort. Reach out to the boy. She pushed it back down, out of feeling's range.

She did not look at him. She did not need to. Margret felt those blue eyes upon her. Theo's eyes! He was so much like her lost love. His calmness and his strength of character. She often felt Theo in Tom. That was the moment when all her emotions turned into hostility. That was the time when she wanted to hurt Tom. She knew she did hurt him deeply. When she could feel his anger, a strange calmness entered her body.

Margret smiled at Clara and got up. She walked through the garden towards the door of the hospital. She did not look at her son.

Clara let go of Tom's knee and went to help Margret, who just waved her away.

"Go back to Tom. He will need you!"

"You know, Margret, Tom does love you."

She said nothing and kept on walking.

Back at the table, Clara found Tom smiling tightly.

"She has done it now! Yes, she has!"

He looked at her and softened.

"I love you and that is all that matters. Now I will take you home and then I have some business to attend to."

"What are you going to do? Can I come?"

"I don't think you will enjoy watching me phoning people."

He gave her another kiss. Releasing his grip, he laughed. It sounded sarcastic.

"I will be ringing the removal company to have my furniture moved into the small flat, then I will cancel the booking at Sissi. I have a better plan for tomorrow. Surprise!"

Andrea Coder was arranging her flowers on the windowsill as she watched the situation between Tom and his mother unfold.

She decided to skip her late lunch. Talking to Margret now

was crucial. She slipped into her shoes and with the sharp click-clack of her heels went in search of Margret.

She found her sitting on her bed, hands clasped in her lap. Pulling up a chair Andrea placed herself next to her. Somehow she liked this strange, complicated woman. Neither talked. Margret's hands slowly relaxed.

"I do not know why such hate swells up in me!" Margret said, staring at the wall. "I just want to hurt him! Push a red-hot poker into his chest! It is very scary this hate."

She turned to Andrea.

"What shall I do?"

Andrea sat in silence. With the utmost concentration she searched for an answer. It was paramount that she found the right one.

"Margret, can you remember what Tom did to make you so angry?"

Feeling the old woman's hands cramp up again, Andrea hoped the question was the right one.

"He…" Margret hissed. "He should have been the one who went, not Theo! He should be in love with me, not with that young girl!"

Margret started talking louder and faster.

"He will break the promise he made. He will leave me to fend for myself! He will follow that girl! She is wrong for him. He needs a good, uncomplicated woman. Someone who helps him run the business! Someone who gives him children! Clara is a spoiled child! Unstable and complicated! One day she will just leave him, break his heart! Tom was educated to run the firm, not to gallivant about making music! From a small child he was trained to take over the company!"

Her hands turned into fists. She pressed them so hard together that her knuckles turned white.

"He should not have those blue eyes, his father's eyes! He has taken Theo's place, but he does not love me. He loves that girl and his stupid music. He should be where he belongs, with his workers and with the company! Not in this fancy world of music and concerts!"

She had wrapped her dress around her hands. Margret was moving her face closer to Andrea.

"I gave Theo and his father a son. A son, they said. 'Dolmer's Engineering will now continue!' To have a son was so important!"

She was becoming more and more agitated. Andrea needed to change the subject. But Margret kept on talking.

"Never have I been of importance. Never!"

She looked back at the wall and quietly continued.

"Only Theo loved me, cared for me, made me feel valued. He made me feel strong. I felt safe so safe with him. Until the boy arrived! *My sunshine* he called him."

Looking back at Andrea.

"Oh, why did he have to die? That was not in our plan! We were going to grow old together. Tom would take over the factory. Marry a suitable girl, have children. Theo and I would be happy again, being together, just the two of us! It is just not right! It is all wrong! Wrong! We did not plan our life like that!"

Her hands relaxed. Margret went limp and sank into herself.

"I am so afraid, Andrea. So very afraid!"

Lifting Margret's legs onto the bed, Andrea helped her lie down. Margret curled up. Andrea covered her.

She stayed sitting by the bed: looking, thinking,

'The circumstances that change our life's plans!'

Tears were running down her face leaving little marks on her make-up.

Back in her office, Andrea started making notes. The death of Theo was the problem, the culprit in bringing up this hate towards her son, who was so much like him. Margret saw Theo in her son. Especially now that he was a young man! She wanted Tom to become her Theo.

But why did she behave so civilly towards Clara? She was

obviously jealous. Maybe she thought that Clara would just fade away and Tom be hers again.

Andrea put her notes down and paced in her office. She stopped at the vase bursting with colourful, fresh flowers. She rearranged them.

"I must, I will, get this right!" she said to the flowers. "Margret is frightened of having to face yet another change in her life. I will have to convince her that everything will be fine. But for now it's down to Tom."

The phone rang.

"Andrea? It's Tom."

"What a coincidence! I was just thinking about you."

"Can you arrange a meeting for me with the two country women? I'm free tomorrow morning and all Thursday.

It is very important that there is someone in the flat when my mother comes back on Monday. I am moving out over the weekend. I cannot live with her. Don't worry, I will not neglect her. I will honour the promise I made!"

"Tom, put your anger aside. She is very frightened of what is ahead of her. You will have to arrange your life so that you can be with her for a little while."

"But I am moving into the little flat this weekend. The removal people are coming in two days! I can NOT live with her. She hates me! How can I live with a person who hates me? Sorry, Andrea, I have made up my mind. I am moving out."

"Well, you have to undo your decisions and all your other appointments! Sorry, Tom. Just for a few weeks until Margret has settled into her life."

"What about the ladies you were talking about? Are they on or off?"

"One of them will be there with you. I will look after that. Please, Tom, this is very important. Only a week or two of your life to help Margret."

There was a long silence on the other end of the line.

"What about Clara. What about me? No, sorry Andrea, I cannot live with a person who hates me. I have tried. Believe me, I have tried. No, sorry, no."

"It will kill her, you know that!"

She heard Tom hang up. She wondered what he would do.

SIXTY

Like a child counting the days and the hours for the arrival of Christmas, Tom was adding up how many more monotonous lunches he was going to consume in the hospital café. He watched his mother slowly stir her soup. Having finished his meal, he ordered coffee and a cup of tea.

"How is your soup, Mum? I will miss this little place."

Tom settled back in his chair and lit a cigarette. He took a drag and then said,

"Tomorrow I am moving some of the furniture into my flat. I don't need much. I am taking grandfather's bed and desk, and a few personal odds and ends."

He looked at her. There was no reaction.

Only a short "Oh."

"On Friday the cleaner from the factory will come and tidy your flat. I thought I might turn grandfather's room into your sitting room. My bedroom can then be used as a spare."

No reaction from Margret.

"I have got the phone connected in my flat; so we can talk over the phone. You can get in contact with me any time."

"Oh, that's a great comfort!"

Margret looked up, her eyes just a slit, her hands tight fists. Sweetly she asked,

"Is Clara moving in with you?"

Tom shook his head.

"Clara will be busy for quite a long time. Maybe until the end of the year."

"So, you are not getting married then?"

He shook his head.

"I hadn't thought about getting married. Not at this stage anyway."

"You are disgusting!" she barked. "You are treating this beautiful, vulnerable girl as if she was your whore!"

She saw the words hit a soft spot. She saw his deep hurt.

It felt as if his chest was being crushed, all the air pushed out. Tom's heart pounded in his throat and temples. Combing his fingers through his hair he tried to pull his anger out of his body. All the while, with hard, darkened eyes, he smiled at his mother.

"Let me take you back to your room, Mother," he said politely.

She shook her head.

"I am going to stay in the garden and enjoy the air of the longest day of the year."

"Excellent. Excellent. What a good idea."

He got up and kissed her forehead.

"Enjoy this day. From now all our days will be getting shorter. I'll see you tomorrow. Maybe Clara can come as well."

Hands in pockets, Tom slowly sauntered through the garden. He hoped he looked calm and relaxed. He found a tune and started whistling. He looked up and saw, behind a large bunch of flours, Andrea watching. He waved to her and mouthed, "Hi".

Tom sat on a bench at the railway station. He was deeply depressed and brooding about his mother's comment. He looked up to see a ray of sunshine walking towards him.

He watched it become Clara in her light, short summer dress, violin case in one hand, a smart leather satchel for her music in the other. Her hair had escaped the comb, the light wind blowing it behind her. She saw him sitting and started skipping. Was it excitement? Or was she showing off?

Tom was ashamed of his thoughts.

"What's wrong?" she asked as he passionately hugged her.

"Nothing that you cannot set right!"

"No, please Tom, what is the matter!"

He had buried his head in her hair, breathing in her scent, her aroma, her smell. Suddenly he pulled away.

"Let's get you home. You must be tired."

Taking her bag, he started walking towards the car.

"Tom! What about the dinner at Sissi's and the fireworks and the bonfires on the river? I was so much looking forward to all that."

Opening the door to the car for her he just smiled.

"Let's get you home. Hop in."

"Please, Tom, at least stay for dinner," Clara begged him as they pulled up at her home.

He shook his head.

"I'm not good company today."

Her mother opened the door for Clara and looked in to Tom.

"How is your mother, Tom?"

She saw the tension in him, the brooding look.

"Are you alright? Is something wrong?"

"No, no, nothing is wrong. And my mother is in fine form. She's coming home on Monday. I still have lots to do before then. I'd better get going. There is a lot for me to do tomorrow. Thank you for asking, Gudrun."

She looked across her shoulder and waved Michael over. He too, saw the tension in Tom.

"Come and have a drink, Tom. A chat. A smoke. Some of that fine Schnapps your gypsy friend makes so potent. Come on, just a quick one!"

The sun had left the garden, the air was still warm. The bottle was almost empty.

"We'd better finish it off," Michael said. "Are you going to the fireworks?"

"I will be able to see it from my bedroom window."

"Surely you will be going out, joining the rest of humanity celebrating this night, the longest in the year? We are going up river with friends. They have built a huge pile of wood for a bonfire to be lit at midnight. Come with us. We are going to have a lot of fun."

Tom shook his head.

"I have a lot on tomorrow. Then I just want to go home."

"Will Clara go with you?"

Again, Tom shook his head.

"Not tonight."

He felt his mother's shocking words seep through him. How could he touch Clara's beautiful body, make love with her harbouring this memory? With every heartbeat, he heard his mother's words, again and again, and again! It was pounding in his head like a huge hammer. Tom got up.

"I have to go."

"One for the road? Another cigarette?"

Tom did not sit down again. He took the cigarette, lit it, and started to walk away.

Michael barred his way.

"My dear, dear friend I know, I can feel it. Something has happened. You can talk to me. I would like to help."

"No, I could not possibly talk to anyone about it. My mother is a monster. I do not know what I did to get her to say such a vile thing. I must go. I have a headache!"

"You have had too much to drink! You cannot drive!"

"I'll call a taxi."

Gudrun joined her husband.

"My dear, dear boy. I cannot bear to see you so unhappy, so upset."

Stepping back she put her hands on Tom's face.

"Don't go home to be alone with your thoughts. Stay with us. We all love you. It would be better for you to stay."

She led Tom into the living room, where he fell into one of the armchairs and started to weep. Clara wanted to comfort him, but Gudrun waved her away.

Rubin, who had been snoozing in the cellar flat, came panting up the stairs wondering what was going on.

Tom took no notice of his teacher. Weeks of tension came silently flooding out of his eyes. With an empty, expressionless voice, Tom said, "No matter what the circumstances, I will start my new life, my own life, this coming week."

He sank back, staring into the void.

Clara started to cry,

"Where are you, Tom! Where?"

Tom just looked at her with his cold light-blue eyes. All he could hear was his mother's voice.

Suddenly Gudrun smacked his face, leaving the imprint of her hand on his cheek. Then she pulled him to her.

"Talk Tom! Talk to me. Tell me!"

"I can't."

"Yes, you can!"

Blankly, looking at the wall, Tom hesitantly said,

"My mother told me that I had made Clara my whore."

Clara gasped. Her hands went to her face.

He turned and looked at Gudrun's gentle face. After a long pause he continued,

"She said: 'You are treating this beautiful, vulnerable girl as if she was your whore!'"

The room was silent. Gudrun and Tom stared at one another. Clara was weeping. Gudrun's outrage showed in her suddenly tight mouth. She shook her head, holding his hands.

"Let that thought go. It is not true!"

Tom shook his head.

"It is so deep in there! I hear it all the time!"

He started hitting his head.

"Do you want me to slap you again? Do you want me to belt that thought out of your brain?"

He shook his head.

"I doubt that would do it."

"Come with us to the party, please. You will make Clara happy!"

With a loud, booming voice Michael called,

"For pity's sake! Who is coming to the bonfire party?"

It was getting close to nightfall when they arrived at the enormous pile of wood and timber, broken chairs and all sorts of flammable bric-a-brac. The lights of the fires across the river competed with the setting of the sun. On the river, boats of all sizes were lit up in festive colours. Large paddle-steamers crowded with jovial tourists slowly paddled upstream. The river and its banks were a scene of joy and laughter.

Tom helped Rubin out of the car. A short distance from the cars were tables and folding chairs. Gudrun and Michael had brought food and placed the plates on the table. Their friends greeted them with joyous laughter. Then someone called from the crowd,

"Let's get on with it!"

All around the pile were stacks of kindling and paper to help start the bonfire. Matches and lighters appeared. With squeals and shouts, the fire took and began to eat its way into the large jumble of timber.

Clara took Tom's hand and got him to join the ring of people dancing around the flames. Rubin declined, finding himself a seat well away from the heat of the fire. The rest of the crowd started to sing a song, its words weaving around fire-spewing demons. Tom soon picked up the melody. The stamping of feet and the skipping; the laughing and shouting as they danced around the now enormous fire took Tom away from his sombre thoughts. As the fire grew larger, so did the circle of people. With arms stretched out, they kept on dancing until one person broke the chain. A number of the party kept on dancing and singing. Some created smaller rings, others danced in pairs; here and there someone by themselves. Everyone was engrossed in the rhythm of their movement.

Clara was with Tom. They were both singing their tune. Something they had made up, just now, for themselves.

"Oh, I love you!" Clara hugged Tom. "We will slay each other's demons. Tom, please tell me that you love me, forever and ever and ever!"

"Clara, will you marry me?"

With a sharp movement she pulled away from him.

"No! Why?"

"I love you! That much! Forever and ever and ever!"

Holding hands they walked to the river's edge. They watched the fires from the other side of the river mirrored in the water. Large boats, small boats, all filled with people singing and laughing, drifting through the yellow-red reflections. Above them, sparks and stars mingled. The longest day had come to an end.

SIXTY-ONE

Great fear grew within Margret. She felt herself lashing out like a cornered beast. She had not been this frightened since she was a little girl. The little girl left with the nuns and the rules and the silence, the discipline. She did not like feeling that fear growing within her.

What would life bring her now? Why did her life have to change? Why could she not just go home and pick up her chores where she left them? The shopping, the lunch packets for Tom, the ironing, cooking, cleaning, knitting, a few chats at the hairdresser.

She sat on the bench in the hospital gardens. She had been sitting there, her mind full of anxious thoughts, since Tom left. The sun had long gone, the light of the longest day still lingering. She wrapped her woollen cardigan around her thin, bony body. Swaying backward and forwards she started to hum. With her thin arms, she hugged herself; swaying and humming.

Slowly, slowly Margret relaxed. She got up stiffly from the hard bench and slowly and aimlessly walked about the courtyard garden. Stopping at one of the large trees she wrapped her arms around its trunk. Quietly, she started to cry.

"Oh mother, come and sing to me. Oh, my love, my Theo come and hug me, hold me. I need you so much!"

She felt utterly alone. Abandoned. Deserted.

A gentle hand took her arm.

"Let's go up on the roof and watch the fireworks," Andrea Coder said to her.

The view over the town and the river; the fires along its banks; the small boats and ships ablaze with lights; the joyous shouts of people in the streets; excited Margret. The sombre thoughts started to leave her. She put her hand on Andrea's shoulder.

"You are a good friend, Andrea."

The hissing sound of a rocket piercing the still night air made them both look around.

"Drinks, drinks!" Andrea shouted excitedly.

She filled the glasses.

"To St John's Day. May all our demons leave us!"

She lifted her glass to Margret. The sky was filled with brilliantly bursting colour.

With a laugh, like a child, Andrea stretched her arms up in the air. The nurses around them started to dance and sing. The joyous atmosphere caught Margret. Stiffly she stretched out her arms and waved them to the music. Soon she picked up the tune, but the words of the song eluded her. She had never heard of St John. But then she had never participated in the solstice celebrations.

The nuns would have called it a party for the Devil. Her in-laws were strict Catholic. Margret did not want to show her ignorance by asking who this particular St John was and what did the demons have to do with this, the longest day? So, she just stood there waving her arms and humming. She had not felt this happy since Theo swirled her about on the dance floor.

Her thought went to her son. Was Tom dancing and singing? Was he getting rid of his demons? Was she his evil spirit?

Slowly her arms stopped swaying. She stood amongst the laughter and cheering, the dancing, the noise of the rockets, the exploding lights above her in the black sky. Total loneliness filled her body, fear started to engulf her.

"I am tired," she said to Andrea.

"Just have a bite to eat, then I will take you back to your room. Please?"

Reluctantly, Margret sat down and had a sip of wine.

"Well, let's see if my demon has left me!" Andrea laughed. "What about you?"

After a long silence, Margret quietly answered,

"Do you think Tom feels that I am evil; some kind of demon? I have been treating him rather badly. What do you think? Please be honest."

Andrea Coder settled back in her seat. As if waiting for an answer from the powers above, she looked up into the now black sky. The celebrations were over. The town was starting to fall back into the quietness of the night. The nurses had returned to their duties.

"Margret, this is the beginning of a new season. Why don't you look upon your new life like that? A new, clean page. No. A new book to be filled with a new life. New is good! New is exciting! Close the old book. You will never forget its content, its story. But you can choose what you would like to remember! Remember; underline the happy parts of your old book."

Margret was picking at the food, breaking up a bread roll. It was too dark to see her expression. Andrea could see her reaction by the way Margret's body became stiff.

"My dear friend," Andrea continued. "Even though you are the most difficult person I have ever met, I do love you. I know Tom loves you. Yes, he does. You must understand that Tom is a grown man. He needs, just like we all did, to start his own life. That does not mean that you are not included in it. You must not push him away! He is a very caring young man with a huge responsibility on his shoulders. He is in love with a wonderful young girl. If it is forever, time will tell."

She took Margret's hand and slowly continued,

"My dear friend you cannot expect life going on the way it always has. You cannot forcefully mould life to your liking! We cannot plan every detail of our lives. Life is peppered with circumstances that hurl us in different directions."

A small squeeze from Margret's hands showed that she had acknowledged what Andrea told her.

Silently, each with their own thoughts, they sat together on the roof terrace of the hospital. The town was silent under the black sky. Only a few fires along the river were still glowing. The boats had gone.

SIXTY-TWO

Arm in arm with Andrea, Margret walked towards the car parked outside the front doors of the hospital. The nurse carried the suitcase. Andrea turned towards Margret and the two women hugged.

"I will come and see you tomorrow with your new companion. I am sure you will like her. She is a lovely young woman. Her name is Barbara."

As Tom helped his mother into the car, he could see a little smile on her face.

"It will be good to get home," she said, without looking at him.

"Yes, Mum," he answered. "The place has been rather quiet without you."

They took the lift up to the flat. Margret was tired from all the goodbyes at the hospital, from the sleepless night full of fear. She could feel how Tom had grown up in the few months she had been away. She also knew that her boy, now a man, had flown the nest. Slight panic set in. What was ahead of her?

"Cup of tea, Mum? I myself am dying for a cup of coffee."

He put the kettle on the gas. On the kitchen table she noticed a bowl of fruit intermingled with some lemons. Looking through the door into the dining room she could see the table had been moved into the middle of the room. On it a large vase filled with shining, white marguerites.

"You have made some changes then?"

Margret walked into the dining room. From there, through the double glass doors, she entered the living room.

"What did you do with granddad's ugly furniture? The room looks lovely now. We might as well have our tea here."

With a sigh, she sat down in her armchair. She saw the basket with her knitting by her seat. Next to the door was a bookshelf partially stacked with new books. She noticed the photo of Tom with his dad. They had been out fishing, both of them looking so happy with their catch. The other armchair was on the other side of the window, facing her. The room was filled with sunshine.

Tom came in with a tray.

"Gudrun made you some biscuits. She's also prepared dinner for us. All I have to do is fry the schnitzel and steam the vegetables. I should manage that. If not, you can tell me how."

He put the cup of tea on the little table next to her. Offering her a biscuit, he laughed.

"You need to put on some weight! You are only skin and bones!"

Tom took his cup and a biscuit and walked to his chair.

"We need some little plates so that the crumbs don't fall all over the clean carpet," Margret said.

Jumping up from his seat Tom waved his arm and, with a smile, declared,

"I am not trained in these matters!"

They sat together sipping their drinks, saying nothing. Margret picked up her knitting, Tom listened to a record through the headphones. Everything seemed to have fallen back into the way it was. Margret was happy.

Tom could hear quiet snores coming from his mother's room. He sat on his bed in his old room, now stripped of its treasures from the past. The wardrobe was empty. The maps and books had gone. His violin was waiting in his new flat; his new life. Oh, how he missed her. And Clara, and the life he had lived the last few weeks. And where had Esther been? Tom felt so far away from that time. But he had decided to stay with his mother until the young woman moved in. Next week. How many times had he said that? Next week life would start anew.

SIXTY-THREE

The clatter of dishes woke him. Tom was lying curled up, fully dressed, on his bed. He could see it was early morning. He got up and realised that there were no clean shirts in his wardrobe. All his clothes were at his flat. He tried to flatten his clothes by running his hands over them. In the bathroom he saw a pressed white shirt neatly place over the stool by the sink.

'Where did she conjure that from?' Tom thought, smiling.

He had a quick wash and shave. Walking down the corridor he could hear soft, quiet singing from the kitchen.

Margret had laid the breakfast table. The kettle was whistling, the tea and coffeepot sitting close by. Margret had brought the vase of marguerites into the kitchen. They stood on the windowsill above the sink. Still humming she was looking at them. Sneaking up behind her Tom gently put his hands on her shoulder and kissed her on the back of her neck. With a jerking movement Margret got up, turned around and hugged her son, pressing her thin, stiff body onto his. Tom hugged her back. Both could feel the love for each other. A feeling never before shown, never given permission to express itself.

Margret let him go, opened her mouth, and spoiled the moment.

"Andrea says that a hug a day keeps you happy and healthy. She is a clever woman and a good friend."

They ate their breakfast in silence.

Tom cleared away the dishes, then left the flat. He needed to walk. It was Tuesday and Clara would be home today. He wanted to feel her love, her softness, her gentle personality. How different his mother was to the Gilles family. As he strolled through the streets of his neighbourhood Tom examined himself. Was it his fault, his behaviour that made Margret the way she was? Was he too sensitive? Was he expecting too much of her? There was no answer forthcoming.

When he returned to the flat from his walk there were three women sitting in the living room, chatting and laughing. Tom stood at the door listening. He could hear his mother and Andrea Coder but could not identify the third.

'Maybe it is because I am not a girl? She always wanted a girl! She always said so when she saw Kira.'

Tom ran his hands through his curly hair, straightened up and walked into the noisy room.

"What a lovely gaggle of happy ladies!" he said.

Andrea jumped up.

"Gaggle, indeed!" she laughed. "How are you, Tom? What a lovely day! What a beautiful flat!"

She pointed at a young woman sitting in Tom's chair.

"This is Barbara, your mum's helper."

Dark blue eyes looked at him. Her jet-black hair was cut short. 'Just like Susanna,' Tom thought. She wore loose summer trousers, a shirt, and sensible flat shoes. She stood up and gave him a strong hand-shake and an honest smile.

"Mr Dolmer," she said. "Pleased to meet you."

Tom watched her as she walked into the kitchen. He noticed her well-built, strong body. 'How old?' he thought. 'Maybe Kira's age? Between thirty-five and forty?'

Coming back into the room Barbara carried a tray with cups and a plate with slices of cake. Tom got up to get the coffee and teapot, but she waved him away, picked up the used cups and returned with the beverages.

Handing Tom his cup she smiled at him.

"Strong and black!"

Tom felt embarrassed. To be served in his own house made him feel uneasy. Subservient people always made him edgy. Even this young woman seemed to have this behaviour inborn. He got up and reached for a slice of cake. Barbara jumped out of her seat to hand it to him.

"Thank you, I am fine! Did you make the cake?"

Settling back she nodded.

"So, when can you start, Barbara?" he asked her. "Obviously there'll be a trial period."

"I was hoping to move in on Thursday as I am free at the moment. I suppose Dr Coder has told you how we work?"

He smiled and nodded.

"Yes. Have you been shown through the flat yet? If not, let me give you the tour."

"Thank you," she said, getting up.

As they walked down the corridor he said,

"It would be good if you moved in as soon as possible. Thursday at the latest. I've got to get back to work. As you know mother will be living here by herself. I have a flat closer to work and I'll be available any time you need me."

"Thursday suits me," she said. "I share this job with my older sister, Linda. We are both married. We both enjoy looking after and helping the elderly. At home in our village, we do not have the opportunity to do so. Also, there is no work to be had where I live. I have a very talented child, she is now fourteen. I would like to get the funds together to send her to university. She wants to become a schoolteacher. Linda lives with us. She has no children. Her husband was killed in an accident."

"I'm sorry to hear that. And your husband?"

"He is a farm worker. Gets jobs here and there. We also have a small farm."

He showed her his old room and she looked in and smiled.

"I like the view. And it has a desk and a bookshelf."

Barbara turned to him.

"I am studying for a certificate to be able to look after the elderly. So a desk and bookshelf would be very useful."

Tom smiled and offered his hand.

"Do you want a written contract, or will you trust my handshake?"

She looked straight at him. Her head slightly cocked to one side as she took his hand.

"I do think I trust you, but will you trust me?"

Taking her hand in both of his Tom laughed out loud,

"I'll take that chance!"

Back in the living room they saw Andrea sitting on the armrest of Margret's chair. They were in deep concentration as Margret knitted. A ball of wool had rolled into the middle of the room. Tom laughed and picked it up.

"Whoever invented knitting was a genius. Very clever making garments with two sticks!"

Andrea looked up.

"Have you two come to an agreement? Margret is very happy having Barbara stay with her. We will still have to meet Linda. So, when can you start?"

"Thursday," Tom said. "It's all sorted."

SIXTY-FOUR

O utside Tom's office window the river moved slowly along. The summer had been hot. He had missed the leisurely flowing water carrying its stories from faraway countries. It rekindled his longing for travel into the unknown. But this time his yearning did not spring from a feeling of wanting to run away. This time it originated from a craving; a craving to learn, to see, to feel all that was new. Foreign countries and their people, their customs, their music.

His body was remembering the evening — the whole night — with Clara in his new flat. They had made love in grandfather's bed and woke up looking out at the untidy garden. They lay there planning, scheming. She was so happy. He was happy. They were happy together.

Suddenly a sweet-smelling breeze surrounded him, its smell almost sickly; it started to choke Tom. He felt threatened, fenced in! Walking away from the window it followed. He knew who it was. Why was Esther so unpleasant? So angry?

"What have I done to make you angry?"

"Clara," a voice whispered.

He felt faint and dizzy. He sat down, his body was both cold and sweaty. His face had gone as white as a sheet.

He poured himself a glass of water. Esther was back, the perfumed air surrounding him. Now she tried to allure him with her music. The music got louder, the smell stronger. A violin reaching high in the air. It sounded like Clara playing.

'But she is in the city having her lesson! I took her to the train this morning!'

He shook his head. He reached for the phone to summon Joyce.

But the phone beat him to it. It rang loudly.

"Hello?" he asked nervously.

Joyce said, "I have Mrs Gilles on the phone. She says it is urgent."

"Gudrun," he said. "What is it?"

"Oh, Tom, I am sorry to call you at work, but I am really worried about Clara. Her teacher, Oskar Bulgakov, just rang. Clara had one of her episodes and will be on the midday train. She was crying and she won't let us meet her. She says it has to be you. But you are at work?"

"I'm on my way," he said.

He arrived at the station far too early. He bought a sandwich but was too tense to enjoy it. Time seemed to stand still. The fingers on his wristwatch had hardly moved. There was no one on the platform. He checked the platform number. He checked his watch again.

Eventually he heard the sound of a train approaching. It pulled in and only one passenger got off. A young, distressed woman carrying a violin case. She threw herself into his arms.

"Let me get you home," he said into her hair.

Her head shook against his cheek.

"No. No," she said. "Take me to our little home."

"Your mother is very worried. She would want to see you, to find out what happened."

"We can ring her. I just want to be with you," she said.

They sat in his untidy little garden. The sun was still high, brightening the brown grass and the flower bed full of weeds, some still in flower, some displaying spectacular seed heads. Clara had changed into loose summer trousers and shirt. She undid Tom's tie.

"You look uncomfortable and hot."

He took hold of her hands.

"What happened?"

"I don't want to talk about it. It is too embarrassing. Please don't ask me to talk about it!"

"But I do! Please tell me what happened."

Pulling her hands away, Clara folded them tight in front of her chest.

"Oskar Bulgakov made me play to some top persons of the college. There was a whole panel of people waiting for me. I felt I was not ready to play in front of a panel of, whatever they were, of judges. I got frightened. My hands started to sweat. My teacher put his hand on my shoulder and asked me to play."

She looked at Tom.

"You know what it is like when you start to play, when the music enters your body, when it fills you up with sound, when it takes you away?"

He took her hands and put them to his face.

"Yes, I know what it is like. When it is over you have to come back. So what happened when you came back?"

"There was this deep black hole. On the bottom I was confronted by a panel of old men. I must have run out of the room. I could not find you! I was so angry that you were not there. Oh, Tom, why does this happen to me? All the time! All the time! They'll look upon me as a failure. I will never be able to play professionally!"

He pushed Clara's hands hard to his face.

'There must be a solution. There must be a way!' he thought.

Letting go of her hands he jumped up.

"Would you be prepared to try something?"

She looked at him and nodded uncertainly.

They stood outside a jeweller's shop.

"Something that will connect us together all the time," he said. "Something to remind you of my love."

"I will not wear a ring! It gets in the way! I could not play wearing a ring!"

Tom pointed at a small necklace, a thin gold chain with a pendant in the shape of a four-leaf clover. She looked at him and smiled and they entered the shop.

Tom bought two pendants.

Along with the pendants the shopkeeper brought a velvet-covered tray displaying an array of sparkling rings.

"Would you like to have a look at the engagement rings?" he said, putting on his sweetest smile. Tom shook his head.

"We will look at the rings at a later date. Don't worry about wrapping the pendants, we will wear them."

Tom bent down so that Clara could fasten the gold chain around his neck. It felt foreign on his body. Then he put the pendant around her neck. She hugged Tom.

"Now we are connected!"

She laughed and skipped out of the shop.

They could see the shopkeeper smiling behind the display of jewellery.

SIXTY-FIVE

Rubin and Gudrun were sitting in the garden playing cards. Clara and Tom watched them for a while. Rubin was arguing, waving his arms around.

"It is only a game!"

Gudrun laughed.

"Everything is a game to you! Nothing is a game. Winning is a deadly serious business! Who wants to be a loser?"

He threw his cards on the table and glanced at her slyly.

"Life gave you some pretty good cards. Did you play them right, my dear Gudrun?

And where is that girl of yours? The Ace of Hearts to us all."

The two young people were standing on the small overgrown path leading to the backyard. Clara looked at Tom.

"I know nothing about cards. What is the Ace of Hearts?"

Tom just smiled and walked into the garden.

"Who is winning?"

Gudrun got up and hugged her daughter.

"My clever, clever girl. What about some afternoon tea?"

Mother and daughter walked arm in arm towards the house, Clara showing off her pendant and telling her about Tom's experiment.

Rubin and Tom settled down in the garden. When Tom remarked on the beautiful day, the wonderful summer they'd had and were still having, Rubin mockingly remarked,

"You know, my boy, talking about the weather mostly means that one's dictionary of interesting talk is closed. Any other topics?"

"Scales, then?" Tom asked

"No, no, no! What's going on with that gorgeous girlfriend of yours?"

He noticed the pendant.

"And what on earth is this? Jewellery on a man? Really, Tom! What next!"

Before Tom could reply, Gudrun and Clara returned with the afternoon tea.

They all sat in silence, Clara and Tom playing with their pendants. Gudrun watched her daughter intently.

"Poor Oskar got a real fright when you suddenly ran out of the room."

In embarrassment Clara started to play with her hair.

"Who were those men and why was I not told that I had to play in front of them? It was all very intimidating!" she said hotly.

Gudrun took Clara's hand away from her hair and held it gently.

"Yes," she said. "They were judges. They wanted to see if you were ready, good enough to be entered into the competition. You would be representing their college. One of them is also a psychologist. He will be on hand to help you overcome your troubles."

"Well, am I good enough? Tell me."

She put her hand on her pendant.

"And I don't need a shrink! I have this. Tom will be with me all the time!"

"Then you will have double safety! And yes, they were very impressed with your playing. You are going to represent the college as their first violinist."

"Really? Really?"

Clara jumped up and danced across the garden. Now and then she would stop, stamp her feet and shout, "Yes, yes, yes!"

Rubin took Gudrun's hand in both of his.

"Please be careful. She is very precious to me. She is still very vulnerable. I just cannot stand the thought of her stuck in that blasted black hole! Stuck forever!"

Squeezing his hands Gudrun shook her head.

"Now we know that such a place exists we will be able to avoid the repetition of such events. Please, Rubin, trust me."

She pointed at Tom, who was now chasing the squealing Clara around the pool,

"She's in safe hands with that young man. He is very grounded. He'll keep her on the level."

"He is a gift from heaven; or perhaps somewhere else?" Rubin whispered.

The sound of Michael's car announced his arrival. Susanna came running into the garden.

"I'm in! I'm in!" she shouted, grabbing Tom and Clara by the arms. "Mummy, can I have a proper drink to celebrate? Please!"

Michael, pushing the overgrown shrubbery aside, ambled into the backyard.

"Did I hear the word drink?"

Susanna danced around her father.

"Please Daddy, can I have one of yours."

"Certainly, my dear. When you can afford to buy your own. Drink, Tom?"

He hugged and kissed Gudrun, greeted Rubin and pointed at the young people.

"What's all this! Dancing and squealing! You're not happy about something, are you?"

He went into the downstairs flat and came out with a bottle of Scotch and two glasses.

"What about us?" Susanna pouted.

"I've worked all day. Wine is upstairs in the 'fridge."

Grabbing Tom, Michael settled down in his cane chair.

"Cheers, Tom. So, what is this all about?"

"Clara will be first violin at her academy."

Michael laughed.

"Is that all? One does get used to hearing about success in this family. But I tell you, my boy, I am just so proud of them! Susanna has been accepted into the university. She is going to study Medicine."

Tom looked puzzled.

"So, she is not going to become a chef?"

Again Michael laughed.

"Susanna is very stubborn. Tell her not to do something and she will do it. So, we all congratulated her on her cooking career and hoped that she would study medicine. You'll see when you have children one day."

He offered Tom a cigarette.

"Somehow I will be glad when they all are settled. This house at the moment is like a circus. I admire Gudrun; how she takes it all with such grace and calmness. The incident this morning rattled her a little. I am so grateful to you for picking Clara up from the train. That girl did not want any of us. Only you would do."

He settled back in the chair and chuckled.

"You know, Tom, when I met Gudrun I did not know that she came with an attachment: her fiddle teacher, Rubin!"

"Has he always taught?"

Michael shook his head.

"He was once a well-known virtuoso. He played all over Europe in the best concert halls. But something happened in his life and he never performed again. He became a teacher, hid from the concert scene and his musical friends.

A blessing for Gudrun, because he was sure that she, coming from a musical family, would extend her talents to the concert halls. But she fell pregnant."

Michael smiled and looked at Tom.

"Gudrun then became mine! She never completely withdrew from music making, but she retired from the concert scene. Thanks to this we became a family. Later she started her women's string orchestra. Then we established the Gilles Quartet, mainly playing privately. So, you see, Tom, music has been with us for a long time. Music for enjoyment, not for winning competitions!"

Again, Michael looked at Rubin.

"Don't take me wrong, my dear boy, I do like Rubin. Even though sometimes I do wish he'd never became part of our life. I hold some fears for my daughter. I am frightened that one day she will be stuck in that black hole with no one there to help her out! It has happened to others."

Susanna interrupted them by sitting on Tom's lap and sniffing his glass of Scotch and breathing in the cigarette smoke. Then she started to play with his pendant.

"Great idea this pendant thing. Where did you learn that? It is sort of spiritual, but you're such a down-to-earth guy. Never thought of you dabbling in that field."

She ruffled Tom's curly hair.

"So when are you and Clara getting hitched?"

Before the uncomfortable Tom could issue a denial, she laughed.

"I will never get married. I am going to have lots of lovers and no children."

Giving Tom a quick peck on his cheek she hopped off his lap and joined the others at the table for a glass of wine.

"Are you going to stay for dinner, Tom?" Gudrun called from the table under the walnut tree.

SIXTY-SIX

$\int$omehow this time Margret felt different sitting there on her little stool watching Tom arrange the flowers on her husband's grave. At her last visit, she'd been extremely low-spirited; deeply unhappy and feeling deserted. This time she came with happy tales, with joyful feelings. She told Theo about her new friend; about her relationship with Andrea. She quietly talked about the new experiences she had during the solstice. With joy in her voice Margret talked about Barbara, her live-in helper, saying she almost felt like a daughter. And how happy she was to be back in her own home.

Margret hooked her arm into Tom's and they slowly walked away from the cemetery, along the little brook towards the café. He could feel how fatigued she was.

"Are you tired, Mother? I'll go and get the car."

"Of course not," she snapped back. "I'm fine."

He felt her pull away and struggle to disguise her weariness.

In the café backyard she picked their usual table where she could sit facing the entrance. She always wanted to know what was going on, who was entering the café. They ordered the same cake and drinks, making the waiter smile.

"Extra dollop of cream on your coffee, sir?"

Across the table she watched Tom scooping the whipped cream off his coffee. She watched him but held back her usual criticisms. The cake sat in the middle of the table, two forks next to it.

"I think," she slowly said, "I think I would like to go to my father's grave one of these days. Could you take me? And I would like Clara to come. Maybe she can sing that song for me? I did like it very much. Could you ask her?"

He stared at her in surprise and then slowly nodded.

"Of course," he said. "She would be, and I would be, delighted."

Tom was still smiling when he opened the Mercedes door for his mother outside her home.

"I'll go find a park," he said. "Please wait for me and whatever you do, don't start climbing those stairs. We'll take the lift."

Margret just nodded. There was no energy left in her. She pushed the doorbell and Barbara buzzed the door open.

It was an ornate and heavy old front door. Its little windows heavily barred against very thin intruders. Tom always joked about its fortifications, but now Margret could not see anything funny. However hard she tried, the door did not want to open for her. With a click it locked itself again.

Barbara came and let her in. She took Margret's arm and led her to a seat inside the building.

"This is ridiculous!" Margret shouted. "I must get my strength back. Where is my son?"

She heard his key in the lock.

"Right here. Let's go up."

Tom took her arm and Barbara helped by holding the other.

On his way back to the car Tom passed Jason's shop. It was locked and empty. An agent's For Leas sign hung in the window. There was no sign on the door to indicate where Jason had gone. He looked sadly across the road to the wine bar where he first met Clara; remembering her ridiculous drink in its silly fluted glass with the olive on a stick. He thought about the *Lark Ascending* and how it had affected him; about his first meeting with his pretentious teacher, Rubin. Jason gave him the courage to buy his beloved Steiner violin. This little corner shop had so much to do with his new life. It all felt so long ago, yet only a few months had passed.

Returning to his own little flat he was greeted by wonderful smells coming from the kitchen.

"Honey, darling, welcome home. Look, I am making you dinner! Honey-bunny!"

The small kitchen was in total disarray. Clara wore a very short, frilly apron and very little else. She was dipping something into a bowl.

Tom stepped back.

"What's this *Honey-bunny* thing all about? And where is my drink, woman?"

"Coming up, Honey!"

She gave him a glass and the bottle.

"It's the latest thing to call your lover. It is all over American TV! Do you like it?"

He shook his head bemusedly and took the bottle and the glass into his bit of dirt that they called a garden. What a change!

When he first met Clara after her lesson with Rubin, the little birds in the vine were just about to make their nest. The trees were starting to sprout their leaves. Now this same person was literally cooking up a storm in his kitchen, wearing an apron and very little else and calling him, *Honey*! He looked up into the tree at the end of his garden. The leaves were still strong and green. Autumn was a long way away.

"How was your day, Hon?"

Clara sat down on Tom's lap, covering his shirt in flour.

"I can see you don't like me calling you Honey. I hate it too. Just thought I'd test you. How was your day? Mine was fantastico!"

Before he could answer she disappeared back into the kitchen.

"Did you know that Jason's shop is closed and empty?" he called to her.

She reappeared.

"Yes, he has run away! No, he is off to see the world. He said that he had no attachments and as I would not have him he was a free man. Dinner is on. Where would you like to eat?"

They sat outside with the plates on their laps.

"What are they?" Tom asked, fascinated by the long, thin oblongs she served.

"I'm a far better cook than my silly sister, you know. No. Actually, these are called fish fingers. I saw them on the television. All the way from the USA I think. The shops have some amazing stuff. There is an American shop in the city. I'll take you there when you come with me one day."

"What a great idea," he said. "I'd love to serve Zita fish fingers! But why all that flour?"

"Oh, just pretending. You might just have thought they were home made!"

She reached over and took off his tie.

"No more Mr Dolmer, Director!" she said.

He kissed her

"I do like your outfit. Not much to remove!"

"That's the idea Honey!"

SIXTY-SEVEN

'Monday!' Tom whispered to himself as he walked with a swift, springy step towards the town's main park. Today was going to be the first day of his new life. He had taken Clara to the station, gone back to his flat to pick up his instrument, and now was on his way to his violin lesson.

Entering the park Tom noticed a very familiar figure pushing a cart. He put his fingers in his mouth and whistled, just as Jack had taught him. The little old man left his cart and slowly limped towards Tom.

"What's that limp all about?"

Jack looked at Tom with his cheeky eyes and smiled.

"Old age, my lad. Just old age. Nothing death cannot fix! Let's go and sit down. I'd rather talk about you. Long time no see!"

Jack licked his fingers and rolled them through his drooping moustache, making the ends stand up proudly, giving him that happy-Jack face. He sat there concentrating as Tom brought him up to date with his changing life.

"And today," Tom finished, "is the first day of my new life. Nothing, Jack, nothing will deter me from living my life the way I wish it to be."

"Oh dearie me, that sounds really serious! You must have some good connections with Mr and Mrs Fate and all the other spirits up there controlling the future."

With a heavily wrinkled forehead Jack looked up to the heavens.

Twirling the ends of his moustache, he looked hard at Tom.

"Did you not at one time blame your unhappiness, your state

of affairs, on two words. I remember you used them quite a lot. I am pretty sure that you told me about those two words you had pinned up on your wall in your room. One was Disappointment, the other Circumstance. Life is peppered with those two words."

He started limping up and down.

"Never, is another word people throw around like confetti at a wedding! I don't believe in Never, my friend!"

Tom could see that his old friend was in pain as he walked up and down in front of him. What Jack said cut deep. It turned his happy future completely around. Tom suddenly understood that life did not follow a directory. Life did not just start on Monday.

"Sit down, Jack," he said.

"Sitting, standing; there is no difference. I forget when I work. Picking up all that rubbish people drop. But then drinking beer also is great."

He looked at Tom with a twinkle in his eye. Tom took the hint.

They walked across the road to the pub.

The beer helped Jack get his smile and humour back.

"How is Zita?" he asked. "I must go and see her."

Telling Jack about Clara's fish dinner made them both laugh. But then Jack shook his head.

"I am worried about Zita. I don't like the thought of her spending another winter in the old rickety shack. I repaired the stumps a while ago, but it needs more than my handywork to make sure the next flood doesn't wash the building away.

She talks about moving into a small flat, but we all know how unhappy she would be being penned up in a small apartment, jammed in between other people.

She is a Gypsy, you know. I sometimes feel that she would not mind disappearing with her house, her life in the floods of the river."

Tom suddenly felt guilty for having neglected Zita.

"When I'm at work tomorrow, I'll organise someone to go and have a look at the place. It is after all on my property, therefore my responsibility.

Now what about this leg, this limp of yours. Have you seen a doctor?"

Jack laughed.

"There's nothing to be done. It's just part of getting old. Call it a natural falling apart process. I never see doctors."

"Don't be silly. Never is a word to avoid. Circumstances rule your life. Be aware of disappointments."

"You got it, my young friend!"

He gave Tom a slap on the shoulder.

"See you around."

Hawelka's café was, as always, empty. He ordered coffee and a sandwich. He still had a good half hour before his lesson. Having not done his practice, Tom prepared himself to be greeted by Rubin with a tantrum and a telling off.

But he was mistaken. Tom found the door to Rubin's flat open. Rubin sat, in deep thought, in his armchair. The window behind him streamed the sun into the usually dim room. The bright light shone on his teacher's wild hair, creating a spiky halo that slightly moved in the breeze. In his lap, Rubin had sheets of music. He looked up.

"This Oskar Bulgakov is completely out of his mind! Look!"

He grabbed the papers and shook them towards Tom. "Look what he wants Clara to play! He is nuts, crazy, expecting her to play this! And in four months! He is going to kill her!"

He threw the sheets at Tom. Tom picked one up, but all the notes just confused him. No one could play that.

"Give it back!" Rubin shrieked. "This is for the piano that will accompany the violin. It is a transcription of a concerto. The piano will play the part of the entire orchestra."

Pointing at the music he continued.

"It will sound terrible, awful! It will sound horrifying. The judges will all run away, and the girl will die of shame."

"Maybe you should make Clara's teacher aware of the terrible transcription?"

"Telling Oskar Bulgakov? Ha! You try!"

"Are we going to have a lesson?"

"Have you been practising?"

Tom shook his head.

"Well, what's the point? Can you drive me to the Gilles's place?"

"I could, but I'd have to get the car from my flat, then pick Clara up from the station. Why are you going there?"

"It is Monday and I am going to stay the week. Clara will need me at her side. We will have to work hard at getting her to sound good.

And why leave your car at your flat! We'll now need a taxi to get us there!"

Tom was about to say something rude but restrained himself.

Rubin mumbled grumpily to himself as he gathered up the unsatisfactory transcription.

"Order us a taxi," he told Tom. "I'll get my things."

Tom went down the stairs wondering how it was he tolerated this old man. Maybe it was because he loved him?

At the flat Tom let Rubin wander through, looking at everything. He stopped at the glass doors leading out into the small garden and laughed.

"Very basic! Yes, very basic. You should get some of that synthetic grass. Never changes, always green, never grows. I suppose not as comfortable to roll around in though."

"What is synthetic grass?"

Rubin sat down on one of the stools.

"I saw it on The Box; that televisual entertainment machine the Havelka's have installed. I saw a gardening program that featured this synthetic grass. I don't know if it was green because the picture was in black and white."

Rubin laughed.

"Why I watched a gardening program, I do not know. I have no garden. This box somehow grabs you with its moving pictures. Very worrying, very worrying! But a great entertainer for those who cannot make their own entertainment. Perhaps you should purchase one for your mother? They are great for people who have nothing to talk about. You know, Tom, the sort of people who can only talk about the weather!"

They both laughed.

"I like your flat," Rubin continued, waving his arm around the room. "Very masculine! There is nothing here that is not needed. I'd like to see a few more paintings. Maybe you would like one of mine? I have too many!

And I do like your little garden even though it is such a jumble.

And no stairs to climb! Those stairs of mine will either keep me young or kill me." Getting up he had another look around the small flat.

"Well done, son!"

He patted Tom on the shoulder.

SIXTY-EIGHT

Margret could not sleep. First she lay on her bed, then she got up and walked about in her room. She ended up sitting on her bed looking out the window that faced the building across the street. Not that she noticed the ugly view. Her thoughts would not stand still, churning about in her head. The framed enlarged invitation card of Sophia Grete Gallas stood on her dressing table facing the bed. Margret could still feel her son's warm, gentle body and his hug. She could feel her love growing towards her son. He was so much like his father.

'Not his hair, though', she thought, smiling. 'That came from me.'

Looking at the picture she shook her head. There was no way that she could accept Miss Gallas to be her mother.

But then she thought,

'She has the same hair as Tom and me!' And Tom has that love of music and his beautiful voice!

I think I once loved music. I might have even liked to sing. But my mother, if she was my mother, sent me to the convent boarding school and I was not allowed to sing, except in church. I was punished for singing, for laughing, for being happy! I was told I would never go to heaven.

Maybe I should give music a try?'

She got up and walked into the living room. It was now dark and she was not used to the new room. She bumped into a chair and cried out.

Her helper came running. It was now Linda, the older sister, not Barbara.

"Mrs Dolmer? Are you alright?"

"I'm fine! I wanted to hear the record Tom brought me, but I don't know how to operate the gramophone."

"Sit down, Mrs Dolmer. Let me do it. I know how it works. Is this the record?"

She held up the sleeve. It showed a photo of a young woman with her eyes closed, her hair blowing in the wind. Margret nodded.

She heard the machine click on.

"The valves need to warm up," Linda explained as they waited.

The young woman on the sleeve began to sing in a language she did not recognise. She was accompanied by a piano. The tune was familiar. Margret settled down in her armchair, closed her eyes, and listened. Linda went into the kitchen to make her a hot drink of cocoa.

When she returned Margret looked at her, puzzled.

"I know this music," she said. "Tom must have played it. I will ask him. I do like it, though."

"Here's your cocoa, Mrs Dolmer."

"Very soothing," she said as she sipped her drink.

Margret fell asleep in her chair, listening to Franz Schubert's, *Winterreise*. Linda covered her with a woollen blanket and when one side of the LP finished, she turned it over.

Margret held Tom's hand. Tom had his arm around Clara. Stopping in front of the impressive, ornate iron gates Margret again felt them growing in front of her. Or was she getting smaller? Holding on to her son's hand, she looked up at him. Being a little taller than her made Margret feel small. Tom could feel the increased pressure of her hand. She looked up along the raked gravel path. In the distance a man turned into a number of people that became a whole train of people.

Margret blinked and they were all gone.

She felt faint. When they reached the grave she sat down. Both Clara and Tom waited for her to make a move.

She looked at Clara.

"Will you please sing the song for me again?"

"Of course, I will," Clara said, despite her anxiety. Being a professional musician she found it hard to ad lib. Had she known that Margret wanted her to sing she should have practised.

Clara started to clean the white marble while she quietly sang the song to herself, trying to memorise the music and the words. Margret watched her beautiful hands gently remove leaves and other debris. The breeze blew long strands of her hair over the young woman's face. Margret could only just hear her quiet singing.

"Please, Clara, I cannot hear you. Can you sing a little louder! I really would like to hear the words again. Please?"

Clara took a long time tucking her hair behind her ear. She carefully cleaned the poem and the notes, reading them again, humming the tune once more. Her love of performance had deserted her. In trepidation, she stood up and faced Margret. Tom stood there watching

With a bell-like voice Clara sang,

"Good night, good night
Till all shall awake
Sleep away your joy, sleep away your sorrow.

The full moon is rising
The mist dispersing
And the sky above, how boundless it is!"

After she finished the silence was ear-shattering. Nothing moved. Margret stared at Clara. Tom watched her taking hold of her pendant. He knew what space she was in and put his hand on his chest. Finding the pendant, he sent strength and love to her. She had given everything to the music, as she always did when performing.

Margret sat on the bench, her body straight and tight. Suddenly she got up.

"Take me home!" she snapped.

"Did you not like my singing?"

But Margret impatiently waved her arms about and started to walk away.

Clara began quietly to cry. Had she not performed well enough for Margret?

In the car, Margret told them that she had to see Andrea immediately. They drove to the hospital but the therapist was busy. Andrea promised to see Margret after work.

Sitting outside in his little sad looking garden with a cup of coffee, Tom tried to relive the scene at the cemetery. He had allowed his mother to be the lead person, but why kill the beautiful feeling after Clara's performance? Then her strange behaviour at the gate? He was full of questions and there was no one here to answer them. Did he really need to know the answers?

Tom felt that he had done what he could. If Margret wanted, needed, to find out where she came from, what her childhood was like, it was now up to her to continue searching. He knew that his grandparents were resting under that big white stone. He knew that Margret as a little girl had been loved. He also knew where his love for music came from. Not from Esther; it was in his blood.

The phone woke Clara. She could hear Tom talking, his voice annoyed, his sentences short. The conversation was brief and to the point.

"Who was it?" Clara called from the bedroom. There was no reply. She got up and found Tom sitting outside.

"Who was it?"

"Bloody Andrea nosing around! Wanting to know what happened. She's a bit worried about my mother's behaviour.

I told her what I thought of my mother's behaviour. She behaved selfishly and rudely. She behaved as if she was the only person in the world with problems! She should start looking at the world, looking around her, looking at other people's lives! That's what I told her!"

He looked at Clara. Her hair was all over the place, her blouse partially undone. She looked all crumpled up and beautiful.

"I love you, Clara Gilles, I will love you forever. I promise, yes, I promise!"

Clara threw her arms around Tom's neck.

"You truly promise?"

"I do. And I never break my promises!"

SIXTY-NINE

Clara was on the early morning train on her way to the city for her violin lesson. Tom sat at his desk looking at the large pile of mail. Douglas Henshall was on holidays. There was a lot for Tom to do. Joyce put a cup of coffee on his desk and gave him some documents to sign. Tom declined her help with the mail. He wanted to look through it first. Amongst the mail he saw an ornate envelope, the address in a beautiful handwriting. On the bottom the word, Personal. Picking up his grandfather's paperknife he cut the envelope open.

> Dear Mr Dolmer,
>
> Every time I go to the bathroom my thoughts go to you and your kind help in finding a plumber to repair the aging pipes in my home.
>
> In this short letter I would like to thank you for your kindness.
>
> Best regards
> A. Singer Miss

Tom leaned back in his chair and smiled. He put the letter into the envelope and stood it against the desk lamp. The world was full of kind people. Why let one person spoil your life? Does one have to love one's mother? Is it not enough to just like her? Why was he trying to force love out of his mother? He gently touched

Elvira Singer's letter and turned towards the mail. Most of it was of no interest, half of it advertising.

After he had read the letters and documents to be signed, Tom went down to the factory floor, where he was greeted by Angus Henshall. Angus had checked the stores and made sure all the finished work was well packed and ready to go. Putting his arm around the boy's shoulder Tom laughed and said,

"That is supposed to be my job. Well, I can see your father is training you to become manager of this place. Just don't work too hard. Enjoy your youth! I never had the chance to do so. Well done. Thank you for your help."

Tom walked into the storeroom.

"Do you mind if I just have a look? And maybe do a little checking?"

Nervously the boy watched his boss as he looked over the supply of steel. When he saw that Tom had found a gap in one of the stacks of materials, Angus was quick to point out that he had ordered more.

Gary, the foreman, put his roughened hands on Angus's shoulder.

"He is a clever lad and so quick in learning. I can put this young man to use any of the machines and he will do a perfect job. Just like someone I knew."

He looked up at Tom who he'd known as a young apprentice.

"Angus will end up in his dad's office. Not like me all bent with blackened hands. Though I must say I love them machines and they do for me what I ask of them."

Walking amongst the machines and his workers, Tom noticed a new face, a new apprentice. For a while he watched the young fingers work the steel on the lathe.

"Well done. What's your name and how long have you been here?"

"Hugo, boss. I have been here three months," the boy shyly replied.

Tom could see that the presence of the boss was making the boy nervous.

"Good work. Keep it up, Hugo," Tom said to the boy and continued his walk through the noisy room, greeting all his workers, drawing in the smell of turned steel and engine oil. He did miss this odour and the noise of the machines. He missed the creating of intricate parts on the lathe. Before leaving the room, Tom turned around watching, reminiscing.

Now he belonged upstairs in his office, answering telephone calls, talking to clients, getting reminder notes from his secretary, being tied to this factory until Douglas returned from his holidays. Sadly he climbed the stairs back to his prison, his office.

There he stood at the window and looked down onto the slowly flowing river. The water was low and grey-brown. Tom wondered how the little brook was going in the valley where he'd spent that glorious weekend. Did the trout have enough water?

There was so much beauty in the world. Tom wanted to see and feel it all. Looking at the flowing water again created a deep longing in him to travel. He put his hand on his chest and felt the pendant and his deep love towards Clara. Maybe one day they could travel together?

By now the owner of the small cafe close to the railway station knew Tom. He brought him a strong long black and the newspaper of the day. Clara was going to be on the three o'clock train. Sitting by the window, Tom was more interested in watching the people rushing to and fro than reading the news of the day. It was Friday. Most of the public going towards the station were carrying luggage. Maybe they were going on holiday; maybe to the airport to fly to strange foreign places. There was a young man dressed in sturdy walking shoes, carrying a large backpack.

'That will be me one day,' Tom thought.

Clara was walking against the tide of people. He could see her hair and sometimes her face. She was smiling at the crowd bumping into her. The young man noticed her and nodded. Tom felt a slight jealousy rise.

"Did you see me wave? I was almost stuck in the crowd. I was not sure if you could see me," she said as she sat down next to him.

Tom took her face in both of his hands and kissed her on the lips.

'Silly me!' he thought. 'Being jealous.'

Putting Clara's cup of tea on the table, the waiter smiled. For a moment he allowed his mind to wander to his young days and his courtship. He turned his smile to Clara.

"Can I get you anything else?"

"Yes!" she almost shouted, "One glass of white wine and one Scotch. We are celebrating!"

Her whole being radiated excitement.

"I am accepted, and I have been told what I am going to play. I am in, I am in!"

She pulled out her folder and put the sheets of music in front of Tom. He traced his fingers along the five lines of the stave and started to read and hum the black dots. On the top of the sheet, he read: *Mendelssohn, Violin Concerto E-Minor.*

Pointing at a passage he looked at her.

"This is hard to play! You are sure you will be able to play this?"

The drinks arrived.

"As sure as I sit here, as sure as I love you. Cheers!"

Tom looked at his glass.

"I am driving. It is Friday afternoon and the police will be out in force!"

"Not in the backroads I will show you. Come on, cheers!"

The waiter brought them a plate of cheeses and some bread.

"On the house," he declared taking their empty cups. "My little gift of congratulations."

Gudrun was on her knees working in the garden. Next to her some old flowerpots filled with plants, some empty waiting to be packed with more. Her work was so involved that she did not hear Tom and Clara coming into the garden. Clara's squealing approach pulled her back to the real world.

"I know, I know!" she said, removing her gloves. "Oskar rang me. He will be coming on the six o'clock train. He will be staying the weekend." Looking at Tom, she pointed to the pots.

"Those are for your desert garden. I will help you put them in."

Turning to her daughter Gudrun gave her a big hug. Clara took her mother's arms and started dancing through the garden. Hair flying, clothes billowing, they cavorted around the pool, singing, laughing. They moved towards Tom. Clara grabbed him by the arm and included him in their celebratory joy.

Rubin emerged from the downstairs flat and looked at them, puzzled.

"What on earth is going on?"

"I've been accepted. I'm playing Mendelssohn."

He shrugged.

"Is that all? I could have told you that they would choose you!"

Clara stepped over to the old man. With a big embrace she said to her teacher:

"I could not have done it without you! You made mummy let me play! Without your support, I probably would have ended up in an office or something like that!"

With his head pushed hard into her chest, Rubin could not answer. He felt deeply embarrassed and shamelessly proud. Feeling her breasts rise and fall with her breath, made Rubin feel young. His thought went to Esther and her beautiful body, her over-zealous way of being, her music making and their love for each other.

Gudrun called out,

"Clara, don't suffocate Rubin! We'd like him to be with us a little while longer!"

Michael arrived, and with him a tall, shy, silver-haired man.

"This is the celebrated maestro, Oskar Bulgakov."

The maestro waved diffidently. He had a large leather bag and from it produced bottles of champagne.

"These will need chilling," he said.

"My department," Michael said, taking the bag from him.

Oskar looked straight at Rubin and walked to him, his hand extended.

The old man stepped back and looked at his ex-pupil. Keeping a totally straight face he asked,

"Have you done your scales today? All of them?"

Oskar, being a tall man, stepped back. He let his head hang and looked towards the ground. Shyly, with a smile, he answered,

"Yes, Rubin. I do them both in the morning and evening. All of them!"

They laughed and embraced each other.

Everyone around Rubin was tall. All five of them, his students. One of them on the way to becoming a great performer. But as he stood amongst them in his old black suit he felt like a colossus. He called out,

"What about the champagne! Where is it! Let's all of us celebrate!"

The days were starting to get shorter, the evenings cooler. The little lanterns hanging from the walnut tree struggled to light up the table and its happy diners.

The conversation flowed, now and then interrupted by loud laughter. Rubin complained about not being able to see what he was eating. Oskar, Michael, and Tom were in deep discussion about the combination of engineering and music. Clara had sunk into her seat. Gudrun was upstairs making coffee. Rubin sat quietly, with a smile, looking at his young friends. Now and then he would pick up some food, hold it to one of the lanterns, inspect it before putting it into his mouth. After each bite, he would run his hand over his neatly trimmed beard to make sure that not a crumb was left.

"What about being a medico and a musician?" Michael asked.

"No, no!"

Rubin suddenly got interested in their conversation. "No, one can only have one profession, the other is a hobby! And you, Michael, cannot be a hobby-doctor. I am a professional musician. So is Oskar. Your lovely Clara is on her way to becoming professional. The rest of you? Well, you love music, but you just dabble in it!"

Standing up and pointing his finger at Michael, and then at Tom, he continued,

"How long since you have worked on your scales? Practised! Being a professional musician means working on your music. Like an athlete, you train every day. You live music, you become music! No, no!"

Rubin was hanging over the table, stabbing the air with his finger. "Gudrun could have been a musician. She was, she is, a great performer. But she met you, Michael. You made her pregnant and she chose motherhood over being a professional musician!"

He looked at Clara who was pulling his coat, trying to get him to sit down and stop shouting.

"But your union has created a superb violinist; and a wonderful person."

Total silence fell over the table.

Oskar Bulgakov stood up. One could feel anger in his composed persona.

"Rubin! Don't you ever dare to push Clara too hard. Have you forgotten? Have you forgotten about the person that fell over the edge, never to be able to perform again? Don't you ever push Clara to that edge, my dear friend, and my teacher!"

Rubin stared back at his ex-pupil who was now challenging him. Both of them bristling, like two stags in a meadow.

Tom tried to distract them.

"I won't be staying tonight. Tomorrow I have work to do for a wonderful woman. A friend of us all. I will need helpers if any of you are available."

"Who are you talking about?" Michael asked him, as the two stags turned to see what this distraction was all about.

"It's about Zita and her house and her restaurant. She's having a large load of firewood delivered from the country. Jack is getting too old to manage to stack it on his own. I also want to examine the building. It needs major repairs."

"I'm in," Michael said.

"And me," said Oskar.

"Many hands make work lighter!" Michael said with excitement. "We men will get up early and the girls can follow with hampers of food. We'll need gloves. I'd love a bit of physical work. Anybody not agreeing?"

Rubin said,

"I do not agree. What about your hands? What about me? What am I going to do?"

Tom laughed, "You can sit in the sun and charm Zita, the exotic gypsy woman."

SEVENTY

When they arrived at eight in the morning the wood had already been delivered. Jack was loading the split logs into a wheelbarrow. He was delighted when he saw the four of them step out of the car, though he was not too sure that the old man would be of any help. Jack showed the men where and how to stack the wood. Starting along the north side of the house under the eaves then continuing on both sides of the building, giving it a winter coat. The remainder would then be placed on high ground by the gate. He showed them how to make a circular stack. Another load would be arriving later.

Rubin looked uneasily at the enormous pile of wood. He turned and went to the door of the house, where he was confronted by a dark-skinned woman standing by the wood stove, singing and wearing only an apron and underwear. He could see her muscles move as she worked by the stove. Her hair, blue-black with a few grey streaks, was tied up with a colourful scarf. As he looked around the dark room he saw that this person had only the one room to live in. He was not sure if he wanted to enter.

"Do come in, Rubin. I am just making some coffee and a few little sweet buns. Please sit down," she said over her shoulder.

Tom was under the building looking at the repairs that had to be done. He made a quick architectural drawing, on which he marked the problem spots. A lot of the supporting timber had badly rotted. He would have them replaced with steel. The deck was also in bad shape. He was glad that Jack had made him aware of the condition the place was in. It would not have withstood the year's spring flood.

Zita carried cups out on the deck. Rubin watched her with fascination. From behind she was like a young woman. Looking at her from the front certainly took that impression away. Her face was completely crumpled up. But bright young, black eyes looked at him and her smile revealed a set of strong white teeth.

"Coffee!" she called.

They all sat outside. Michael had told Oskar about her coffee.

"You must be Clara's new teacher, Oskar Bulgakov? Am I right?" she asked as she poured the coffee.

Taking off his working gloves, Oskar offered his hand in greeting. He was rewarded with a good strong handshake. Oskar, being a violin teacher, was very much aware of people's hands. These were small-boned and strong. But they were hard working hands with a gentle tenderness in them. He looked at them closely.

"Have you ever played an instrument?"

She laughed a smoker's laugh. Her black eyes sparkled.

"I am a Romani, a Gypsy. We love music. Everyone plays something. I played the violin and the guitar. We lost all our instruments in the flood before we came here. Now I just sing. Then, you know, to make music you need someone to play with, to tease, to charm. Then things happen. Then the music happens. Not sure if you understand. I am different, I am a Romani."

She slid her hand out of his.

"Oh no," Oskar replied. "We are not different. We just have a different background, different education. I'd love to hear you play. I'd love to play with you! There is nothing more enchanting than being teased and charmed by a musical opponent. We could all play together! You might even be able to teach me something. Next time I will bring you a guitar and a violin and you will play with me."

Zita smiled at him.

Jack was edgy. He wanted them to get back to work. Tom showed Zita his plan of her house.

"We will get that work done with as little interruption to your life as possible," he said.

Looking towards the river and the shrubs with their leaves getting a tinge of autumn colour, they both sat in silence for a while.

"I could never live in a flat, Tom. I would feel penned up. I need nature all around. Also the river, I need the river. It does the travelling for me. It calms me. Do you think that a man like Oskar Bulgakov would play with me? They all talk big those important men! I would love to play again."

With a sigh she continued,

"Well, all that was in another life. Now let's get on with this one and help stack the wood. We could do with another wheelbarrow or two."

The arrival of Gudrun and Clara broke the working rhythm of the men. They had taken it in turns to wheel the barrow from the road to the house. The stacking became neater. Only now and then someone would stop and have a good stretch accompanied by a groan.

The women carried the food into the kitchen and together with Zita they created an inviting lunch. Everyone agreed that the food tasted excellent after the hard work. Rubin had spent the morning snoozing in the sun. He complained about feeling slightly burned. Zita offered him a large straw hat, which made everyone laugh.

After lunch, the truck came with the second load. The workers slowed. They were all getting tired. Mid-afternoon Zita made some more coffee.

"Have you ever heard of Django Reinhard? He was a guitar player, a Gypsy. Oh, he could play. You should get a record of the Hot Club of Paris. I think Kira has all his recordings. You should listen to him play. That is gypsy music. My music!"

Zita looked at Tom.

"You find me cheap guitar and we two can make music together.

Just for fun and joy. Drink up and then go home. Jack and I can finish the rest. You have done a great job and if there was any water in my fishing holes, I would cook you some fish. Thank you for the lovely stacking."

Michael looked hard at Zita.

"You make me another cup of that delicious coffee and I will be back tomorrow helping Jack with the rest of the wood. I am not as fit as I should be. And yes, we will bring a guitar. We have one or two at home."

At eight the next morning they returned. Michael and Oskar in Michael's MG with a guitar and violin. Clara drove Tom's car, carrying his violin. Pushing a wheelbarrow he found in the factory storeroom, Tom walked along the road. Then a taxi arrived with Kira. Rubin had gone back to his own place in his tower. He did not enjoy watching the young people at work. It made him feel old and useless.

With two barrows, work sped up. Soon three sides of the little house were clad in firewood. After coffee, Jack showed them all how to make a round wood stack. He felt extremely proud of being a teacher to these academically trained men. Drawing a large circle in the dirt he explained that the round pile would be covered with the remaining wood, like tiles on a roof.

"Just watch me and do as I do. Then we cannot go wrong. We start in the middle. Base first. We stack the wood to a cone and then create a kind of roof."

But his workers were slow and clumsy. Frustrated, waving his arms around, he said,

"No, better you bring us the wood. Kira and I will do the stacking."

By lunchtime, the first cone was finished.

"Now see, with the wood like that, the rain will just run off. The inside will be completely dry."

While the men were working, Zita began playing the guitar. She remembered all the chords and soon the rhythm of her strumming the strings entered her body. Tom heard the music waft out of the house. He could hear himself playing with her. Let the melody run its own course. Loading his barrow higher with wood made the ones stacking complain, but Tom wanted to finish the job so he could join Zita and her music. When there was a big pile of wood waiting to be stacked, Tom got his violin and joined her. They tuned the instruments and Zita started her rhythmic strumming. Tom listened. She began to tease him with a little melody. He picked it up and off they went.

Michael stood in the doorway, moving to the rhythm, clicking his fingers, then clapping. Jack pushed him aside. He started to dance and whistle. He slapped his thighs and stamped his feet to the beat.

"I want to play!" Oskar looked at Michael. "Let's go and get our violins. Can I borrow yours, Clara? Please?"

By the time they came back, Jack had shown Clara how to play the spoons.

"It is just for having fun, my love," he said as he settled down with a large pot as a percussion instrument. Jack would drum and whistle, then dance and stamp his feet.

Zita and Tom were almost on top of each other, their music intertwined. Tom would pick up a tune and invite her to come along, then Zita would take over. They did not hear the others arrive.

Exhausted, she stopped. Tom finished with a flurry and then started to play scales. He looked at Clara and sang,

"Have you done your scales today? Your scales today?"

Still playing he mimicked Rubin by sticking one finger in the air. Slowly he wiggled it back and forth. Everyone laughed.

"Now I can tell Rubin, with a clear conscience, that I have done my scales when I go to my lesson."

SEVENTY-ONE

Sitting on the steps outside Rubin's flat Tom looked out the little window. The plant climbing up the wall of the synagogue next door had turned scarlet. Tom thought of his first visit and how he had watched the birds making a nest. He remembered Clara storming through the door full of anger towards her teacher. What a whirlwind those six months had been.

Every Monday, when waiting for Rubin to call him in for his lesson, Tom's heart ached to be with Clara. Every Monday for the last few weeks he had taken her to the station. They spent weekends in his flat, doing very little, just being together. Every Monday he missed her presence.

Every Monday the door would open and Rubin would say,

"Have you done your scales?"

Tom would laugh.

"Yes! Every day, twice; morning and evening. And the new piece of music!"

After that Rubin would ask him into his domain.

But not this Monday. He walked past Tom and slowly descended the stairs.

In the café, he ordered their coffee and cake. He looked worried.

"That Oskar Bulgakov has made Clara change violin. Now! Two weeks before the competition! Why? Oh, why?"

Vigorously he stirred his coffee.

"This is utter madness! Utter madness to get her, so close to the big day, to switch instrument. She has played on her beautiful Testore all her life. Bulgakov says the other violin has a better tone, is better suited for Mendelssohn. What does he know? I wonder what she is going to play on?"

Noisily he drank his coffee. Looking at Tom he continued,

"We are not to talk about it to her. We are not to talk about any music to her. The weekends are meant to be a relaxation! There are only two more weekends!"

Rubin started walking up and down.

"What about me? I am a total wreck! Day and night the girl is in my thoughts! Am I forgotten? Me, Rubin Goldmark, who has been looking after my dear Clara all her life? I, who taught her everything she knows!"

With a swooshing movement of his arm he stopped.

"Have I been discarded, thrown away. Tossed on the pile of useless old teachers like a bit of scrap?"

Tom got up and embraced the old man.

"No, Rubin, never! Oskar must have his reasons. I am sure he will tell you later."

Looking up at his tall, latest student, Rubin continued.

"And you? You will never make a violinist. You just do not have the discipline. To you this, these scratchings, are just for fun or relaxation from your boring work with machines! Look what has become of me. Rubin Goldmark, once a concert violinist, now teaching engineers! What next?"

From the back room, Mrs Havelka called.

"He does not mean it, Mr Tom. He has been like this for days. Not being able to see Clara is hard for him. Especially after having worked with her so intensively. You must not take offence, please. He looks forward to seeing you."

They both sat in silence. Rubin thinking of Esther and his lost love, Tom wishing it was Friday.

People started to come out of the station. At the very back, Clara came into view. She looked tired. Her small backpack hung on one shoulder. Tom went to meet her. As he took the backpack from her she told him that she just wanted to go home. She wanted to see her mother and go to sleep in her bed in the attic room of her house. Leaving him standing, she walked slowly to the car. He caught her up with her and opened the door for her. There was no reaction. A fear crept into Tom. It seemed as if Clara was not there, only a shell of a body looking like her.

When she got home she went up to her room and closed the door. Having watched her daughter, Gudrun went into the kitchen and, with a mug of hot milk with a good spoonful of honey in it, followed Clara up the stairs.

Tom found Michael in the garden, hugging the last bit of sun, reading the newspaper. He saw Tom's worried look and glanced up at Clara's attic room.

"Don't worry yourself, Tom. Let her have a few hours of rest and she will be her good old self."

"I hate seeing her like that. What can we do to help her?"

"Stop pushing the girl into competitions! I don't know where that ambition to become famous comes from. I personally blame it on Rubin thinking he can recreate some long-lost love of his through her."

"Gudrun could have been a concert performer. Does she miss it?" Tom said, and then mimicked Rubin,

"Oh, and then he made her pregnant!"

Michael lit another cigarette.

"She still has her music! Gudrun has done some wonderful things, especially starting a woman's orchestra, in a time when women were not allowed to play in a symphony orchestra. Then we have our little quartet. There is a lot of music in this house. So, why do we have to have a famous daughter? So that Rubin can fulfil something he is lacking? Sorry Tom, but I also am worried about Clara's state of mind.

But thank you for being so patient with my daughter. She needs you more than I'd realised."

Upstairs a window opened and Gudrun called them to come

inside. The sun had gone, the garden filled with cool air. She was in the kitchen, preparing a meal. Michael walked up to his wife and kissed her on the back of her neck.

"Are you happy?" he asked. "Has life been good to you?"

Gudrun turned around and stared at him.

"Of course! What has brought this on with you?"

"Worrying about Clara and her performance anxiety for one."

Gudrun shrugged.

"That's how it is. You know she wants nothing more than to perform. Playing for her is almost like a drug. Just the coming out of it, that is her problem! You are a doctor, you know how hard it is to let go of drugs!"

Michael stepped back angrily.

"I never wanted my daughters to be affected like this! And now it's too late to stop it progressing. Now all we can do is slow it down!"

"Tom is always there for her."

"We can't rely only on him!"

Tom sneaked upstairs where he quietly opened the door into her room. Clara lay curled up on her bed. He took his shoes and jacket off and lay down beside her. Pushing her back onto his chest she sighed. Tom buried his face into her hair, breathing in her smell. He found her neck and kissed it.

When they woke up it was dark. Someone had been in the room and put a blanket over them.

They found Gudrun sitting in the kitchen. Michael had stretched out on the sofa and was asleep.

Clara stood in the doorway wrapped in a blanket and looked at her mother. Her face was pale and in the dark light she looked older. Behind her stood Tom. Gudrun looked at her daughter with concern.

"I am so hungry," Clara said. "My head is splitting. My legs are so tired. My back is so sore."

"My poor darling, let me get you some food."

"Come with me," Tom said to her. "Come and sit down."

He led her into the living room where she fell into one of the armchairs. He knelt down in front of her and, taking her foot, he slowly started to massage; first one then the other. He had seen a nurse doing this to his mother and noticed the pleasure she got from it.

Working on Clara's foot gave him as much pleasure as it gave her. She started to unwind. Her shoulders dropped. She relaxed her neck and head.

The sound of plates being put on the table brought them both back from their bliss. Clara opened her eyes.

"Food," she said. "Oh, I am hungry!"

Michael stirred and got up from the sofa. Looking at his daughter's exhausted body made him pick up his packet of cigarettes. He walked out the back door and into the garden. Up and down he walked in the dark, the only visible part of him the glow of the cigarette's ember as he angrily pulled the relaxing smoke into his lungs. With a flash of light, he lit another one.

Coming back into the room he found his family sitting at the coffee table eating in the soft light of the candles Gudrun had lit.

"What a lovely scene," he said. "When you're finished, Tom, might I have a word with you in my office?"

Tom had never been in the office before. The desk, bookshelf and other furniture were old and reminded Tom of his grandfather. But the medical equipment was new, gleaming stainless steel. The room felt like a doctor's surgery.

"For emergencies," Michael said, pointing at the equipment.

"Here, sit down, Tom. I want to ask you to do something for me. I know it is a big ask. Gudrun and I have been fighting all week over Clara's situation. I am so afraid that the girl will crack. When she was at home for most of the week the pressure was not so distressing for her. Now? Now? When she is away all week? Look at her!

I sometimes have the feeling that the teachers want to create some musical phenomenon. Something to satisfy their own ambition. To show her off! I hate seeing her like that. This is the worst she has looked.

She is not a bloody poodle who has to learn to dance! Oh, how much I hate to see her like this!"

Quietly Tom said,

"You wanted to ask me something?"

"I was. We were wondering if you could stay with Clara in the city for the next two weeks? You could stay at my mother's place. There's just her and my brother, Edward, there. It is a huge place, that old family home. Think about it. You don't need to tell me now."

"Michael, there is nothing in the world I would not do to help Clara. But Michael, I am running a factory with workers to look after. I have a mother to be visited. I cannot just, as you say, think about it. I have to talk to my manager and my secretary. We are just a small concern. Every man counts! I cannot just get a, what do you call it, a locum, to take my place."

He got up and turned to the door.

"I can't change the circumstances, the complications that exist. That keep on coming up! Keep getting put in front of me."

He controlled his anger.

"I'm sorry, Michael. I will see what I can do. Right now, I cannot do anything. As much as I would love to say, yes. You'll have to let me sort things out with my company first."

Michael watched his angry stride as Tom left. He turned back to the house and saw Gudrun watching. He shrugged apologetically.

"I upset him," he said.

She heard Tom driving off. "Let him think about it," she said. "Give him time to come around."

SEVENTY-TWO

H e would have preferred to take the train to the city, watching the landscape fly past rather than keeping an eye on the road and the increasing traffic. Tom was on his way to the Gilles family estate outside the city, Gudrun beside him, on the back seat a large flat box with Clara's newly drycleaned dress. Next to it a bunch of flowers for Oma Gilles.

This would be Tom's second week in the city, living in the big Gilles family house on the outskirts. He realised that this coming week would not be as uneventful as the one before. On Thursday was the competition.

Being close to her seemed to have calmed Clara's anxiety. The days had passed in a regular rhythm, something that made everyone feel settled. Tom was not allowed to sit in during Clara's lesson. The first day he spent outside the room, listening. Oskar Bulgakov was a patient, kind teacher. He never lost his temper, nor did he ever raise his voice as Rubin did. Quietly he would ask Clara to play the passage again, then praise her. Sometimes they would play together. This way of tutoring kept Clara in balance. She was falling in love with her teacher and wanted to give him her best.

In his free time, Tom visited museums. He strolled through parks, had a look at the Opera House. When he walked into the concert hall, he heard the little boy inside him say,

'Maybe Esther could not come to the market, because she was called away to play in the Golden Concert Hall.'

'Yes, son,' his father had replied. 'Circumstances can change the passage of life.' Holding on to this thought, Tom stayed for a while in this impressive Hall of Music.

As he drove towards the city, towards Clara, the feeling and memories of Esther became stronger. Did she ever play in the big concert halls of the world? Who was she? Why had Clara been given her instrument? How come Esther has chosen him, luring him to play the violin? Tom could hear Rubin's warning not to let her enchant him. Why?

Gudrun's voice tore Tom away from his thoughts.

"Does your mother know that you are with us in the city?"

Tom just shook his head. He did not want to talk about Margret. Had he not been with her this lunchtime, as he was every Monday? He was frightened that she might find out and their easy relationship would be upset. Quickly, he changed the subject.

"I thought your place was big, but that family mansion is huge! It could accommodate all of you, not just Edward and Oma. Do you ever think about moving back in?"

Gudrun laughed.

"Michael would not go back, ever. There is a small scandal attached to this story.

Well, it was not such a small scandal in those days. Old Dr Gilles MD had the unfortunate habit of having affairs. One day Oma Gilles bought the house we now live in and threw him out of the big house, the mansion, out of the city, out of her life.

He had to start a new practice in a new town.

Michael went with his father and Edward stayed with his mother.

It was a dreadful family split, right down the middle.

Only after the old man's death did Michael get financial support from his mother. And by then Michael himself was a doctor."

Gudrun put her hand on Tom's knee and continued.

"Well, as you can see there are now no cracks left in the relationship between mother and son. Time just wiped all the bad memory out. You know, Tom, time is a great healer."

She watched the suburbs approaching. Tom slowed and turned off on the approach road to the estate.

"Originally the big house belonged to an estate run by Michael's great-grandfather. As the city grew, parts of the property were sold off until only a small oasis of parkland remained. That added to the family fortune.

The original iron gates were retained and that big wrought iron fence built around the whole of the property. I always feel like I'm entering a fortification holding back the encroaching suburbs and modernity and its ills."

Tom drove through the open gates. The gardener waved to him from his little cottage next to the impressive entrance. He followed the curving driveway to the imposing facade of the grand old house.

Oma Gilles sat waiting in her wheelchair with Clara at her side. Oma smiling, Clara grinning from ear to ear, hardly containing her pleasure at the sight of Tom's car.

That evening, high up above in the attic flat of the big house, they made love, soaring away into the private world that only lovers can find.

When he opened the wardrobe in the morning, next to his suit he saw a row of new white shirts. Clara laughed.

"You have charmed my grandmother. She ordered Emma, the housekeeper, to go and buy you all these shirts. You know she has offered us this flat. Anytime we are in the city we can come and stay here."

Tom was still staring at the shirts.

"How did she know my size?"

"Old habits. You left one of your shirts lying about in the bathroom," she teased.

Together they took the underground into the centre of the city from where they walked to the privately run academy of music. After Tom had left Clara with her teacher, he decided to visit some more galleries and museums. His first call was to the large building of the Historical Museum, where he spent all morning. After a quick lunch, he strolled through the narrow streets of the inner part of the city, discovering tiny shops selling fascinating, specialised items.

Walking down a narrow lane Tom noticed a handwritten sign advertising a private Museum for Musical Instruments. Following the arrows, he was led to a door held open by a stool. He put his donation into the waiting jar and entered.

He found himself in the corridor of a flat. Along the walls were the displays.

In the first glass case he noticed a reed sewn onto black velvet. Tom looked at the notice.

No.1 Reed, the first musical instrument.

No. 2 showed a simple flute, then there was a Pan Pipe in no. 3.

And so Tom wandered through the history of the wind instruments, then the strings, percussions and many more. Some of the very old instruments were shown in photographs. The labels told him in which countries these instruments were still in use. His dream to travel was rekindled.

At the end of the display was a small bookshop with armchairs inviting the viewer to sit down and look at the books in comfort.

Tom found a number of interesting books and allowed his mind to travel to strange places. He bought four books, one of them large with beautiful colour photographs.

That evening Tom wanted to show Clara his purchases, but she was not interested. The next day was her big day. Everything circulated around her. The books remained on the little bedside table. She had no interest in books at this moment. Her eyes were on a battered old violin case.

"Is that...?" he began.

"My birthday present violin? Yes."

"I thought you didn't like it?"

"I took it to a luthier and he adjusted the bridge height and did some magic with it and restrung it with those expensive strings Rubin gave me and, well, it plays like nothing I've ever played before. It has such a romantic tone! So *Mendelssohn*. Oskar is very keen for me to play it."

He wanted to ask her more about its origins but she was far too nervous, too preoccupied.

SEVENTY-THREE

She looked a picture in her green-blue silk dress. The colour played tricks on one's eyes as she moved. The blue would flash through the green. It was sleeveless with a large strap running along her right shoulder. Her hair had been tamed with many pins and clips; an especially beautiful comb was pushed into it. She wore a little make-up. Tom wanted so much to give her a hug, but was only allowed to look, not to touch. One thing he could do was to bend down and kiss her pendant. Doing so he felt her shivering with the evening chill.

He looked around and saw Emma standing by Oma's wheelchair.

"She's cold," he said. "Can you get her a wrap?"

Emma returned with an elegant shawl. She draped it over Clara's bare shoulder.

"Break a leg," she whispered.

A taxi circled the driveway and parked ahead of Tom's Mercedes.

The taxi driver jumped out, opening the door for her. He could not keep his eyes of Clara.

"Mademoiselle!" he said.

Tom and Oma watched him whisk their delicate child and love away. Tom checked his pockets for his own keys and his wallet. He kissed Oma on the forehead.

"I'll pick Rubin up at the station," he said.

"I do so hope everything goes well," Oma said. "I wish I could be there."

"So do I, but there's to be no audience for this show, just judges, her teachers, and me as her gofer."

"*Gofer*? What is a gofer?"

"You know. Go fer this, Go fer that. Another Americanism!"

He laughed and got in his car and waved goodbye.

Only the stage was lit. In the dark the judges were waiting. Clara, Oskar, and Tom stood in the wings. She had been warming up, running scales and exercises. She was right, the old violin sang so deeply, so romantically.

Tom thought of Esther.

"Please be with her!" he whispered.

A soft breeze floated around him. He felt it caress his neck and face. Before he could whisper her name, she was gone. Clara turned and looked at him. From her carefully styled hair a strand escaped and gently touched her neck and head. She did not notice. Clara touched her pendant and walked out. She was a picture of total concentration. Behind her came Oskar Bulgakov. He would accompany her on the piano. They bowed to the darkness and were greeted by a few hands clapping. They sounded lost in the auditorium.

Tom opened two buttons of his shirt and found his pendant.

The piano began. It introduced the piece's theme. Then Clara put her instrument to her shoulder and her music filled the small hall. Oskar's accompaniment was discrete. Often the two of them looked at each other. Tom had the feeling that they were making love to each other with their music. Oh, if he was only able to do that. What had Rubin said about his relationship with Esther? How they made love with their music and their bodies? The violin Clara played had the most bewitching tone. It wrapped him up, like an invisible ribbon. He told himself that it was only his romantic love for music that made him believe that he had heard this instrument sing to him before. The feeling of Esther had left him. She was not with him! The strand of hair gently swayed. Clara did not seem to notice. Was Esther with Clara?

Holding on to his pendant Tom looked at Clara playing. She stood erect, her legs slightly apart, hardly moving, just playing, making her violin sing. He shut his eyes and let the music take him away.

With a strong downstroke on the final deep note, Clara finished the concerto. From out of the darkness came enthusiastic applause. Someone in the back of the room called, "Bravo!"

Tom saw Rubin next to him with an enormous bunch of yellow roses.

Clara and Oskar left the stage. The small audience called them back. Taking her hand Oskar gently pulled Clara back on stage. Rubin emerged out of the dark backstage and strutted with the flowers behind them. He bowed deep, handed the bunch to Clara and retreated. Clara took the bunch of roses and, with a provocative gesture, threw them into the dark towards her judges, bowed and walked off stage.

She fell into Tom's arms. With her make-up smudged and her eyes wet with tears, she asked him,

"Do you think I was good enough? Do you think they liked my playing? Do you think I have passed?"

"My darling, darling Clara you did better than you ever can imagine. Did you not hear the clapping and the calls of bravo?"

She shook her head and held him tight.

"Please hold me, hold me, stop me from falling. Oh, I am so cold."

Finding the shawl, Tom wrapped it around her shivering body and held her until she started to calm and relax.

Rubin stood in the background with his hands over his eyes. Oskar Bulgakov had joined the audience and was being congratulated. They could hear the shouting and laughter of the audience congratulating the maestro.

Tom and Rubin led Clara out through the back door to Tom's car.

Rubin had fallen asleep. He sat in the front seat of Tom's car. It was late Sunday afternoon and they were on their way back home. It was a good long drive. There was hardly any traffic on his side of the road. Everyone was going back into the city after having been out in the countryside for the weekend. Clara had stayed behind in the big old house with her grandmother for a few more days.

Suddenly Tom pulled into a side road and stopped the car. After getting out he lit a cigarette. Thinking of Clara's distress made his heart hurt. Taking deep drags of his cigarette did not help him relax. He lit another one.

"Why have we stopped? Oh dear, chain-smoking now?"

Rubin stood in front of Tom, whose eyes were now two deep-blue pools. He could see the anguish in the young man's face. Tom turned away. 'Big men don't cry,' he could hear his mother say.

Rubin took hold of Tom's chin and turned his face back towards him.

"Talk, my dear friend. Talk to me."

"I think," Tom slowly said, "that I have come to the end of my ability to cope with all the situations put in front of me. Oh Rubin, how can I help Clara? How? Then how can I cope with my mother? How can I run a company when my mind is full of hurt and confusion?

I feel so happy amongst the Gilles family and then stifled by my mother's company.

I feel like a chameleon changing colour all the time. I am being looked upon as the stable one. What did Gudrun call me? Our rock! She called me. Well, Rubin, this rock is near crumbling!"

Dropping his cigarette stub, he ground it aggressively into the earth. He pointed into the back seat of his car.

"In my car are four books I bought. One of them is called *Traveling the world with music*. That is what I long for. Travelling with my instrument, meeting other musicians, seeing the world, experiencing all kinds of music!"

He began to pace alongside his car.

"I love Clara too much to leave her. I cannot break the promise to my father about looking after my mother. That takes me to my work which gives both me and Margret the possibility to live well."

Stopping before his old teacher, Tom looked down at him.

"I am so worried about Clara. I thought she had managed to retreat slowly from her high. But she had not! She just hovered on the top, so everyone would think that she had managed her problem. Clara told me it was like holding her breath, holding it in, frightened to let go, to show the judges that she had a problem. What would have happened if I were not there to hold her?"

Angrily Tom pointed his finger at Rubin.

"And who's idea was it to invite a reporter! A music critic! It was supposed to be a closed shop. Then Clara finds that article in the following day's paper. That was shock number two for Clara. Who invited him?"

Rubin pressed himself against the car. He took hold of Tom's finger and gave a high-pitched shout.

"Not me! Not me! Did you read the article? Well, did you?"

Tom shook his head. Being busy calming Clara after she saw her name there, he did not have a chance to read it.

"Well, then, you missed the fact that the story was about Oskar Bulgakov, that charming, good-looking teacher of Clara's. He had found the new talent, Clara Gilles, the young girl of beauty both in looks and playing. Oh, Tom, this man is ambitious for himself. He has never made it to the top. Never was quite good enough. Did you know that he was going out with Gudrun, but Michael came along and snatched her away from him. Now that imbecile is trying it on with her daughter! I know him, I taught him. Yes, him and Gudrun and Michael. None of them made it! Only Gudrun could have."

Rubin moved to the bonnet of the car and tried to sit on the fender.

"It is too late to get Clara away from Oskar, but I will have to make Michael and Gudrun aware of his scheme. This small article will bring great changes. Did you know that he also invited the director of the Philharmonic Orchestra? You know what that means. Before next year is over, she will hold her first concert. Oh, she can do it! But at what expense? I have experienced a collapse in a talented violinist before. That woman never played again in public."

With his old polished, black shoes Rubin started to push the dirt of the ground about. Round and round his shoe went, creating a small circle. Putting his hand into his pocket he pulled out a crumpled old handkerchief. Tom noticed that the old man was weeping. Slowly Rubin said,

"I am not allowed to talk about it. One day I will tell you! Now we better go on. My legs are getting tired."

They got back in the car and, in silence, drove on.

SEVENTY-FOUR

Chaos greeted Tom when he walked into the entrance of Dolmer's Engineering. Joyce was behind the receptionist's desk, on the telephone. The top of the desk was piled high with small parcels. A young man impatiently walked up and down in front of her. Tom immediately stepped in and talked to the agitated man. He needed a signature for the delivery. Taking the book, he signed. He mouthed to Joyce,

"Where's Angus?"

She put her hand over the receiver.

"Angus is sick. So is his father."

Tom put his head in the machine room and waved Gary over.

Together they took the parcels to the storeroom, unwrapped them and put the delivered components in their rightful places.

He returned to Joyce at reception, but she waved him away. She looked stressed.

On his desk was a stack of mail. Documents were lying in a neat pile. Next to them were letters to be signed. After reading and signing the letters, Tom started on the large pile of mail.

Joyce came into the room with two cups of coffee.

"Do you mind, if I join you?"

She placed the strong, black coffee before him.

"You need a shave," she said. "You only look half awake."

"You don't look much better," he said. "What is going on? How long have Douglas and Angus been away?"

"Last Wednesday, but that's not the main cause for panic. We lost our new receptionist!"

"How do you lose a receptionist?"

"I sacked her. She was hopeless! When Angus and Douglas rang on Wednesday, I was running the show on my own!"

"You should have rung me."

"And what good would that have done? You would have felt torn between Clara and here. No, no it never even crossed my mind to ring you!"

She picked up the empty cups and walked towards the door.

"Let's just get on with it!" she said, walking out.

The first thing he did was ring his mother to cancel lunch.

"Why?" she demanded. "What is the reason?"

"Chaos at work, Mother. Joyce sacked the receptionist while I was away. Douglas and Angus are ill…"

She cut him off.

"I'll be there," she said, and hung up.

She arrived with her new help mate, Linda, while Tom was going through the factory and speaking to the men, sizing up the situation.

He returned to his desk and was still ploughing through the pile of mail when the phone rang. To his surprise, he heard his mother's voice.

"Clara on the line, will you talk to her?"

"Is that you, Mother?"

"It's me. I'm answering the phones. Linda is dealing with deliveries. Do you want to talk to your young lady?"

"Can you ask her to please ring back in half an hour?"

He walked out of his office and looked over the balustrade to the reception area. Sure enough, behind the desk sat his mother with Linda. Joyce came and stood next to him.

"Leave her," she whispered. "Leave her be!"

When Clara rang back she was agitated.

"Why did I have to wait so long to talk to you? I'm coming home today. Can you please fetch me from the station? Maybe at five after your lesson with Rubin?"

"Rubin? Oh God, I clean forgot. Look, work is frantic. All sorts of issues. Please take a taxi to my place and can you get some food in? I don't know when I can get away."

"What about Rubin?"

"I'll have to cancel him." "He won't like it."

Tom sighed.

"I miss you," she said.

He couldn't think of anything to say. His mind was a whirl of problems. He hung up without replying.

"Joyce?" he called. "Can you ring Mr Goldmark and give him my apologies? I can't meet him today because of the work situation."

He went down to check on his mother at reception, but she'd left Linda in charge after giving her a short induction in phone manners. He found Margret in the small office behind the desk going through the books.

She looked up, nodded, and went back to the accounts.

Joyce brought her a cup of tea. They smiled at each other, but no words were exchanged.

Lunch had been ordered from a restaurant close by. Tom decided to close the office for an hour. He, Margret and Joyce sat outside in the courtyard overlooking the river.

"How was your time away? How did Clara go with her performance?"

He looked at her in surprise. How did she know? Then he looked at Joyce. She shrugged.

"What should I have done? Lie? I am not good at making up stories."

Margret laughed. Tom felt cornered. He ran his hand through his hair.

"It was a very busy time and she did really well. Really, really well."

"Why don't you both come for lunch on, say, Thursday? You can tell me all about it then. Together. Let me know, so we can get organised."

Margret did not wait for an answer. She turned to Joyce.

"We must get a new receptionist as soon as possible. Do you advertise or use an agency?"

Tom suddenly felt redundant. He got up and walked back to the factory, wondering how he could possibly keep up with his mother's changing moods.

SEVENTY-FIVE

Clara was in the kitchen getting ready to cook a meal. Her mother had written down a recipe for risotto.

"You look terrible!" she said.

Looking at her over the incredible chaos of food on the table Tom blew her a kiss.

"Yes, and I love you too. You look, as always, beautiful."

But Clara was busy cooking. Tom went out in the dark and sat amongst the sad-looking plants Gudrun had so carefully planted. To keep the warmth of the day in the flat he closed the door into the garden. Settling into one of the chairs he lit a cigarette and thought about the strange events of the day. The confusion in him was heightened by coming home to find Clara happy and calm, cooking up a storm. Maybe he had walked into a time warp, maybe something had happened to one of the constellations of the stars?

"Dinner is on. Now! Or it will be spoiled."

The table had been cleared and laid for dinner. In the middle a candle and an uncorked bottle of red wine. Clara was furiously stirring the pot. With a big spoon she dropped a solid blob of something made of rice, with intermingled vegetables, on his plate.

"It will taste better than it looks," she said, unconvincingly. Tom gingerly put some in his mouth. It did taste good. He smiled.

"More please. It is good. Is there a salad?"

"Oh, drats. I forgot. It's in the fridge. We can have it afterwards. Do you mind? Mummy made a dressing."

After dinner they sat in bed well covered by the duvet. The nights were cold now. Tom would have to talk to the property manager about getting the central heating going.

She snuggled up to Tom, who was half asleep.

"How was your day? Mine was full of exhausting and scary happenings."

She nudged him.

"Are you listening? Do you want to know about my day?"

"I need a shower and then sleep. I'm exhausted. Excuse me while I clean myself up."

When he returned, showered and groomed, he found Clara waiting for him with expectations. But there was no energy left in his body. As soon as he touched the pillow he fell into a deep sleep.

Next day they walked down the narrow street to the luncheon date with Margret.

"I'm not sure about this," he said. "I feel like it's a trap."

"Don't be silly. It's a good sign. Maybe it's the beginning of being accepted?"

She stroked his arm, feeling him tense as they approached the door.

He rang the bell.

"Don't you have a key?"

"Yes, but it's not my house any more. It would seem foreign to just walk into the house."

The lock buzzed and Tom pushed the heavy door.

They entered. Margret called down the stairs.

"Haven't you got a key?"

A beautifully laid table greeted them in the dining room. Linda took the flowers Clara brought and put them into a vase. Margret pointed towards the window. She liked to see the sun shine through the blooms.

The three of them settled down in the living room. Margret turned to Clara.

"Tell me about your competition. How was it conducted? Were there many people? How did the other competitors fare?"

"Well, I won!"

Clara smiled at Margret.

"There were five competitors. I did not meet any of them. It was what they call a closed competition. No family, no friends attended. Only Tom, who was there to help me afterwards."

"Afterwards? What happens afterwards?"

Clara frowned. She looked down into her lap.

"I fall apart, basically. I collapse. I...I fall down a deep, dark hole. They have psychologists and what-not to help, but Tom is the one who, through his love and his personality, stops me from falling all the way.

But that is not the reason why I love him!"

She looked up to Margret. "I just love him. I cannot explain."

She settled back in her seat. Looking into her glass she continued.

"Yes, I won. My teacher, Oskar Bulgakov, smuggled a reporter and the Director of the Symphony Orchestra into the room where I played. He was not supposed to do that, and I am not sure why he did. The result was a small article in the arts page of the daily paper. Something that upset me.

On Monday I had a meeting with the Director. My teacher was there as well. I wanted my mother to come. She was busy rehearsing with her orchestra. Daddy had to go back to work and Tom was not there either."

She struggled for a moment. Tom could sense the anxiety rising.

"They wanted me to sign a contract to play with the Symphony Orchestra! I did not know what to do, so I did nothing. I just walked out of the meeting. Back at the house I got my violin, a few personal things and took a taxi to the station. Tom was busy and could not pick me up. But I did manage to cook some sort of gluggy risotto for us."

Even Clara smiled, Margret noticed her eyes becoming watery.

"You poor child! This is all too much, going too fast for a person as young as you. Take your time, my dear, and never, never sign anything until you are sure what you are signing."

Linda called them in for lunch. As always it was a hot meal. Again, something delicious from the farm.

SEVENTY-SIX

B etween the three of them he felt they should be able to choose
the right receptionist. Clara was manning the desk and tele-
phones downstairs. Margret, Joyce and Tom were waiting for
the first person to be interviewed. A row of young women sat
outside the board room.

Margret talked about the days of her father-in-law and how
they chose staff, especially receptionists.

"Look at their hands. You don't want to employ someone with
brightly painted fingernails, particularly if they are long. Also,
too much make-up shows someone who is more concerned about
themselves. Then watch out how they talk. They are the face
of your business! Kind eyes that look straight at you. Well, you
know what I mean."

Margret settled back in her seat. Joyce asked the first candidate
into the room.

Downstairs Clara and Linda were sitting behind the desk.
Clara was taking a call. Linda noticed a small yellow car drive
into the car park. A tall lady, looking very much like Clara, came
into the building. She saw Clara and headed for her. Her face was
grim. Clara waved her away, pointing at the phone in her hand.
Linda quickly sized the situation up.

"Madam, what can I do for you? Sorry, but everyone is busy at
the moment. Please take a seat. We will be with you in a moment."

Gudrun did not move. She looked past Linda to her daughter.

"I have been looking for you everywhere! I need to talk to you
and it is urgent."

"Please take a seat," Linda said.

The first of the interviewees came down the stairs. Her skirt was so tight she had to walk sideways. She had the most amazing hairdo. Clara could not help but point. They all stared at her. Another young woman followed her down.

"Five went up," Clara said. "Three to go."

"Your father and I need to talk with you, young lady," Gudrun said to her.

"I'm at work, can't you see! Can't it wait? At least until Joyce gets back from the interviews."

Another young woman came down the stairs.

"I'll wait," Gudrun said.

"Let me get you a cup of coffee," Linda said to her, placatingly.

They met in Tom's office after the last interviewee had departed. Margret gave Gudrun a cool, polite nod. Neither spoke to the other. Clara stood uncomfortably by the desk.

Tom looked them over.

"Any of you like a job as a receptionist?"

Gudrun gave him a tight smile.

"Sorry, Tom, I need to talk to Clara. She walked out of a meeting yesterday with a very important man, the Director of the Symphony, Sir Richard. Just walked out on the Director of the Symphony Orchestra. It is just not done!"

"I was not prepared for it! I was thrown to the lions once again!"

Margret sat back in one of the armchairs and watched as Clara defended herself.

"Why am I not warned about these things?! I just find myself in situations. I cannot do that, I need to prepare myself! Oskar was so kind and gentle before the competition, I loved him for that. Now he suddenly is pushy and forceful!"

With tears in her eyes she shouted at her mother,

"You know they wanted me to sign a contract! I have no idea what it means when you sign a contract. Oskar got all smoochy and sweet and kept on pointing at the bottom of the document.

It was all too creepy, so I just walked out, got my things and went to the station. I just wanted to be with Tom!"

Gudrun went to hug her daughter, but Clara pushed her away.

"You had no time to come. Daddy had to go to work. Suddenly I am all grown up. Not too long ago Daddy pointed out to me that I was still too young for this and that. Suddenly when I turned twenty-one, I was grown up, to make my own decisions, to do as I pleased. If it was not for Tom, I would have got terribly lost!"

Margret smiled at Clara.

"Clara, mothers are humans, you know. They make mistakes. Some of them…some of us…make big mistakes."

Gudrun nodded understandingly.

"So true, so true!" she said to her. Then she looked to Tom.

"I need to sort this mess out! Do you mind if we talk about it here? It is not private. We have to work out how to handle this. You, Tom, and also Margret might have some ideas. I am not experienced when it comes to business and what Oskar Bulgakov is planning is to use my talented daughter as a business proposition. He wants to be the presenter of this young, talented musician to the world and I don't like it. I know him too well!"

Tom thought a moment. He drummed his fingers on the desk.

"We need to involve Rubin," he said. "He might be a temperamental old bugger, but he knows a lot. We need to find an independent manager for Clara, someone involved in classical music, someone with a good reputation. Oskar seems to be an excellent teacher. I think Clara likes him?"

Clara nodded.

"Clara will have to think what direction she wants to take. I don't know enough about music. Usually in business one needs to be clear about one's direction. Diddle-daddle just confuses the issue. If I may suggest that Clara, Rubin and I get together and find out where Clara wants to go. But first I think, Clara needs to ring Oskar Bulgakov and apologise for her actions. I am sure he will understand."

He looked around the room, sensing that the meeting had reached a resolution.

"Thank you, Tom," Gudrun said. "Thank you very much."

As Margret and Gudrun walked down from the office, Gudrun asked her,

"How did the interviews go? Anybody suitable?"

Margret nodded.

"There were two good candidates."

She stopped at the foot of the stairs to chat with Gudrun.

"You see, the person has to be liked by the staff as well as being a good representative of the firm. The lady I liked the best was more mature then the rest. She had worked in a warehouse, then had a family and is now ready to come back to work. I cannot continue to come. I get too tired. The wonderful Linda does everything for me when we get home."

She walked Gudrun to the door.

"We must get together soon," she said. "Our children are already behaving as if they are married. Oh, how I wish Tom would marry. We'll see, time will tell."

Gudrun took her arm.

"And the same for my daughter. Thank you for the invitation. I'll ring you and we'll make a time."

SEVENTY-SEVEN

Tom and Rubin met over coffee the next Saturday afternoon at Havelka's cafe.

"This is a surprise," Rubin said. "You made whatever it is you want to see me about sound distinctly urgent." "It is urgent and it is about the young woman we both love. Clara."

"Why? What has she done?"

"It's more like what is being done to her. You did warn me about Oskar. Now he wants her to sign an unread contract. There was an argument about it between her and her mother in my office. I was the meat in that sandwich! She needs a manager: a real, experienced performer's manager."

Rubin smiled.

"You are a good man, Tom," he said. "You should be a diplomat, not an engineer. You are absolutely right. Clara needs a manager. A good one, who understands her problem, who can help and guide her. I will have to think hard to find the right person. Someone does come to mind. A woman, a bit younger than myself. The only problem is that she had a run-in, a serious argument, with Oskar. She has very good connections, yes, very good connections."

Rubin stroked his little perfectly trimmed beard.

"It is remarkable that you have walked into our lives. I sometimes think of the strangeness of it. So glad I took you on as my student. Student — ha — student! I almost did not. You will never make a violinist, but you are perfect for Clara. You helped her grow up."

He ordered another coffee and a jug of water.

"All her life Clara has been wrapped up in cotton wool. The early talent of the child scared Gudrun. There had been madness in her family. No...madness is probably too harsh, a little unfair. Let's say a severe breakdown, a collapse which started with the fear of falling. Clara had already shown it often as a child."

Suddenly the old man became quiet.

"Let's not talk about it. Let's talk about what is ahead. Move forward with what we have got. Make the best of it. Yes, improve! After all, Clara is still a child. Very little does she know about life. She is very dear to me. She does remind me of my youth."

Rubin dug his old handkerchief out of his pocket and with an overemphatic noise blew his nose.

All of a sudden he got up.

"Are you by any chance going to go out to the Gilles's house? If you do, can I please come? We might just be able to work something out."

He strutted towards the door.

"Don't move, I am just getting my address book, and my toothbrush."

In the Gilles's garden Rubin approached Clara with outstretched arms.

"Congratulation, my darling!"

He wrapped himself around her, burying his face between her breasts.

"And any excuse for a hug, my dear!"

He drew in her smell, felt her soft body, sensed her escaped strand of hair and yearned for his lost youth. Esther also had been a tall woman. They made a strange looking pair. He small, sporting a mop of untameable black hair. She tall with beautiful long blonde hair. When they hugged, he could nestle his face between her breasts and smell her skin.

He felt Clara push him away.

"Thank you, Rubin. I am quite chuffed. It was good to play and win. But now? I feel like I am in a vacuum. I sort of do not know what to do, or where to go."

He tapped his nose with his finger.

"Rubin has a plan," he said. "That's the reason I am here."

He pulled his well-worn address book from his coat pocket.

"In here," he said, "are the addresses of everyone who is anyone in the musical world. I have rubbed out the dead ones. All of us will put our heads together and work out something. But you, my dear girl, will have to tell us what you want out of life. I can give you examples and advise you what direction to take."

Tom had been watching from the sidelines. Now he stepped forward.

"What is it you want from life?" he asked her.

She shrugged her shoulders.

"Do you want to marry me?" he asked.

He knew she would decline.

She shook her head.

"So, do you just plan to spend your time as you have up till now?"

"Are you making fun of me?"

"I'm asking what you like doing. What you love doing."

"I love playing my violin and I love sleeping with you."

Clara smiled at Tom.

Rubin cleared his throat nervously. He was suddenly embarrassed.

"Maybe playing in an orchestra would be just the thing for you to do?" Tom continued. "Or becoming a music teacher? There are many possibilities in this world for a musical mind."

She looked around. She looked at Tom, at Rubin, to where her mother waited anxiously inside the house.

"I do love performing. I do love sharing my music making. I love the high I feel when playing. I am terrified though about what happens to me afterwards. The feeling of falling is so frightening. The feeling of having no control, of not being able to avoid the drop into the blackness. That blackness which is trying to suck the life out of me. I know I have had lots of help trying to overcome this problem. Only Tom can catch me and hold me until I am able to become myself again. But can I expect him to be there every time I play?"

"Yes, you can!" he said. "And Rubin and I are going to find you the world's best manager for your career! So, let's join your parents and have a drink and talk about it."

Inside, around the table, Rubin laid out his plan.

"I have looked at a number of candidates. I keep on coming back to the same person. There is just a small problem. This lady had a bad falling out with Oskar. I do feel that he should still remain Clara's teacher, if she agrees. Her name is Leslie Dawson. You might have heard of her, Gudrun? She is about ten years younger than me. The problem between her and Oskar can be ironed out. The main thing is to see if Clara likes her."

Proud of having kept the same professional tone as Tom, Rubin leaned back in his chair and smiled at his listeners.

"The final decision is Clara's. And I too, will always be here to support her."

"Thank you, Rubin," Gudrun said. "Thank you very much. How can I repay you for your wisdom?"

"A little supper, perhaps? Some bread and cheese?"

"Come, Clara," Gudrun said. "Come and help me. And we'll have a little chat about things."

Rubin waited until they'd left. He turned to talk with Tom, but Tom smiled at him and walked out into the garden, fingering his cigarette packet open.

Rubin followed him out.

"Is everything all right, Tom?"

Tom blew smoke into the evening air.

"I'm getting in deeper and deeper," he said. "I am her lover and her protector. But I don't understand what you expect from her? Do you want to be her lover, too?"

In the kitchen, Clara was close to tears.

"I don't know what I want!" she burst out to her mother. "I'm confused. I'm frightened. And I find Rubin's clinginess and his body hugs....embarrassing!"

"Rubin is just a soppy old man. He has known you ever since you were born. He looks upon you almost as the child he never had with the woman he loved so much."

"Who was she?" Clara asked.

But Gudrun took the tray and walked into the living room. Clara followed her.

It was hard for her to imagine Rubin having a lover. She decided the woman would have been very short and deferential. He was such a self-important, opinionated old man.

"Rubin, have you ever been married or engaged?"

Rubin looked at Clara in total astonishment. He shook his head.

"No. Neither," he said.

"But you must have been, well, sort of, in love with someone when you were younger?"

He blew Clara a kiss.

"Yes, my dear child, I have been in love many times. Once fatally. Like you are with Tom. With my body and with my soul. Completely, incurably in love."

"What happened to your lover?"

"She left me. She just left. One day she was gone, and I never saw her again."

Gudrun got up and walked back into the kitchen. Tom saw her sitting by the bench with her head in her hands and he went to her. She felt his arm around her shoulders.

"Are you alright, Gudrun?"

She shook her head. Her answer shocked him.

"Her name was Esther. Rubin's love was my mother's twin sister."

She turned towards him.

"You must never tell Clara! Never! You must never talk about her!"

"I met her once when I was a child. It was a meeting that changed…"

"What is going on? Hugging my mother now?"

He looked up as Clara came into the kitchen.

She stopped laughing when she saw that her mother had been crying.

Letting go of Tom, Gudrun stood, turned towards the door and wished them, "Good night."

"What was that all about?" Clara asked him.

"You. We're all concerned for you."

"I'm going to bed," she said. She looked at him from under lowered lids. She pouted a kiss.

He shook his head and smiled.

"I'll join you later. I need to clear my head. And have a smoke."

Passing through the living room he saw Rubin still eating and drinking. He kept going out into the chill of the night.

He lit a cigarette and inhaled.

So many situations now fell into place for Tom. The likeness. The way that Clara and Esther intertwined in his mind. Did Esther lure him to fall in love with Clara rather than with the violin?

Tom stubbed out his cigarette. He looked up into the black sky. 'Did it matter?' he thought.

'I'm happy with my life. Never did I imagine that I could love someone so much as I love Clara. And now, somehow, my mother has found her own pleasant self. Work is demanding, but I like its challenges. The only thing I miss is the possibility of playing my violin. That and the dream of travel still live there, strong in my heart.'

Walking back into the room Rubin greeted him with a hiccup. "Nice smoke?"

Rubin had finished the bottle of wine. He was close to being drunk. He offered Tom a glass. Realising that the bottle was empty he started laughing.

"All gone, all gone. Everything is gone. Nothing is forever. Only the longing stays in your heart, in your chest and in your groin. It aches and aches and aches. It is torture. And now I look at the beautiful Clara and see Esther, in every way. Her body, her hair, her music making. Not her eyes. They are Michael's."

He lifted his now empty glass.

"Cheers, my boy. To love and pain, to loss."

Tom lifted his.

"No, my friend, my teacher! To the future."

"Ha!" was Rubin's answer. "What future. I am an old man! How much future have I got left. My future is Mr Death!"

Getting up he swayed a little and slowly shuffled to the door. Tom helped him get down the stairs to his bedroom. He put him to bed and then climbed up all the stairs to the loft room where Clara was sitting up in bed.

"Where have you been? I have been waiting for ages!"

"Waiting heightens the excitement," was his answer as he slid into bed.

SEVENTY-EIGHT

Tom joined Gudrun on her morning walk in the park across the road from the house. The little dog was running in front of them, reading the messages left from other dogs. Now and then he lifted his little leg to tell his opponents he also had visited this spot. He constantly looked back at Gudrun, making sure that she followed. Tom never had a pet. He asked the name of the dog.

"Michael called him Gorky. A silly thing to call this small creature after such a great man. He was a Russian writer."

She smiled at Tom.

"Michael admires Maxim Gorky. The great man apparently once said: 'Only mothers could think of the future — they give birth to it in their children.' Michael gave me the tiny, little puppy adorned with a pink ribbon. Later he discovered that the little girl dog was a boy dog."

Gudrun laughed out loud.

"I am so glad we did not have sons. He wanted to call his son, Maxim Gorky Gilles! A great name for a man who one day will be famous, he said. I am so glad we have a Clara and a Susanna. Oh, just imagine."

Little, scruffy Gorky heard his name and came, tail wagging, to see what his mistress wanted.

"What kind of a dog is he?"

"I think his DNA would show you that the dogs from the whole neighbourhood took part in fathering him. He is a faithful little fellow."

She bent down and gave Gorky a gentle pat and scratch behind his ear.

"Where is Michael?"

"In the city with his mother. She is a bit poorly."

He is very close to her, even though he chose his father after the separation."

Before they returned to the house Gudrun put her hand on his arm.

"Please do not mention Esther's name. Not to Clara or Rubin or myself. It just brings up a time I would rather forget."

The table was laid. Clara had boiled some eggs. They were wrapped in a small, clean towel in a basket. Having used the timer she hoped that they all would be nicely soft boiled.

"I like my egg hard boiled!" Rubin called from the living room. "Soft eggs upset my beard!"

"Tittle-tattle! Breakfast is on," Clara responded.

One could see that Rubin had slept in his clothes. Tom had only taken off his shoes when he put him to bed. He felt embarrassed undressing his teacher.

Whilst complaining about the terrible night he had; how he spent all night trying to resolve Clara's future; he attacked his egg, making the yolk run over his hand onto the plate. Like a child confronting something very scary, he pulled a face and pushed the plate away.

"All night I was planning and worrying about how to get Leslie and Oskar to be friends again. Did I tell you that Leslie Dawson was born in Australia? Yes, I know, a barbaric country. She was sent to England to get a proper education. She never went back to live in Australia. She visits, but never stays. I met her when touring England. She is a lovely lady, maybe a bit rough, but honest and thorough."

Rubin laughed, almost choking on his bread.

"When there was a problem she always said, *No warries — she'll be all-right.* I was never quite sure who the she was, but we all laughed — not wanting to show our lack of knowledge."

Tom ignored the old man's ramblings.

"Getting to the point," he said. "We need to make an appointment with Leslie Dawson. If you could give me her number, I'll get in contact with her and arrange a meeting. Make them aware that this should be handled in a businesslike manner."

He looked to Clara.

"Excuse my manner. I am not intending to look upon you as a bit of merchandise, but we need to keep things clear and precise.

I have to go to work both Monday and Tuesday. I'll do my best to take the rest of the week off. I have to be back Sunday evening."

He looked back to Rubin.

"So give me her phone number. I'll contact Miss Dawson."

Shocked Rubin looked at him. He wanted to organise the meeting, be the coordinator, be important!

"I want to come!" he said sharply. "No, I will come!"

"You can come, but I will do the talking."

"Oh, how kind of you, Mr Dolmer, engineer, numbers-man. What do you know about music? Except the few scratchings you can produce on your Steiner violin, which is just a copy!"

Rubin got up and stomped about the room. Tom faced him.

"This is not a competition between us! It's a very serious situation dealing with Clara's future."

Rubin shook his head.

"You know nothing, nothing about music! I am the person who should be the mediator!"

Putting her hands on the two men, Gudrun guided them into the living room.

Clara had left and was sitting in the garden. She suddenly felt like an object being fought over. Tom could see her next to the swimming pool slowly moving her hands through the water. She was still wearing her night dress. Her hair was unkept. She looked beautiful. Quietly he promised to help make her dream come true.

"I never break my promises," he said to himself.

Gudrun pushed Rubin into a chair.

"Now listen to me, my good, old friend. Times have changed from the days when you and I were involved in the music world. We need to realise that! We need to step aside and let the new generation step in. Tom will be the right person to take care of Clara. He loves her. And this is also a business transaction. Yes, it sounds very hard. But it is. So please, Rubin, let go of your pride."

Tom had picked up a woollen blanket and left the room. He could see that Clara was upset and cold sitting out there in the chill of the morning air.

Gudrun led Rubin to the window and together they watched as Tom put the blanket around Clara's shoulder, then he bent down and kissed her. She got up and cuddled into Tom.

Gudrun looked at Rubin.

"Do you want to destroy that? You have had your time, your love. You have been successful. You have been on top of that wave, surfing it for many years. Step back, give Tom the information. Please!"

Slowly Clara stopped shivering. She was barefoot. The ground was covered in cold dew. She did not want to go back into the house.

"I am not a piece of meat!"

"Oh yes, you are. All lovely and soft and so good-smelling. A very large piece of meat! And I love every bit of it! And now I am going to eat you!"

He picked her up and hung her over his shoulder. Going through the front door they avoided Rubin and Gudrun. He carried her all the way up to the attic room. They did not appear until lunchtime.

When Tom came down into the living room, he found both Gudrun and Rubin reading. On the table was a sheet of paper. Written on it was the address and telephone number of Leslie Dawson.

SEVENTY-NINE

By now the car almost knew the way to the city and the big house of the Gilles family. Rubin was comfortable lying, supported by a number of cushions, on the back seat. Clara was driving. The last two days had been very stressful for Tom. He was leaning up against the window asleep. To avoid the worst of the traffic they decided to leave Tuesday in the evening.

During lunch with his mother on Monday, Tom was told that both Barbara and Linda had to stay on the farm for most of the following week. Tom had to organise his life around it. He probably would have to stay with Margret. It all depended on what happened during the interview with Leslie Dawson.

The noise of the wheels on the gravel driveway woke Tom. Clara parked the car in the garage. Emma, the housekeeper, was already waiting for them. She took some of the luggage. They helped Rubin out of the back seat. He was stiff and complaining.

Tom would have liked to go for a walk in the garden, but it started to rain. Smelling the beautiful odour of wet earth, he stopped in the doorway of the house and looked out into the dark. Small lights were showing the way into the garden. Never would one have guessed that just at the end of the path new houses had been built on land that once was part of a vast estate.

Inside, supper was waiting for them. Oma Gilles sat at the end of the table; next to her a young nurse.

"Please excuse me for not coming to greet you. I feel the cold rather badly these days. It creeps into my bones."

She waved to Clara and demanded a kiss.

"No hugs!" Michael had walked into the room. "She is still a little sore after her operation. Nothing to worry about. Just at her great age it takes a little longer to get over a medical procedure, no matter how small."

Tom kissed her on the other cheek, making the old lady smile.

"Now I am totally in balance. How are you, you two beautiful children? I just want to look at you. I get very tired quickly and talking does exhaust me a little. Please sit next to me."

The nurse pulled the chairs closer to her and, holding Tom and Clara's hands, Oma sat there smiling, looking around the table at her family.

"Please eat!" she urged.

Emma brought her a bowl of broth.

Feeling the slender, cold hand of the old lady, Tom started to think of his grandparents. He could have met his grandfather. He only died about ten years ago. How did they live? His grandmother must have come from a very good family, an educated family, maybe a wealthy family.

He felt a slight pressure from the hand that held his.

"A penny for your thoughts, Tom."

He gave her a gentle kiss on her cheek.

"I was wondering if you might become my substitute grandmother."

"I will think about it, my boy. I will let you know tomorrow. Now I must retire." Turning towards the nurse she smiled at everyone and was rolled out of the room. Michael went with her. Clara had tried very hard not to show Oma her distressed state of mind. As soon as Oma was out of the room, she started weeping. She could not imagine her life without her Oma.

The appointment with Leslie Dawson was scheduled for nine in the morning. Rubin was going to stay behind. He took it quite gracefully. But Clara was nervous.

They arrived at Leslie Dawson's flat just before the appointed hour.

A young woman showed them into a very large room with a grand piano. She asked them to be seated and pointed to a group of comfortable armchairs situated in a corner of the room. Then she left. The walls were covered in bookshelves. The street trees outside growing right up to the window made the room rather dark.

The woman came back with coffee, cups and a small bowl of chocolates. She poured the coffee, offered them milk and sugar, smiled and left again. Tom took his coffee and walked to the window. Outside, below him, a tram was rattling past, then another. On the opposite side of the road he could just make out a park. The tree outside the window was incredible dense.

"It's an elm," someone said behind him in a rather deep, husky voice. The woman standing behind him held out her hand for a greeting.

"You must be Tom Dolmer. And the young lady hiding in the big chair, Clara. Well my child, your reputation is galloping in front of you. I have heard lots about you; all good things."

"But I must ask," she said sternly, "if you have apologised to Oskar for your sudden departure from the meeting with the Director of the Symphony Orchestra?"

Clara nodded.

"Excellent! We have a clean start."

Leslie was a strong-looking woman, of medium height, with a round face. Her black hair was pulled back in a neat bun. Tom liked her immediately. Her language was impeccable, without any hint of an accent.

"Now, Mr Dolmer, what can I do for you? I believe that you are representing Clara. Is she your wife, fiancé, girlfriend?"

Clara jumped up.

"We are not married. I am more than his girlfriend. I don't think a word had been invented for our relationship."

"I get it. You are madly in love," she continued, taking a cigarette out of a wooden box. "Please Mr Dolmer let me know a bit about yourself. Who you are?"

"I'm an engineer and Director of a family firm, Dolmer's Engineering. And I am a student of the violin."

"And your family? Are there musicians in it?"

He shook his head.

Clara protested.

"His grandmother…"

He interrupted her.

"I understand Miss Dawson's need to know my background, but this meeting is about you, not about me. I do not know of any musicians in my immediate family. What we are here for is to discuss you and your future."

Miss Dawson smiled and held up a hand.

"Well, Mr Dolmer you certainly know how to get to the point of the matter. You are more than just an engineer, aren't you?"

"He runs an engineering works. He is the Director of Dolmer's Engineering in our town. The business has an impeccable reputation!"

Clara had walked up to Tom's side.

"All Miss Dawson needs to know is that I am, as Rubin so diplomatically puts it, a numbers man, not a musician, and not involved in the music industry. I am here as your mediator. I am simply here to get you someone suited to take care of your career, to help you, to lead you. I am not the important one, you are. So please let's get on with it."

Leslie Dawson smiled and turned towards Clara.

"Young lady, how do you see your future?"

Clara was clear and precise.

"I do not wish to be buried in the back row of an orchestra. I wish to perform. Up front where people can see me and hear me."

"I believe you have a small psychological problem which could create difficulties."

Clara stared at her. Miss Dawson smiled again.

"You see, dear, I like to do my homework. I spoke to Oskar, and to Rubin. They praised your talent, your technique and your precise playing, your memory and your perfect ear. Then my dear girl, you have had the best teacher in Rubin. There is no better, even though he can be a little difficult at times. It was a good choice of him to make you continue playing under Oskar. But watch that man, he is very ambitious and can be ruthless — as I myself have discovered. But that is water under the Harbour Bridge. And now you have your lover, Mr Dolmer, who will look after you."

She lit another cigarette and shook Clara's hand.

"Now my dear, now it is up to you to decide if you would like me to be the one to look after your affairs. Maybe you would like to think about it, talk it over with Mr Dolmer? If you'll excuse me, I will be back in a little while."

With that she got up and left them.

Tom went back to the window and watched the trams rattle past below. He liked Leslie Dawson. If only everyone he had to deal with was like that: straight to the point. Yes, he liked her. She would be good for Clara. He felt Clara next to him.

"What did you think of her?" she asked.

"I like her."

"At first I felt she was a bit cold and stern. I wasn't sure if I could warm to her. Then I thought she was all right. Then I did not know. In the end I decided I've never met anybody like her. So...I can't decide."

The door opened and Miss Dawson entered the room.

"Well? Did you come to a decision?"

She looked at Clara, who smiled shyly at her. Miss Dawson could see that Clara was not sure what to decide.

"I have rung Oskar and we are all going out for lunch so I hope you have no appointments. He will be here soon."

She went to the wooden box and took a handful of cigarettes which she put into a silver cigarette case.

A table for four was reserved for them. The establishment looked like it had been built many centuries ago. The curtains, made from heavy, brown velvet seemed to be as ancient as the building. The head waiter, in a well-worn, black suit. greeted Oskar by name. It was obviously his favourite café restaurant. At the table the waiter pulled out a chair for Clara.

"Mademoiselle."

And then gave them all a menu.

"The usual wine, Mr Bulgakov?"

He nodded, then helped Clara to choose a meal.

Over coffee, and after they had consumed two bottles of white wine, the conversation became relaxed. Oskar pointed at Leslie. With a laugh he told Tom that under the serious exterior of his friend lived a simple Australian farmer. She let the comment pass her by, but then she looked at Clara, then at Tom.

"My family actually owns two properties. One of them is bigger than your country! We run sheep for wool and beef cattle. Our sheep have won many prizes for their fine fleece. These places are called stations not farms. We are known as station owners and we employ a large number of people. We are not simple farmers. Lesson over.

I would like some cake, please."

She waved to the waiter.

Tom wanted to know more about her country, her life on a station. She shook her head.

"Today we do business. Some other time we talk about Australia. I will show you pictures of my beautiful home in the outback and tell you about my childhood and you will tell me about that secret you are carrying inside you. We will peel each other's armour off like onions. But today we have to keep a head for business. Today after lunch we will work out how we can help Clara."

Clara handed the sheet of paper to Tom to read. She did not quite know how to handle the situation. On the top of the document, in beautiful handwriting, the word: *Agreement*.

Then Leslie's name, address, and contact telephone number.

"I like to have things in writing. This is not a binding document, only an agreement, so we all know where we are heading. You have to excuse me being so meticulous. That's just how I am."

There was only one sentence:

"I, Clara Gilles, will employ Leslie Dawson to be my adviser in all matters of my musical career."

Tom thought it to be a strange document. Then Leslie Dawson was not an ordinary person.

"My first advice would be to reconvene a meeting with the Director of the Symphony Orchestra. What do you say to that, Clara?"

Clara nodded.

"The only reason I left the last meeting was due to not having been warned by Oskar that I was being interviewed.

Please, Miss Dawson, I need to have time to think about situations I have to confront. Perhaps this comes partly from my musical education, from one of Rubin's rules: never to ad lib, always be prepared."

Clara signed the Agreement between her and Miss Dawson.

"Mr Dolmer, would you like to be part of the meeting?"

He shook his head.

"I have to be back by Sunday evening. The week after that I'll be occupied with matters at home. But I would very much like to meet the orchestra's Director."

The sun was low, and a few rays had found their way into the room. Tom detected some ginger streaks in Leslie's black hair. She had blue eyes and the excitement of the afternoon, plus the lunchtime drink, had given her shiny red cheeks. She looked much younger now the light was shining on her.

She got up and offered her hand.

"Can I call you Tom? I will try to get Sir Richard to see us this week. Goodbye."

Walking over to Clara she smiled.

"Goodbye, Clara. Do keep up your lessons with Oskar Bulgakov. You also have Rubin to help you. And with your charming lover by your side all will move along splendidly. I will do my best to help."

EIGHTY

They drove home, Rubin asleep in the back seat, Clara beside Tom. Tom drove in silence, wrestling with how to get to the meeting with Sir Richard — who could only spare them time on the Friday of the following week.

And this, of all times, was when neither of Margret's helpers could come down from the farm. The harvest had to be got in.

"You look worried," Clara said to him, putting her hand on his knee. "What is it?"

"How do I get to this meeting, this important meeting with Sir Richard when I will be the only one able to look after my mother that day?"

"But Oma said Margret could come with us and stay in the guest room. I'm sure she can entertain Margret for a few hours while we're at the meeting."

She studied his frowning face a moment.

"Just ask Margret. Just ask her if she would like to come? All she can do is say no. We could go to an exhibition or a museum or whatever. Just ask her."

Clara was quite right, Tom thought. Yes, all she could do was refuse or have some sort of a tantrum. And she did seem to be getting stronger.

He sighed.

"I'll will have to move in with her for the week. I can still feel the marks of her whip on my heart!"

"You'll be fine. She seems to be much more mellow now than when I first met her. She has really improved all round."

Tom dropped Rubin off at his flat and Clara off at the shops to get some groceries. With a sinking heart he made his way to his mother's apartment building.

Barbara was just about ready to leave when he arrived. They exchanged a few words. She promised to be back on Sunday evening.

"I am really sorry to put you into this situation. It is harvest time and both of us have to help."

She made him a strong black coffee and left. He found himself alone in his mother's home. He now felt like a stranger there. Tom carried his coffee into the spare bedroom, where he was going to spend the nights. Opening the window he was confronted by the grey wall of an airshaft. The room was dark and it felt unused.

He remembered his mother doing her ironing and sewing here. In those days it smelled of ironed clothes and of his mother. As a little boy he always wanted to help. There was a small bottle of water that Margret used to moisten her clothes with before ironing them. It had an attachment on the top that splashed the water evenly over the fabric. She would never allow him to use it, to help her. He remembered the little chair he had to sit on. From there he watched the iron glide over the crumpled-up fabric. He was fascinated how flat the clothes became. And he loved the smell. Discovering the little chair on top of the wardrobe, he touched it, smiling, then slid it back and went in search of his mother.

Tom found her in the living room with her knitting and sat down next to her. He put his coffee cup on the small table beside her basket of wool.

"I was just remembering when you used that room for your sewing and ironing and how I used to watch you."

She smiled, never losing focus on her clicking needles.

"You were always full of questions. What made the iron hot? What was electricity? Why can we not see it? Why, why, why? I never did know what to say. Your father was so good in making up believable answers. Electricity was the most interesting thing.

How this, how that, how did it manage to change wire? How did it manage to flow through a ninety-degree angle? I remember Theo telling you that there was a little man sitting in the corner bending the electricity over his little knee. You would try so hard to see him, wondering if he had a coat in the winter. Yes, you and your dad. Like two peas in a pod."

She looked up and smiled at her son, now only a few years older than Theo when they married.

"How did Clara go with her interviews or whatever it was?"

Margret did not want to think any more about her past; even though Andrea had pointed out to her that life was also filled with good and beautiful moments. They should not be lost.

"Thank you, it went extremely well."

Margret did not listen to Tom's report. Her eyes had moved to the daily newspaper on the small table next to her. She put aside her knitting and showed him an article on Adult Education.

"I'm thinking about enrolling in a History course. You know, Tom, I have always been interested in, I've always liked, history. I feel I would like to learn some more. But maybe studying books would be better than evening classes? Could you maybe get me some?"

"I've visited the Historical Museum in the city. They have an excellent bookshop. Would you like to go one day?"

She looked doubtful.

"I am not sure. It would be very tiring. I don't know."

She picked up Tom's empty cup and took it into the kitchen where she stood for a long time by the window.

'Historical Museum,' she thought. One of her favourite places when she was a girl.

"Why not?" she said to the window. "Yes, why not!"

She saw Tom's reflection in the window. Turning around she said,

"Why not! Yes, I would like to go and visit the museum again."

Tom's delight showed on his face.

"Let's go next week, while your ladies are away."

She looked a little unsure. He hurried to convince her.

"So, let's make a plan. We would have to stay the night. That is no problem, there are plenty of hotels in the city. You tell me when and I will book one. It would be towards the end of the week. I am busy at work at the moment."

He heard the doorbell and hurried off to answer it. He paused by the hall mirror and looked at himself. There was a smile greeting him in the reflection.

"Yes, yes. Thank you whoever you are. Circumstances, happy circumstances. I will be able to be with Clara when she has to see Sir. Richard. Yes, yes!"

The doorbell chimed again. It was Clara carrying bags of shopping.

"I hope I got the right food," Clara said nervously to Margret. "This is what my mother recommended. But please, please don't make me cook. I am terrible in the kitchen. Just ask Tom!"

Tom had an image of Clara in a frilly apron and nothing else, with flour on her nose. He turned away to hide his smile.

Margret unpacked the bags and put the food away in its allotted spaces.

"This is all fine," she said. "Your mother knows her way around a kitchen, I can see. And don't you worry. I like cooking. You will be eating with us?"

Clara nodded and looked at Tom.

"I would love to. I will do the dishes. Tom can do the drying!"

"It's settled," Margret said. "Dinner and then we can discuss my visit to the city."

Over dinner Margret talked about going to the Historical Museum in the city. She sounded genuinely excited about the idea. Clara immediately joined in.

"You can stay at my grandmother's house! She has a guest room with an attached bathroom. You could come and go as you please. The room has a door into the garden. My Oma would love to meet with you."

With a big smile Clara looked at Tom. Putting his finger on his lips, then scratching under his nose, Tom shook his head. He could see Margret react to the thought of staying with a stranger.

"Yes," Margret answered, unsurely. "Yes, that sounds very tempting. I will think about it."

"You stay there," Clara said. "Tom and I will clear the table."

Tom put the plates on the kitchen sink and then passionately kissed her.

She untangled herself from Tom's heated embrace. Clara called out to Margret:

"I have some pudding, but it needs to be warmed up. Mummy cooked it for us."

After Margret had gone to bed, Tom walked Clara back to his flat. She was going to stay there for the week. From there it was not far to walk to Rubin, who was going to help her choose music in case Sir Richard wanted to know of her favourite composers. In the flat Clara would be able to do her practice. Tom could pick her up on his way home. Hopefully Wednesday evening they would be on their way to the city; hopefully together, hopefully with Margret. She would love Tom's mother to meet her family.

EIGHTY-ONE

Wednesday after work Tom drove over to pick up his mother. Clara had helped Margret to pack; to make sure she had her medication. When Tom turned the key in the door Margret was busy making sandwiches for the trip.

"I am parked on the footpath!" Tom called down the corridor. "Have you two ladies finished? Are you ready?"

He took Margret's case.

"Mother you will need to take a coat. It gets chilly now when the sun has gone!"

He could feel her nervous tension in the corridor. It spilled out as Margret argued over who was going to sit in the back. She thought she might have a bit of a sleep on the way.

When Tom opened the back door for her, she saw Rubin leaning against his pillow.

"I think I would like to sit in the front after all!" she said sharply.

She got in clutching her pillow. In the confusion over seating Clara put the sandwiches in the boot with the luggage, next to two violins carefully wedged on their sides.

Both Margret and Rubin slept all the way.

The days were getting shorter. It was dark when they arrived. As the week before, Emma was there to help them. She smiled at Margret and took her case. A safely paved path took them to her apartment.

When Emma asked Margret if she should hang out her clothes, Margret shook her head and put her hand on her case. She was not going to have a stranger meddle with her belongings. Emma showed her the door into the rest of the house and went out to help Rubin. Tom followed Margret into her room.

Clara ran into the house looking for her Oma. The table was set for supper. No one sat at the end of it. Then someone hugged her from behind.

"She is on her way," Michael told her as he kissed her on her head. "She is just getting ready."

Turning her around he held her at arm's length.

"Let me look at you. You have become so grown-up, my darling daughter. Bit scary! I miss you all terribly."

He pulled her close. Clara could sense that something was amiss.

"How is Oma. Please be honest. Is she very ill? Is she going to die?"

"No, no. She just has a hard time getting over her operation. And yes, one day she will die. But not now. I will make sure of that."

Michael brushed her tears away with his fingertips.

"Now go and freshen up. Your smile will make anyone better."

Tom brought his mother into the house through the front door. He was worried that she would feel intimidated by the grandeur. But she walked in calm and relaxed and stood in the hall and let Emma take her coat. Tom had informed her about the history of the place. Now he explained the set up of the interior.

"Welcome, Margret!" Michael said. "My family's ancestral nest is now yours to enjoy!"

She smiled and nodded, looking up at the high ceiling and the ornate fittings.

Tom thought Michael looked tired, his face drawn.

He ushered them into the living room where Clara and Edward waited.

"Clara, pour our guests some drinks. I do need to attend to my mother and her nurse. She'll join us in the dining room for a light supper."

Clara offered Margret a glass of wine and poured Tom a Scotch.

"This is my Uncle Edward," she said.

He shook Tom's and Margret's hands. Margret felt a gentle warmth in his grip. His scholar's eyes smiled at her.

"I live in the flat above us. I am Edward; child number one. I get to boss my little brother around."

With a "Hi Sis!" Susanna ran to Clara and hugged her. She did not notice Margret.

She got herself a glass of wine and sat with Clara.

Everyone sat in silence, except the two sisters chatting away to each other about their lives.

Rubin quietly slid into the room. He felt the sombre atmosphere in the house. He poured himself a drink and chose a seat as far away from Margret as was possible. She didn't notice as Edward had discovered a mutual love of history with her.

Margret sat in an extremely comfortable leather armchair and observed the Family Gilles. Michael and his brother seem to have very little in common, and the girls, one angel-like with long blonde hair, the other much more masculine with far too short thick, black hair. As if they had different fathers.

Emma's call for supper pulled them out of their thoughts. In the dining room Oma was sitting at the end of the table. She asked for Margret to come closer.

"Welcome to my house and my family. I do hope you will find your room comfortable and the company agreeable. You have to excuse me for not being able to be a good host. I have been unwell."

The two granddaughters had settled next to her. She held their hands.

"But youth gives me strength. Please help yourselves to some food."

Emma and the cook entered with platters of cheese, cold meats, pickles and salad. The nurse put a bowl of broth in front of Oma. She looked at Michael.

"I wonder if I could have a glass of wine? Just so I can join in the cheer of the company."

Margret was unsure of where to sit, but Edward smiled and patted the seat next to him. Tom placed himself on her other side.

Oma Gilles had not asked for a kiss from him. She was worried Margret might object to her love towards Tom. She lifted her wine glass to her family.

"Please children, tell me about your week. My life at the moment is rather uneventful. I need your stories to brighten it up. Where shall we start? Maybe with the youngest."

Having listened to her children telling about their days, Oma Gilles turned towards Margret.

"May I call you Margret? You certainly will call me Irene."

Margret smiled at the old lady who had an aristocratic air about her. Somehow Margret had the feeling that she had experienced people like that. 'Probably saw it on television when in hospital', she thought.

"Yes, please. Call me Margret, please. That is much more personal, Irene."

"I would like to raise my glass to your son. One can see that he comes from a caring home. Everything about him shows the nobility of his family background."

Irene's eyes were sparkling, but her hand started to shake. The nurse gently took her glass and placed it back on the table in front of her. Michael squirmed in his chair. But Irene had not finished.

She turned towards Tom.

"You, my dear young friend will have a very exciting and successful life in front of you. Hopefully with my dear Clara. Time will tell. Life is full of circumstances. One never knows, but one can always hope. Cheers to you, Margret. I hope we will become friends."

Not being able to lift her glass, she just smiled and touched it.

"And now my dear family, please carry on, I must retire. I will see you all in the morning."

The nurse gently pulled the wheelchair away from the table and wheeled her out of the room. Michael followed them.

Margret broke the silence.

"What a wonderful, noble person! Yes, I do hope we can be friends. Now, I need to retire as well. Please, Tom?"

Edward helped her get up. Emma offered to accompany them, but Margret just wanted Tom to come along.

"My dear boy, what lovely people. I am still not too sure about Michael and that Rubin I can certainly do without. Little creepy man he is. But then he is not a relation."

Margret had been to the bathroom and was in her nightdress and dressing gown. The central heating had been turned on, making the room extremely comfortable. She climbed into bed, asking Tom to please get her in the morning.

"I will wait for you. By the way where are you sleeping?"

"I'll show you tomorrow. Clara and I are in the attic flat. Good night, Mum."

He walked out into the cold night air and lifted his arms to the heavens.

'Thank you,' he thought. 'Thanks whoever brought these changes to her!'

After having spent the morning at the Historical Museum, Tom and Clara took Margret to the same café restaurant they went with Leslie Dawson. Tom liked the food, the wine and the atmosphere. Looking around for a free table Tom noticed Oskar Bulgakov in deep conversation with Leslie Dawson. Before he could decide if they should find another place, Oskar had noticed him and Clara.

"What an amazing coincidence! We are just talking about you and your meeting tomorrow. Do come and join us."

Tom looked at his mother and then introduced her to Leslie.

"Oh, you probably will be eating. Sorry Mrs Dolmer, I did not know that you were with them. You probably would like to just enjoy the company of your son and Clara. But maybe Clara could sit with us for a little?"

"What meeting?" Margret asked.

Walking to a large table, she suggested that if Leslie and Oskar did not mind watching them eat, they could all sit together. That way she would know what was going on as well.

On the table was a Reserved sign. Leslie laughed as Oskar put it on another. He called the waiter, ordered more coffee, a bottle of wine and asked for the menu.

"And a cake for Miss Dawson. Put it all on my tab. Thank you."

Margret repeated her question.

"What meeting?"

Leslie, who had introduced herself as Clara's adviser, explained the situation.

"We are very lucky to be able to see Sir Richard. He is a busy man. We are seeing him tomorrow morning."

Looking at Tom she continued, "Are you coming, Tom?"

Tom looked at his mother.

"If you are needed, you must go. You are good at negotiating."

She looked at the menu and ordered soup and bread.

The conversation flowed freely. Margret enjoyed being involved and able to contribute. They talked about everyday events. Towards the end Leslie turned to Clara.

"Did you bring your violin?"

Clara nodded.

"Just be yourself my dear child. And please, Clara, do not expect to be chosen immediately. He will probably put you on the backburner. You will carry on as you have up till now. You will continue to play in your mother's orchestra and in your family's quartet. It is all experience and exposure. Sir Richard heard you play. He knows you are good. I would like you to continue your lessons with Oskar. Maybe twice a week, the rest of the time with Rubin. Don't forget to keep fit!"

She looked at Tom.

"We still have to have our talk! The one about the peeling of onions. Now I must go. Nice meeting you, Mrs Dolmer. You have a great son. See you tomorrow."

'A person to my liking,' Margret thought. 'No fuss. Straight to the point!'

Margret looked at Tom.

"What was that about onions?"

"Oh, nothing really. And nothing to do with cooking."

Margret looked tired. The museum, the enjoyable company, the wine all contributed. Tom asked the waiter to order a taxi.

EIGHTY-TWO

When Margret got up the next morning, Tom and Clara had already left. She put on her coat and walked out into the garden. Emma found her sitting on a bench in the sun, dozing. She asked if Margret had had breakfast, and if she preferred tea to coffee. She had just made a fresh pot for Mrs Gilles. Following Emma into the dining room she heard someone ringing a bell in the living room.

Margret followed the sound.

"Good morning, Margret. Have you had some breakfast? The children have left. What an exciting day!"

Irene rang the bell again. Emma came in pushing a trolley on wheels, on it a teapot, cups and a small bowl with sliced lemon.

"Would you like something to eat, Mrs Dolmer? Maybe some toast with jam or cheese?"

Margret got up and poured the tea. Questioningly she held up a slice of lemon. Irene nodded and smiled.

"You have not been too well either? You are too young not to be well. Forgive my inquiry, but you could not be very much older than Michael. You must get better and strong again. Our children need us, even though they pretend they don't."

Falling into deep thought, Irene Gilles sipped her tea.

"You know, Margret, I am going to get better, I am determined! I want to see Clara play. I want to see Susanna with her doctor's degree. Once they get the medication right, I will be running again. No, I will never be running. I can hardly walk."

Suddenly she laughed.

"Your wonderful son carried me all the way up to my box when we went to the opera to see *The Magic Flute.* Everyone stared! People are so conventional in this town. He is a wonderful young man. You must be proud of him."

Margret was silent. Tom never told her anything, but then she never asked him about his life outside work. Both of them had been very polite to each other. One Monday lunchtime was like the other, cold and polite. Every Monday Tom would bring the same bottle of wine and the same bunch of flowers. Now and then they would visit Theo's grave and go out for coffee. Even the waiter knew what they wanted. They always ordered the same.

Emma came in with a small tray, upon it a plate with toast, a small bowl of butter and some slices of cheese.

"It must be wonderful to have a large family. Has your son Edward a family? And what does he do?"

"No, Edward never married. There were plenty of lovers. Probably never the right one. He is a publisher. Mainly travel books and books on history. Not the best market for such specialised books. But then as long as I am alive, he can live out of my pocket. And I don't mind."

Irene Gilles gave a little laugh.

"And your parents?" she asked. "Still around?"

Margret shook her head. She did not know what to say, how to handle the situation. But then Oma Gilles looked at her with her sharp, lively, black eyes and Margret found herself saying,

"I did not know my mother. I am very confused about who she was. According to documents my mother died when I was four years old. But my memory tells me otherwise. In the hospital I had long sessions with the counsellor, Andrea Coder, trying to get to understand and to learn how to deal with my childhood. Together we decided to close the book on it. My life started the day I met Theo, the man I loved, and his parents."

Irene looked at Margret in astonishment.

"But you must have known your maiden name? You can use

that name to find out who your parents were; where you came from. Oh, Margret, you must find out! I can help you. Truly and discretely."

Michael entered the room, carrying a syringe.

"How are you, Margret? I am here, if you need anything. Please excuse us. Time for Oma's shot. She will be back on deck at lunchtime."

Margret went out and slowly walked in the garden. Oh, why, oh, why, did Irene rattle the tin of her past? But this tin, or box, in which she had put the memories of her past would never completely disappear. Not until she had opened the container and solved all the problems it held.

The path took her to the end of the garden, to an impressive wrought iron fence. Through the bars she could see large, modern houses.

"Depressing." Edward had come up behind her. "Once upon a time there were fields beyond these bars. Yes, truly depressing. Oh, I'm sorry if I startled you. You were obviously in deep thought."

"Yes," Margret found herself saying. "I was delving into my past, my strange history."

"Have you written about it? Personal stories at the moment sell well. I can publish it for you."

Margret smiled.

"There's nothing to write about. Just a life."

"Well, writing about it is a good start. Just putting your thoughts on paper can help a lot. You can always burn the paper. You don't need to keep it. I do a lot of that sort of thing. I must have written volumes and volumes of books that way. Nothing published, of course."

He laughed and took her arm.

"I have actually come to tell you lunch is on. My mother is waiting. Clara rang. They have gone off celebrating. Will be interesting to hear their story. Unpublishable of course."

They slowly wandered back to the house, Edward informing Margret about the history of the property, its highs and its lows.

"When mummy goes, I will have to buy a tent. I could not afford to live here. But we will see. You see Margret, history does not sell. Not real history. Only the history of people living now, famous people that is. It is all trash. Those books will not survive history. But they help me make money."

The nurse wheeled Irene Gilles into the dining room.

"In this house we have a hot midday meal. I hope you don't mind, Margret. I get too tired to eat in the evening. Then it is really not good for you to have a big meal before you go to bed."

She pointed at the chair next to her.

"Please sit next to me, then we don't have to shout."

Margret excused herself for a moment. The pills next to Irene reminded her that she had been neglecting her medications. She hurried off to her room.

Back at the table, Irene asked her what she was going to do about her problematic past.

"Write about it!" Edward called across the table. "Truly! Write about it. Get it out of your system, by writing. Not everyone can open up through talking. That is just the system psychologists use. It keeps them in business!"

Michael bristled.

"Psychology is a science! Writing is fiction!"

Oma waved at them.

"Boys! Sit down! Margret will decide what to do. She is a grown woman!"

To change the subject, Margret asked how Clara went.

"Well, they are celebrating. I think that answers your question?" Michael said with a smile. He continued,

"It is so good to have you here in our home, Margret. I have not had much time to welcome you."

He looked at his mother: "I am sure I have sorted out mummy's medication. She will now grow from strength to strength. I have promised to keep her going until Clara gives her first concert."

The family was sitting around the table, in the middle was a large bowl of fruit. Candles created a cozy atmosphere. No one had tried to find out how the meeting with Sir Richard went. Suddenly Michael got up.

"For God's sake will you tell us about your morning?"

Clara looked at her father coyly.

"It was OK."

"And where are Tom and Rubin! What's going on?"

Rubin, pushing a trolley, stood in the doorway. He wore the most ridiculous large top hat. On the trolley was a cake. Tom was trying to light the candles, but Rubin would not stand still. He was completely engrossed in his role, in his element. He was performing.

Oma Gilles clapped her hands and laughed.

"Oh, Rubin, you funny man. Always the entertainer. I wonder who the cake is for? I wonder what we are celebrating?"

'Always having to steal the show!' Margret thought. 'Showing off at his age, really!'

Everyone else laughed and clapped.

Rubin rolled the cake to Clara. Tom had just managed to light the candles. The cook and Emma came into the room carrying glasses and bottles of champagne.

Margret suddenly felt completely left out. She could not understand such theatre. Why did Clara not just simply tell them how she went.

Rubin and Tom started singing a tune they had made up. Like professional singers they stood in front of Clara; Tom tall and handsome, Rubin trying to look bigger by wearing the very tall top hat. Margret was ashamed to see her son playing the fool. She felt like leaving.

"Champagne! Champagne, please," Rubin called, waving his arms about.

The Gilles family were all laughing and cheering. Margret really wanted to leave.

Rubin handed her a glass, "Madame!"

She returned him an ice-cold look.

When everyone had a glass Rubin made a speech, talking about Clara's life, her incredible talent and her exiting future.

"To our Clara's future!" they all called out

In his excitement Tom went to his mother and gave her a kiss. As he was bending down, Margret hissed at him,

"I would like to go home tomorrow!"

Tom shrank back from her. The next day Clara was going to play for her grandmother. He had planned to stay until Sunday. He turned away from his mother and rejoined the party.

"Hello!" Michael called. "Please could someone tell me how the meeting went? I can see we are celebrating. I just would like to know a few details. Please!"

Clara, eyes sparkling, went over to her father and sat on his lap.

"Sir Richard liked my playing. No one told me that he came to Oma's 90th birthday and saw me play. Also, he was impressed with the amount of violin pieces I know. Shortly he said, I am on his books."

She looked at Rubin.

"He was especially amazed about me having tackled the Sibelius Violin concerto and he was happy that I love Brahms, but he felt I should also learn some more modern pieces. He did mention some, but I have forgotten."

She lifted her glass.

"Cheers to Rubin! And thank you. Truly, truly."

Rubin had pulled one of his disgusting handkerchiefs out of his pocket and wiped his eyes.

Margret noticed. She could not understand how this horrid little man could have wormed himself into this noble family.

"Thank you, my darling girl. You have no idea how much you have given me!"

He loudly blew his nose and asked for more champagne.

Everyone cheered and laughed.

Margret had enough. She excused herself and went to her room.

Tom did not go to say good night.

EIGHTY-THREE

I t was a chilly morning. Margret had packed her case and was ready to leave. Walking into the house she was greeted by Emma, who offered to make her some tea.

"Mrs Gilles is in the living room," she said politely. "I can bring the tea to you there."

With a friendly smile Irene wished her a good morning.

"The older I get the less sleep I need."

Emma brought the tea and some toast for Margret.

"What a wonderful evening we had. I am so proud of Clara. Then, you know, Margret, Clara showed her talent for music at a very early age. I think she got her first violin at the age of four. Rubin has been coaching her all her life. He is an excellent teacher. You know, in his younger days he was a very well-known performer."

"How did Rubin become such a good friend of your family?" Margret found it hard to say his name.

Irene told her about his relationship with Gudrun's aunt, Esther, and her sudden disappearance. Margret started to think more kindly of him. But liking him was impossible. She told Irene so.

"Oh Margret, Rubin is the kindest man you could wish to know. He is a wise man, an old man who has not lost the child in him. He can be so funny. Yet there is a deep serious side to him. Also, he is totally honest. He speaks his mind. Rubin might be small and slightly scruffy but he is part of this family; as you now are."

Margret shook her head.

"I just do not like him and I find it rather embarrassing having

470

to watch an old man like him play the fool. I am not used to people like that."

She gave a loud sigh.

"I will be leaving this morning."

"You can't leave! This afternoon we are having a concert. The Gilles quartet is playing. You must not miss that!"

Irene was visibly upset.

Clara and Tom came into the room, arms around each other.

Oma looked at them, the shock visible on her face.

"Margret is leaving us today!"

"We know," Tom said coldly. "Mother told me last night. I will take her to the station. I am not going to miss the concert."

He looked coldly at Margret.

"All you have to do is tell me when you would like to go."

"Good morning all. Someone leaving?" Michael walked into the room. "No one is allowed to leave until after the concert. Clara has been promoted to first violin. She has pushed Rubin one notch down. Ha!"

"Did I hear the word leaving. Who?"

Edward had entered the room.

All fingers pointed at Margret. She was now standing, but frozen in place.

"You can't go!" Edward said. "There is a book on history I would like to show you. And you cannot possibly miss the performance.

The Big Room is being made ready for it as we speak! We could not under any circumstance have an empty seat. Come on, Margret, what would be more important than enjoying the Gilles Quartet play in our little theatre? No, we could not have an empty seat!"

"Why don't we all go and have breakfast," Irene interrupted. She waved to the nurse to wheel her into the dining room.

Edward smiled and pulled out the chair for Margret by the dining table. With a simple, determined gesture he pointed at it.

"Margret, please."

She stood there, looking at him. She did enjoy his company; his determination to make her stay; his shy charm. She looked at the others. She wasn't sure what to do.

Entering the Big Room, as they called it, was like entering a small theatre. Its interior was almost over-decorated. The walls were painted as if there was a mezzanine filled with faces looking down on them. On the sides were the boxes. The smallest of spaces were painted. The thirty seats covered in deep red velvet stood out from the dark blue carpet. On each side of the stage was a floor-to-ceiling curtain held back with a gold rope from which big gold tassels hung. The stage was covered in a red carpet. Four gold-painted chairs stood on it in readiness. On the side, pushed out of the way, was a gleaming black grand piano.

"My grandmothers folly. She loved to entertain." Irene laughed. "And we love using it. Come, children, find your seats. The ushers are all paintings. They have been unable to help for many years. As a child I thought them scary. They look so real."

She asked the nurse to take her to the right-hand side of the stage; from there she would be able to observe her granddaughter.

Margret was looking for Tom. She felt insecure in this strange environment. Edward walked up to her and showed her to a seat in the middle of one of the front rows.

"You know, Clara had her first public appearance on this stage. She was four years old."

He noticed Margret looking about her.

"Tom is on stage helping. Don't worry, he is not performing, just helping out. Do you mind if I sit with you?"

Looking around, he told Margret that his mother had invited a few friends of hers. He wondered who they were. He suspected they would be very important people. But Margret was still looking at the interior. Above her she noticed a chandelier. It was adorned with tiny little lights. The chandelier was painted, the lights real.

"It is all an illusion," Edward said. "The room is not as high or as big as it appears. Everything is painted, very cleverly and convincingly, with a forced perspective to give this appearance."

Rubin walked on stage and called, "Lights please."

"Is he playing?" she asked.

Edward nodded.

The lights dimmed. Only the stage lights stayed on.

Standing in the middle of the stage Rubin bowed and welcomed the family members, their friends and also the friends of Mrs Irene Gilles. He made a bow and thanked her for her impeccable hospitality. Then he announced the piece they were going to play.

"I know we have played this wonderful, melodic piece by Brahms before. This time we will perform with a slight change in the order of players. Our wonderful and talented Clara Gilles has pushed me off my seat. She will now be playing the first violin."

He bowed and smiled.

"Ladies, Gentlemen, Johannes Brahms String Quartet No 2 in A minor, op. 51.

Played by the Gilles Quartet, led by Clara Gilles."

With a big bow he left the stage.

Clara walked in, carrying her violin, Esther's violin, but no sheet music. Behind her Gudrun, Michael and then Rubin. They bowed to the audience and sat down, Clara nodded, and they began to play.

Margret's hands had knitted themselves together, knuckles showing white. She could not get over the beauty of mother and daughter, together in blue satin.

Even Rubin looked respectable. Though she did feel his trousers would have improved with an ironing. Michael, who always seemed to clown about, was now totally concentrating. Gudrun looked so beautifully serene playing the 'cello.

Margret was wrapped up in the music. She closed her eyes and floated away. When it stopped, she wanted to clap and cheer, but Edward took her hands and shook his head.

"This is the first movement. There are two more to come. Then you can clap and whistle."

As always Clara gave it her all. She played magnificently. Rubin kept looking at her as she led the group.

Tom was ready for her. They had decided to only play the one piece; but there could be a demand for an encore. He would have to manage to get her back on stage.

He had asked Rubin not to have an encore. All he wanted was a cigarette to calm his nerves.

'Oh Esther, help Clara, help me,' he thought. Suddenly he thought that Esther could have performed on this stage. It was quite possible. And maybe Rubin as well? Who knew who had given private performances for Oma Gilles's grandmother?

The music stopped. He saw the musicians get up and bow. Rubin was holding Clara's hand. He was stopping her from running off stage.

Clara noticed Tom and he sent her a kiss. She was holding on to her pendant. He was digging amongst his shirt buttons to find his. When Clara came off stage she fell into his arms. She stayed until she felt grounded.

Tom whispered, "One step at a time. Slowly, one step at a time."

The audience called for more. Rubin walked out on stage.

"I can play for you. Anything you like, but for Clara on her first day as leader of this quartet her wonderful performance was quite enough. Thank you."

The quartet came back on stage. Again, Tom noticed the way Clara was carrying her violin. Just like Esther all those many years ago. From the back of the audience he could hear a loud, "Bravo". It came from Oskar Bulgakov. Who else had been invited?

Clara left the stage and cuddled up in his embrace.

"One step at a time, slowly, slowly. Like a ladder. Descend one step at a time until I can feel the ground. Don't look down," she mumbled.

"Good girl, good girl," Tom whispered as he covered her shaking body with a shawl.

Rubin looked at him.

"When you are ready. We will be in the living room. Take your time."

"I'm fine," Clara said.

But Tom could see in her eyes that she had not quite come down from her high. He held her, rocked her, quietly sang to her until she was warm again and had stopped shaking. Until her eyes were calm. He held on to her, feeling her warm relaxed body melt into his.

'We have done it. No, she has done it', he thought.

By using a simple mantra, Clara had managed to avoid falling, falling into the black void she so much feared.

When Clara and Tom came into the living room, everyone cheered and clapped. Carrying one yellow rose Sir Richard walked towards Clara. He gently took her hand and kissed it. No words were exchanged. None were necessary.

Emma and the cook brought plates of beautifully presented hor d'óeuvres. Edward and Michael were busy with the champagne.

Tom took two glasses of champagne and handed one to his mother. She had been standing alone watching the excitement. After having taken her glass mother and son stood together in silence. He put his arm around her shoulder and together they remained in their own spaces, their own worlds. Yet they both felt they belonged. Margret had stopped feeling like an outsider. The music had changed everything. It had unlocked the box of her deep past. Though the lid was still closed. Would she be able to open it? Margret relaxed into Tom's embrace.

Irene Gilles rang her little bell. The room fell into silence.

"Thank you for coming to my home to help me enjoy my dear Clara's rise to lead violin in our little quartet. The Gilles Quartet might not be honoured with a worldwide reputation, but I am sure Clara will rise and rise to conquer the world with her talent and her beauty.

Please excuse me. This old body is tired. Keep on enjoying yourself. There is plenty to eat and drink.

There is just one more thing. I would like to see my family, all of them and that includes Margret and Tom, for a late supper at about eight.

Please carry on."

Edward approached Margret and Tom.

"Clara is looking for you, Tom," he said.

As Tom left he gestured to Margret.

"Would you like to sit down, Margret?"

He took her arm and led her to one of the big armchairs.

"Can I get you another drink? Maybe a bite to eat?"

He picked up a small plate and filled it with the small, delicious-looking hors d'oeuvres. He took a seat next to her.

"Have you been to see some of our museums? Maybe the Historical Museum?"

Margret nodded. She liked Edward. He was a gentle, polite man.

"I myself love to dig into the history of families. Maybe one day, when my mother is not with us any more, I will publish my account of the rise and demise of Admiral Frantz Benedict von Staden and his descendants, including myself. Most aristocratic families have a number of skeletons in their cupboard.

To our forgotten, unmentioned skeletons."

He raised his glass and looked at Margret.

"And you, have you uncovered your own family past?"

She didn't look at him. She shook her head, keeping her eyes averted.

"What was your maiden name?"

She mumbled, "Lamberg."

She did not want to talk about her family, but Edward kept on digging, as if he already knew the answers and was waiting for her confirmation.

"Lamberg?," he prodded. "A well-known family in the trading world."

She got up.

"Please excuse me," she said. "I am tired and will go and have a rest. I've not been too well lately. But I will be back for the supper at eight."

He smiled and nodded and watched her walk from the room.

EIGHTY-FOUR

All eyes were on Oma Irene Gilles. She had rung her little bell and called them all to silence. It was eight o'clock.

"As you all know I am a very old person who might not be with you for much longer. My life has been extremely long and is filled with memories of joy, excitement and sadness. Over the years many secrets had been handed to me, some of which I need to let go, need to talk about... Need to hand on to you.

My dear son Edward, who had always been looked upon as an amateur historian, started to research our family. And with the seemingly unreasonable fanaticism of a hound he has discovered happenings which became his and my secrets. Some of them will remain so, some will have to be revealed."

She looked at Margret.

"Your past has been extremely interesting. You see, my dear, it is very easy to discover the history of one's family. Edward is an expert in doing so. Your married name, Dolmer, took him to your maiden name, Lamberg. Wolfgang Lamberg married Sophia Grete Gallas. In the archives Edward found an invitation card to a concert. A concert here, in this little theatre."

She looked around the room. She had everybody's attention. Her eyes came finally to Margret. Margret's gaze was on her.

"This concert was held in our little theatre long before you were born, and some years before Sophia met Wolfgang. She was a singer, known for her talent in performing Lieder. Her favourite composer was Franz Schubert.

If Sophia was your mother, then I met you as a tiny baby, in about 1902. If your mother was Sophia, you will have noticed

478

that one of the stillborn babies was named Irene, after me. Her second child, a boy, was also stillborn. The third a daughter she called Margret. This little girl was her love and joy. Even though Sophia was older than me, we were the best of friends.

To my mind there is no doubt that she was your mother. You look a little like her. Life's circumstances have taken you along a different path to hers. It hurt you and made you hard and suspicious. I do know though, that she is in you, because you were created in love with the gentlest person one could wish to know.

If you are Margret Lamberg, then you had the most handsome, caring father. The Lamberg family have always been in trading. Therefore I think he would have been involved in his father's import-export business and been a very busy man.

I can see both of your parents in your son. I am not too sure where those blue eyes are from. They must be Tom's father's. I believe he was a wonderful man."

Margret had taken Tom's hand. He bent down and kissed her on the cheek. She did not shy away. Tom gently freed his hand and put his arm around her shoulder. She snuggled into his chest and started quietly to weep.

"I don't know what to think. I don't know who I am," she muttered.

Tom just held her. No one spoke.

Margret composed herself and sat up.

"Thank you, Irene," she whispered.

Edward smiled, got up to fill her glass.

"Not for me, thank you."

"Just a small drop?"

She nodded, trying very hard to keep back her tears.

Irene's little bell rang again.

"There are other matters I would not like to take to my grave. My dear son has dug deep. No doubt one day he will publish a book about this family. I just do hope he changes the names."

Irene looked at Gudrun, then Clara, then back to Gudrun.

"The reason I need to bring the next family story to light is because of my beloved granddaughter Clara. We all witnessed her talent this afternoon. This young person is music. She soars away to a world none of us know. There was another, in her family, with that talent. This person also became music. But anything that can take us beyond ourselves is filled with danger. Most of us would need guidance to find our own self again, to find the ground, to be grounded."

All of a sudden Rubin jumped up from his seat, overturning his wine on the white table cloth, creating a large, blood-like stain.

"No! You are not allowed to talk about her. You are not!"

Michael gently pushed him back in his seat. Rubin looked at Gudrun pleadingly. A deep fear started to fill Tom's chest. He removed his arm from his mother's shoulder.

"Rubin," Irene continued. "You also must let your ghosts go, let them rest, free yourself!

Where was I? Yes, Clara. Clara is the image of her. From an early age the child showed talent. With the memory of her aunt still fresh, Gudrun did not permit to have Clara treated like a Wunderkind. She was brought up like any other child."

Having freed himself from Michael's grip, Rubin stood up again.

"Why don't you say her name! She this and she that. None of you can say her name. It hurts too much. Doesn't it?"

With surprising agility he climbed onto his chair. Like a hurt beast he called out,

"Her name was Esther Asplin and she was the most beautiful woman on earth. Oh, how we made music together! Oh, how we loved each other!"

He turned towards Tom.

"And you my friend, Tom, are in love with her double; our Clara! Don't you dare hurt that girl! Don't you dare let that girl fall! How could I have known about Esther's incredible highs and lows? How could I have helped her? And one day she just left, just disappeared. Puff, gone! Nobody told me where to. Nobody."

Rubin stepped off his chair muttering nobody. Tom, who felt the man's pain, got up and stood next to Rubin. All he could say was,

"My dear Rubin, I know how you feel. I truly do!"

Rubin spun around and looked up at Tom.

"You have met her! You have met Esther. Come on and tell your story and then maybe someone will release me from my pain and tell me what happened to her."

Tom stepped back. Oh, he needed a cigarette. He needed to walk. He needed to get away. He ran his hands through his hair. He could not talk. He went back to his seat. Clara joined him. With her arms around his chest she stood behind him. She was frightened, and she was shocked about what Rubin had said.

Gudrun got up and faced Rubin.

"We tried to save Esther by taking her away from you. Her state of mind became more and more confused. She told my mother, her twin sister, about her highs and lows. There was no Tom to catch her, to help her back to her normal self. You Rubin, fell also. But you seemed to bounce and enjoy the highs and lows. Esther fell and fell. Her black hole becoming deeper and deeper until one day she could not get out. It was Michael's father who realised that Esther, after every one of her great performances fell into a deep depression. It happens to quite a lot of performers, but Esther, my dear aunt, had no help."

Gudrun started quietly to weep.

"We took her away from you. Yes, we did. She went into an institution. My mother would not allow us to let you know where she was. Esther was never allowed to play again. When she was released from the clinic, my mother left us all and took her to Norway. Her violin stayed here with us. Esther met someone; he was a nice kind man. She came back to show him the life she once had. She also wanted him to meet the family. We did not tell you, Rubin. We did not dare. Esther found her violin. I think she only played once in public again and we do not know where. Then she went back to Norway. Twelve months after that she died. My mother soon followed her. They were identical twins. One could not live without the other."

Looking at Michael she continued,

"Esther was the most remarkable musician. She conquered everyone's heart with her beauty and her kindness. I did not only lose Esther, I also lost my mother."

Gudrun looked at Tom. She looked at Clara standing behind him, clasping his chest, her long hair trailing over his shoulder. "Why, oh why did Esther not meet a man like Tom?"

Clara kissed Tom on his neck and whispered that she loved him more than anything in the world.

Rubin looked at Tom.

"Tell them. Come on, tell them where you saw Esther. She played for you. Did she not? She wrapped you up with her music. Tell them how she lured you to play the violin. Lured you away from your life! To me, to Clara, to become part of this family!"

Tom looked at the faces of the people he had learned to love so much.

He found it hard to tell his story. How does one explain feelings? How does one put smells, strange whispers, music arriving with a breeze into words?

"Esther, Esther!" Tom hesitantly started. "Never did I think that I could say her name out loud. She has been my deep secret since I was nine years old, when I met her at the market. Her music bewitched me. She made me love the violin. My ambition was to play, to make my violin sing like Esther did. I fell completely in love with her. Her hair, the comb, the way she held her violin. Everything. Her kind eyes, her movements when she played. I wanted to be like her. Her music filled me with a longing. This longing never left me. With my first wages I bought my violin. I had no idea how to play. But Esther was always there; pushing me, teasing me. Then I met Rubin. Her presence became stronger. Every time I thought of giving up, she would tease me with her music. Through Rubin I met Clara. Esther stayed around me, made me play my violin.

The more I talk about her, the more I feel that her spirit led me to Clara. You all might think I am making this up, or that I have lost my mind. I do not come from a family where music is appreciated. I am an engineer. I believe in facts. Ghosts live in fairytales. Esther showed me her spiritual side, showed me… Oh, how can I explain to you what it is like to stand in still air and yet be caressed by a sweet-smelling breeze filled with music, wrapping you up, encapsulating you? How can I explain that feeling?

Esther was the one who put the longing for being able to make music into me.

Esther took me to Clara.

Esther became Clara.

Now she is gone. She has put me where she wants me to be. She has lured me here to stop Clara from experiencing her pain, her demise."

He picked up Clara's hands which were still clasping his chest and kissed them.

"Esther promised to be at the following market, but no matter how hard I looked I could not find her."

Turning around Tom looked at Clara

"Little did I know that one day she would be here right next to me."

BOOK TWO

My dearest Clara   March 1971

As you can see on the stamp I am back 'home', if there is
such a thing for me lately. Ever now my life is filled with
travel, filled with following you and your music making all
over the world. My little flat feels somehow like Home, full
of beautiful memories.

You were missed at Rubin's funeral and memorial. As
he wanted it the farewell was, in Rubin-style, grand and
flowing with champagne. Somehow, I did not feel like
making a speech. I played for him. Played my violin,
probably very badly. I just made up a tune, sang, whistled,
danced and copied some of his funny little gestures. You
know, Clara, I could not help myself in finishing my dismal
performance with scales! All of them. By the laughing, you
could tell who really knew Rubin. Your dad and Oskar
clapped. I felt very honoured.

Now I have the job of sorting out his piles and piles of
'stuff' and also his Will. I am pretty sure that he left all his
instruments to you. Also, his tower-flat. But I will let you
know when I have seen the solicitor.

Rubin asked me to take his ashes and put them next to
Esther. Gudrun will accompany me to Norway. She knows
where Esther is resting. For me, it will be an opportunity
to thank Esther for having brought me to you, my darling
Clara.

My mother is well and happy in the absolutely fabulous
Home on the other side of the river. She is sharp and often
sarcastic, as ever. We went to both of the graves. She had a
long chat with her mother.

Oh yes, I must tell you. She sees quite a lot of Edward,
sharing her interest in History. I wonder how long that has
been going on? Edward is still living in the big house. He
has rented out the ground floor flat to a conductor. That

seems to bring in enough money to keep the house going. Also, his publishing business is going well. He is writing a book about his family. Wonder, if he is brave enough to put us in?

Went to Oma Gilles grave with flowers from you. I know that her passing has deeply distressed you.

I will see you after having been in Norway. Before I come back to you, I would like to see the country and experience that strange violin they play. So, it could be well into April. I will be back for your next concert — PROMISE!

Everyone here misses you. Please give my regards to Leslie Dawson.

Take care my darling. I miss you. All my love is with you, always.

Tom

My dearest Clara,   September 1995

I have only been away for a few days and already I miss you.
Somehow, I am glad that you decided not to come. It seems
that my homecoming is filled with sad moments.

Zita's passing was peaceful. Kira found her mother in
bed. Zita must have known that her end was near. She had
surrounded herself with items she loved and wanted to take
with her to the other side, as she called it. There was a small
pile with Kira's name on it, one for me and a small wrapped
up box for you. She wanted to be cremated, her ashes put on
her boat with her favourite belongings and then she asked
to have the boat burned on the river's side-arm where she
used to go fishing.

There was only a small crowd. Your parents came, and
Oskar. Kira was there and Jack. As we watched the boat
burn, we played what we thought was gypsy music. Then
we were told to go back to the little house where a number
of bottles of Schnapps stood on the table. Oh, my dear
Clara, we all got terrible drunk. I had to think of Rubin
and how much he liked his Schnapps.

Otherwise? Angus, the son of my ex-manager, has taken
over the big flat. He is now my business partner. Douglas
died last year. I did not manage to get to his funeral. I was
touring with you. In a few years, I am planning on handing
the business over to Angus. He has a family of two boys.

I will stay until mother's birthday at the end of the
month. She is going to be ninety-two. Still fit and bossy.
She will out-live us all! She sends her love.

As I am writing this, you are sleeping. Oh how, I am
looking forward to being with you, feeling your soft skin,
smelling you.

All my love forever
Tom

My darling, darling Clara,   Late September. 1995

Life is full of sadness. Oh, how much I wish you were with me, helping me through my sorrow. Darling, you must come back, even if it is just for a very short visit. Your father has had a stroke. Gudrun needs you to be at her side. She is not that strong herself. Michael is at home. Susanna and her husband are doing what they can. Then you know what Michael is like. Stubborn and independent. He keeps on sneaking into the little garden shed where he has a stash of cigarettes and drinks. I cannot see any harm in letting him have that enjoyment. He is only half a man without them. I suppose it must be hard for Gudrun to let him go. I could never let you go, my love.

My mother's birthday party was as jolly as it could be. Every time I visit her, she asks me if I have found myself a wife and how many children I have.

Oh dear, a hard question to answer.

Well, my darling, darling Clara I will close for today.

I don't know when I will be back 'down-under'. I do not particularly like to stay here for the winter.

Love you and miss you.
Tom

My darling Clara,   Late autumn 2004

I am really sorry I could not come back to Australia with you after your exhausting last tour of Europe. It was wonderful to be with you, to experience your beautiful playing, to witness the excited crowd. Inside I am sad that these concerts will be the last for me. There will be no more standing in the wings watching you. There will be no more catching you, holding you, stopping you from the frightening fall.

Often have I felt these last few years that this was the main reason why you are still with me. I have never understood why you did not go and see your sick mother before she passed away. Or, for that matter any of our so close friends.

My mission these last few years has been to go home burying friends and then sorting out their estates. Rubin. You never even came to get his instruments or make any decision what to do with his flat.

Now that my mother has gone I have decided to completely divorce myself from the business. I do not like the way Angus runs the place. I still own the building and the land. His rent and my investments will keep me financially comfortable for many years. I have offered to sell him the big flat. The little one, our flat, will remain ours. Also, now that my mother is not with us anymore I am free of my promise to my father.

Oh, my darling Clara. This place is so full of memories, so full of ghosts. I sat under my willow the other day, thinking of them all. The only one left is Kira, my childhood friend, my gypsy queen. Zita's little house is still there. In his last years Jack would come and do repairs. The funny little man told me he looked upon it as a shrine to a beautiful human being.

The river has been regulated. There is a big dam just above our town. The water is used for making electricity. The river is working so hard that downstream its energy has become slow-moving. It is too tired to flood the planes, and Zita's fishing hole is just a deep crater. I have had offers in selling this land for development. I cannot think of having the big tree removed and Zita's house pushed over.

Sitting at the water's edge I realised that I have neglected my dream of traveling and making music. My darling Clara, yes, I have neglected my dream. You became my life. With you I travelled, you made the music, you filled my being with music, you made your violin sing like Esther did

I am sitting here in our little flat, sipping a Scotch. Through the one door I can see my study and the map of rivers, or as I called it: My Map of The World.

The little boat is glued onto one of the rivers next to my first two big words: Disappointment and Circumstance. Well, there have been many of both of them.

Looking through the other door I see Grandfather's big bed. Oh, my sweet, sweet Clara. I promised you my love and as you know, I never break my promise.

It is so hard being away from you. The country you have chosen as your home is so vast, so endlessly big and so far away from everything. I need the feeling of history. I need confined spaces. I need water. I need a splashing river full of life and youth.

Oh, my darling love where has our carefree youth gone.

My dreams will be with you and our youth when I go to sleep tonight in Grandfather's big bed.

All my love goes to you,
Your Tom

My darling, darling Clara   Spring 2013

If I could have known that my goodbye to you and your
beautiful setting in the Australian bush was going to be
the last one, I would have made it into a 'Rubin-style'
celebration. My last check-up at the hospital showed that
I have a heart murmur and was advised not to fly. So, my
darling it looks like you will have to come to me for my
ninetieth birthday.

I have given myself a grand present. I bought a small
farmer's cottage just a short walk from the village where
you celebrated your twenty-first birthday. Nothing here
has changed. Not like in our town. It breaks my heart to
go there.

My grandfather's factory is no more. The building
was saved and is now a health gym. In the machine room,
different machines stand. Loud music blaring instead of
the clanking of the lathes. The smells are not of turned
iron but perfume mixed with sweat. There is a café on the
ground floor of the office wing. I do not know what happens
upstairs. I am just glad about having taken my furniture out
and the Miro print. I have that here with me alongside the
Chagall in my little cottage. The garden area has been turned
into a carpark. The river is tamed and runs sluggishly in a
concrete channel. Downstream from the factory is nothing.
Oh, darling, how I cried when I saw the land flattened in
readiness for some apartment buildings. Now I feel that my
childhood has gone. Remember the first time I took you
down the river? I think I already loved you then.

I decided to go back to the country. Finding myself
driving past the yellow flowers, over the water on the road
and the bridge to the village which stood there unchanged,
my heart ached for the beautiful weekend we spent there.

Yes, my darling Clara, I am still driving and yes, the old

Mercedes is still going. I am an old man and I drive not as fast as I used to, and I stop often. You know, my love, when I saw the yellow flowers, I could see you hopping through the little waterfall. What wonderful memories I have.

As you know, my birthday is in the middle of March. There is still time for you to come and join me. Kira has offered to help me celebrate. She might stay with me over the summer. I thought of fetching her in town. We will see. Do you remember Hannah? She is still working at the hotel and has promised to cook me something special. I will have Schnapps in memory of Rubin, a glass of beer to remember my good friend Jack, and a bottle of the best wine to celebrate the Gilles family — who showed me the other side of life. Then I will slowly walk home and think of you, only you; the way you made music with your violin and your body. Oh, my darling, I might be almost ninety, but I can still feel you and smell you. This memory will never leave me.

Yours forever,
Tom

P.S.: I do realise that you are having great problems in committing yourself to write down your thoughts. Still a small letter or card from you on my birthday would mean the world to me.

Fels & Gruenewald
Rechtsanwalt
Baden a.d. Thaya
OESTERREICH
Dezember 2018

To
Clara Gilles
25 Toronto Lane
Melbourne
AUSTRALIA

Madam,

The late Mr Tomas Alexander Dolmer has requested that we look after his affairs both here in Austria and in Australia.

In his last will, he states that all the properties he has purchased in Australia will go to you. There is also a small parcel containing a river stone and a gold necklace with a four-leafed clover pendant. We will send it to you by registered mail.

Mr Tomas Alexander Dolmer's Austrian investments have been placed in a trust fund for the upkeep of the family estate belonging to Dr of Medicine, Susanna Leopold.

Mr Dolmer requested to inform you that his wish was to have his ashes scattered amongst the yellow flowers by the small waterfall. The two ladies attending his funeral will honour his wish.

In the near future, you will be contacted by our Australian partners.

With best regards
Walter Gruenewald

Clara   Christmas 2018

In my deep sadness at the loss of Tom, and this now deep
loathing I have for you I cannot address you as 'dear' or
'siss'. This is a parting letter. Parting from you and all the
times we had together. The good has been wiped out by
your behaviour over the last forty-plus years.

One week before his 90th birthday Tom rang me every
day to see if there was a letter or card from you. Every day
he walked to the village Post Office, but no message from
Australia. Tom made us aware of your phobia about writing;
of giving away something of yourself. But ask yourself, how
much did Tom give you?

Still, he forgave you. But deep down he started dying.
His daily walks to the river or the little waterfall over the
summer months became less and less until during the most
glorious autumn he stopped going out altogether.

Kira and I helped Tom celebrate his birthday. We
arranged it as he wished it to be. He tried to be cheerful,
but he was deeply unhappy. After his birthday Kira, now
almost 100 years old, stayed with him until his death at the
beginning of December.

Kira told me that Tom suddenly stopped playing his
violin.

Sometime in November, he summoned his solicitor to
change his will. He took off his pendant, laid it on a stone
from the river and asked to have it sent to you after his death.

Oh Clara, why are you so cruel? He gave you his life.
He was there for every one of your concerts, helped you
down from your incredible highs, stopped you from
following Esther's fate. You could not have survived as a
world-renowned violinist without him. Did you love him?
Or just use him?

There is no forgiveness for the way you treated your own

parents. Daddy so much wanted to see his Botticelli Angel. He was in his hospital bed crying for you. Then after his death, Mummy went back to her home country. She fell ill and soon was gone too. She never spoke of you again. I had her buried close to her mother and aunt Esther. Rubin's ashes are there as well.

All these people, who adored you, helped you, loved you dearly. All of those people you let down. A lifetime of people and you just threw them away.

I will never be able to forgive you. Hating you is too kind. I will wipe you out of my life.

Dr Susanna Leopold M.D.

P.S.: When the yellow flowers by the little waterfall are blooming, I will go and spread his ashes into the flowing water and onto the yellow flowers.